SCANDALOUS RISKS

SCANDALOUS RISKS

A NOVEL BY

Susan Howatch

ALFRED A. KNOPF

NEW YORK *1990*

THIS IS A BORZOI BOOK
PUBLISHED BY ALFRED A. KNOPF, INC.

Copyright © 1990 by Leaftree Limited
All rights reserved under International and
Pan-American Copyright Conventions. Published in the
United States by Alfred A. Knopf, Inc., New York,
and simultaneously in Canada by Random House of
Canada Limited, Toronto. Distributed by Random
House, Inc., New York.

Owing to limitations of space, acknowledgements for
permission to reprint previously published material
appear on page 389.

Library of Congress Cataloging-in-Publication Data
Howatch, Susan.
Scandalous risks / Susan Howatch.
p. cm.
ISBN 0-394-58886-X
I. Title.
PS3558.0884S29 1990
813'.54—dc20   90-53076 CIP

Manufactured in the United States of America
Published November 2, 1990
Reprinted Once
Third Printing, November 1990

Contents

PART ONE

THE
GARDEN

"For the true radical is not the man who wants to root out the tares from the wheat so as to make the Church perfect: it is only too easy on these lines to reform the Church into a walled garden. The true radical is the man who continually subjects the Church . . . to the claims of God in the increasingly non-religious world which the Church exists to serve."

JOHN A. T. ROBINSON
Suffragan Bishop of Woolwich,
1959–1969
HONEST TO GOD

I

"We all need, more than anything else, to love and be loved."

JOHN A. T. ROBINSON
writing about Honest to God *in the*
Sunday Mirror, *7 April 1963*

I

I NEVER meant to return to the scene of my great disaster. But one day, after yet another wasted weekend among alcoholic adulterers, I took a wrong turn on the motorway and saw the sign to Starbridge. Immediately I tried to escape. I drove up the next slip-road, but as I crossed the bridge to complete the U-turn I made the mistake of glancing south, and there, far away in the gap between the hills, I saw the spire of the Cathedral.

1988 dissolved into 1963. I glimpsed again my Garden of Eden, and as I hesitated at the wheel of my car, the rope of memory yanked me forward into the past. I forgot the U-turn, I forgot the motorway, I forgot my wasted weekend. On I drove to Starbridge along that well-remembered road which snaked between the hills before slithering to the floor of the valley, and ahead, appearing and disappearing with each twist of the road like some hypnotic mirage, the Cathedral grew steadily larger in the limpid summer light.

The city stood in the heart of the valley, but it was the Cathedral, eerie in its extreme beauty, which dominated the landscape, and as I stared at the spire I saw again that vanished world where the Beatles still had short hair and skirts were yet to rise far above the knee and the senior men of the Church of England still dressed in archaic uniforms. Then as I remembered the Church in those last innocent days before the phrase "permissive society" had been invented, I thought not only of those scandalous risks taken by Bishop John Robinson when he had written his best-seller *Honest to God,* but of the scandalous risks taken by my Mr. Dean as he had run his Cathedral and dallied with disaster and indulged in his dangerous dreams.

I reached the outskirts of the city.

It was very old. The Romans had built their city Starovinium on the site formerly occupied by the British tribe the Starobrigantes; the Anglo-Saxons had converted Starovinium into Starbrigga, a landmark in King Alfred's Wessex; the Normans had recorded the town as Starbrige in Domesday Book, and Starbrige it had remained until the author of an eighteenth-century guidebook had fabricated the legend that the name was derived from the Norman bridge across the river Star. Starbridge then acquired its modern spelling, but the link with its remote origins lingered on in the Bishop's official designation. In theory married to his diocese, he was entitled to use "Staro" as his surname whenever he wrote his signature. I had no idea who the current Bishop of Starbridge was, but I could remember the Bishop of twenty-five years ago as clearly as I could remember the Cathedral's Dean.

I drove into the city but it was not as I had known it. Starbridge had been raped in the later years of the 1960s, like so many other dignified county towns. The new housing estates now stretched to the cemetery; there was a by-pass, a shocking aberration on concrete stilts—how my Mr. Dean would have hated that!—and in the oldest part of the town I found a one-way traffic system so baffling that I had to circle the market-place three times before I could find my way out. Then I got lost in the network of streets I had known so well, the streets around St. Martin's-in-Cripplegate. Butchers' Alley was a pedestrian precinct; Chasuble Lane was blocked by a NO ENTRY sign. Completely confused I fled down Mitre Street only to find a hideous multi-storey car-park leering at me as I flashed by Marks and Spencer's, but ahead I could see the traffic lights of Eternity Street and with relief I realised that the past was finally at hand. Seconds later, still swearing and sweating after my excursion in the maze, I was driving through the arched gateway into the Cathedral Close.

At once the constable on duty flagged me down. I was told that no parking was available unless I was calling on diocesan business or visiting a resident. I almost declared: "I've come to see the Dean!" but somehow I hauled myself back to 1988, produced a five-pound note and said instead: "Would this do?" The constable was deeply shocked. He said: "I'm afraid not, madam," and in rage I retired to the multi-storey car-park, but I felt cheered to learn that even now, in the heart of Mrs. Thatcher's England, there were still some things which were not for sale.

I left my Mercedes sulking by a down-market Ford and emerged from the car-park into a street which ran down to the Crusader Hotel. I was progressing at last. The Crusader faced St. Anne's Gate, the pedestrian entrance to the Cathedral precinct, and a minute later I was entering the huge walled enclosure of the Close.

The Cathedral rose from the lawn of the churchyard like a vast cliff towering upwards from a beach. The building still had the power to bring me gasping to a halt, but no sooner had I told myself that nothing had altered than I realised the place was awash with tourists. The Japanese, the Americans, the Germans, the French—all were on parade with their cameras and their guides, and amidst the flotillas of foreigners the English drifted idly, grey-haired ladies on outings, hikers with backpacks, even a bunch of teenage bores with beercans, their ghetto-blasters silenced by the Constable of the Close. I was just marvelling at the diversity of these superfluous people when I became aware that they were united by their behaviour: they were all constantly looking up, and at last I looked up too; I looked beyond the slim windows, beyond the gargoyles, beyond the roof of the nave to the great cross which marked the summit of the spire.

That at least was unchanged.

But soon I felt the crowds were oppressive, and in the hope of escaping from them I tried to enter the Cathedral. The main doors of the west front were closed. So was the door in the north porch. Between the hours of ten and five, I discovered, all tourists were channelled through a side door by the cloisters where turnstiles heralded a request for money. "It's only a voluntary contribution, of course," said the dragon on duty at the cash-register. I flung her the five-pound note which the constable had refused. In shock she gabbled her thanks but I ignored her and stalked into the Cathedral.

It was infested with tourists. They swarmed and buzzed and hummed and clattered. Official guides droned. Cameras flashed illicitly. In horror I fled down the side-aisle of the nave and re-entered the cloisters by the door in the south transept, but even in that secluded quadrangle it proved impossible for me to be alone with my memories. A bevy of matrons declared that everything was "awesome" and "wondrous" and far better than that cathedral they had seen yesterday or was it the day before. Elbowing my way past them I tried to find the wooden seat where my Mr. Dean and I had sat so often, but it had been removed. Tears stung my eyes. I felt I was engaged in an exercise of overpowering futility. My Garden of Eden had been ploughed under. Here I stood, in one of the greatest cathedrals in England, and it was no more than a Disney theme-park. God was absent. There was no whiff of holiness, no whisper of religion and not even a clergyman in sight.

But then I saw my clergyman. I glanced down the north colonnade at the moment that he entered the cloisters by the transept door. It was not my Mr. Dean; he was long dead. It was the man I had labelled my Talisman. He recurred in my life. I thought of him as a portent, sometimes heralding disaster but often merely signifying change. Some years had elapsed since we had last met, but now here he was again, a tall thin man some five or six years my junior with straight brown hair and a strong-boned face. He was no longer wearing glasses but I recognised him at once. He had more trouble recognising me. I saw him look in my direction, glance away, then stop to look back. The tourists swarmed between us, but as he moved forward they automatically stepped aside to make way for him.

"Venetia?" he said amazed, and at once as I saw myself through his eyes I realised how odd my presence must have seemed. It was surely not often that a raddled wreck of a society woman was washed up on such a beautiful but polluted shore.

"Hullo, soothsayer!" I said, instinctively assuming a synthetic gaiety, although why I attempted to deceive him about my state of mind I have no idea. I should have realised that the passing years would only have heightened his intuitive powers.

"This place is worse than Piccadilly Circus," he said, ignoring my pathetic attempt to be debonair. "Want to be rescued?"

"Passionately."

"Follow me."

With an unutterable relief I hurried after him as he led the way around the quadrangle. The door on the south side was marked PRIVATE but my Talisman, that human amulet who could achieve extraordinary results, ignored the sign and drew me into the stonemasons' yard beyond the wall. Various workmen, engaged in the unending task of restoring the Cathedral's fabric, were moving among the blocks of stone, but no one queried our presence. My companion's clerical collar was no doubt sufficient to rebuff any thought of a challenge. On the far side of the yard we reached a second door. This one was marked CHOIR SCHOOL ONLY, but once again my Talisman, ignoring the sign, led me through the doorway into another world.

"It's the garden of the old episcopal palace," he said. "Ever been here?"

"No." The palace had been ceded to the Choir School after the war, and by the time I had started moving among the ecclesiastical elite of Starbridge, the Bishop had lived in the house known as the South Canonry on the other side of the Close.

I suddenly realised there were no other human beings in sight. A silence broken only by birdsong enveloped us. The garden shimmered bewitchingly in the hot bright light.

"Where are all the choirboys?" I said, hardly able to believe such peace was not in imminent danger of destruction.

"On holiday. Relax," said my Talisman, and led the way past a shrubbery to a newly mown lawn which stretched to the river. Weeping willows trailed their branches in the water, and beyond the far bank meadows strewn with buttercups unfolded towards the hazy blue outline of the hills which surrounded the valley. The only building in sight was a farmhouse a mile away. Although we stood in the heart of Starbridge, nothing had changed on this flank of the city where the river looped around the mound on which the Cathedral stood. The water-meadows had been preserved as common land since the Middle Ages and protected in recent years by the National Trust.

As we sat down on a weathered bench by the water I said: "How clever of you to bring me to a place where the past survives intact!"

"You were looking for the past?"

"God knows what I was looking for."

"The past can survive in many forms," said my companion, "and unlike this beautiful view, not all those forms are benign."

"Quite. Hence the massive fees commanded by psycho-analysts."

"There are other liberators."

"Don't you mean con-men?"

"No, con-men can't open the prison gates once the past has become a jail."

"No magic wand?"

"No magic password."

"And what, may I ask, is the magic password of the true liberator?"

" 'Forgive.' "

The conversation ceased but the river glided on, the brilliant light glittering so fiercely on the water that my eyes began to ache. Looking away I saw that my right hand was gripping the arm of the seat. The paint on my fingernails was the colour of blood, and suddenly I saw myself as someone who had long suffered a debilitating haemorrhage but had abandoned all hope of a cure.

"You're wasting your time," I said. "I'm beyond liberation. Run away and liberate someone else." And then before I could stop myself I was exclaiming in despair: "I wish I'd never come back to this place! Usually I never even think of that bloody, *bloody* year—"

"Which year?"

"1963, but I don't want to talk about it."

"That was the year of *Honest to God,* wasn't it? I remember it well— and I remember you too, full of *joie de vivre*—"

"Oh yes, that was me, oozing *joie de vivre* from every pore—"

"So what went wrong?"

There was another silence before I answered: "Well, you see . . ." But I was unable to finish the sentence. Then I said: "Well, to put the matter in a nutshell . . ." But again I had to stop. It was only after yet another silence that I heard myself say in a voice devoid of emotion as I confessed the emotion I could never forget: "Well, the trouble was . . . I became so very, very fond of my darling Mr. Dean."

2

MY Mr. Dean had been christened Norman Neville and during the course of his career he had possessed various clerical titles, but I shall refer to him throughout this narrative by his surname, Aysgarth, because it was the one designation which never changed. He had left the name Norman behind in infancy when his mother decided to call him Neville, and he had left the name Neville behind in the 1940s when his ghastly second wife insisted on addressing him as Stephen; she had declared that the name Neville had been ruined by the unfortunate Mr. Chamberlain, and that only a pure, noble, serious name such as Stephen could ever be good enough for the man she intended to marry. It had apparently never occurred to her that these dreary adjectives hardly did her husband justice, but Aysgarth, whose tolerance of his wife's peculiarities bordered on the masochistic, had raised no objection to this despotic rechristening, and after his second marriage in 1945 the number of people who knew him as Neville had steadily declined.

"If any woman tried to alter *my* name I'd put her in her place pretty damned quickly, I assure you!" my father declared once to my mother when I was growing up, although in fact Aysgarth's Christian name was irrelevant to him. My father was old-fashioned enough to call all men outside our family by their surnames, so although he and Aysgarth were close friends the relationship sounded more formal than it was. For years after their first meeting Aysgarth had addressed my father as "my lord" or "Lord Flaxton," but in 1957 after Aysgarth received his great preferment my father had said to him: "Time to dispense with the title—address me as Flaxton in future." This invitation, so condescendingly delivered, was intended—and received—as a compliment. Indeed Aysgarth, who was the son of a failed Yorkshire draper, was so overcome that he blushed like a schoolboy.

"Dear Mr. Aysgarth!" mused my mother long ago in the 1940s when I was still a child. "Not quite a gentleman, of course, but *such* a charming way with him at dinner-parties!"

My father and I first met Aysgarth on the same day in 1946. I was nine, my father was fifty-five and Aysgarth, then the Archdeacon of Starbridge, was forty-four. I had been sent home early from school after throwing an inkpot at some detestable girl who had called my father a "barmy peer." I hated this local hell-hole and longed for a governess, but my father, whose idealism forced him to subscribe to the view that patricians should make efforts to mix with the plebeians, was resolute in sending all his daughters to school. The schools were private; my mother would certainly have balked at the prospect of her daughters being sacrificed on the altar of state education, so I never met the so-called "lower orders," only the infamous middle classes who, I quickly learnt, considered it their mission in life to "take snooty, la-di-da pigs down a peg or two." If the middle classes hadn't been so busy conquering the world for England in the nineteenth century I doubt if the upper classes would have survived into the twentieth.

"You did quite right to throw the inkpot!" said my father after I had defended my behaviour by telling him how he had been abused. "One can't take insults lying down—I've no patience with Christians who waffle on about turning the other cheek!"

"And talking of Christians," said my mother before my father could give his well-worn performance as an agnostic lion rampant, "don't forget the Archdeacon's calling on you this afternoon."

"What's an archdeacon?" I said, delighted that my father had supported me over the inkpot and anxious to retain his attention.

"Look it up in the dictionary." He glanced at his watch, set me firmly aside and walked out.

I was skulking sulkily in the hall five minutes later when the doorbell rang and I decided to play the butler. I opened the front door. In the porch stood a short, broad-shouldered man who was dressed in a uniform which suggested an eccentric chauffeur. He had brown hair, rather bushy, and the kind of alert expression which one so often sees on the faces of gun-dogs. His eyes were a vivid blue.

"All chauffeurs should go to the back entrance," I said, speaking grandly to conceal how unnerved I was by this curious apparition in gaiters.

"I'm not a chauffeur—I'm an archdeacon," he said smiling at me, and asked my name. To put him to the test I answered poker-faced: "Vanilla," but he surmounted the challenge with ease. "How very charming and original!" he exclaimed, not batting an eyelid, and told me I reminded him of Alice in Wonderland.

I was hardly able to believe that any adult could be so agreeable. "If I'm Alice," I said, testing him again to make sure I was not mistaken, "who are you?"

"If you're Alice, I think I'd like to be Lewis Carroll," said my future Mr. Dean, exuding the charm which was to win my mother's approval, and that was the moment when I knew for certain that he was my favourite kind of person, bright and sharp, quick and tough, yet kind enough to have time for a plain little girl with ink-stained fingers and an insufferable air of grandeur.

My father's reaction to Aysgarth was startlingly similar to mine. "I like that man," he kept saying afterwards. "I *like* him." He sounded amazed. Hitherto he had regarded all clergymen as the victims of an intellectual aberration.

"You'll never believe this," said my mother that evening on the telephone to my elder brother in London, "but your father's fallen violently in love with a clergyman—no, not the local parson who's gone round the bend! Your father complained about the parson to the Bishop, and the Bishop sent the Archdeacon to investigate, and it's the *Archdeacon* who's won your father's heart. Your father's even saying he's seen the Virgin Birth in a new light—he's dreadfully unsettled, poor dear."

This evidently alarmed my brother very much. Outraged squawks emerged from the telephone.

However the truth was that my father was neither suffering from the onset of senility nor undergoing a religious conversion. He was merely having to upgrade his opinion of clergymen because Aysgarth, an Oxford graduate, was one of those rare beings, my father's intellectual equal. A clergyman who had won a first in Theology could be dismissed; theology was not a subject which my father took seriously. But a clergyman who had been at Balliol, my father's own college, and taken a first in Greats, that Olympian academic prize which even my father had had to toil to achieve—there indeed was a clergyman who defied dismissal.

"I've come to the conclusion that Mr. Aysgarth's a great blessing," said my mother to me later. "Clever men like your papa become bored if they don't have other clever men to talk to, so perhaps now he's discovered Mr. Aysgarth he won't be such a crosspatch whenever he's obliged to leave London and spend time at Flaxton Hall."

I said: "If I read Greats up at Oxford, would Papa like me better?"

"Darling, what a thing to say! Papa adores you—look how he stood up for you about the inkpot! Papa and I love all our children," said my mother vaguely, wandering away from me to attend to her plants in the conservatory, "and you're a very lucky little girl to belong to such a happy family."

I stood alone, staring after her, and wished I could be one of the exotic plants to which she paid so much devoted attention.

AYSGARTH had a brother, who taught classics at a minor public school in Sussex, and a sister, who lived in the south London suburbs, but these siblings were rarely mentioned; he was fond of them but they had no place in the world he had carved out for himself since he had entered the Church. He had decided to be a clergyman when he was up at Oxford on his scholarship. This had been a brave decision, since he had had no money and no influential clerical connections, but Aysgarth was capable of great daring and possessed the iron nerves of a successful gambler.

"Aysgarth may look the soul of propriety in his clerical uniform," my father remarked once to my mother, "but by God he takes scandalous risks!" My father often talked riskily, particularly when he succumbed to the childish urge to shock people he disliked, but in fact he lived a very conventional life for a man of his class. If he had been Aysgarth, obliged to make his own way in the world, he would have played safe, using the Oxford scholarship to follow an academic career. To enter the Church, where salaries were risible and worldly success for any self-made man was unlikely, would have struck my father as being reckless to the point of lunacy. Outwardly opposed to Christianity but inwardly attracted to the aspects which coincided with his own old-fashioned, sentimental liberal humanism, he was enthralled by the madcap idealism which seemed to him to characterise Aysgarth's choice of a profession.

"It was such a courageous step to take, Aysgarth!"

"Nonsense! God called me to serve Him in the Church, so that was that. One doesn't argue with God."

"But your intellect—surely you were obliged to give rational consideration to—"

"What could be more rational than the decision to use my gifts in a way which would most clearly manifest my moral and intellectual convictions?"

My father was silent. Unable to risk believing in knowledge which his arrogant intellect deemed unknowable, he was speechless when confronted by Aysgarth's act of faith. No rhetoric from an evangelist could have dented my father's agnosticism, but Aysgarth, never speaking of Christianity unless my father raised the subject, presented the most powerful apologetic merely by revealing his life-story. My father was baffled but respectful, disapproving yet filled with admiration.

"But how did you have the nerve to marry when you were still a curate? Wasn't that an absolutely scandalous risk for a penniless young man to take?"

"I'd been engaged for seven years—wouldn't it have been even more of a scandalous risk if I'd waited a day longer?" retorted Aysgarth, and added to my mother as if he knew he could rely on her sympathy: "I regarded my first wife as the great prize which lay waiting for me at the end of my early struggles to get on in the world."

"So romantic!" sighed my mother predictably.

"Mr. Aysgarth," I said, fascinated by his unembarrassed reference earlier in the conversation to the Deity whom my family felt it bad taste to discuss, "did God tell you to marry, just as He told you to be a clergyman?"

"Be quiet, Venetia, and don't interrupt," said my father irritably. "Sophie, why isn't that child in bed?"

But my Mr. Dean—my Mr. Archdeacon as he was then—merely winked at me and said: "We might talk about God one day, Vanilla, if you've nothing better to do," and when both my parents demanded to know why he was addressing me as if I were an ice-cream, I realised with gratitude that he had diverted them from all thought of my bed-time.

According to various people who could remember her, Aysgarth's first wife had been beautiful, intelligent, charming, religious and utterly devoted to her husband and children. Aysgarth seldom mentioned her but once when he said: "Grace was much too good for me," he sounded so abrupt that I realised any question about her would have exacerbated a grief which was still capable of being painfully recalled. The marriage had produced five children, four boys and a girl, Primrose, who was my age. The children were all either brilliantly clever or remarkably good-looking or, as in the case of Christian and Norman, both. James, the third son, was good-looking but not clever, and Alexander, the youngest, was clever but not good-looking. Primrose, who had a face like a horse, was brilliant and I became close friends with her, but I shall return to the subject of Primrose later.

Then in 1942 when Christian, the eldest, was fifteen and Alexander was little more than a baby, the first Mrs. Aysgarth died and my Mr. Archdeacon became entangled with the appalling creature who was to become his second wife. She was a society girl, famed for her eccentricities. Everyone declared that no woman could have been less suitable for a clergyman, but Aysgarth, bold as ever, ignored this judgement and lured his *femme fatale* to the altar soon after the end of the war. Everyone then proclaimed that the marriage would never last and he would be ruined, but "everyone," for once, was wrong.

A year after the marriage came the vital meeting with my family. "All clergymen with balls should be encouraged!" pronounced my father, and proceeded to throw his weight about at Westminster in an effort to win preferment for his new friend. Having devoted many years of his life to politics in the House of Lords my father was not without influence, and the Church of England, under the control of the Crown, was always vulnerable to the meddling of the Crown's servants in the Lords and Commons. Usually the Church succeeded in going its own way without too much trouble, but although on ecclesiastical matters the Prime Minister took care to listen to the leading churchmen, he was not obliged to act on their advice. This situation occasionally reduced eminent clerics to apoplectic frenzy and led to chilly relations between Church and State.

Into this delicate constitutional minefield my father now charged, but fortunately it proved unnecessary for him to charge too hard because Aysgarth was well qualified for a choice promotion; he had been appointed archdeacon at an unusually early age after winning the attention of the famous Bishop Jardine who had romped around Starbridge in the 1930s. Jardine had retired before the war in order to swill port in Oxfordshire, and without a powerful benefactor a self-made man such as Aysgarth might well have languished in the provinces for the rest of his career, but he did have an excellent *curriculum vitae* and my father did have the urge to play God. In consequence Aysgarth's transfer to London, where his talents could be fully displayed to the people who mattered, was hardly a big surprise.

"If you're an agnostic," I said to my father at one stage of his campaign, "why are you getting so mixed up with the Church?"

"The Church of England," said my father grandly, "belongs to all Englishmen, even unbelievers. It's a national institution which for moral reasons deserves to be encouraged, and never forget, Venetia, that although I'm an agnostic and even, in moments of despair, an atheist, I remain always an exceedingly moral man. This means, *inter alia,* that I consider it my absolute moral duty to ensure that the Church is run by the very best men available."

"So it's all right for me to be interested in the Church, is it?"

"Yes, but never forget that the existence of God can't be scientifically proved."

"Can the non-existence of God be scientifically proved?" I enquired with interest, but my father merely told me to run away and play.

Aysgarth was still too young to be considered for a bishopric or a deanery, and when it was agreed by the Church authorities that a little London grooming was necessary in order to eliminate all trace of his modest background, a benign Prime Minister offered him a canonry at Westminster Abbey—although not the canonry attached to St. Margaret's church where so many society weddings took place. (This disappointed my mother, who was busy marrying off her eldest daughter at the time.) The canon's house in Little Cloister had been badly damaged by a bomb during the war, but by 1946 it had been repaired and soon Aysgarth's frightful second wife had turned the place into a nouveau-riche imitation of a mansion in Mayfair.

I must name this woman. She had been christened Diana Dorothea but her acquaintances, even my father who shied away from Christian names, all referred to her as Dido despite the fact that they might be socially obliged to address her as Mrs. Aysgarth. She was small, slim and smart; she dressed in a bold, striking style. Numerous falls from horses (the result of a mania for hunting) had bashed her face about so that she was ugly, but possibly she would have been ugly anyway. She always said exactly what she thought, a habit which regularly left a trail of devastation in her wake, and her wit—overrated, in my opinion—was as famous as her tactlessness. "Dido can always make me laugh," said my Mr. Dean—my Canon, as he had now become. He was amazingly patient with her, always serene even when she was crashing around being monstrous, and his reward was her undisguised adoration. "Of course I could have married anyone," she declared carelessly once, "so wasn't it too, too sweet of God to keep me single until I'd met darling Stephen?"

"Is any further proof needed," muttered Primrose, "to demonstrate that God moves in mysterious ways?"

Primrose hated her stepmother.

"Really, Primrose . . ." Those syllables always heralded some intolerable remark. "Really, Primrose, I can't understand why you don't invest in some padded bras. I certainly would if I were unfortunate enough to have your figure . . ." "Really, Primrose, we must do something about your clothes! No wonder no man asks you out when you look like someone from a D.P. camp . . ." "Really, Primrose, you must try not to be so possessive with your father—possessiveness, I've always thought, is inevitably the product of a low, limited little nature . . ."

"If she were my stepmother," I said to Primrose after witnessing one of these verbal assaults, "I'd murder her."

"Only the thought of the gallows deters me," said Primrose, but in fact it was her love for her father that drove her to endure Dido.

Aysgarth wound up fathering five children in his second marriage, but three died either before or shortly after birth and only a boy and a girl survived. Elizabeth was a little monster, just like her mother, but Philip was placid and gentle with an affectionate nature. Not even Primrose could object to little Pip, but she had a very jaundiced opinion of Elizabeth, who would scramble up on to her father's knees, fling her arms around his neck and demand his attention at every opportunity. Aysgarth complicated the situation by being far too indulgent with her, but Aysgarth was incapable of being anything but indulgent with little girls.

My father had naively thought that once Aysgarth was ensconced in the vital Westminster canonry peace would reign until the inevitable major preferment materialised, but before long Aysgarth's reckless streak got the better of him and he was again taking scandalous risks. Having run a large archdeaconry he quickly became bored with his canonry, and as soon as he had mastered the intricacies of Abbey politics he decided to seek new worlds to conquer in his spare time. He then got mixed up with Bishop Bell of Chichester, a remarkable but controversial celebrity who was always tinkering with international brotherhood and ecumenism and other idealistic notions which the more earthbound politicians at Westminster dubbed "hogwash." The most dangerous fact about Bishop Bell, however, was not that he peddled hogwash from the episcopal bench in the House of Lords, but that he was loathed by Mr. Churchill, and as the Labour Government tottered in slow motion towards defeat, it became increasingly obvious that Mr. Churchill would again become Prime Minister.

"Think of your future, Aysgarth!" implored my father. "It's death to get on the wrong side of these politicians!"

"Then I must die!" said Aysgarth cheerfully. "I refuse to be an ecclesiastical poodle."

"But if you want to be a bishop or a dean—"

"All I want is to serve God. Nothing else matters."

My father groaned and buried his face in his hands.

"What's the difference between a bishop and a dean?" I demanded, taking advantage of his speechlessness to plunge into the conversation, and Aysgarth answered: "A dean is the man in charge of a cathedral. A bishop is the man in charge of a diocese, which is like a county—a large area which contains in addition to the cathedral a number of churches all with their own parishes. A bishop has a special throne, his *cathedra,* in the cathedral and sometimes he goes there to worship, but often he's looking after his flock by attending services all over the diocese."

"It's as if the bishop's the chairman of the board of a group of companies," said my father morosely, "and the dean is the managing director of the largest company. Aysgarth, how I wish you'd never got involved with that POW camp on Starbury Plain during the war! I can quite see how useful you are to Bell when he needs someone to liaise with the German churches, but if you want to avoid antagonising Churchill you've got no choice: you must wash your hands of all those damned Huns without delay."

"I'm a disciple of Jesus Christ, not Pontius Pilate!" said Aysgarth laughing. "Don't talk to me of washing hands!" And when my father finally laughed too, I thought what a hero Aysgarth was, unintimidated by my formidable father, unintimidated by the even more formidable Mr.

Churchill and determined, like the star of a Hollywood western, to stand up for what he believed to be right.

However, real life is far less predictable than a Hollywood western, and contrary to what my father had supposed, Aysgarth's work with the Germans failed to result in a lethal confrontation with Mr. Churchill as the clock struck high noon. Bishop Bell was undergoing that metamorphosis which time so often works on people once judged controversial, and in the 1950s he became so hallowed that any hand-picked confederate of his could hardly fail to acquire a sheen of distinction. With Bell's patronage Aysgarth became renowned as an expert on Anglo-German church relations. He formed the Anglo-German Churchmen's Society; he raised funds to enable German refugees in England to train for the priesthood; he kept in touch with the numerous German POWs to whom he had once ministered in the Starbridge diocese. Like Bell, Aysgarth had been uncompromisingly opposed to Nazism, but he saw his post-war work with the Germans as a chance to exercise a Christian ministry of reconciliation, and in the end it was this ministry, not his canonry at Westminster, which in the eyes of the senior churchmen made him very much more than just a youthful ex-archdeacon from the provinces.

"It was a terrible risk to mess around with all those damned Huns," said my father, "but he's got away with it." And indeed Aysgarth's failure, once he turned fifty, to receive his big preferment lay not in the fact that he had aligned himself with the pro-German Bishop Bell; it lay in the fact that he had a disastrous wife.

Dido prided herself on being a successful hostess. Her dinner-parties were patronised by an astonishing range of distinguished guests who enjoyed her eccentric remarks, but clerical wives are hardly supposed to toss off letters to the newspapers on controversial issues or make withering remarks about the Mothers' Union during an interview with a women's magazine. The press were rapidly enthralled with appalling results. Dido stopped giving interviews but could seldom resist a tart comment on any matter of public interest. ("What do you think of the conquest of Everest, Mrs. Aysgarth?" "Thank God someone's finally done it—I'm bored to death with the wretched molehill!" "Do you believe in capital punishment, Mrs. Aysgarth?" "Certainly! Flog 'em and hang 'em—and why not crucify 'em too? What was good enough for Our Lord ought to be good enough for mass-murderers!" "What do you think of the Suez crisis, Mrs. Aysgarth?" "The Archbishop of Canterbury should declare that the entire disaster is a Moslem plot to humiliate a Christian country, and all the soldiers going to the Canal should wear crosses, like the Crusaders!")

"Aysgarth will never receive preferment now," said my father in deepest gloom after the Suez comment had been plastered over William

Hickey's Diary in the *Daily Express.* "How could that woman ever be a bishop's wife? She'd outrage everyone in no time."

Hating to abandon hope I said: "Could he still be a dean?"

"Perhaps in one of the minor cathedrals a long way from London."

"Dido will never leave London except for Canterbury or York," said my mother dryly, but she was wrong. Late in 1956 after the Suez crisis had reached its catastrophic conclusion, Dido gave birth to her fifth and final child, a stillborn boy, and promptly lapsed into a nervous breakdown. From time to time in the past she had suffered from nervous exhaustion, but this episode was so severe that she was completely disabled. She had to spend a month in an establishment which was tactfully referred to as a convalescent home, and even when she emerged she could do no more than lie in bed in a darkened room.

"I think she fancies herself as Camille," said Primrose. "I'm just waiting for the first little consumptive cough."

"Maybe she'll commit suicide," I suggested.

"Not a hope. That sort never does. Too damn selfish."

The day after this conversation Aysgarth turned up on the doorstep of our London home in Lord North Street, a stone's throw from Westminster Abbey and the Houses of Parliament. My mother was out at a charity coffee-party, my father was downstairs in his study and I was lolling on the sofa in the first-floor drawing-room as I reread *Middlemarch.* By this time I was almost twenty and had recently returned with relief to England after enduring weeks of exile with family friends in Florence.

When I heard the doorbell I laid aside my book and padded out onto the landing. In the hall below me the butler had just opened the front door and Aysgarth was saying: "Lord Flaxton's expecting me," but from the tone of his voice I realised I should abstain from cascading down the stairs to offer him an exuberant welcome. I paused, keeping well back from the bannisters. Then as soon as the hall was empty I sped noiselessly down the staircase and pressed my ear to the door of my father's study.

". . . and since you've always taken such an interest in my career," I heard Aysgarth say, "I thought you should be the first to know that I have to leave London. There's no choice. Dido's health demands it."

My father at once became apoplectic with horror. I too was horrified but I did rouse myself sufficiently to check that my eavesdropping was unobserved. Fortunately a gossipy drone rising from the basement indicated that the servants had paused for elevenses. With confidence I returned my ear to the panel.

". . . and now that I've spoken to the psychiatrist," Aysgarth was saying, "I can clearly see that she needs to make a completely fresh start somewhere else. The tragedy is that back in 1946 she so desperately wanted to come to London because she felt that here she could play a major part in advancing my career. The present situation—and of course we all know my career's ground to a halt—is very hard for her to bear."

"Quite. But nonetheless—"

"The death of the baby was the last straw. Dido now feels she's a failure at everything she undertakes in this city, and she's convinced that she has no chance of happiness until she leaves it."

"But Aysgarth," said my father, trying to mask his despair by assuming a truly phenomenal gentleness, "that's all very well for Dido, but what about you?"

"I couldn't live with myself unless I'd done everything in my power to make Dido feel successful and happy."

There was a silence while my father and I boggled at this extraordinary statement. I was too young then to feel anything but a massive outrage that he should be acquiescing without complaint in the wrecking of his career, and it was only years later that I realised this was my first glimpse of the mystery which lay at the heart of his marriage.

"It's clear to me that I'm not meant to move any further up the ecclesiastical ladder," said Aysgarth at last when my father remained silent, "and I accept that. I confess I'd be happy to stay on in London and devote myself to my German interests, but obviously it's time for my life to take a new turn."

My father managed to say in a voice devoid of emotion, "I'll see what I can do about a Crown appointment."

"That's more than good of you, but quite honestly I think you'd be wasting your time if you tried to pull strings in Downing Street. I'm sure I must have the letters 'W.I.' against my name in the clerical files."

" 'W.I.'?"

" 'Wife Impossible.' "

"Ah." There was a pause. Obviously my father was so appalled that he needed several seconds to frame his next question. It was: "Surely Bell can do something for you?"

"Unfortunately no canonry's likely to fall vacant at Chichester at the moment, and apart from Chichester Bell's influence is mostly abroad—which is no use to me, since Dido couldn't possibly cope with the stress of living in a foreign country. I'll talk to Bell, of course, but—"

"If he can't produce anything suitable, Aysgarth, I believe your best bet would be to go straight to the top and talk to the Archbishop of Canterbury."

"He's been implacably opposed to Dido ever since she criticised the hat Mrs. Fisher wore at the Coronation."

"Oh God, I'd forgotten that disaster! All right, pass over Fisher. What about the Bishop of London?"

"He's fairly new and I still don't know him well."

"In that case you must approach his predecessor. Dr. Wand's not dead yet, is he?"

"I seem to have the knack of alienating even the nicest Anglo-Catholics."

"Then your Dean at Westminster—"

"He's been cool towards me for some time. I've been paying too much attention to my international concerns and not giving enough time to the Abbey."

"But there must be someone who can rescue you!" said my father outraged. "I thought Christians were supposed to be famous for their brotherly love!"

Aysgarth somehow produced a laugh but before he could reply my father said suddenly: "What about your old diocese? Can you approach the Bishop of Starbridge?"

"He's another man I don't know well. You're forgetting that I left Starbridge before he was appointed."

"But *I* know him," said my father, who was one of the largest landowners in the Starbridge diocese. "He's a dry old stick but we're on good terms. Just you leave this to me, Aysgarth, and I'll see what I can do . . ."

<h2 style="text-align:center">4</h2>

NEITHER my father nor Aysgarth hoped for more than a canonry, and both of them were aware how unlikely it was that any choice position would fall vacant at the right moment, but within twenty-four hours of their secret conference the Dean of Starbridge suffered a stroke and it was clear he would be obliged to retire. At once my father plunged into action. The deanery was a Crown appointment, but my father, undeterred by the thought of those hideous letters "W.I." in Aysgarth's file, started swamping the Prime Minister's clerical advisers with claret at the Athenaeum. He was helped by having an eligible candidate to promote: Aysgarth knew Starbridge well from his years as Archdeacon, and as a first-class administrator he was more than capable of running one of the greatest cathedrals in England. My father beavered away optimistically only to be appalled when the Prime Minister admitted to him during a chance encounter at the Palace of Westminster that since the deanery was such an important appointment he intended to let Archbishop Fisher have the last word.

"Oh my God!" I said in despair when my father broke the news. By this time I had insinuated myself into the crisis so successfully that my father was taking the unprecedented step of treating me as his confidante. "Mrs. Fisher's Coronation hat!"

"If Aysgarth fails to get that deanery," said my father, "just because Dido made a catty remark about a hat—"

"We can't let it happen, Papa, we simply can't—Fisher must be tamed." It was now 1957 and the entire summer stretched before us. "Is he interested in racing?" I demanded feverishly. "We could offer him our box at Ascot. Or what about tennis? We could offer him our debenture seats for the Wimbledon fortnight. Or cricket—you could invite him to the Pavilion at Lords—"

"My dear girl, Fisher's hardly the man to be swayed by mere frivolities!"

"Then what's his ruling passion in life?"

"Canon law."

The problem seemed insuperable.

After a pause during which we racked our brains for inspiration I asked: "Who, technically, has the power to overrule the Archbishop of Canterbury?"

"The Queen and God. I mean, the Queen. I really can't start believing in God at my age—"

"Never mind God, let's concentrate on the Queen. Why don't you pull a string at the Palace?"

"What string? I don't have a string—you know very well that I've never been the courtier type!"

"Now look here, Papa: are you a peer of the realm or aren't you?"

"I'm beginning to feel like the inhabitant of a lunatic asylum. Venetia, the Queen would only refer the matter back to the Prime Minister, and since we already know Macmillan's determined to pass the buck to Fisher—"

"Then we've just got to conquer that Archbishop. Let's think again. He's an ex-headmaster, isn't he? If you were to invite him to dinner with the headmaster of Eton and throw in the Bishop of Starbridge for good measure—"

"This has all come to pass because back in 1945 Aysgarth married that bloody woman!" exclaimed my father, finally giving way to his rage. "Why on earth did he marry her? That's what I'd like to know! Why on earth did he do it?"

It was a question I was to ask myself many times in the years to come.

OUR fevered plotting resulted in my father's decision to give a little all-male dinner-party at the House of Lords. This made me very cross as I had planned to charm the Archbishop by begging him to tell me all about his life as headmaster of Repton, but my father merely said: "Women should keep out of this sort of business. Why don't you start training for a decent job instead of loafing around smoking those disgusting cigarettes and reading George Eliot? If you'd gone up to Oxford—"

"What good's Oxford to me when all public-school Englishmen run fifty miles from any woman who's mad enough to disclose she has a brain bigger than a pea?"

"There's more to life than the opposite sex!"

"It's easy for you to say that—you're tottering towards your sixty-sixth birthday!"

"Tottering? I never totter—how dare you accuse me of senility!"

"If you can spend your time making monstrous statements, why shouldn't I follow your example?"

My father and I had this kind of row with monotonous regularity; I had long since discovered that this was an infallible way of gaining his attention. The rows had now become stylised. After the ritual door-slamming my long-suffering mother was permitted to play the peace-maker and bring us together again.

However on this occasion events failed to follow their usual course because before my mother could intervene my father took the unprecedented step of initiating the reconciliation. He did it by pretending the row had never happened. When I returned to the house after a furious walk around St. James's Park he immediately surged out of his study to waylay me.

"Guess what's happened!"

"The Archbishop's dropped dead."

"My God, that's close! But no, unfortunately the dead man's not Fisher. It's the Bishop of Starbridge."

I was appalled. "Our best ally!"

"Our only hope! I feel ready to cut my throat."

"Well, pass me the razor when you've finished with it."

We decided we had to be fortified by sherry. My mother was out, attending a meeting of the W.V.S. In the distance Big Ben was striking noon.

"What the devil do I do now?" said my father as we subsided with our glasses on the drawing-room sofa. "I can't face Fisher without Staro on hand to make his speech about how well Aysgarth ran the archdeaconry back in the forties. In Fisher's eyes I'm just a non-churchgoer. I was absolutely relying on Staro to wheel on the big ecclesiastical guns."

"Personally," I said, "I think it's time God intervened."

"Don't talk to me of God! What a bungler He is—if He exists—collecting Staro at exactly the wrong moment! If Aysgarth ever gets that deanery now it'll be nothing short of a miracle, and since I don't believe in miracles and since I strongly suspect that God is an anthropomorphic fantasy conjured up by mankind's imagination—"

The doorbell rang.

"Damn it," muttered my father. "Why didn't I tell Pond I wasn't at home to callers?"

We waited. Eventually the butler plodded upstairs to announce: "Canon Aysgarth's here, my lord."

"Oh, for heaven's sake show him up!" said my father crossly. "You know I'm always at home to Mr. Aysgarth!"

Pond retired. My father was just pouring some sherry into a third glass when Aysgarth walked into the room.

"Sit down, my dear fellow," said my father, "and have a drink. I assume you've heard the disastrous news."

"Abandon your sherry!" said Aysgarth. "Send for the champagne!"

We gaped at him. His eyes sparkled. His smile was radiant. He was euphoric.

In amazement my father exclaimed: "What on earth's happened?"

"Fisher summoned me to Lambeth Palace this morning. He said: 'Let's forget all the nonsense those women stirred up. We can't let the Church suffer in 1957 just because my wife wore a certain hat in 1953.' "

My father and I both gasped but Aysgarth, now speaking very rapidly, gave us no chance to interrupt him. " 'Starbridge is suddenly without either a bishop or a dean,' said Fisher, 'and both the cathedral and the diocese have problems which need solving urgently by the best men available—' "

"My God!" said my father.

"My God!" said my voice at exactly the same moment. I had a vague picture of an anthropomorphic deity smiling smugly in a nest of clouds.

"He offered me the deanery," said Aysgarth. "By that time, of course, I was almost unconscious with amazement, but I did somehow manage to open my mouth and say 'thank you.' "

For a moment my father was silent, and when he was finally able to speak he could produce only a Latin tag. It was an emotional: *"Fiat justitia!"*

Aysgarth tried to reply and failed. Mutely they shook hands. English-men really are extraordinary in their ruthless pursuit of the stiff upper lip. If those men had belonged to any other race they would no doubt have slobbered happily over each other for some time.

"Venetia," said my father at last, somehow achieving a casual tone, "ring the bell and we'll ask Pond to conjure up the Veuve Clicquot."

But I ignored him. Taking advantage of the fact that women were permitted to be demonstrative in exceptional circumstances, I exclaimed to Aysgarth for the first time in my life: "My darling Mr. Dean!" and impulsively slipped my arms around his neck to give him a kiss.

"Really, Venetia!" said my father annoyed. "Young women can't run around giving unsolicited hugs to clergymen! What a way to behave!"

But my Mr. Dean said: "If there were more unsolicited hugs in the world a clergyman's lot would be a happier one!" And to me he added simply, "Thank you, Venetia. God bless you."

In ecstasy I rang the bell for champagne.

II

"We need to be accepted as persons, as whole persons, for our own sake."

JOHN A. T. ROBINSON,
writing about Honest to God *in the*
Sunday Mirror, 7 April 1963

I

AYSGARTH drank quite a bit. Not quite a lot. But quite a bit. There's a difference. "Quite a lot" means serious drinking twice a day. "Quite a bit" means serious drinking occasionally and moderate drinking in between. Aysgarth was apparently the kind of drinker who seldom touched alcohol during the day but who regularly had a couple of whiskies at six o'clock. If he went to a dinner-party later he would then drink a glass of sherry before the meal, a couple of glasses of wine with the food and a hefty measure of port once the cloth was drawn. This was by no means considered a remarkable consumption in the political circles in which my father moved, and probably the upper reaches of London ecclesiastical society also regarded such drinking habits as far from excessive, yet by 1957 my father was afraid a rumour might circulate that Aysgarth was a secret drinker.

"He keeps his bottle of whisky behind the Oxford Dictionary in his study!" my father said scandalised to my mother after this eccentricity had been innocently revealed to him. "What a risk to take! He's paying lip-service, of course, to the tradition that clergymen shouldn't indulge in spirits, but what are the servants going to think when they discover the clandestine bottle? He'd do better to keep it openly on the sideboard!"

"Since Mr. Aysgarth hasn't had a lifetime's experience of dealing with servants," said my mother delicately, "perhaps he thinks they won't find out about the bottle."

"I disillusioned him, I assure you, but he didn't turn a hair. 'I'm not a drunk and my conscience is clear!' he declared, not believing a word I said, and he even had the nerve to add: *'Honi soit qui mal y pense!'* He's quite incorrigible."

My father also disapproved of Aysgarth's occasional trick of drinking too fast. On that day in 1957 as we celebrated the offer of the Starbridge deanery, he downed three glasses of champagne in a series of thirsty gulps and sighed as if longing for more. It was not offered to him. "Fancy drinking champagne like that!" said my father shocked to me afterwards. "No breeding, of course. Not brought up to drink champagne properly."

I opened my mouth to remind him of his blue-blooded friends who regularly consumed champagne as if it were lemonade, but then I decided not to argue. I was in too good a mood. Instead I merely proffered the opinion that Aysgarth was more than entitled to a quick swill after enduring his wife's nervous breakdown and the agonising worry over his future.

I was still savouring my relief that the crisis had ended when I learnt that a new cloud had dawned on the ecclesiastical horizon. Calling on us the next day Aysgarth confessed his fear that an old adversary of his might be appointed Bishop of Starbridge.

It was six o'clock. (Aysgarth always timed his visits to coincide with the possibility of refreshment.) My mother was attending a committee meeting of the Royal Society of Rose-Growers. Once again my father and I joined forces to support our harassed cleric.

"Have a whisky, my dear fellow," said my father kindly. "We'll pretend you're not wearing your clerical collar and can drink spirits with a clear conscience. Who's this monster who might be offered the bishopric?"

"Oh, he's no monster!" said Aysgarth hastily, sinking into the nearest armchair as my father added sodawater to a shot of Scotch. "He's just someone I'd be happy never to meet again."

"Your sworn enemy!" I said, reading between the Christian lines.

"Don't be facetious, Venetia," said my father. "This is serious. Do you have no power of veto, Aysgarth? Surely the Dean and Chapter are always consulted about the appointment of a new bishop?"

"Unofficially, yes, but officially we have to take the card we're dealt—and bearing in mind the fact that I've only just won the deanery by the skin of my teeth I'm hardly in a position to raise even an informal objection to this man."

"But who on earth is he, for God's sake?"

"The rumour bouncing off the walls of Church House," said Aysgarth after a huge gulp of whisky, "is that Charles Ashworth's been approached for the job."

"Oh, him! In that case you've nothing to worry about. He'll never take it."

"I know he's already turned down two bishoprics, but this could be the one bishopric he's unable to refuse. He'd rank alongside the bishops of London, Durham and Winchester—there'd be a seat available immediately in the House of Lords—he'd be only ninety minutes by train from the centres of power in the capital—and as if all these advantages weren't sufficient to seduce him, he'd have the challenge of pulling the Theological College together, and he's an expert on theological education."

"I've never heard of this man," I said. "Where's he been hiding himself? What's he like?"

"Oh, he's the most charming fellow!" said my father with enthusiasm. "Very keen on cricket. A first-class brain. And he's got a nice little wife too, really a *very* nice little wife, one of those little women who listen so beautifully that they always make a man feel ten feet tall—"

"The Reverend Dr. Charles Ashworth," said Aysgarth, ignoring this sentimental drivel as he responded to my demand for information, "is Lyttelton Professor of Divinity at Cambridge and a Canon of Cambridge Cathedral."

"So what's wrong with him?"

"Nothing. We're just temperamentally incompatible and theologically in different camps."

"Maybe he'll turn down the job after all!" I said brightly after we had all observed a moment of heavy silence. "Why did he turn down the previous bishoprics?"

My father commented: "Being a bishop isn't every clergyman's idea of heaven," and Aysgarth said: "Ashworth preferred life in his academic ivory tower." However as soon as this statement had been made he modified it by adding rapidly: "No, I shouldn't say that. Ashworth came down from his ivory tower in '39 when he volunteered to be an army chaplain. That was something I never did. Then he was a prisoner of war for three years. I never had to endure that either. After the war he did return to academic life but not, I'm sure, because he wanted to escape from the world. He must have felt genuinely called to resume his career of writing and teaching, and I'm sure this call is why he's turned down the previous bishoprics."

"So why should his call now change?"

"Because the offer's alluring enough to make him wonder if God might have other plans for him."

"Let's get this quite straight, Aysgarth," said my father, always anxious to eliminate God from any conversation. "Have you actually had a row with this man or is this just a case of polite mutual antipathy?"

"In 1946," said Aysgarth, "we had such a row that he smashed his glass in the fireplace and stormed out of the room."

"Impossible!" said my father, balking at the thought of a clergyman behaving like a Cossack. "Ashworth's such a charmer! What on earth was the row about?"

"The theology of redemption and the theology of the Incarnation."

"Impossible!" said my father again. "Two highly intelligent men going berserk over *theology*—of all subjects! No, no, Aysgarth, I refuse to believe it, you must be romancing!"

"I assure you I'm not—although to be fair to Ashworth," said Aysgarth with an effort, "I should explain that at the time he was obviously still suffering from his experiences as a POW."

Unable to restrain my curiosity I asked: "What exactly do you mean when you talk about the theology of redemption and the theology of the Incarnation?" but my father at once cried imperiously: "Stop!" and held up his hand. "I refuse to allow theology to be discussed in my drawing-room," he declared. "I value my collection of glasses too highly. Now Aysgarth, I'm sure you're worrying unnecessarily. Ashworth's not going to bear you a grudge just because you once drove him to behave like a hooligan during some bizarre tiff, and besides, you're now both such distinguished Christian gentlemen! If you do indeed wind up living in the same cathedral close, then of course you'll both have no trouble drawing a veil over the past and being civil to each other."

"Of course," said Aysgarth blandly, but he downed the rest of his Scotch as if he still needed to drown his dread.

2

THE appointments were eventually announced within a week of each other in *The Times*. Ashworth did accept the bishopric, although it was whispered on the Athenaeum's grapevine that he nearly expired with the strain of making up his mind.

"I think I must now give a little men-only dinner-party for him and Aysgarth at the House of Lords," said my father busily to my mother. "It might be helpful in breaking the ice if they met again in a plain, simple setting without a crucifix in sight."

"Anything less plain and simple than that baroque bastion of privilege would be hard to imagine," I said, furious at this new attempt to relegate me to the sidelines, "and why do you always want to exclude women from your dinner-parties?"

"Don't speak to your father in that tone of voice, please, Venetia," said my mother casually without pausing to glance aside from the flowers she was arranging. "Ranulph, you needn't be afraid to hold the dinner-party here; Dido won't come. When I telephoned yesterday to enquire how she was, her companion said she was still accepting no invitations."

"And besides," I said, turning over a page of *Punch,* "if you stick to your misogynist principles, you won't be able to ogle that 'nice little wife' of Professor Ashworth's at the dinner-party."

"Nice little wife?" echoed my mother, sufficiently startled to forget her flower arrangement and face us. "Well, I've only met her a couple of times at dinner-parties, but I thought she was tough as nails, the sort of chairwoman who would say to her committee: 'I'm so glad we're all in agreement,' and then effortlessly impose her views on the dissenting majority!"

"For God's sake let's have both Ashworths to dinner as soon as possible," I said, tossing *Punch* aside. "I can't wait."

The dinner took place a fortnight later.

3

MY mother invited Primrose to accompany her father to the dinner-party, and she also extended an invitation to Aysgarth's third son, James, who was stationed with his regiment in London. Any young man in the Guards who can look dashing on horseback in a glamorous uniform will always be popular with mothers of unmarried daughters, but twenty-four-year-old males with the cultural limitations of a mollusc have never struck me as being in the least amusing.

"I wish you'd invited Christian and Norman as well as James," I grumbled, but my mother said she had to avoid swamping the Ashworths with Aysgarths. The Ashworths did have two teenage sons but at the time of the dinner-party Charley was doing his National Service and Michael was away at school.

I regretted being deprived of Christian; like every girl I knew I had gone through a phase of being madly in love with Aysgarth's eldest son, and although I had by this time recovered from my secret and wholly unreciprocated passion for this masculine phenomenon who looked like a film star and talked like a genius, a secret hankering for him lingered on.

Meanwhile, as I hankered in vain for Christian's presence at the dinner-party, my mother was obliged to add to the guest-list my brother Harold, an amiable nonentity, and his wife, Amanda, an expensive clothes-horse. They were in London on holiday but would eventually return to Turkey, where Harold had a job shuffling papers at the British Embassy and the clothes-horse fulfilled her vocation to be ornamental. Their combined IQ was low enough to lay a pall over any dinner-party, and to make matters worse my other brother—the one who on his good days could be described as no genius but no fool—had to speak in an important debate, a commitment which excluded him from the guest-list. Oliver, the Member of Parliament for Flaxfield, was also married to an expensive clothes-horse, but unlike Harold's ornament, this one had reproduced. She had two small boys who made a lot of noise and occasionally smelled. My three sisters, all of whom had manufactured quiet, dull, odourless daughters, were united in being very catty about Oliver's lively sons.

My eldest sister, Henrietta, lived in Wiltshire; she had married a wealthy landowner and life was all tweeds and gun-dogs interspersed with the occasional hunt ball. My second sister, Arabella, had married a wealthy industrialist and now divided her time between London, Rome and her villa at Juan-les-Pins. My third sister, Sylvia, had been unable to marry anyone wealthy, but fortunately her husband was clever at earning a living on the stock exchange so they lived in a chic mews house in Chelsea where Sylvia read glossy magazines and tended her plants and told the *au pair* how to bring up the baby. My mother disapproved of the fact that Sylvia did no charity work. Henrietta toiled ceaselessly for the Red Cross and even Arabella gave charity balls for UNICEF when-ever she could remember which country she was living in, but Sylvia, dreaming away among her plants, was too shy to do more than donate clothes to the local church.

I was mildly fond of Sylvia. She was the sister closest to me in age, but since we were so different there had been no jealousy, no fights. Having nothing in common we had inevitably drifted apart after her marriage, but whenever I felt life was intolerable I would head for her mews and sob on her sofa. Sylvia would ply me with instant coffee and chocolate digestive biscuits—an unimaginative response, perhaps, but there are worse ways of showing affection.

All my sisters were good-looking and Arabella was sexy. Henrietta could have been sexy but was too busy falling in love with gun-dogs to bother. Sylvia could have been sexy too but her husband liked her to look demurely chaste so she did. They all spoke in soprano voices with the affected upper-class accent which in those days was beginning to die out. I was a contralto and I had taken care to speak with a standard BBC accent ever since I had been teased by the middle-class fiends at my vile country preparatory school for "speaking la-di-da." My sisters had escaped this experience. They had attended an upper-class establishment in London before being shovelled off to an equally upper-class boarding school, but in 1945 my parents were able to reclaim Flaxton Hall, which had been requisitioned during the war, and they were both anxious to spend time in the country while they reorganised their home. I was then eight, too old for kindergarten, too young to be shovelled off to boarding school. Daily incarceration at the hell-hole at Flaxfield, three miles from our home at Flaxton Pauncefoot, proved inevitable.

Possibly it was this torturous educational experience which set me apart from my sisters, but it seemed to me I had always been the odd one out.

"That child gets plainer every time I see her," said Horrible Henrietta once to Absolutely-the-Bottom Arabella when they rolled home from Benenden for the school holidays. "Those broad shoulders are almost a deformity—she's going to wind up looking exactly like a man."

"Maybe she's changing sex. That would explain the tomboyish behaviour and the gruff voice . . ."

"Mama, can't something be done about Venetia's eyebrows? She's beginning to look like an ape . . ."

"Mama, have you ever thought of shaving Venetia's head and giving her a wig? That frightful hair really does call for drastic measures . . ."

My mother, who was fundamentally a nice-natured woman whenever she wasn't worshipping her plants, did her best to stamp on this offensive behaviour, but the attacks only surfaced in a more feline form when I reached adolescence.

"Can't someone encourage poor darling Venetia to take an interest in clothes? Of course I know we can't all look like a fashion-plate in *Vogue,* but . . ."

"Venetia, my sweet, you simply can't wear that shade of lipstick or people will think you're a transvestite from 1930s Berlin . . ."

Even my brothers lapsed into brutality occasionally.

"Oliver, you've got to help me find a young man for Venetia—"

"Oh God, Mama, don't ask me!"

"Harold, do explain to Venetia how ill-advised it is for a young girl to talk about philosophy at dinner-parties—she simply takes no notice when I tell her it's so dreadfully showy and peculiar—"

"Certainly, Mama. Now look here, Venetia old girl—and remember I speak purely out of fraternal affection—your average man doesn't like clever women unless they're real sizzlers, and since you'll never be a real sizzler . . ."

"Poor Venetia!" said Absolutely-the-Bottom Arabella to Horrible Henrietta when she knew quite well I was within earshot. "No sex-appeal."

"Well!" said my father with a sigh of relief once his third daughter was married. "Now I can sit back and relax! I don't have to worry about Venetia, do I? She'll never be a *femme fatale*."

". . . and I can't tell you how glad I am," I overheard my mother confiding to her best friend, "that Venetia will inevitably have a quieter life than the others. When I think of all I went through with Arabella—not to mention Henrietta—and even dearest Sylvia was capable of being a little too fast occasionally . . ."

I remembered that remark as I dressed for dinner on the night of the Aysgarth-Ashworth reunion, and wished I could be a sizzler so fast that no one would see me for dust. I slid into my best dress, which was an interesting shade of mud, but unfortunately I had put on weight with the result that the material immediately wrinkled over my midriff when I dragged up the zip. I tried my second-best dress. The zip got stuck. My third-best dress, which had a loose-fitting waist, was wearable but hopelessly out of fashion, and my fourth-best dress transformed me into a sausage again. In rage I returned to number three in the hope that I could divert attention from its unfashionable lines by swathing myself in jewellery.

"Darling, you look like a Christmas tree!" exclaimed my mother aghast as she glanced into the room to inspect my progress. "Do take off those frightful bracelets—and what on earth is Aunt Maud's diamond hatpin doing in your hair?"

I sank down on the bed as the door closed. Then in despair I tore away all the jewellery and began to wallop my impossible hair with a brush. Eventually I heard the guests arriving, and after a long interval Harold was dispatched to drag me into the fray.

"Come along, old girl—everyone's thinking you must have got locked in the lavatory!"

Loathing the entire world and wishing myself a thousand miles away I followed him downstairs. The sound of animated conversation drifted towards us from the drawing-room, and as I pictured everyone looking matchlessly elegant I had to fight the urge to run screaming through the streets to Sylvia's house in Chelsea.

"Here she is!" chirped idiotic Harold as I finally made my entrance.

All heads swivelled to gaze at my dead dress and diabolical hair. I had a fleeting impression of an unknown couple regarding me with mild astonishment, but just as I was wondering if it were possible to die of humiliation, my Mr. Dean exclaimed warmly: "My dear Venetia, how very delightful you look!" and he held out his hands to me with a smile.

IT was Aysgarth's kindness which first attracted me to Christianity; the contrast between his attitude and the callous remarks of the non-believers in my family was so great that I felt the explanation could only be theological. It was small wonder that I hero-worshipped him from an early age, but I must make it clear that I was never in love with him. Such a possibility was inconceivable, first because he was a married clergyman, a creature permanently unavailable for a grand passion, and second because he was over fifty years old and therefore incapable of being classed by my youthful brain as an object of sexual desire. Moreover Aysgarth had become considerably plainer since I had first met him in 1946. By the time of the Ashworth dinner-party eleven years later his springy brown hair was smoother, straighter and a shop-soiled shade of white, while his deeply lined face was marred by pouches under the eyes. He was also much heavier, not repulsively fat but markedly four-square. "Aysgarth's built like a peasant," my father remarked once, not meaning to be unkind but unable to abstain from that insensitive frankness which can be such an unfortunate trait of the aristocracy.

However after Aysgarth's heroic kindness to me at the beginning of that dinner-party, I would hardly have cared if he had been built like an elephant, and as soon as Primrose and I had the chance for a quick word I said to her enviously: "You're so damned lucky to have a father like that."

"Isn't he wonderful? All other men seem so dreary in comparison."

Immediately I felt annoyed with myself for giving her the opportunity to drool; once Primrose started flaunting her Elektra complex she was nauseous. "Professor Ashworth doesn't look too bad," I said in the hope of diverting her. "In fact I'd say he was rather well preserved for a man of his age."

After my embarrassing entry into the room my mother had cursorily introduced me to the Ashworths, but afterwards the Professor had been button-holed by Harold while Mrs. Ashworth had been cornered by my fascinated father so I had had no opportunity to converse with them. I now paused to inspect the Professor with care. He was a tall man who had kept his figure; I learned later that he had excelled at games in his youth and still possessed a single-figure handicap as a golfer. Middle age had given him a receding hairline, but his curly dark hair was streaked in just the right places with just the right shade of glamorous silver. He had brown eyes, a straight nose, a firm jaw with a cleft chin, and deep lines about his strong mouth. These lines, which immediately suggested past suffering, reminded me he had once been a prisoner of war.

I opened my mouth to remark to Primrose how rare it was to encounter a handsome cleric, but at that moment we were interrupted by James, Aysgarth's soldier-son, and I was obliged to endure a lot of jolly talk about nothing. Nevertheless I kept an eye on the Professor. He was gliding around, displaying a formidable social technique as he talked to everyone in turn. From various syllables which reached my ears I gathered he was even able to talk to Harold's clothes-horse about fashion.

Eventually Primrose was unable to resist abandoning me to move to her father's side, jolly James decided to take a hand in passing around the canapés (our butler Pond was most put out) and I was just pretending to inspect my mother's somewhat constipated flower arrangement when the future Bishop of Starbridge materialised at my elbow and said with such a polished charm that I even thought for a moment that he was genuinely interested in me: "I hear you've been visiting Florence. It's a beautiful city, isn't it?"

"Possibly," I said, determined not to simper at him merely because he was one of the most distinguished churchmen in England, "but I don't like Abroad."

"In that case I assume you're glad to be home!"

"Not specially, but don't let's waste time talking about me, Professor. I'm not a bit interesting, although it's very kind of you to pretend that I am. Why don't you tell me all about you?"

I had pierced the cast-iron professional charm. "Ah, so you're a listener!" he exclaimed with a seemingly genuine amusement. "How delightful!"

Mrs. Ashworth, slender and sleek in a black dress, chose that moment to interrupt us. My first impression had been that she was much younger than her husband, but now I saw that she was probably his contemporary; her neck had that crepe-like look which afflicts women past the menopause, but she was so immaculately made up that one barely noticed the tell-tale signs of age. Her dark hair was swept back from her forehead and drawn into a bun at the nape of her neck. Her rimless spectacles gave her a chaste, schoolmistressy look which was curiously at odds with the wicked little dress which clung to her svelte figure, and at once I decided she was far more interesting than her husband. The Professor seemed a very typical product of the best public schools and universities, but Mrs. Ashworth, whom I found impossible to place against any definitive background, didn't seem typical of anything.

She was saying lightly to her husband: "Vamping young girls again, darling?"

"Indeed I am—I've just discovered Miss Flaxton's a listener."

"Ah, a *femme fatale!*" said Mrs. Ashworth, regarding me with a friendly interest as I mentally reeled at her choice of phrase. "How clever of you, Miss Flaxton! Men adore good listeners—they have a great need to pour out their hearts regularly to sympathetic women."

"I do it all the time myself," said the Professor, effortlessly debonair. "Apart from golf it's my favourite hobby."

"How very intriguing that sounds!" said Aysgarth, sailing into our midst with his champagne glass clasped tightly in his hand. "Am I allowed to ask what this hobby is or should I preserve a discreet silence?"

There was a small but awkward pause during which I was the only one who laughed—a fact which startled me because although the remark could have been classed as risqué it could hardly have been described as offensive. Yet both Ashworths were as motionless as if Aysgarth had made some error of taste, and Aysgarth himself immediately began to behave as if he had committed a faux-pas. "Sorry," he mumbled. "Bad joke. Silly of me."

The Professor made a lightning recovery. "No, no!" he said, smooth as glass. "I was merely startled because you seemed to materialise out of nowhere!"

"Just thought I'd seize the chance for a quick word before we all go in to dinner—"

"Of course—I was thinking only a moment ago that I'd talked to everyone in the room except you—"

"Seems ages since we last met—"

"Yes, it's certainly a long time—"

"Oxford '52, wasn't it?" said Aysgarth, having regained his equilibrium with the aid of a large swig of champagne. "That weekend when we were both guests of the Master of Balliol."

"No, you've seen Charles since then," said Mrs. Ashworth. "We met in London when we all helped the Dean of Westminster recover from the Coronation."

"So we did! I'd quite forgotten . . . I'm sorry, I can't quite remember—dear me, I'm beginning to sound like an amnesiac—but did I ever call you Lyle?"

"I really have no idea," said Mrs. Ashworth, as if such a feat of memory was well beyond her capabilities, "but please do in future. Did I ever call you Neville?"

"Neville!" I exclaimed. "But no one calls him Neville nowadays—he's always Stephen!"

"Ah," said Mrs. Ashworth, "but you see, I met him before the war when Bishop Jardine appointed him Archdeacon of Starbridge. I was Mrs. Jardine's companion at the time."

Much intrigued I said: "But how romantic that you should now be re-turning in such style to the house where you were once a mere companion!"

"It would indeed be romantic if it were true, but the Jardines lived in the old episcopal palace which is now the Choir School, whereas Charles and I will be living—thank goodness!—in the South Canonry. I wouldn't have wanted to return to the palace," said Mrs. Ashworth serenely. "Too many"—she hesitated but for no more than a second—"poignant memories."

Aysgarth said: "Do you regret the loss of the palace, Ashworth?" but the Professor replied promptly: "Not in the least—and my dear fellow, if you're going to call my wife Lyle, I really don't see why you should now fight shy of calling me Charles! I only hope I have your permis-sion to call you Stephen in the interesting times which I'm sure lie ahead for us all."

Aysgarth at once became almost inarticulate with a shyness which I suspected was triggered not only by his social inferiority complex but by his gratitude that Ashworth should be making such a marked effort to be friendly. He could only manage to say: "Yes. Stephen. Fine. Please do," and toss off the remains of his champagne.

Appearing in contrast wholly relaxed Ashworth observed: "It really is most remarkable that our careers should have coincided like this—in fact, if you knew how often Lyle and I have been telling ourselves recently that God moves in mysterious ways—"

"Darling," said Mrs. Ashworth, "if you quote that ghastly cliché once more I shall be tempted to strangle you with your brand-new pectoral cross."

"More champagne anyone?" enquired jolly James, still playing the butler.

His father at once held out his glass. " 'Well, I don't mind if I do, sir!' as Colonel Chinstrap used to say on *I.T.M.A.*—"

"Oh, how I adored *I.T.M.A.!*" said my mother, drifting over to us and eyeing her constipated flower arrangement as if she had suddenly realised it needed a laxative. "Venetia, can you pass around the cigarettes? Pond seems to have disappeared in a huff for some reason . . ."

"That bishop-to-be is going to look simply too heavenly in gaiters," Harold's clothes-horse was drawling as she demolished her third dry martini.

"Can someone stop young James playing the butler?" muttered my father. "Pond's taken violent umbrage."

". . . and what I absolutely can't understand," idiotic Harold was burbling in a corner, "is how Pater, who can't bear going to church and has always said 'Boo!' to God, has got himself mixed up with these high-powered clerical wallahs."

"He'll probably wind up taking the sacrament on his deathbed," said Primrose, "like Lord Marchmain in *Brideshead.*"

"Brideshead?" said Harold. "Where's that?"

"I'm damned hungry," said my father to my mother. "Are they all dead drunk in the kitchen?"

"Dinner is served, my lord!" thundered Pond reproachfully from the doorway, and with relief we all descended to the dining-room.

5

THE next evening Aysgarth called at six o'clock with a note of thanks and a bunch of carnations for my mother, but found only me at home. My mother had travelled down to Flaxton Pauncefoot that morning and my father was attending a Lords' debate on education. Harold and the clothes-horse had not yet returned from a day at the races.

When Pond showed Aysgarth into the drawing-room I was reading Professor Ashworth's latest book, *St. Augustine and the Pelagian Heresy: The Origins of His Theology Concerning God's Grace,* which I had borrowed from the library. The Professor wrote in a cool, lucid prose which created an impression of scholarly detachment and yet succeeded in being surprisingly readable—but perhaps that was because he was writing of St. Augustine's fight to master his sex-drive, a fight which was to have immense repercussions both for Christianity and for the bluff heretic Pelagius who had said (more or less) that man could jolly well pull himself up by his own bootstraps and conquer sin not by God's grace but by will-power and a stiff upper lip.

Pelagius, it is hardly necessary to add, had been a Briton.

"Oh, I've read that book," said Aysgarth as we settled down for a delectable discussion of the dinner-party. "I thought it very bad. Like St. Augustine Charles's twin obsessions are heresy and sex. Apparently up at Cambridge all his divinity undergraduates refer to him as Anti-Sex Ashworth."

"How extraordinary! He seemed quite normal."

"No, no—rabid against fornication and adultery. Such a mistake! In my opinion there are far worse sins than the sexual errors, and—whoops! Here's Pond with the drinks."

Pond deposited the sherry and whisky decanters, the soda-siphon and a suitable selection of glasses on the side-table and waited for orders, but I waved him away.

"Help yourself, Mr. Dean."

"Well, perhaps a little soupçon of sherry—"

"Oh, go on—have a whisky! You don't want to go down in history as Anti-Alcohol Aysgarth!"

"That possibility," said my Mr. Dean, helping himself to a modest measure of Scotch, "is so remote that I don't think we need consider it seriously. And I must guard my tongue about Charles, who was certainly more than civil to me last night—even though I nearly shocked him to death with my opening remark—"

"But only a second before you arrived Mrs. Ashworth had been teasing him about vamping young girls! I don't think you shocked him at all—he was just taken aback because you slunk up behind him and—"

"—hit him over the head with a double-entendre! I must have been mad."

"I thought you were sensational. And so was Mrs. Ashworth, making that little black dress look like a hundred-guinea model from Harrods just by wearing one piece of jewellery—and choosing rimless spectacles instead of glasses with distracting frames—and dyeing her hair so cunningly that no man would ever dream it had been touched up—"

"*Dyeing her hair?* But no clergyman's wife would ever do that!"

"Yes, I expect that's what the Professor thinks too whenever he's not busy conquering everyone in sight by exuding that synthetic charm of his. But tell me: who *is* Mrs. Ashworth? Where did she come from? And how did the two of them meet?"

"Ah!" said Aysgarth, settling down cosily for a gossip. "Now that's quite a story . . ."

6

APPARENTLY Mrs. Ashworth had grown up in a remote Norfolk parish where her great-uncle had been the vicar; her parents had died young. This clerical background had enabled her to obtain the post of companion to Bishop Jardine's wife when Jardine himself, rocketing racily up the Church's ladder of preferment, had been appointed Dean of Radbury in the '20s. Five years later in 1932 he had become the Bishop of Starbridge. In 1937, the young Charles Ashworth, already a doctor of divinity, had decided to visit Starbridge to do some research in the cathedral library, and since he was the protégé of Archbishop Lang he had been invited to stay at the episcopal palace. Crossing the threshold he had fallen instantly and violently in love with Mrs. Jardine's companion.

Since Mrs. Jardine had been an ineffectual woman who had relied on her companion to run the palace for her, this *coup de foudre* had caused chaos, but Ashworth, much to the Bishop's fury, had refused to be deflected from his romantic charge to the altar.

"The whole trouble was," said Aysgarth, "that Lyle's departure was a bereavement for the Jardines as well as a crippling inconvenience. They were a childless couple who'd come to regard her as a daughter, and they'd reached the stage where they couldn't imagine life without her."

"Presumably they were all reconciled later?"

"Oh yes, but back in 1937—"

"—the Jardine dragon had to be vanquished before St. George could carry away the maiden on his shining white horse!"

"As a matter of fact whether he was a saint and she was a maiden was hotly debated later when the two of them produced a baby only seven months after the wedding, but since the infant was very small and delicate, just as a premature baby should be, everyone eventually agreed that the maiden's purity had been unsullied prior to her marriage."

"Rather tricky to be a clergyman," I said, "and produce a baby a shade too fast."

"Most embarrassing for poor Charles! However I never had any serious doubt that he'd behaved himself—he was always too ambitious to do anything else." As an afterthought he added: "He was married before—his first wife was killed in a car crash—but although he was a widower for some time before he met Lyle you can be sure he kept himself in order. The first thing a successful young clergyman learns to acquire, if he wants to continue as a success, is an immaculate self-control in dealing with women."

"At least nowadays clergymen can get married, which is more than poor St. Augustine could—although actually I don't understand why St. Augustine couldn't marry. Why did he have to be celibate?"

"Well, in the days of the Early Church . . ."

We embarked on a fascinating conversation about the origins of clerical celibacy, and Aysgarth promised to lend me his copy of St. Augustine's *Confessions.*

"My dear Venetia," he sighed at last as he finished his whisky and rose reluctantly to his feet, "how very much I enjoy talking to you!"

I smiled radiantly at him and felt like a sizzler.

7

I SHOULD perhaps make it clear that contrary to the impression I may have created while describing the turning point of his career, I did not see Aysgarth often. He led a busy life at Westminster, and I was often away.

After leaving boarding school I had been obliged to endure periods of exile in Switzerland and Italy, and even when I returned to England I often sneaked down to Flaxton Pauncefoot in order to escape from the ghastly London social events where I was either ignored or treated as a freak. Life drifted on. I had no idea what I wanted to do. My métier seemed to consist of sipping drinks, smoking cigarettes and reading books. There was no calling, no summons from God written in the sky in letters of fire, and increasingly often it seemed to me that my career as an adult was incapable of beginning so long as I remained condemned to the sidelines of life by my unfortunate looks and my embarrassing intellectual inclinations.

Sometimes I gave way to despair. Supposing I had to suffer the ultimate horror of not marrying? Then I would be "poor old Venetia," that pathetic freak, till my dying day. The prospect was intolerable. My depression deepened. My parents found me increasingly difficult, and soon after the Aysgarth-Ashworth dinner-party they decided that something would have to be done.

It was unusual for my parents to stage a joint-attack. My mother preferred to leave the bombastic behaviour to my father and take refuge in the conservatory, but on this occasion she was apparently desperate enough to decide that I was more important than her plants.

"We just thought we'd have a little word, darling," she said soothingly after we had all assembled for battle in the drawing-room of our house in Lord North Street. "Your father's actually quite worried about you."

"Worried?" said my father, bristling with rage. "I'm not worried, I'm livid! I shouldn't have to deal with a recalcitrant daughter at my age—it's bad for my blood pressure."

"You should have thought of that," I said tartly, "before you frolicked around with Mama in Venice in 1936."

"*Frolicked?* What a damn silly word—makes me sound like a bloody pansy!"

"Oh, do stop screaming at each other!" begged my mother, fanning herself lightly with the latest edition of *Homes and Gardens.* "What happened in '36 is quite irrelevant—except that here you are, Venetia, and we have to help you make the best of your life—which means we simply must insist that you now stop frivolling and—"

"Frivolling?" I mimicked. "What a damn silly word! Makes me sound like a bloody butterfly!"

"Oh my God," said my mother, taking refuge in *Homes and Gardens.*

"Just because you happen to be reading St. Augustine's *Confessions,*" said my father, storming into the attack, "you needn't think you're not frittering away your time—and I must say, I think Aysgarth should have asked my permission before he lent you that book. Parts of it are most unsuitable for an unmarried young woman."

"If you mean that incident in the public baths when Augustine was fourteen—"

"What a lovely picture of a cyclamen!" murmured my mother, gazing enrapt at a page of her magazine.

"If you'd gone up to Oxford," said my father to me, "as I wanted you to, you wouldn't be lying around sipping gin at odd hours, smoking those disgusting cigarettes and reading about fourteen-year-old boys in public baths!"

"If I'd gone up to Oxford," I said, "I'd be studying the work of Greek pederasts, ordering champagne by the case and damn well *looking* at fourteen-year-old boys in public baths!"

"Now look here, you two," said my mother, reluctantly tossing her magazine aside, "this won't do. Ranulph, you must try not to get so upset. Venetia, you must stop talking like a divorcée in an attempt to shock him—and you must try to remember that since he watched his own father die of drink and his brother die of—well, we won't mention what he died of—your father has an absolute horror of the havoc wealth can cause among people who lack the self-discipline to lead worthwhile, productive lives. The truth is that people like us, who are privileged, should never forget that privileges are always accompanied by responsibilities. We have a moral duty to devote our wealth and our time to worthy causes and live what the lower orders can see is a decent upright life."

"Hear, hear!" bellowed my father.

"I'm sure you think that was a dreadfully old-fashioned speech," pursued my mother, encouraged by this roar of approval to sound uncharacteristically forceful, "but believe me, it's neither smart nor clever to be an effete member of the aristocracy. You *must* be occupied in some acceptable manner, and fortunately for you, since you live today and not yesterday, that means you can train for an interesting job. I do understand, I promise you, why you chose not to go up to Oxford; being a bluestocking isn't every woman's dream of happiness. But since you've rejected an academic life you must choose some other career to pursue while you fill in your time before getting married. After all, even Arabella had a job arranging flowers in a hotel! I know she wound up in a muddle with that Italian waiter, but—"

"I don't want to arrange flowers in a hotel."

"Well, perhaps if you were to take a nice *cordon bleu* cookery course at Winkfield—"

"I don't want to take a nice *cordon bleu* cookery course at Winkfield."

"You don't want to do anything," said my father. "It's an absolute waste of a first-class brain. Awful. Tragic. It makes me want to—"

"Ranulph," said my mother, "don't undo all my good work, there's a pet. Venetia—"

"I think I'd like to be a clergyman."

"Darling, do be serious!"

"All right, all right, I'll take a secretarial course! At least that'll be better than arranging bloody flowers!"

"I can't stand it when women swear," said my father. "Kindly curb your language this instant."

"You may have spent a lot of your life declaring in the name of your liberal idealism that men and woman should be treated equally," I said, "but I've never met a man who was so reluctant to practise what he preached! If you really believed in sexual equality you'd sit back and let me say 'bloody' just as often as you do!"

"I give up," said my mother. "I'm off to the conservatory."

"And I'm off to the Athenaeum," said my father. "I simply daren't stay here and risk a stroke any longer."

"How typical!" I scoffed. "The champion of equality once again takes refuge in an all-male club!"

"Bloody impertinence!" roared my father.

"Bloody hypocrite!" I shouted back, and stormed out, slamming the door.

8

IF I had been living in the sixties I might then have left home and shared a flat with cronies; I might have taken to drink or drugs (or both) and chased after pop singers, or I might have opened a boutique or become a feminist or floated off to Nepal to find a guru. But I was living in the fifties, that last gasp of the era which had begun in those lost years before the war, and in those days nice young girls "just didn't do that kind of thing," as the characters in *Hedda Gabler* say. (*Hedda Gabler* was one of Aysgarth's favourite plays; he adored that clever doomed sizzler of a heroine.)

It was also a fact that in between the acrimonious rows my life at home was much too comfortable to abandon in a fit of pique. My parents, exercising a policy of benign neglect, were usually at pains to avoid breathing down my neck, ordering me about and preaching nauseous sermons about setting an example to the lower orders. I was waited on hand and foot, well fed and well housed. In short, I had sufficient incentives to postpone a great rebellion, and besides, like Hedda Gabler, I shied away from any idea of not conforming to convention. If I flounced around being a rebel I knew I would only earn the comment:

"Poor old Venetia—pathetic as ever!" and wind up even worse off than I already was.

So after that row with my parents in 1957 I did not rush immediately upstairs to pack my bags. I gritted my teeth and faced what I saw as the cold hard facts of life: no longer could I sit around sipping gin, smoking cigarettes and soaking up the sexy reminiscences of St. Augustine. The day of reckoning for my refusal to go up to Oxford was at hand, and just like any other (usually middle-class) girl who considered that the hobbies of flower-arranging and playing with food were far beneath her, I had to embark on a secretarial training.

However as I reflected that night on my capitulation to parental bullying, I thought I could face my reorganised future without too much grief; a secretarial course could well be my passport to what I thought of as Real Life, the world beyond my mother's gardens and my father's clubs, a world in which people actually lived—swilling and swearing, fighting and fornicating—instead of merely existing bloodlessly in charity committee meetings or in cloud-cuckoolands such as the Athenaeum and the House of Lords.

I decided to go to Mrs. Hoster's Secretarial College because Primrose had attended a course there while I had been fighting off death by boredom in Switzerland and Italy. Like me, Primrose had been encouraged by her school to try for a place at Oxford, but she had convinced me that an Oxford education was the one thing we both had to avoid if we were to have any hope of experiencing Real Life in the future.

"Christian told me frankly it would reduce my chance of marrying to nil," she had confided, "and there's no doubt spinsters are always regarded with contempt. Besides, how on earth could I go up to Oxford and leave poor Father all alone with Dido? He'd go mad if he didn't have me to talk to whenever she was driving him round the bend." Primrose had never been away from home. She had attended St. Paul's Girls School in London while I had been incarcerated at Cheltenham Ladies' College, and I had always secretly resented the fact that her father had considered her indispensable while mine had been willing to consign me to an institution.

Although Primrose was anxious to marry eventually, just as a successful woman should, she never seemed to mind having no boyfriends. Instead she channelled her gregarious inclinations towards forming a circle of female friends whom her brothers condescendingly referred to as "the Gang." Some of the Gang had been at school with her, some had been debutantes with us in 1955 and some had been her classmates at Mrs. Hoster's. Aysgarth adored us all. Dido used to refer to us as "Stephen's Little Harem" and look indulgent. "Name your favourite of the day!"

we would tease him as he sat beaming on the sofa and we lounged on the carpet at his feet, but he would sigh: "I can't decide! It's as if you were asking a chocolate-addict to select from a row of equally luscious peppermint creams!"

When the Aysgarths moved to Starbridge in 1957, it was thought the Gang might drift apart, but Starbridge was an easy journey by train from London and the core of the Gang kept in touch. Abandoning all thought of a secretarial career in London, Primrose landed a job at the diocesan office on Eternity Street, and in order to avoid constant clashes with Dido she had her own flatlet in the Deanery's former stables. Time ticked on. I completed my secretarial training and drifted through a series of jobs in art galleries and antique shops and publishing houses. Then with the dawn of the new decade the Gang at last began to disintegrate. Penny and Sally got married, Belinda joined the Wrens, Tootsie became an actress and was expelled from the Gang for Conduct Unbecoming, Midge dropped out to grow daffodils in the Scilly Isles, and by 1963 only I was left in "Stephen's Little Harem"—"The last peppermint cream left in the box!" as my chocolate-loving Mr. Dean put it so saucily, much to his wife's annoyance.

"You really should make more effort to get married, Venetia," she said soon afterwards. "In the game of life women who don't marry are inevitably regarded as such amateurs, and you wouldn't want people to look down on you pityingly, would you, my dear? That's one thing a clever girl can never endure."

I could have withstood that woman better if she had been merely mad and bad. But it was her talent for disembowelling her victims with the knife of truth which made her so thoroughly dangerous to know.

It was 1963. The innocent days were almost over, and in the early spring, just after John Robinson, the Suffragan Bishop of Woolwich, published the book which was to shake the Church of England to its foundations, the foundations of my own world were at last rocked by the earthquake of change. Exasperated by my failure to stay in any job longer than a year, my father went to great trouble to obtain a post for me at the Liberal Party's headquarters. I handed in my notice a week later.

"How dare you do this to me!" shouted my father, who was now seventy-two and even less capable of managing a recalcitrant daughter.

"My dear Papa, I'm the victim, not you! I was the one who actually had to work at that ghastly place!"

"Well, if you think you can loaf around under my roof doing nothing for the next six months—"

"Nothing would induce me to loaf around under your roof a day longer!" I said, almost twenty-six years old and finally summoning the strength to burst out of my luxurious prison. "I'm off to Starbridge to meditate on God and contemplate Eternity—which is exactly what you ought to be doing at your age!"

And having delivered myself of this speech, which could be guaranteed to infuriate any humanist past endurance, I embarked on my journey into adventure.

III

"But now 'God' is news!"

JOHN A. T. ROBINSON,
writing about Honest to God *in the*
Sunday Mirror, *7 April 1963*

I

AT Waterloo Station I encountered Charley Ashworth, the Bishop's elder son, whom I had occasionally met in Starbridge during my visits to the Aysgarths. He was a year my junior, small, chatty and bumptious. It was generally agreed that the bumptiousness masked an inferiority complex which had arisen because he was plain while his brother Michael was handsome. After completing his National Service Charley had gone up to Cambridge, where he had taken a first in Divinity, and in 1961 he had entered a theological college, also in Cambridge, to learn how to be a clergyman. This exercise, which hardly seemed compatible with his pugnacious personality, was still going on.

"Good heavens—Venetia!" he exclaimed, speeding towards me with a suitcase in one hand and a copy of Bishop Robinson's *Honest to God* in the other. "What are you doing here?" He made it sound as if I were trespassing.

"Just admiring the view from platform twelve." I had set down my bags in order to rest my wrists; I never managed to travel light. Around us throbbed the echoing noise and mouldy smell of a mighty station. I had been gazing at the inert train nearby and trying to decide which end would have the best chance of offering me a solitary journey.

"But I'd heard you were running the Liberal Party!" Charley was protesting as I realised my hopes of solitude had been dashed.

"I decided I wasn't political."

"Good for you! Personally I think women should keep out of politics."

"And what do you think they should keep in?"

"The home, of course." He heaved open the door of the nearest carriage and flung out his hand generously towards the interior as if he were offering a child a treat. "In you go!"

"Could you deal with my bags?" I said. "We girls are such delicate little flowers that we have to rely on strong brave boys like you to help us whenever we're not sitting at home being plastic dolls."

"Very funny!" said Charley good-humouredly, my sarcasm quite lost on him, and without complaint turned his attention to my bulging suitcases.

"How are you getting on with *Honest to God*?" I enquired as he tossed his book onto the seat.

"Oh, have you heard of it?"

"I can read, you know. 'Our image of God must go, says Bishop—'"

"That article in *The Observer* was a disgrace!"

"Did you think so? I adored it—such fun when a Church of England bishop declares to all and sundry that he doesn't believe in God!"

"But that's not what Robinson's saying at all—"

"That's what laymen think he's saying."

"And that's exactly why the book's a disgrace! It's so bad for laymen. My father says that Robinson's being thoroughly irresponsible as well as intellectually slipshod, and I agree with him," said Charley, exuding outraged virtue as he heaved my bags up on to the rack. "My father and I always agree on everything." Closing the carriage door he pulled down the window and began to scan the platform.

"Tedious for you," I said. "My father and I are in perpetual disagreement. Life's just one long glorious row." But Charley, leaning out of the window, was too absorbed in some private anxiety to reply.

"Bother the infant," he said at last, glancing at his watch. "He's cutting it very fine."

"What infant's this?"

"I doubt if you'd know him—he's only twenty. He's supposed to be staying tonight with us at the South Canonry." Again he hung out of the window in an agony of suspense but a moment later he was bawling "Hey!" in relief and wildly waving his arm.

A tall, pale youth, earnest and bespectacled, appeared at the door and was hustled into the carriage. He wore very clean jeans and a spotless blue shirt with a black leather jacket. All he was carrying was a duffel-bag. "Sorry I'm late," he said. "I got lost on the underground." Unaware that Charley and I knew each other he wasted no time looking at me but removed his glasses and began to polish them with an exquisitely ironed white handkerchief. In the distance the guard's whistle blew and after a preliminary jerk the train began to glide out of the station.

"Venetia," Charley said, remembering his manners, "this is Nicholas Darrow. Nick, this is the Honourable Venetia Flaxton."

"I find it more comfortable these days to drop the Honourable," I said. "Hullo, Nick."

Replacing his spectacles he looked me straight in the eyes and at once I felt as if I stood in a plunging lift. "Hi," he said politely without smiling. His eyes were an unnaturally clear shade of grey.

"Have we met before?" said my voice. I sounded as unnerved as I felt, but I knew that the obvious explanation for my loss of poise—sexual bewitchment—was quite wrong. He was a plain young man. Yet somehow he contrived to be compulsively watchable.

"No, we haven't met," he was answering tranquilly, opening his duffel-bag and pulling out a book. It was *Honest to God.*

"Nick's father was principal of the Starbridge Theological College back in the forties," Charley said. "Maybe Nick's jogging your memory of him."

"No, that's impossible. I wasn't involved in Starbridge ecclesiastical circles until the Aysgarths moved to the Deanery in '57."

Charley obviously decided to dismiss my confusion as a mere feminine vagary. "Nick's reading Divinity up at Cambridge just as I did," he said, "and—good heavens, Nick, so you've bought *Honest to God!* What's your verdict so far?"

"Peculiar. Can it really be possible to reach the rank of bishop and know nothing about the English mystics?"

"Maybe he can't connect with them," I said. "I certainly can't. I think Julian of Norwich's description of Christ's blood is absolutely revolting and borders on the pathological."

The grave grey eyes were again turned in my direction and again I wondered why his mysterious magnetism should seem familiar.

"Well, of course it's very hard for a layman to approach these apparently morbid touches from the right angle," Charley was saying with such condescension that I wanted to slap him, "but if one takes the time to study the mystics with the necessary spiritual seriousness—"

"You're a churchgoer," said Nick suddenly to me.

"Now and then, yes."

"But you're not a communicant."

"I watch occasionally." I was still trying to work out how he had made these deductions when Charley exclaimed in delight: "In College we debate about people like you! You're from the fringes—the shadowy penumbra surrounding the hard core of Church membership!"

"I most certainly am not!" I said, concealing my fury behind a voice of ice. "I've been christened and confirmed—I'm just as much a member of the Church of England as you are!"

"But if you're not a regular communicant—"

"I've never been able to understand why chewing a bit of artificial bread and sipping some perfectly ghastly wine should confer the right to adopt a holier-than-thou attitude to one's fellow-Christians."

"Shall I give you my best lecture on the sacraments?" said Charley, allowing a sarcastic tone of voice to enhance his nauseous air of condescension.

"No, read *Honest to God* and shut up. It's narrow-minded, arrogant believers like you who give the Church a bad name."

Charley flushed. His pale brown eyes seemed to blaze with golden sparks. His wide mouth hardened into a furious line. "If all so-called believers were a little more devout, we might have more chance of beating back sin!"

"Who wants to beat back sin?" I said. "I'm mad about it myself." And opening my bag I casually pulled out the famous unexpurgated Penguin edition of *Lady Chatterley's Lover*.

That closed the conversation.

The train thundered on towards Starbridge.

2

"SORRY," said Charley to me an hour later. "I didn't mean to offend you. Since you don't come from a religious family, it's very praiseworthy that you go to church at all."

"Oh, my father's devoted to religion," I said. "He just has trouble believing in God."

"So he didn't mind your being baptised and confirmed?"

"Mind! He insisted on it! In his opinion all loyal English people ought to go through the initiation rites of the Church of England—it's part of our tribal heritage, like learning about King Alfred burning the cakes and memorising the patriotic speeches from *Henry V* and singing 'Land of Hope and Glory' at the last night of the Proms."

"This is most interesting, isn't it, Nick?" said Charley. "When one comes from a religious home one doesn't realise what extraordinary attitudes flourish elsewhere."

"What's so extraordinary about them?" I said. "Isn't the main purpose of our glorious Church to reassure us all that God is without doubt an Englishman?"

"You're teasing me!" said Charley. But he sounded uncertain.

I suddenly became aware that Nick was gazing at me. I had intercepted his gaze more than once during our hour of silence, and as I caught him in the act yet again I demanded: "Why do you keep staring at me as if I'm an animal at the zoo?"

He lowered his gaze and shifted uncomfortably in his seat. "Sorry." His voice was almost inaudible. "It's the aura."

"Nick's a psychic," said Charley serenely as my jaw sagged. "That's how he knew you were a churchgoer but not a communicant."

"No, it wasn't!" said Nick angrily. "Her knowledge of Dame Julian suggested she was interested enough in Christianity to be a churchgoer, and her repulsion towards the description of Christ's blood suggested she was unlikely to take part in any symbolic ritual involving it. The deduction I made was completely rational and involved no psychic powers whatsoever!"

"Okay, but you can't deny you're a psychic—think what a whizz you were at Pelmanism!"

"Shut up, I don't want to talk about it."

"I always thought it was such a shame when your father stopped you telling fortunes—"

"*Shut up,* Charley!" Jumping to his feet the youth heaved open the door into the corridor and stalked out in a rage.

"It's not my day, is it?" said Charley with a sigh. "Why do I always put people's backs up? I can't understand it. I only want to be sociable and friendly."

Leaving him brooding with touching innocence on his abrasive personality I prowled down the corridor to the buffet where I found Nick slumped at a table and sipping Coca-Cola. After buying some liquid which British Rail had the nerve to market as coffee I sat down opposite him.

"Now look here," I said sternly, trying to take advantage of my years of seniority. "You've made a disturbing statement and I want an explanation. What's the matter with my aura? Is it exuding gloom and doom?"

He failed to smile. He was a very serious young man. "No, turbulence," he said. "You must be very unhappy. You look so self-assured in your expensive clothes, and you talk so carelessly as if you hadn't a worry in the world, but underneath you're throbbing with pain."

"Supposing I were to tell you that you're dead wrong?"

"I don't see how I can be. As soon as you mentioned your revulsion towards Dame Julian's description of Christ's blood I sensed *your* blood, spattered all over your psyche, and I knew you were in pain."

I boggled but recovered. "Here," I said, shoving my hand palm upwards across the table. "Read that and tell me more."

"I don't do that sort of thing nowadays." But he glanced at my palm as if he found the temptation hard to resist. "Anyway I'm not trained in palmistry. I just hold the hand and wait for the knowledge."

I grabbed his fingers and intertwined them with mine. "Okay, talk. You owe it to me," I added fiercely as he still hesitated. "You can't just make gruesome statements and go no further! It's unfair and irresponsible."

Sullenly he untwined our fingers, set my hand back on the table and placed his palm over mine. There followed a long silence during which he remained expressionless.

"My God!" I said, suddenly overwhelmed by fright. "Am I going to die?"

"Oh no," he said. "You're going to live." And for one long moment he stared at me appalled before blundering out of the buffet in confusion.

3

I CAUGHT UP with him just before he reached the carriage. "What the hell did you see?"

"Nothing. I just don't like meddling with psychic emanations, that's all, and I promised my father I wouldn't do it. If I seem upset it's because I'm angry that I've broken my word to him." Diving into the carriage he collapsed in a heap on the seat.

Charley, who had been dipping into my copy of *Lady Chatterley's Lover,* hastily shoved it aside but I paid him no attention. I remained in the corridor and stared out of the window at the smooth hills of the Starbridge diocese. The train was now hurtling towards our journey's end.

"Nick and I are down here for Easter, of course," said Charley, appearing beside me as the train slowed to a crawl on the outskirts of the city. "Nick stayed on after the end of term to begin the swot for his exams, and I delayed my return to Starbridge in order to make a retreat with the Fordite monks in London . . . Are you staying with the Aysgarths or are you heading for home?"

"The former." As the train lurched over a set of points on its approach to the station I stepped back into the carriage and said abruptly to Nick: "Are we going to meet again?"

"Oh yes. And again. And again. And again."

"What a terrifying prospect!"

"No, it's okay, you don't have to worry. I'm benign."

"I see," I said. "A recurring phenomenon which ought to be entirely harmless. Like Halley's Comet."

Finally I saw him smile. I noticed that he had good teeth, very even, and that when his mouth was relaxed he lost the air of solemnity conjured up by his spectacles. Again my memory was jogged, and as it occurred to me that he was as watchable as a gifted actor I at last solved the riddle of his familiarity. "Wait a minute," I said. "Are you any relation of Martin Darrow, the actor?"

"He's my half-brother."

I relaxed. Although I'm not averse to paranormal puzzles I much prefer mysteries that are capable of a rational explanation. "My mother's mad on him," I said agreeably, "never misses an episode of his comedy series, stays glued to the TV. But surely he must be at least thirty years older than you are?"

"My father had a rather peculiar private life."

"Come on, chaps!" exclaimed Charley, plunging bossily back into the carriage as the train finally halted at the platform. "Get a move on! Nick, as you've only got a duffel-bag, could you give Venetia a hand with her suitcases?"

I stepped down onto the platform accompanied by my psychic porter. The sun was shining and far away in the distance beyond the train, beyond the railway yard, beyond the roofs of the mean little villas which flanked the tracks, I saw the slim straight spire of the Cathedral.

Blazing with energy Charley bounded ahead and by the time Nick and I emerged from the station he was bouncing towards the episcopal car, a black Rover, as Mrs. Ashworth emerged from the driver's seat. I knew now, six years after our first meeting, that she was the same age as Aysgarth, but on that day she looked more like forty-five than sixty-one. It was not only her slender figure which made her seem youthful but the smooth straight hair coiled simply in a bun; an elderly woman who has the guts to flout fashion by refusing a permanent wave really does deserve to look a long way from the geriatric ward.

Ever since our first meeting when she had boldly identified me as a *femme fatale* despite the massive evidence to the contrary, I had secretly labelled her my heroine and now, once again, my admiration for her was renewed. She was wearing a pale lilac-coloured raincoat, unbuttoned to reveal a straight grey skirt and a sky-blue blouse—unremarkable clothes, but on her they looked as if they had arrived by special messenger that morning from Paris. Her navy shoes, so different from the old ladies' "support" footwear which my mother favoured, were notable for the elegance of their stiletto heels. Mrs. Ashworth might have turned sixty, but this boring fact had evidently long since been dismissed by her as trivial. Her triumph over the ravages of time was superb.

"Hullo, Nicholas!" she exclaimed warmly after she had given Charley a peck on the cheek, but I knew she was much more interested in me.

"Venetia—what a surprise! I saw Dido Aysgarth earlier today but she didn't mention they were expecting you at the Deanery."

"They're not expecting me. To be quite honest, Mrs. Ashworth, I'm not exactly sure why I'm here. I'm a bit *bouleversée* at the moment."

"How exciting! Come and have tea. I've got a prayer-group turning up later and there's a visiting American bishop who comes and goes like the Cheshire cat's smile, but at the moment I'm absolutely free."

My spirits rose, and accepting her invitation with gratitude I slid into the back seat of the Bishop's Rover.

4

THE South Canonry, where the Ashworths lived, was an early Georgian house far smaller than the old episcopal palace but still too large for a modestly paid executive with a wife and two adult sons. The garden consisted almost entirely of labour-saving lawns; full-time gardeners were no longer an episcopal perk, and the Ashworths were aided only by a man who came once a week to civilise the lawns with a motor-mower. Mrs. Ashworth hated gardening and kept no plants in the house. I always found the bare, uncluttered look in her home immensely appealing.

As I was almost the same age as Charley I had been invited to the house occasionally in the past along with various Aysgarths and other young people in the diocese, but the visits had been infrequent and I had never come to know the Ashworths well. Neither had my parents. My father respected the Bishop's intellect but found Ashworth was fundamentally unsympathetic to his sentimental, old-fashioned brand of humanism. Whereas Aysgarth was tolerant of agnostics Ashworth seemed hard put to conceal his opinion that agnosticism was an intellectual defect—and there were other differences too, as we all discovered over the years, between the Bishop and the Dean. Aysgarth was gregarious with an apparently inexhaustible supply of good humour, whereas Ashworth, behind his cast-iron charm, was a very private, very serious man. Laymen like my father dubbed Ashworth "churchy"—that sinister pejorative adjective so dreaded by clerics—but Aysgarth was unhesitatingly labelled "one of us." Ashworth, isolated to some degree by the eminence of his office, was held to resemble Kipling's cat who walked by himself; his close friends had been left behind in Cambridge in 1957, and perhaps this was one of the reasons why he was so close to his wife. It was widely observed how well attuned they were to each other. They seemed to generate that special harmony which one finds more often among childless couples, the harmony of two people who find each other entirely sufficient for their emotional needs.

Considering that the marriage was successful, people found it immensely interesting that the two sons should have undergone such obvious problems: Charley had run away from home when he was eighteen while later Michael had been thrown out of medical school. However, these embarrassing episodes now belonged to the past. Charley had been rescued, sorted out and replaced on the rails of conformity, while Michael had been steered into the employment of the BBC with happy results. Why Charley should have run away from home no one had any idea, but Michael's hedonistic behaviour was universally attributed to a desire to rebel against his father's puritanical views on sin.

"There's a screw loose in that family somewhere," Dido would say darkly, "you mark my words."

The irony of this statement was that Aysgarth had the biggest possible screw loose in his family—Dido herself—yet all his children were turning out wonderfully well. This fact must have been very galling to the Ashworths as they struggled to surmount their problems at the South Canonry.

When I arrived at the house that afternoon I was immediately soothed by its well-oiled serenity. The drawing-room was notably dust-free and arranged with a tidiness which was meticulous but not oppressive. A superb tea was waiting to be served. The telephone rang regularly but was silenced almost at once by the Bishop's secretary in her lair by the front door. Dr. Ashworth himself was out, fulfilling an official engagement, but if he had been present he too would have been running smoothly, just like the house. I could remember him appearing during my past visits and saying to his wife: "What did I do with that memo on the World Council of Churches?" or: "Whatever happened to that letter from the Archbishop?" or: "What on earth's the name of that clergyman at Butterwood All Saints?" and Mrs. Ashworth, indestructibly composed, would always know all the answers.

After tea Charley went upstairs to unpack, Nick wandered outside to tune into the right nature-vibes—or whatever psychics do in gardens—and Mrs. Ashworth took me upstairs to her private sitting-room. Unlike my mother's boudoir at Flaxton Hall there were no dreary antiques, no ghastly oil-paintings of long-dead ancestors, no boring photographs of babies and no vegetation in sight. The air smelt celestially pure. On the walls hung some black and white prints of Cambridge and a water-colour of the Norfolk Broads. The only framed photograph on the chimney-piece showed her husband as an army chaplain during the war.

"Sit down," said Mrs. Ashworth, closing the door. "Now that we've got rid of the men we can relax. Cigarette?"

"I do like this room," I said, accepting the cigarette and sinking into a comfortable armchair. "It's all you, isn't it? Everything's your choice.

All my life I've had to put up with revolting inherited furniture and now I've finally reached the point where I'm determined to have a place of my own."

"Splendid! All young people need to express themselves through their surroundings. You should have seen Michael's room when he went through his Brigitte Bardot phase!"

"I bet Charley puts up all the right pictures," I said, not daring to ask what the Bishop had thought of the Bardot pin-ups.

"Fortunately Charley only has space on his walls for books. My former employer Bishop Jardine left Charley his entire theological library—no doubt because Charley always said he wanted to be a clergyman when he grew up . . . But let's get back to you. So you're seeking a room of your own! But why seek it in Starbridge?"

"I'm not sure that I will—I've only drifted down here because I've got a standing invitation to use the Put-U-Up sofa in Primrose's flat. I'm such a drifter, Mrs. Ashworth! I despise myself for drifting but I don't seem able to stop. It's as if I'm marking time, waiting for my life to begin, but nothing ever happens."

"When will you consider that your life's begun? At the altar?"

I was grateful for her swift grasp of my dilemma. "Well, I know marriage shouldn't be the be-all and end-all of a woman's life, but—"

"It certainly was before the war. Perhaps this is a case where 'the more things change the more they remain the same.' "

"I think it must be. As I see it, I really do have to get married in order to live the kind of life I'd enjoy, but here I am, almost twenty-six, and I'm beginning to think: supposing I never marry, never win respect and status, never stop drifting—I could wind up wasting my entire life."

"A nightmarish prospect."

"Terrifying. And then I start to feel desperate—*desperate,* Mrs. Ashworth, I can't tell you how desperate I feel sometimes—and now I'm convinced I've got to act, got to get out of this rut—"

"Well, it sounds to me as if you're making progress at last! You're looking for a place where you can express your real self; you've embarked on an odyssey of self-discovery . . . Do you have to worry about money?"

"No, I've got a hefty income because I came into money from both my godmothers when I was twenty-one. Maybe that's part of the problem? If I were penniless—"

"—you'd hate it. I did. Now let's consider your situation carefully—"

"I don't have a situation, Mrs. Ashworth, I just have a non-event." The words suddenly began to stream out of my mouth. "I want to live—I mean *live*—I want to swill gin and chat about philosophy with a gang of brilliant people and smooch with handsome men and dance till dawn and burn the candle at both ends, but all I get are boring nine-to-five jobs, social events where I'm an embarrassing failure, no love-life and evenings spent swilling gin on my own while listening to Radio Luxemburg. I've never had a boyfriend. I did belong to a gang of clever people but they were all girls. Here I am, bursting to join in the Great Party of Life yet confined to the margins by my utter lack of sex-appeal, and it's awful, Mrs. Ashworth, absolutely *awful,* so utterly vile and unfair—"

"But anyone," said Mrs. Ashworth, "can have sex-appeal. It's simply an attitude of mind."

I stared at her. She gave me a sphinx-like smile. Enrapt I tried to speak but failed.

"It's all a question of confidence," said my heroine, flicking ash from her cigarette casually into the nearby tray, "and in your case it would be confidence in your appearance. You want to be able to walk into a room and think: I'm glamour personified—how lucky all those men are to see me!"

"But I'm not beautiful!"

"Neither was Cleopatra."

"Yes, but she was Queen of Egypt—"

"—and she made the most of it. That's what you have to do too—make the most of your assets. Stand up for a moment."

I stood up.

"Revolve."

I revolved.

"Yes," said Mrs. Ashworth tranquilly, waving her cigarette to indicate I could sit down again, "it's all very simple. Wear plain, tailored clothes which emphasise your waist and hips. Never wear flat shoes even though you happen to be tallish. Favour V-necks to distract the masculine eye from your shoulders and take care not to stoop—that only makes the shoulders more noticeable. And grow your hair."

"Grow it? But Mrs. Ashworth, I'll turn into a sort of yak!"

"Nonsense, men adore the pre-Raphaelite look. Oh, and go to a beauty salon and get advice on make-up. You have the most beautiful eyes. Make them a focal point."

"But do you really think that if I do all this—"

"That's just the beginning. Then you must plot how to get in with a crowd of clever, interesting people by exploiting a clever, interesting person who's already known to you. How about Christian Aysgarth? You can't be much younger than his wife."

"Well, yes, I do know Christian and Katie, but—"

"Splendid! They're your passport to your new life. Don't linger in dull old Starbridge. Seek that room you want in Oxford and wangle your way into Christian's set."

"But Christian just sees me as one of Primrose's gang of virgin spinsters!"

"He won't when you arrive in Oxford flaunting glamorous eye make-up and pre-Raphaelite hair. I think that you and Primrose," said Mrs. Ashworth, careful in her choice of words, "may have reached the parting of the ways." Before I could comment she was adding with regret: "I wish I could invite you to stay tonight, but thanks to Nicholas and our visiting American bishop, we've got a full house."

I said with curiosity: "What's Nick's connection with your family?"

"His father and Charles have known each other for many years, and since Jon Darrow's now very old Charles likes to keep a paternal eye on Nicholas to make sure he's all right."

"Isn't there a mother?"

"She died. There's a half-brother in London—"

"The actor."

"That's right—and there was a half-sister, but she's dead now too and Nicholas never had much in common with her children."

"He's very . . ." I tried to find the right word but could only produce a banality. ". . . unusual."

"Yes, isn't he? Sometimes I think he needs a substitute mother, but I never feel my maternal instinct can stretch far enough to take him on—although I must say, my maternal instinct seems to have stretched out of sight during this conversation! I seem to have forgotten I'm a bishop's wife. Instead of advising you to vamp the intellectuals of Oxford I should be telling you to get a job at the diocesan office and help me with my charity work in your spare time!"

I laughed but before I could reply the front door banged far away in the hall. "That'll be either Charles or our American bishop," said Mrs. Ashworth, rising to her feet, "and let's hope it's Charles. I do like Americans, but all that sunny-natured purring's so exhausting."

"Darling!" shouted the Bishop downstairs.

"Coo-ee!" called Mrs. Ashworth with relief, and added indulgently to me: "Isn't he funny? He so often arrives home and shouts: 'Darling!' like that. It's as if he has no idea what to do next and is waiting for instructions."

In walked the Bishop, looking like a film star in a costume melodrama. The old episcopal uniform of apron, gaiters and frock-coat, so suitable for the eighteenth-century bishops who had had to ride around their dioceses on horseback, was finally giving way to more modern attire, but for his official engagement that afternoon Dr. Ashworth had decided to be conservative, and he looked well in his swashbuckling uniform. He was two years older than Aysgarth, but like his wife he appeared younger—not much younger, perhaps, but he could still have passed for a man on the right side of sixty.

"How are your parents?" he said to me agreeably after the greetings had been exchanged.

"Seething. I've just left home and embarked on a new life."

He gave me his charming smile but it failed to reach the corners of his eyes. Perhaps he was trying to decide whether I could be classified as "wayward" or "lost" or even "fallen." Smoothly he fell back on his erudition. "This sounds like a case of metanoia!" he remarked. "By which I mean—"

"I know what it means. The Dean told me. It's a turning away from one's old life and the beginning of a new one."

"In Christ," said the Bishop casually, as if correcting an undergraduate who had made an error in a tutorial. "I hope the Dean didn't forget to mention Christ, but these liberal-radicals nowadays seem to be capable of anything." He turned to his wife and added: "I lost count of the times I was asked about *Honest to God* this afternoon. People were deeply upset. It's a pity Robinson wasn't there to see the results of his ill-informed, half-baked radicalism."

"I thought Robinson was supposed to be a conservative," I said. "After all, he wasn't invited to contribute to *Soundings,* was he?"

The Bishop looked startled. "Who's been talking to you of *Soundings*?"

"The Dean was very enthusiastic when the book was published."

"I'd have more confidence in Stephen's bold espousal of the views contained in these controversial books if I knew he was a trained theologian," said Dr. Ashworth. "However, as we all know, he read Greats, not Theology, when he was up at Oxford."

"But since he's been a clergyman for almost forty years," I said, "don't you think he might have picked up a little theology somewhere along the way?"

The Bishop was clearly not accustomed to being answered back by a young female who had never even been to a university. Possibly he was unaccustomed to being answered back by anyone. He took a moment to recover from the shock but then said suavely enough: "Good point! But perhaps I might draw a parallel here with the legal profession. Barristers and solicitors are all qualified lawyers, but when a knotty legal problem arises the solicitors refer the matter to the barristers, the experts, in order to obtain the best advice."

"Well, I'm afraid I must now leave you to your expertise," I said politely, rising to my feet, "and descend from the mountain top of the South Canonry to the valley of the Deanery." I turned to my hostess. "Thanks so much for the tea and sympathy, Mrs. Ashworth."

"Drop in again soon," said my heroine with a smile, "and if there's anything I can do, just let me know."

"Yes indeed," said the Bishop, suddenly becoming pastoral. "If there's anything we can do—"

"I'll see you out, Venetia," said his wife, and led the way downstairs to the hall. As she opened the front door she added: "You won't want to lug your suitcases to the Deanery—I'll ask Charley to bring them over later in the car."

I thanked her before saying anxiously: "I do hope I didn't upset the Bishop when I answered back."

"My dear, he was enthralled! Such a delightful change for him to meet someone who doesn't treat him as a sacred object on a pedestal." She looked at me thoughtfully with her cool dark eyes before musing: "Maybe you've been concentrating on the wrong age-group; very few young men have the self-assurance or the savoir-faire to cope with clever women. Try looking for something intelligent, well educated and pushing forty."

"It'll be either married or peculiar."

"Not necessarily . . . Didn't I hear a rumour once that Eddie Hoffenberg was rather smitten with you?"

"Oh, for heaven's sake, Mrs. Ashworth—I'd rather die a virgin spinster!"

Mrs. Ashworth merely smiled her enigmatic smile and said: "Do keep in touch."

I drifted away down the drive towards the Deanery.

5

EDDIE HOFFENBERG emerged from the Deanery just as I approached the front door, so there was no possibility of avoiding him. My father had once referred to him as "Aysgarth's poodle—that bloody Hun," but my father, who had lost his best friends in the First War, was notorious for his anti-German sentiment. Other people, less outspoken than my father, were content to regard Eddie with a polite antipathy. "It's my cross," Eddie would say with gloomy relish, and sometimes he would even add: "Suffering is good for the soul."

"It's clergymen like Eddie Hoffenberg," I had said once to Primrose, "who make Christianity look like an exercise in masochism."

"It's Germans like Eddie Hoffenberg," said Primrose, "who encourage the belief that we were doing them a favour by trying to kill them in the war."

However although there was no denying that Eddie was a German, he was hardly typical of Hitler's so-called master-race, and the fact that he had eventually acquired British citizenship marked him out as a very unusual German indeed. He was tall, bald and bespectacled; his faintly Semitic cast of features had caused him to be bullied by Aryan monsters in the Nazi army, but since he had no Jewish blood in him, this experience had provided him with additional evidence that he was doomed to special suffering. Fortunately his army career had been brief. In 1944 at the age of twenty he had been captured by the British in Normandy, imported to England and dumped in a prison-camp on Starbury Plain. Two weeks later Aysgarth, then Archdeacon of Starbridge, had paid a pastoral visit to the camp and naturally Eddie had been quite unable to resist the opportunity to moan to him about how awful life was.

It was not difficult to understand why Eddie had chosen to adopt Aysgarth as a hero, but it was far harder to understand why Aysgarth had chosen to return Eddie's devotion. "Aysgarth has five sons," my father remarked once to my mother. "Why should he want to play the father to a Teutonic disaster who's perpetually encased in gloom?" My mother had no answer, but Primrose eventually produced an explanation. "Eddie changed Father's life," she told me. "It was Eddie who wrote to Bishop Bell and said how wonderful Father was with the POWs, and since that letter led to Father's vital friendship with Bell, Father can't help being sentimental about Eddie and regarding him as a mascot."

Eddie came from Dresden, which had been devastated by fire-bombing in 1945. None of his family had survived. After the war he had quickly reached the decision that he had to begin a new life elsewhere, and when he thought of the one friend he still possessed he sought Aysgarth's help. Aysgarth encouraged him to be a clergyman. Eddie had been a Lutheran once, but that was in the old, vanished life. Once Aysgarth had extracted the necessary money from the new Anglo-German Churchmen's Fellowship, Eddie began his studies at the Starbridge Theological College and spent his holidays with the Aysgarths in London.

Ordination as a clergyman of the Church of England followed and a curacy was squeezed out of a Westminster parish. (A German was lucky to get any job in Westminster, but the Bishop of London caved in after Aysgarth and Bell staged a joint assault.) When Aysgarth became Dean of Starbridge he at once approached the new bishop on Eddie's behalf, and Dr. Ashworth, striving to exercise a Christian spirit after his own years as a POW, proved unwilling to make any move which could be construed as anti-German. Possibly he also saw the chance of unloading his current diocesan problem, a seedy Starbridge parish in the area of the city known as Langley Bottom where there was a run-down Victorian monster of a church, an equally run-down Victorian monster of a vicarage and a working-class congregation of twenty.

Eddie the masochist embraced this challenge with zest. Having been trained at the Starbridge Theological College in its Anglo-Catholic heyday under Nick's father, Jonathan Darrow, he had no hesitation in resorting to the most florid ritualism (traditionally popular among the religious members of the working classes), and before long the parish was rising from the dead. Consolidating his success Eddie slaved on, organising clubs, running Bible classes, raising money. The parishioners, who had at first regarded him with suspicion, came to the conclusion they preferred the attentions of a foreigner, even a German foreigner, to the ministrations of some toffee-nosed English gentleman who had been educated at a public school. (The plebs are such dreadful snobs.) Eddie flourished. The parish boomed. The Bishop was both amazed and admiring. When a residentiary canonry at last fell vacant at the Cathedral, he had no objection to Aysgarth's suggestion that Eddie's talents should now be employed in a more elevated sphere, and so Eddie became a canon, working hard at his Chapter duties and beavering away on various diocesan committees. He had arrived. Franz Eduard Hoffenberg, that pathetic young German prisoner of war, had been transformed into a pillar of the English ecclesiastical establishment. All he now had to do was live happily ever after.

Of course being Eddie he remained gloomy but it was impossible for him to dispute that his life was now very comfortable. He had a snug little house in the Close, a surrogate family, the Aysgarths, a reasonable income and a pleasant amount of prestige. No one was surprised when he made a success of the canonry. Discarding without difficulty the Anglo-Catholic trappings which he had used to conquer Langley Bottom, he fitted easily into the Cathedral's middle-of-the-road pattern of worship. In theological matters he was more conservative than his hero, but like Aysgarth he was an idealist prone to talk soppily about the brotherhood of man when he had downed a couple of drinks. His odd, ungainly, pear-shaped figure was always carefully dressed. He observed English customs rigorously, even declaring how devoted he was to Walls pork sausages and Dickens when we all knew he must be hankering for bratwurst and Goethe. Priding himself on his mastery of slang he spoke English almost flawlessly except when he began to ponder on the mystery of suffering. Those were the occasions when I thought he was a joke. Otherwise I just thought he was a thundering bore.

As we encountered each other outside the Deanery that afternoon I inwardly recoiled but nevertheless achieved a passable smile.

"Hi Eddie," I said and automatically added: "How are you?" but that was a mistake. One never asked Eddie how he was. He was all too likely to reply in excruciating detail.

"Well, as a matter of fact my back's playing me up again," he began, "but I've found this wonderful osteopath who—"

"Super! Is the Dean in?"

"Yes, but we're just off to Evensong. I say, Venetia, I had no idea you were about to visit the Aysgarths!"

"Ah well, ignorance is bliss, as the saying goes . . ." I was trying to edge past him but his bulk was blocking the way. The Deanery, a rambling medieval concoction enhanced by Georgian meddling, had no formal drive up to the front door; instead a pebbled lane at the side of the house led to the old stables, while a flagstone path flanked with lavender bushes led through the front garden. Eddie was planted on the flagstones and I was trying to slink past the lavender.

"Are you here for long?" Eddie was enquiring, apparently unaware of my attempts at circumnavigation.

"No, I'm heading for Oxford."

The front door swung wide. "Venetia!" cried Aysgarth in delight. "What a marvellous surprise!"

"Mr. Dean!" I said as my spirits soared, and firmly pushing my way past Eddie I clasped Aysgarth's outstretched hand.

6

"MUST see you!" I hissed. "Top secret!"

His bright blue eyes at once became brighter and bluer. He loved being conspiratorial with young women. "You go on ahead," he called to Eddie. "I'll catch you up."

"We're late already, Stephen—"

"I'll run all the way to the vestry!" said Aysgarth lightly, and with reluctance Eddie sloped off through the front gate.

Wasting no time I said: "I've left home and I need advice. Any chance of a quick word without half the Close breathing down our necks?"

"Meet me in the cloisters after Evensong."

"Wonderful! Thanks so much . . . In that case I might as well go to Evensong, mightn't I?"

"Why not?" said the Dean amused. "It would help to pass the time!"

As it occurred to me that Dr. Ashworth would have responded far more coolly to my lukewarm attitude to worship I exclaimed: "How glad I am you're not the Bishop! I've just been hobnobbing with him at the South Canonry."

"How on earth did you end up there?"

"I got mixed up with Charley on the train. Mr. Dean, what do you think of *Honest to God*?"

"Superb! Quite splendid! A breath of fresh air sweeping through the Church of England!"

"Yes, I thought it probably was. The Bishop's decided it's absolutely the bottom."

"The trouble with Charles," said Aysgarth as we left the garden, crossed Canonry Drive and entered the churchyard of the Cathedral, "is that he was trained as a theologian. Such a pity! A theologian's approach to religion is nearly always much too cerebral and he inevitably becomes cut off from ordinary believers."

"But isn't this book supposed to be bad for ordinary believers?"

"Rubbish! It's the best thing that's happened to them for years. Robinson's realised that the ordinary believers are waiting for a new comprehensible interpretation of Christianity which will relate to the lives they're living right now in the 1960s—they're not waiting for cerebral restatements by theologians in their dead, dry, alienating academic language!"

"But if the book's too radical—"

"Nothing could be too radical! Let's have this New Reformation Robinson talks about! Let's have this New Morality! Now that we're finally emerging from the long shadow of the war and shedding the millstone of the Empire, we need to celebrate our psychological liberation by making everything new—so why not start by flinging religion into the melting-pot, as Robinson suggests, and recasting our beliefs in a bold, creative, dynamic style that's thoroughly attuned to our day and age?"

I began to feel excited—insofar as one can ever feel excited about a subject such as theology. I was, in fact, very much in the mood for revolution and I deeply fancied the thought of an iconoclastic assault on any part of the established order. "Long live Bishop John Robinson!" I declared, making Aysgarth laugh, and we quickened our pace across the sward to the Cathedral.

AT the north porch we parted, Aysgarth walking on to the Dean's door, the special entrance for the clergy, and I wandering through the porch into the nave. A sidesman showed me to a seat in the choir. This was not an unusual favour to bestow prior to a weekday service when few laymen would be present, but nevertheless it made me feel privileged.

The Cathedral was quiet. By that time the tourists had left and it had reverted to the inhabitants of Starbridge, most of whom preferred to admire it loyally from afar. However the congregation did eventually mount to thirty. I sat gazing up at the vaulted ceiling and trying to think noble thoughts, but I was pondering on Mrs. Ashworth's advice about eye make-up when the organ marked the beginning of the service.

I liked the weekday choral Evensong. It required no effort apart from kneeling down and standing up at regular intervals, and there was no sermon either to stretch the brain or induce *rigor mortis*. The choirboys sang in their unearthly voices; the vicars-choral bayed with authority; the vergers marched around providing touches of ceremonial; the clergy lolled meditatively in their stalls. I thought it was all so luxuriously restful, like a hot bath garnished with an expensive perfume, and as I watched the sun slant through the great west window I thought how clever God was to have invented the Church of England, that national monument dedicated to purveying religion in such an exquisitely civilised form.

Aysgarth was looking untidy as usual. His shop-soiled white hair always seemed to need trimming. Wearing a dignified expression he rose to his feet to read the lessons, while in the intervals Eddie, crammed into his canon's stall at the other end of the choir, intoned the versicles and recited the prayers. I was always surprised by how well Eddie did this, but no doubt Aysgarth had trained him not to sound as if he was fathoms deep in depression. Aysgarth himself read the lessons beautifully in his deep, resonant voice. In fact I was so busy thinking how well he read that I forgot to listen to what he was reading. Appalled by my lack of concentration I was on the point of making a new attempt to focus my mind on the service when I saw Nick Darrow staring at me from the opposite side of the choir. I supposed I had been too busy thinking about eye make-up to notice him earlier.

As soon as our glances met he looked away but I went on watching him and wondering if he was destined to be my lucky mascot. But "mascot" seemed the wrong word to describe someone like Nick. It was too cosy, too banal. For Nick Darrow I needed a word which implied magic, extraordinary happenings, paranormal phenomena—

"Ah-ah-ah-men!" sang the Choir, winding up the service.

The organ trilled and fell silent for a moment before embarking on a fugue. Everyone hauled themselves to their feet. The Choir tripped out jauntily, mission accomplished, and the clergy followed, looking inscrutable. Aysgarth never once glanced in my direction.

Wandering towards the transept I found Nick had fallen into step beside me.

"Ah!" I said, finally grasping the word I wanted. "It's my Talisman! I shouldn't be surprised to see you again, should I, but why are you on your own?"

"Charley's busy with his father."

"Mrs. Ashworth was telling me about yours. I hear he's very old."

"Yes, but he's okay."

"How old is 'old' exactly?"

"He'll be eighty-three in May. But he's okay."

"Compos mentis?"

"Yep."

"Super! I often think my father's mad as a hatter. Is your father able to do much?"

"Yep. He prays."

"Ah. All the time?"

"No, he does see people occasionally."

"He sounds like a hermit!"

"He is a hermit. But he doesn't mind me being with him because we don't have to talk."

I suddenly realised I was gazing at him as if he were a creature from another planet. "How restful!" I said, not sure what to say. "My father's the very reverse of a silent hermit!"

"He might become one later. My father only became a recluse after my mother died." He turned abruptly towards the nave. "So long."

"When are we due to meet again?"

He shrugged and walked away.

I gazed after him in fascination. Then heaving open the massive door in the south transept I passed at last into the cloisters.

8

IN the centre of the quadrangle lay the lawn beneath which in previous centuries the eminent men of Starbridge had been buried, and overshadowing this ancient graveyard an enormous cedar tree towered above the roof of the colonnade. There was a faint breeze. The cedar's dark upper branches were stirring against the pale, limpid sky.

I was still gazing at this tranquil scene when the door creaked behind me and Aysgarth slipped out of the transept. Unlike Dr. Ashworth he had entirely rejected the archaic uniform of a senior churchman, but perhaps that was less because he wanted to be modern than because his thickset figure was unsuited to fancy dress. On that evening he was wearing a black suit, slightly crumpled, and the black clerical stock which was worn over an ordinary shirt and secured by ties at the back beneath the jacket. He had no pectoral cross; he belonged to the generation of Protestant churchmen who thought such papist adornment pardonable only when adopted by bishops. His hair, perhaps disarranged when he had removed his surplice after the service, swooped wildly over his ears in undisciplined wings and bumped against the back of his stiff white clerical collar. He looked like an eccentric scientist who has just made an important discovery.

"Let's go and sit on Lady Mary Calthrop-Ponsonby!" he suggested blithely as I moved to meet him.

"I *beg* your pardon, Mr. Dean?"

With a laugh he led the way to a wooden seat on the northwestern corner of the lawn, and as I drew closer I saw that the back of the seat bore a brass plaque inscribed: "In memory of Lady Mary Calthrop-Ponsonby, 12th February 1857–8th November 1941. FIGHT THE GOOD FIGHT WITH ALL THY MIGHT."

"Three cheers for Lady Mary," I said as we sat down, and I told him how I had decided to abandon London in search of a new life. ". . . and I've now reached the point where I'm trying to decide what to do next," I concluded. "Mrs. Ashworth thinks I should go to Oxford, park myself on Christian and Katie and wangle my way into their set, but I'm not sure I have the nerve to exploit them so brazenly."

"I don't see why you shouldn't stay with Christian and Katie for a few days while you decide if Oxford has anything to offer you, but I can't quite see why Lyle is pointing you in that direction."

"She thinks I'd enjoy mixing with an intellectual *jeunesse dorée.*"

"On the contrary I think you'd soon be bored stiff with all those academics."

"Would I? Are you sure? I just feel that if only I could get in with the right set—"

"In my experience right sets tend to be much too fast."

"When one's been crawling along like a tortoise, Mr. Dean, the idea of pace begins to seem attractive."

He laughed. "Was London really that bad?"

"Yes, it really was. I've been a failure there. Don't just tell me to go back and try again."

"Very well, let's be more imaginative. This could be a great opportunity for you, Venetia! A fresh start is always a great opportunity, but you should remember that happiness isn't ultimately dependent on getting in with the right set; it's about serving God by using your God-given gifts in the best possible way."

"I only seem to have a God-given gift for drifting in and out of boring jobs."

"It's obvious that you haven't yet found your métier, and in my opinion pondering on the right métier, not choosing which city to live in, should actually be your number-one concern at the moment. You need to escape to somewhere very quiet and very remote for a few days so that you can ponder in peace and see your situation in perspective . . . Come on holiday with me after Easter!"

I nearly fell off Lady Mary. "What a breathtaking suggestion!"

He laughed again before adding: "Dido's not coming but Eddie's accompanying me and Primrose is joining us twenty-four hours later. Come up on the Wednesday after Easter with Primrose!"

"Where's 'up'?"

"The Outer Hebrides."

"*Is* there an Outer Hebrides?"

"Apparently. The new Earl of Starmouth has very kindly lent me his hunting-lodge on Harris."

"Don't Elizabeth and Pip want to go?"

"Dido's taking them to her sister in Leicestershire where they'll ride horses with her and be blissfully happy."

"*Chacun à son goût,*" I said. "Personally I'd rather live it up in a Caledonian Shangri-la."

"My sentiments exactly!" said Aysgarth, and as he smiled I suddenly wondered if he, like me, was seizing the chance to escape from intractable private problems.

IV

"What is most real to you? What matters most for you? Is it money and what money can buy? I doubt it, deep down. For you know that you 'can't take it with you.' And seldom does it bring real happiness. Is it love? That's a good deal nearer, because it has to do with persons, not things."

JOHN A. T. ROBINSON,
writing about Honest to God *in the*
Sunday Mirror, *7 April 1963*

I

AFTER staying the night in Primrose's flat, I caught a train the next morning to my country home at Flaxton Pauncefoot, a village which lay ten miles from the port of Starmouth in the south of the diocese. Here I sorted out some appropriate clothes for the holiday, selected a couple of books and dumped my current stock of dirty laundry on the housekeeper who returned it, faultlessly washed and ironed, that evening. Nowadays there are very few advantages in being a member of the aristocracy, but at least one never has to worry about laundries. Nor does one have to waste time shopping for food or sweating over a hot stove. I said to the housekeeper: "I'd like baked beans on toast with a poached egg on top, and tell Pardoe to look out a half-bottle of that nice St. Julien, the one with the picture of the purple vineyard on it." That solved the problem of dinner.

Afterwards, greatly fortified, I phoned my mother to inform her I would be heading for the Hebrides, retired to the blue drawing-room where the television set lurked behind a fire-screen, and watched the latest episode of the comedy series *Down at the Surgery* in which two doctors have their virtue constantly assailed by a stream of diverse nymphomaniacs. The elder doctor was played by Martin Darrow with a professional deftness which prompted me to giggle so hard that I dropped cigarette ash all over the floor. He was far better-looking than his young half-brother, but nevertheless I was conscious of the strong resemblance between them. I wondered idly what their father, the ancient hermit, thought of his elder son's career as a television star.

The next morning I extracted my red MG from the stables, heaved my bags into the back and returned to Primrose's flat. I had remembered it was Sunday but somehow I managed to arrive too late to attend Matins, so taking advantage of the spring sunshine I lounged on the seat in the Deanery's garden as I waited for everyone to return from the Cathedral. Unfortunately Primrose and the Dean stayed on for the Sung Communion service. I should have remembered that possibility and removed myself, but I was still lolling in the sunshine when Dido turned up to torpedo me.

"So there you are, Venetia! Primrose was under the impression you'd be back in time for Matins. I do think you might have telephoned to say you'd be late, but then that's the upper classes, isn't it, my dear, always expecting the entire world to fall into step beside them, and personally I've always been devoutly thankful that I was merely the daughter of a self-made Scottish millionaire and irredeemably *nouveau riche* because at least I was taught consideration for others from the cradle. Now"—she paused for breath as she parked herself purposefully on the bench beside me— "I'm so glad I've got the chance for a word alone with you, because I think it's time that an intelligent, *honest* older woman—and as you know, my dear, I always pride myself on my candour—I think it's time," said Dido, without even pausing for breath after this parenthesis, "that I gave you a piece of sensible and I hope not unaffectionate advice— because of course I'm very fond of you, Venetia, just as Stephen is, although I do see all your little faults and foibles *rather* more clearly than he does, because darling Stephen's so noble that he always sees the best in everyone, whereas I, being a realist—and I'm always being complimented on my realism—I, being a realist," said Dido, battling her way out of the jungle of this monstrous sentence, "take a much more pessimistic view of humanity, and having been a rich young girl myself I know all about the pitfalls waiting to ensnare rich young girls who drift around without any proper *direction*—which brings me to what I want to say."

I raised an eyebrow and looked hopeful.

"What you have to do, my dear, is not simply to drift hither and thither like a piece of flotsam—or is it jetsam?—on the sea of life while you dabble in antiques and publishing or sidle off on little holidays to the Hebrides with an elderly clergyman who really should have known better than to invite you—although, of course, I do understand that darling Stephen, so soft-hearted, only wanted to be kind—but I'm afraid he didn't stop to think, did he, that suggesting a holiday was actually only offering you a way of escaping from your problems, and what you really have to do, Venetia my dear, is not to *escape* from your problems but to *face* them. To put matters absolutely candidly, if you can't find a husband you must find a suitably worthy cause to which you can devote your energies, and quite honestly—and I know it's unfashionable to say this, but since I always believe in calling a spade a spade—"

I raised the other eyebrow and looked even more hopeful.

"—I think you need to find God. I began my search for God when I was about your age—it was after my favourite sister died—and once I'd started I was always so cross with myself that I'd never started before because religion's so absolutely fascinating and I can't understand why it's not taught properly in schools, especially when they go to such lengths to teach useless things like algebra and hockey. Anyway, once I'd started looking for God I met Stephen and lived happily ever after, and I think the same sort of thing might happen to you if only you could stop being so self-centred. As it happens I know the most wonderful clergyman in London who specialises in spiritual direction, and I'm quite certain that if I were to ring him up and tell him about you—"

"How terribly kind of you, Mrs. Aysgarth, but I'm afraid I've absolutely had it with London."

"Oh, that won't last, you'll go back, you're a London person. Now my dear, I do hope you're not thinking that darling Stephen will give you spiritual direction in the Hebrides, because Stephen's not at all spiritual on holiday, he just likes to sit around eating and drinking and reading detective stories, and I honestly think he'd be most put out if you started chatting to him about God. Anyway, Stephen really can't start giving spiritual direction to young girls, even here in Starbridge, because he's much too busy running the Cathedral and keeping the Chapter from murdering each other, and even if he wasn't much too busy he prefers to exercise his pastoral skills these days among men—and usually German men, as Eddie Hoffenberg will be the first to tell you. And talking of Eddie, I do think you might be kinder to him, he's *such* a nice man and he's had such awful tragedies in his life and he just doesn't deserve to have you and Primrose poking fun at him behind his back. God only knows what the two of you will get up to in the Hebrides—I can just see you egging each other on and smirking in corners—and in fact to be quite candid and to cut a long story short, I think this holiday is a thoroughly bad idea for all concerned. Why don't you and Primrose run off to Cornwall and leave those two clergymen to recharge their spiritual batteries in peace?"

"I don't think Primrose would care for that idea at all, Mrs. Aysgarth."

"Oh, Primrose! If that girl were to spend a little less time doting on her father and a little more time being nice to Maurice Tait her life would be vastly improved—and so, God knows, would mine! In fact in my opinion you'd be doing us all the biggest possible favour, Venetia my dear, if you lured Primrose away to—no, not Cornwall, too unoriginal, how about the French Riviera? Take her to your sister's villa at Juan-les-Pins!"

"I don't like the French Riviera."

"Well, you certainly won't like the Hebrides. Dr. Johnson thought it was quite awful, he told Boswell so."

"I don't like Dr. Johnson."

"Venetia dear, don't you think you're being just the teensiest bit negative?"

"I'm sorry, Mrs. Aysgarth. It really is so kind of you to worry about my spiritual welfare, and I'll think very carefully about everything you've said, I promise."

We looked at each other. Her hard dark eyes bore a sharp, shrewd, sceptical expression, and although I tried to exude a docile respect I knew she was not deceived. Rising to her feet abruptly she said: "I must see about lunch. Why don't you come indoors and have a chat with Elizabeth? She always feels so hurt when you and Primrose go out of your way to ignore her."

Smiling meekly but seething with rage I followed her into the house to talk to her daughter.

2

PRIMROSE usually ate her meals in her flat, but for Sunday lunch, that sacred British institution, she joined her family in the Deanery dining-room, and on that Sunday before Easter I sat with her at the long table. As usual on such occasions, a crowd turned up. In addition to Dido's two children—not only Elizabeth, who was now a precocious fourteen, but little Pip, who was a nine-year-old pupil at the Choir School—there was a female called Miss Carp, known within the family as Polly (in memory of Polycarp, a bishop of the Early Church); she kept the household running while Dido poked her nose into everyone else's business, popped up to London to patronise Harrods and pampered herself with the occasional attack of nervous exhaustion, a condition which Primrose described as "sheer bloody-minded self-indulgence." There had been a succession of *au pair* girls who had looked after the children, but these creatures had been dispensed with once Pip had begun his career at the Choir School.

The other guests at lunch that day consisted of Aysgarth's second son by his first marriage, Norman, who lectured in law at King's College London, Norman's wife, Cynthia, who always looked as if she might sleep with everyone in sight but probably never did (although my sister

Arabella always said Cynthia was the vainest, most sex-mad girl she had ever met—and coming from Absolutely-the-Bottom Arabella that was really something), Aysgarth's third son, James, the jolly Guardsman who was so good at talking about nothing, James's girlfriend, whose name I failed to catch although it was probably Tracy or Marilyn or something non-U, Aysgarth's fourth and final son by his first marriage, Alexander, known as Sandy, who was doing post-graduate work up at Oxford, a chum of Sandy's called Boodle (I never found out his real name either), two elderly female cousins of Dido's from Edinburgh who appeared to be quite overwhelmed by all the English, Primrose, me and—inevitably—Aysgarth's most devoted hanger-on, Eddie Hoffenberg. The two people whom I most wanted to see—Aysgarth's eldest son, Christian, and his wife—were conspicuous by their absence.

"They were here last weekend," explained Primrose.

All Aysgarth's children visited their home regularly and all appeared to get on well with their father who was unfailingly benevolent to them. The contrast with my own family could hardly have been more marked. My elder brother, Harold, was too stupid to hold my father's attention for long, and although my brother Oliver was no fool—no genius but no fool—he too was uninterested in intellectual matters. Henrietta, Arabella and Sylvia could only be regarded by my father as pretty little playthings. I drove him up the wall. In consequence family gatherings were notable for my father's impatience and irritability, my mother's valiant efforts to pour oil on troubled waters, and my siblings muttering to one another in corners that "Pater" really was getting a bit much and Mama had to be some kind of saint to stand him and only a liberal supply of champagne could save everyone from going completely and utterly bonkers.

At the Aysgarths' lunch that day everyone talked animatedly, Dido inflicting her usual outrageous monologues on her defenceless cousins—with occasional asides to Eddie Hoffenberg who took seriously his Christian obligation to be charitable—Norman commenting on some judge named Denning (this was just before the Profumo affair made Denning famous), Cynthia describing the work of some besotted artist who yearned to paint her portrait, James saying: "Really? How splendid!" at intervals, Sandy and Boodle arguing over the finer points of Plato's dialogue "On the Soul," Elizabeth throwing out the information that actually she was an Aristotelian and that Plato simply rang no bells for her at all, Primrose arguing that the whole trouble with the Roman Church was that St. Thomas Aquinas had based his *Summa* on Aristotle's philosophy, and my Mr. Dean chipping in to observe that the world was always divided into Aristotelians and Platonists, and wasn't the treacle-tart absolutely first-class. In the midst of all these stimulating verbal fireworks, little Pip, who was sitting thoughtfully on my left, turned to me and said: "Do you like the Beatles, Venetia?"

"They're a little young for me, Pip, but I liked 'Love Me Do.' "

"I think they're fab," said Pip. "Much better than Plato or Aristotle."

One of the most attractive aspects of life with the Aysgarths was the wide range of the topics discussed. I doubt if my parents and siblings had heard of the Beatles in the spring of '63.

Later in the drawing-room I had an interesting talk about politics with Norman but Cynthia became jealous and winkled him away from me. By this time the Dean had shut himself in his study for his post-prandial snooze, but Eddie Hoffenberg was still hovering as if eager to tell me about his osteopath, so I slipped away to take refuge in Primrose's flat. Primrose herself had departed after lunch with her boyfriend Maurice Tait, one of the vicars-choral who sang tenor in the Cathedral Choir and taught at the Choir School. In fact she cared little for Tait (a damp, limp individual whose hobbies were stamp-collecting and supporting the Bible Reading Fellowship) but she liked to keep him around so that she could talk about "my boyfriend" and look worldly. I didn't despise her for this. I wouldn't have minded a neutral escort myself, if only to silence the fiends who muttered: "Poor old Venetia!" behind my back, but no limp, damp individual had presented himself for acquisition. I didn't count Eddie, of course. Not only was his Wagnerian gloom intolerable but he was so ugly that if I had accepted him as an escort the fiends would merely have gone on muttering: "Poor old Venetia!"

I also had to face the fact—an unpalatable one for my ego—that Eddie had never actually tried to do more than trap me in corners and talk about his health. He had never invited me to his house on my own or suggested a visit to the cinema—or even invited me for a walk on a Sunday afternoon. Tait always took Primrose for a walk down by the water-meadows after he had lunched with his mother. Primrose would sigh beforehand and say what a bore these walks were, but I suspected that if Tait had failed to appear one Sunday she would have been very cross indeed.

The rest of the day passed most agreeably, providing a tantalising glimpse of what fun life could be when one was accepted by a group of congenial people; at least at the Aysgarths' house I was never left out in the cold. After tea we all played croquet and I beat everyone except Boodle. There was much laughter as we languished on the lawn. Then having completed my odyssey among the croquet hoops I ate baked beans on toast with Primrose in her flat and we discussed Life, a ritual which involved reviewing the day's events, pulling everyone to pieces, putting a few favoured individuals together again and tossing the rest on the scrap-heap. This was fun. Primrose had her faults (priggishness, intolerance, intellectual snobbishness) but she was witty and seldom bored me. I only became bored when she was either talking soppily about her father or droning drearily about her work at the diocesan office on Eternity Street. Every time she began a sentence with the words "The Archdeacon and I," my teeth automatically gritted themselves, so when at ten o'clock that evening the dread words tripped off her tongue I waited until she had finished her sentence and then immediately asked if I could have a bath. Half an hour later I was stretched out on the Put-U-Up sofa, now transformed into a bed, and tuning in to Radio Luxemburg on my transistor.

"Good heavens, Vinnie!" exclaimed Primrose, appearing crossly in curlers as I was smoking a final cigarette and wriggling my toes in time to Elvis Presley. "You're not still listening to that drivel, are you? I can't understand why you're so keen on pop music!"

"No, you wouldn't. You're not fundamentally interested in sex."

"Honestly, Venetia! What a thing to say!" She flounced back to her bedroom.

Elvis quivered on vibrantly. As I stubbed out my cigarette I wondered—not for the first time—if anyone would ever invite me to have sexual intercourse, but it seemed like a forlorn hope. Switching off the transistor I pulled the bedclothes over my head and allowed myself to shed a single furious tear of despair.

3

EASTER was the following weekend. In the interval I loafed, smoked and vegetated, unwilling to think deeply about the future and telling myself I needed a few days of absolute rest in order to recuperate from the horrors of London life. I did toy with the idea of reading *Honest to God* but the desire to escape from my problems by being intellectually mindless was so strong that I could only reread Primrose's childhood collection of Chalet School books.

Finally I was roused from my torpor by the spectacle of Easter in a great cathedral. I avoided the Good Friday services but attended Matins on Sunday morning and was rewarded when Aysgarth preached a most interesting sermon about how Christianity was all set to undergo a dynamic resurrection, recast and restated for the modern age. The Bishop, who was ensconced in his *cathedra* at one end of the choir, spent much time gazing up at the east window as if he were wondering how it could possibly be cleaned.

The next day Aysgarth was obliged to supervise the conclusion of the special services, but on Tuesday he was free to depart for the Hebrides; he and Eddie planned to drive to Heathrow airport and leave the car in the long-term car-park. At half-past eight that morning after Primrose had departed for her office I wandered across the courtyard of the stables to say goodbye to him, but no sooner had I entered the house by the side door than I heard Dido's voice, throbbing with emotion, in the hall. Automatically I stopped dead. I was still well out of sight beyond the stairs.

". . . I'm sorry, I'm sorry, I absolutely *swore* I wouldn't break down like this, but I do so wish you were coming to Leicestershire—I know horses bore you, but you could read quietly in the library and—"

"Darling—"

"—and at least you'd be *there.* I just think it's so sad for Elizabeth and Pip that we're never together on our own as a family—"

"But that's not true!"

"Not on our *own,* Stephen—there's always someone from your first marriage there—all right, we won't talk of Primrose, but it just seems so wrong that we're not going to be together—"

"But when Lord Starmouth offered me the lodge the first thing I did was ask you to come with me!"

"How could I when I'm ill every time I try to go in a plane?"

"I was quite prepared to go overland, but since you were adamant that nothing would induce you to go to the Hebrides—"

"I thought you'd back down and come to Leicestershire. I never dreamed you'd run off instead with Primrose and Eddie and—my God!—Venetia—"

"What's wrong with Venetia? Isn't she Primrose's best friend and the daughter of one of my own oldest friends?"

"I don't give a damn who she is, that girl's sly, not to be trusted, a trouble-maker—"

"My dearest, I really don't think this conversation does you justice—"

"Oh, I'm sorry, I'm sorry, it's just that I feel so depressed, so alone, so utterly *abandoned*—"

There was a silence. I guessed he had been driven to silence her with an embrace. Pressing my back against the wall of the passage I held my breath and waited until at last she said tearfully: "How I hate separations!"

"I'll write every day."

"If only there was a phone at this stupid place—"

"I'll try and phone from the nearest village."

"Promise?"

"Of course I promise."

"Oh Stephen . . ." Another silence elapsed before Aysgarth said abruptly: "Here's Eddie with the car. Quick, take my handkerchief and dry your eyes—where are the children?"

"I don't know . . . Elizabeth! Pip! Your father's leaving!"

At once I slipped silently away.

4

PRIMROSE and I began our journey north twenty-four hours later after the day-long diocesan conference of the Young Christians for Peace, an event which Primrose had helped to organise and which apparently could not take place without her. Primrose had always been an enthusiastic organiser. She had acquired the taste for power when she had become a Girl Guide leader, and since then the local branches of the Student Christian Movement, the Bible Reading Fellowship, the Missions to Africa Fund and the Inter-Faith League had all benefited from her efficient interference.

"You really ought to get interested in some worthwhile cause, Venetia!" she exclaimed as she returned, flushed with triumph, from her conference. "If I were to do nothing but read dated schoolgirl books, watch television and listen to Radio Lux, I'd go mad in no time!"

I refrained from argument; I was all for a quiet life, and since I was a guest in her flat I had a moral obligation to be docile, but I realised then that Mrs. Ashworth had been correct in deducing that Primrose and I had reached the parting of the ways.

Meanwhile we had to go on holiday together. Driving to Heathrow in my MG we caught a late-morning flight to Glasgow and arrived in the town of Stornoway, the capital of the Outer Hebrides, in the middle of the afternoon. Although it was the largest settlement on the island of Lewis and Harris, the town was small and the airport was primitive. On stepping out of the little plane I felt a soft damp wind on my cheek. A vast vista of white clouds and green treeless wastes stretched before me, but when I had an immediate impression not of desolation but of peace I realised my mood of torpor was at last beginning to dissolve.

"There's Eddie," said Primrose.

Eddie's ungainly figure was clad in the English holiday uniform of grey trousers, a casual shirt and a tweed jacket, but he still managed to look like a foreigner; the uniform was much too well tailored. He was driving a hired car, a faded white Morris which had seen better days but which bucketed along the narrow roads with surprising spirit. Lewis, I realised as I stared out of the window later at Harris, was the tame, domesticated part of the island. Harris was all bare hills and sinister peat-bogs and glowering little lakes with hardly a croft in sight. Yet I was intrigued. It seemed light-years away from London, and beyond the village of Tarbert we appeared to leave civilisation behind completely. A single-track road adorned with the occasional hardy weed wound through brutal hills. Now and then the sea was visible as a lurid strip of midnight blue. Squalls of rain swooped down from the hills and swept away along the coast. Rainbows appeared fleetingly during improbable bursts of sunshine. The car groaned but battled on. I began to be excited.

"Is there really anything at the end of this road, Eddie?"

"Wait and see!" He pulled the car round a hairpin bend, and a second later Primrose and I were both exclaiming in wonder. Before us lay a small bay, shaped like a crescent moon and fringed with pale sand. Overlooking this idyllic seascape stood an Edwardian house, not too big but solid and well proportioned. Beyond a walled garden the brown-green moors, dotted with rocks, rose towards mountains capped by cloud.

"Just like Wuthering Heights!" remarked Primrose. "True romantic isolation! All we need now is Heathcliff."

The front door opened as if on cue, and the Dean of Starbridge stepped out into the porch to welcome us.

5

DESPITE its remoteness the house turned out to be very comfortable, in that plain tasteful style that always costs a lot of money, and this comfort was enhanced by a married couple who did all the boring things such as cooking, shopping, cleaning and keeping the peat fires burning. At that time of the year in the far north the weather was still cold, particularly in the evenings, but having spent so much of my life at Flaxton Hall, where the heating was either non-existent or modest, I took the chill in my stride. In contrast, wretched Eddie was soon complaining of rheumatic twinges and saying that whenever he was in pain he was convinced he was going to die young.

"In that case," said Primrose, "please do die now and save us from listening to any more of your moans," but at that point Aysgarth intervened, reminding Eddie lightly that life had been much worse in the POW camp on Starbury Plain and begging Primrose not to encourage anyone to die because it would be so annoying to have to cut short the holiday.

Our days in the wilderness began with breakfast at nine. Eddie then walked to the village and collected the specially ordered copy of *The*

Times; on his return he studied it for twenty minutes. Another brisk trot followed, this time up and down the beach, but finally he allowed himself to relax in the morning-room with *The Brothers Karamazov.*

In contrast Aysgarth followed quite a different pattern of activity. After breakfast he sat in the drawing-room for a while and gazed at the sea. Then he dipped into one of his newly purchased paperbacks (all detective stories) and read a few pages. More sea-gazing followed but at last he roused himself sufficiently to pen a letter to his wife. ("The daily chore," commented Primrose to me once in a grim aside.) By the time the letter was finished Eddie had returned from the village but Aysgarth refused to read the newspaper in detail after Eddie had discarded it; he merely glanced at the headlines and tried to do the crossword. Despite his intellect he was very bad at crosswords, almost as bad as he was at bridge, and had to be helped by Primrose and me. The completion of the puzzle took at least twice as long as it should have done because we all spent so much time laughing, but once the last letter had been pencilled in Aysgarth invariably announced with regret: "I suppose I ought to take some exercise." He then staggered outside, inhaled deeply a few times and staggered back indoors again. As soon as the clock in the hall chimed twelve he declared it was time for drinks. Eddie, who preferred to abstain from alcohol till the evening, remained in the morning-room with *The Brothers Karamazov* but Aysgarth and I would swill champagne while Primrose toyed with her customary glass of dry sherry.

At some time during the morning Primrose and I would have been out, either scrambling along the rocky coast or following the path up into the stark wild hills. It rained regularly, but since we always wore macks and sou'westers the weather was never a serious inconvenience. Besides, the rain never lasted long. When the sun did shine we continually marvelled at the colours around us: the sea was a sapphire blue, the waves bright white, the sands dark cream, the moors green-brown mixed with ash-grey rock. Primrose took numerous photographs while I tried to impress the scenes on my memory and wished I could paint. Often as we scrambled along the low cliffs we saw seals playing near the beach, and several times in the hills we glimpsed deer. There were never any people. As the days passed my sense of peace increased until I even began to wish I could have been one of those ancient Celtic saints, dedicated to a solitary life in a remote and beautiful place in order to worship God. At least I would have been spared the rat-race in London and the hell of attending the Great Party of Life as a wallflower.

After lunch every day Aysgarth retired for "forty winks," which usually lasted half an hour, Primrose and I read *The Times* and Eddie wrote letters. Then at three o'clock we departed with a picnic tea for an outing in the car. All over the long island we rambled; on two consecutive days we stopped on the road to Leverburgh at a point above the vast sands which stretched across the bay towards the distant range of blue mountains, and twice we visited the remote church at Rodel on the southernmost tip of Harris. Then I, who was so very bad at worship and so very reluctant to be "churchy," found myself thinking of Jesus Christ, living thousands of miles away in another culture in another millennium, writing nothing, completing his life's work in three years, a failure by worldly standards, dying an ignoble death—yet still alive in the little church at Rodel on the remotest edge of Europe, still alive for his millions upon millions of followers worldwide, not a despised, rejected failure any more but acknowledged even by non-Christians as one of the greatest men who had ever lived, etched deep on the consciousness of humanity and expressing his mysterious message of regeneration in that most enigmatic of all symbols, the cross.

"What are you thinking about, Venetia?" said that pest Eddie, ruining my rare moment of feeling religious as I stood staring at the church.

"Elvis Presley," I said to shut him up. Eddie loathed pop music.

By then I was missing my daily dose of the pops on Radio Luxemburg which seemed to be unobtainable in the Hebrides; perhaps the weather conditions were unfavourable—or perhaps Luxemburg was merely too far away. The BBC in those days devoted little time to musical trivia so my deprivation was severe, but on the other hand there was little time to tune into the wireless. When we returned from our picnic the moment had arrived for a gin-and-tonic for me, whisky for the men and another glass of sherry for Primrose. During dinner we sampled a claret or a white burgundy—or possibly, depending on the menu, both; Aysgarth was taking seriously his absent host's invitation that we should help ourselves to his well-stocked cellar. After dinner we played bridge or, if we were feeling frivolous, *vingt-et-un*. Conversation, spiked by all the drink, sparkled. Even Eddie shuddered with mirth occasionally.

"Father," said Primrose late one evening after Eddie had scooped the pool of matchsticks at *vingt-et-un* and Aysgarth had suggested a nightcap of brandy, "isn't this holiday turning into a distinctly Bacchanalian orgy?"

"I hope so!" said Aysgarth amused.

"So do I!" I said at once. "Primrose, these poor clergymen spend months on end being saintly and strait-laced—why on earth shouldn't they let their hair down on holiday?"

That idiotic Eddie was unable to resist sighing: " 'Eat, drink and be merry for tomorrow we die.' "

"Well, I'm not dying yet!" declared Aysgarth robustly. "I've still got a lot of living to do!"

A chord twanged in my memory. " 'I've gotta—*whole* lotta living to do!' " I sang, imitating Presley. " '*Whole* lotta loving to do—and there's-uh no one-uh who I'd rather do it-uh with-uh than you—COME ON, BABY!' "

"*Venetia!*" exclaimed Eddie, appalled by the vulgarity, his eyes almost popping out of his head.

"*Venetia!*" cried Primrose scandalised, casting an embarrassed glance at her father.

"What a splendid song!" said my Mr. Dean naughtily, unable to resist the urge to shock them still further. "Does it come from the repertoire of those young men Pip likes so much?"

"The Beatles? No, it's an Elvis Presley number."

"Ah, Mr. Presley! The Bishop thinks his records ought to be banned—which inevitably means they're first-class fun. 'Charles,' I said to him after I'd supported the publication of *Lady Chatterley's Lover,* 'the real obscenity in our culture isn't sex. It's violence.' But of course he refused to agree. Funny how Charles takes such a dark view of sex—it's as if he can never forget some very profound sexual sin which affected him personally in some quite unforgettable way."

"Isn't the most likely explanation," said Eddie, who had had a good deal to drink, "that he had a strong sex-drive in his youth and that he was constantly afraid of giving way to temptation?"

"I don't know why you throw in the phrase 'in his youth,' Eddie!" said Aysgarth more naughtily than ever. "Why shouldn't he still have a strong sex-drive even now he's past sixty?"

Eddie went pink. Primrose stood up and said brightly: "Who's for cocoa?"

"I thought we were all going to have a nightcap of brandy," I said. "Go on, Mr. Dean! Do you think the Bishop and Mrs. Bishop go in for Lady Chatterley–style high jinks at the South Canonry?"

"*Venetia!*" chorused the horrified voices of Canon Hoffenberg and Miss P. Aysgarth, Girl Guide leader.

The Dean could barely speak for laughing but managed to gasp: "Eddie, why don't you keep Primrose company while she goes in search of cocoa? Venetia and I are going to discuss D. H. Lawrence!"

"This is all your fault, Vinnie," said Primrose exasperated. "If you hadn't mentioned Elvis Presley—"

"I'd very much like to hear this Mr. Presley," said Aysgarth. "Could we tune into Radio Luxemburg on that radiogram in the morning-room?"

"Not a hope, Mr. Dean—unless the reception's a great deal better tonight than it's been so far."

"Eddie," said Primrose, "let's leave them to their decadence."

Eddie said drunkenly: "We draw the line at rock-'n'-roll, Stephen!" and stalked after her.

"Snob!" I shouted after him before adding to Aysgarth: "The mystery about that radiogram is that there appear to be no records to go with it. Wouldn't you think that the Earl's teenage daughters would keep a supply of old favourites here to wile away the rainy days?"

"Let's have a search!" exclaimed Aysgarth, leaping to his feet.

"Tally-ho!" I cried, leading the charge into the hall. Then I stopped. "But it's no good searching the morning-room," I said, "because I've already done that. I've searched the drawing-room too. Perhaps the attics—"

"What about that cupboard over there under the stairs?"

We bowled over to the cupboard and I dived inside.

"There's probably a light," said Aysgarth as I floundered in the darkness. "Thank heavens this place has a generator and we don't have to rely on candles . . . ah, well done!"

I had found the light switch and was now surveying a jungle of mackintoshes, Wellington boots and bric-a-brac which stretched far back below the stairs. Ploughing forward I nearly disembowelled myself with a fishing-rod. "Bloody hell," I muttered before I remembered the Church. "Whoops! Sorry, Mr. Dean—"

"Oh, did you speak? I didn't hear a word."

The old pet! I adored him. Heaving aside a battalion of boots I struck gold in the form of six cases, all designed to carry records. "Eureka!" I shouted, ripping open the first case of twelve-inch LPs, but found only the Beethoven symphonies with a dash of *Swan Lake*. Attacking the second case I glimpsed the word "Wagner" and slammed shut the lid with a shudder.

"Any luck?" called Aysgarth excited.

"Hang on." I opened the third case—and there, miraculously, was Presley, glittering in gold lamé and slouched in a pose to launch a thousand screams. "Whoopee!" I yelled and staggered backwards past the macks and wellies with the record-case clasped to my bosom.

"Jiminy cricket!" said Aysgarth awed as I showed him the picture on the sleeve.

"Just you wait, Mr. Dean! This is the kind of stuff guaranteed to make the Bishop pass out in the pulpit!"

We plunged into the morning-room where I crammed the LP onto the turntable. Then I hesitated, holding the arm above the revolving disc as I tried to select the most suitable track. I didn't want to bludgeon him into a coma with "Heartbreak Hotel." A milder introduction seemed called for. Finally the decision was made, and the next moment Presley—

Presley before he became decadent and bloated and corrupt—the young, unspoilt, unsurpassable Elvis Presley began to belt out "You're Right, I'm Left, She's Gone."

6

"THIS is wonderful!" cried the Dean. "Wonderful!" And as I lifted the needle from the groove at the end of the track he exclaimed: "It makes me want to catch up with all the fun I missed out on in my youth!"

"Was your youth really so drab?"

"Drab! That's an understatement. Primitive Methodists, no money, working day in, day out, in order to get on—why, the most thrilling moment of my youth consisted of a forbidden visit to the cinema where I watched Clara Bow oozing 'It' as I sank my teeth into a sinful peppermint cream! Never mind, those times are gone now—and how glad I am that I've lived to see the dawn of a new era! Class barriers collapsing, sexual inhibitions being overcome—"

"Good old Elvis! Want to hear some more?"

"I want to hear everything! Play that song you were singing at dinner!"

I rummaged around and found it. "Okay, Mr. Dean!" I cried. "Off we go!"

The beat began to pound. Presley began to celebrate the joy of life. And suddenly Aysgarth rose to his feet.

"Isn't it great?" I shouted, turning up the volume, but he merely cried enthralled: "Let's dance!"

I kicked off my shoes, we grabbed each other's hands, he drew me to the centre of the floor. And there, as Elvis Presley sang his heart out and the boards vibrated beneath our feet, I danced with the Dean of Starbridge to the beat of rock-'n'-roll.

7

AS the final chord throbbed and we clutched each other, breathless with laughter, I saw that Primrose and Eddie were standing appalled in the doorway.

"Honestly!" said Primrose as I abruptly switched off the radiogram. "I've never seen anything quite so undignified in all my life!"

"My dear," said her father, "you mustn't be so serious that you forget how to have fun."

At once Primrose turned her back on us and stalked off across the hall.

"Leave her to me, Stephen," said Eddie. "You go on having fun." And he too withdrew, closing the door behind him.

"That's the nicest thing Eddie's done in a month of Sundays," I said. "But why on earth is Prim being so idiotic?"

"I'm afraid she realised I was cross with her."

"*Cross?* That wasn't being cross! You should hear my father when he roars like a lion—that's what being cross is all about!"

"But Primrose is particularly dependent on me for my love and approval. Ever since her mother died—"

"But her mother's been dead for over twenty years—isn't it time Primrose grew up? God knows, I never thought I'd hear myself say this but sometimes when I see this so-called 'dependence' on you I really feel quite sorry for Dido."

He merely regarded me with grave blue eyes and said nothing.

A panic-stricken remorse assailed me. "Sorry," I mumbled, furious with myself for plunging around in his family problems like an elephant cavorting among eggshells. "Tight as an owl. Rude as hell. Forget I spoke."

"My dear Venetia, there's no need for you to apologise!" he said at once, sloughing off both my tactlessness and his problems as if they were supremely unimportant. "Let's be tight as owls together and go on having the time of our lives!" And as he stretched out his hands to me again I was suddenly transported to the very centre of life.

My world turned itself inside out. In a split second of blinding clarity I saw him at last not as the family friend who was always so kind to me, but as the irresistible stranger whose personality, by some great miracle, uniquely complemented my own. My loneliness was annihilated; my despair exploded into a euphoric hope. Knowing I had to withdraw at once before my emotion could utterly overwhelm me, I blundered across the hall to the cloakroom, sagged in tears against the door and mutely contemplated the vastness of my discovery.

8

"*VENETIA?*"

"Just a sec." I pulled the plug of the lavatory and emerged dry-eyed into the hall. As I saw the anxious expression on his face I realised he thought I was suffering from the effects of too much to drink, but although I opened my mouth to reassure him no words came. I was speechless because his entire appearance had changed. His white hair now seemed not shop-soiled but creamily distinguished. His forehead had assumed exactly the right height and breadth to enhance this impression of distinction, and his nose, formerly large, had become exquisitely and nobly Roman. The lines on his face no longer suggested antiquity but the power of a fascinating and formidable character. His eyes, radiantly blue and steamily bright, made me feel weak at the knees, while his thin mouth, which turned down slightly at the corners, no longer seemed tough in repose but overpoweringly sultry; I felt weaker at the knees than ever. In fact when he smiled I felt so demolished by his sheer sexual glamour that I actually had to sink down on the hall chest. I had forgotten he was sixty-one. Or, to be accurate, I had not forgotten but the fact no longer had any meaning for me. He could have been twenty-one, forty-one or eighty-one. Such a trivial fact was of no importance. All that mattered was that he was the man I wanted to go to bed with that very night and marry the very next morning.

I suddenly realised he was speaking again. He was saying: "How about some black coffee?" and my voice was replying without a second's hesitation: "I think I'd prefer a very large Rémy Martin."

He laughed. Then reassured that I was no longer expiring from an excess of alcohol, he vanished into the dining-room to raid the sideboard.

"What happened?" he inquired with curiosity as he returned with two brandies and sat down beside me on the hall chest. "Were you overwhelmed by Mr. Presley?"

"No, by *joie de vivre*—and by you, Mr. Dean," I said, somehow keeping my voice casual. "You must be the trendiest dean in Christendom!"

He laughed in delight, and I saw then that his attitude towards me was quite unchanged; untouched by any emotional earthquake he was merely savouring the concluding moments of an entertaining evening. "I always regard it as a very great blessing that Pip was born when I was fifty-two," he said. "He keeps me young in outlook."

Primrose chose that moment to return to the hall. "Sorry," she said. "I didn't mean to be such a kill-joy, but I genuinely can't stand that sort of music."

Aysgarth gave her a kiss to signal that her apology was accepted and asked: "Where's Eddie?"

"In the drawing-room. He started talking about the decadence of pop music and then before I could stop him he was holding forth on the decadence of Berlin in the thirties. I walked out when he began to ruminate on the nature of evil."

"I'd better go and rescue him."

"Why not just hit him over the head with *The Brothers Karamazov*? I nearly did."

They wandered off together to save Eddie from his turgid metaphysics. Knocking back the rest of my brandy I reeled upstairs to my room and passed out in a stupor of alcohol, ecstasy and rampant sexual desire.

V

*"The universe, like a human being, is not built merely to a
mathematical formula. It's only love that gives you the deepest
clue to it."*

JOHN A. T. ROBINSON,
writing about Honest to God *in the*
Sunday Mirror, *7 April 1963*

I

THE next day was Sunday and Aysgarth had earlier mentioned that he
would be celebrating Communion in the dining-room at eight. Since
Eddie and Primrose would inevitably attend the service I had decided I
should make the effort to join them, but when Primrose woke me I
realised, as my hangover hit me between the eyes, that my virtuous
decision would have to be revoked.

"There's something so wonderfully moral about alcohol," observed
Primrose as I pulled the bedclothes over my head with a groan. "Punishment always follows excess."

I could have murdered her, but by that time I was too enrapt with my
memories of the previous evening to bother. She departed unscathed and
immediately the door closed I sat up, ready for Day One of my new life.
I tossed off the necessary potion to soothe my liver. Then I flung back
the curtains and exclaimed: "A celestial day has dawned for Venetia
Flaxton!" Outside it was raining, but who cared? The view, wreathed
in shifting mist, seemed more romantic than ever. Sliding back into bed
I lit a cigarette, hummed a verse of Presley's "I Need Your Love Tonight"
and prepared for a delicious hour of meditating on the object of my
desire.

It was immediately obvious that I could never speak of my love. Since
nothing could come of my grand passion there could be no conceivable
point in disclosing my feelings, and besides, there was no one in whom
I could confide—except Mrs. Ashworth, but I could hardly babble to the
wife of a bishop about my newfound adulterous lust for a dean.

Having reached this conclusion I perceived a second obvious truth: not only would I have to keep my mouth shut but I would have to rise to great thespian heights to conceal my secret. No one must ever guess the truth because no one would ever understand the height and breadth and depth of my well-nigh incinerating desire. I pictured my siblings sniggering: "Poor old Venetia! A crush on an elderly clergyman—whatever will she think of next?" And as for Primrose . . . but no, the mind boggled. I had to carry the precious secret to my grave, but I could accept this necessity because I was so happy. I had been granted the power to love; nothing else mattered, and indeed to have wanted more would have been disgustingly greedy. Since it was quite impossible that Aysgarth could fall in love with me it was pointless to hope that my passion might be reciprocated, but I would be blissfully content with his continuing avuncular friendship, and so long as I could live near him, see him regularly and have the occasional little chat about God or Eternity or whatever else might interest him, my life would be indescribably rich and fulfilling.

So be it. I would still die *virgo intacta,* but having experienced passion on a cosmic scale I could at least tell myself that my years in the world hadn't been a complete waste of time.

With a sigh I stretched myself luxuriously and decided I was in paradise.

2

MY next task was to choose what to wear for Day One of my new life, but all my clothes now seemed so dreary, no more than a drab mass of browns, beiges and moss-greens. Then I remembered the red sweater which I had bought on impulse when I had visited Marks and Spencer's to replenish my stock of underwear; I had just had a row with my father and was feeling aggressive, but now the scarlet seemed to symbolise not aggression but passion. I selected the sweater and eyed a pair of earth-coloured slacks. Did I dare wear trousers on a Sunday? Yes. I was in the mood to take a scandalous risk. My mother had brainwashed me into thinking slacks were vulgar on any day of the week, but I had long since realised they suited me. I have longish legs and not too much padding around the hips. It was true that I was usually at least seven pounds overweight, but we can't all be the Duchess of Windsor.

I brushed my horrible hair and clipped it severely behind my ears to curb its tendency to billow around my head in a frizz. Then I slapped on some powder and went wild with the mascara which normally I reserved for evenings. My mother believed only fallen women wore eye make-up during the day, but Mrs. Ashworth had confirmed my suspicion that this piece of folklore was out of date. I tried to recall whether Mrs. Ashworth herself wore eye make-up but the memory eluded me. Dressing the part of a bishop's wife, Mrs. Ashworth was the kind of clever woman who would spend half an hour making herself up to look as if she were not made up at all.

Did I wear lipstick? No. Lipstick was going out of favour. The "look" consisted of emphasising the eyes and hair. Jewellery? No, quite inappropriate for a Sunday morning in the Hebrides, and anyway I had decided to emulate Mrs. Ashworth's uncluttered simplicity of style. Was I ready? Yes. For anything. Forgetting my liver, which was still feeling a trifle battle-scarred, I sailed downstairs for breakfast just as the clock in the hall chimed nine.

They were all seated at the dining-room table. Primrose was pouring herself some coffee, Eddie was spooning sugar on his porridge and Aysgarth was buttering a slice of toast. Immediately in my imagination six trumpets blasted a triumphant fanfare while drums rolled and cymbals clashed.

"Mr. Dean!" I exclaimed with a radiant smile. "Do please forgive me for missing Communion but I was prostrated!"

"Maybe you should be prostrated more often!" retorted Aysgarth, much amused. "You look remarkably well!"

"Sheer mind over matter! As soon as I had willed myself to leap out of bed and sing the 'Ode to Joy,' I felt simply too wonderful to be true . . . Eddie, why are you goggling as if you'd swallowed an octopus?"

Eddie stammered with an uncharacteristically marked German accent: "You look tremendous, Venetia!"

"I *am* tremendous," I said, helping myself to eggs and bacon from the sideboard. "What else is new?"

Aysgarth started to laugh and when I glanced at him over my shoulder he gave me one of his saucy winks which meant, as I well knew, absolutely nothing.

I nearly passed out. Then winking back at him, as befitted a platonic friend of many years' standing, I prepared to toy in ecstasy with a hearty breakfast.

3

"WHY are you made up to the nines and behaving as if you'd just quaffed an entire bottle of champagne?" demanded Primrose baffled as we set out in the rain for our morning walk.

"It's the after-effects of listening to Elvis." I then realised it was time to act the part of my old nonchalant self, but before I could say anything else Primrose was confiding: "I think Eddie's terribly smitten—I've never before seen him turn such a strangulated shade of puce!"

"Oh, people are always saying Eddie fancies me, but I don't believe a word of it! He never makes anything which could be remotely described as a pass."

"Probably too frightened. After all, if you're as ugly as Eddie, you'd be afraid that any girl you approached would simply shriek: 'Dracula!' and run screaming in the opposite direction."

"True. I wonder if he's ever done it."

"Approached a girl?"

"No, had sex."

"Honestly, Venetia, why have you suddenly developed this appallingly one-track mind?"

"As a matter of fact Eddie doesn't strike me as being unsophisticated about sex—look at that cunning remark he made about Bishop Ashworth's sex-phobia."

"Imagine doing it with Eddie!" said Primrose shuddering.

"Imagine doing it with your Maurice Tait!"

"Maurice is actually rather good-looking when he takes off his glasses—"

"Yes, but would he remain good-looking if he took off anything else? God, what a bloody peculiar thing sex is! Do you suppose your father still does it with Dido?"

"Don't be obscene!"

"Yes, I'm sorry, that *was* a bit far-fetched—"

"Of course all that stopped years ago!"

"You mean they have separate bedrooms?" I knew my Mr. Dean was languishing in a ghastly marriage, and I knew it was impossible that he should love the middle-aged gorgon whom I had overheard nagging him so unmercifully, but I saw no harm in establishing beyond doubt that the marriage was entirely nominal.

"They've had separate bedrooms almost from the start," said Primrose, wrinkling her nose in distaste. "That was because of her insomnia. But the separate bedrooms didn't stop her getting pregnant five times."

This was not exactly the news I wanted to hear. "In that case why do you think they've stopped having sex?"

"The doctor told her after number five was born that she mustn't have any more children."

"So what? I can't see that proves anything, the state of contraception being what it is—"

"I'm quite sure," said Primrose firmly, "that an eminent cleric of the Church of England would never engage in anything so sordid as contraception."

"But perhaps contraception's no longer required. If the old hag's had the change of life—"

"I don't think she has. I know she's forty-eight and ought to be absolutely over the hill but she still gets monthly migraines when she has to lie in a darkened room and pretend she's dying."

"In that case you're right and your father must be entirely frustrated."

"He's more likely to be faint with relief! Surely once a man gets past sixty he just wants to go to bed with a good book?"

But I thought of my Mr. Dean regretting his repressed youth, and although I was sure he would recoil from copulating with Dido I did wonder how content he was with his enforced chastity.

"He should never have married her," Primrose was saying, reverting to a well-worn theme. "Well, he never would have married her if she hadn't ensnared him when he was still mad with grief after Mother's death."

I was, of course, familiar with the Primrose Aysgarth version of history, and out of delicacy I had never tried to debate it with her, but I was well aware that other people saw her father's past in a different light and now for the first time I was sufficiently intrigued to throw tact to the winds.

"Primrose, two and a half years elapsed between your mother's death and his marriage to Dido! He couldn't have been mad all the time!"

"Dido kept him mad by chasing him so hard that he had no chance to recover his equilibrium."

"But I've heard it said that he himself was the one who did the chasing—"

"That was simply a rumour Dido put into circulation in order to boost her ego. The truth was she sank her talons into him when he was vulnerable and then clawed away until he agreed to marry her."

"But that makes your father sound absolutely feeble!"

"Nonsense! On the contrary it shows he was strong enough to marry out of compassion and tough enough to survive the inevitable disaster!"

"So are you saying he never loved Dido at all?"

"How could he have done? It was Mother he adored. He just saw Dido as a neurotic, pathetic failure and he was idealistic enough to think he could heal her by marriage. He acted, I assure you, not out of love but out of sheer nobility of soul."

Elektra had spoken. I had no doubt I was supposed to swallow whole this theory which showed her father as a self-sacrificing saint, but I could not help but feel it raised more problems than it solved. There were plenty of neurotic women in the world; why had he allowed himself to be nailed by someone as dreadful as Dido? And why had he been driven to heal a neurotic woman anyway? And why had he felt it essential that the healing should take place within the framework of marriage when it must have been obvious that such a marriage could only prove disastrous? The more I considered the theory the more unsatisfactory it seemed; I could only conclude that Primrose had been carried away by her Elektra complex and that her father's second marriage was a mystery she had never even begun to unravel.

Idly I heard myself say: "Bearing in mind the fact that your father must often have been vilely unhappy with the gorgon, do you think he's ever looked at anyone else?"

"Good heavens, no!" Primrose was genuinely appalled. "Of course, I know one does occasionally hear about vicars who let the side down, but *Father*—the former Archdeacon of Starbridge—a Canon of Westminster—and now the Dean of one of the greatest cathedrals in England—"

"Sorry, forget I spoke."

"I know he talks racily sometimes, but underneath all that he's quite exceptionally serious and devout! In fact you can be one hundred percent certain that ever since he took his ordination vows not a single adulterous thought has ever crossed his mind."

Yet again Elektra had spoken, but this time I was prepared to accept the pronouncement without question; it chimed with everything I knew about my heroic Mr. Dean. I sighed, but I had never seriously thought that my grand passion had a hope of being consummated.

I vowed never to entertain such a futile thought again.

4

"VENETIA," said Eddie that evening as we waited for the others to join us in the drawing-room for cocktails.

"Uh-huh?" I was flicking through the pages of one of the bound volumes of *Punch,* thoughtfully provided by the Earl of Starmouth to ward off any television withdrawal symptoms among his guests.

"Instead of going for a walk with Primrose tomorrow morning, would you come for a walk with me?"

I somehow restrained myself from exclaiming: "Good God!" Turning another page of *Punch* I enquired: "Down to the village to pick up *The Times*?"

"No, later. Are you playing for time while you think of an excuse to refuse?"

"Oh Eddie, don't look so mournful!"

"How am I supposed to look when you respond to my invitation with such a lack of enthusiasm?"

I felt caddish. Poor old Eddie! Why should I make him miserable when I myself was in such ecstasy? I resolved to be benign. "Okay," I said, closing the volume. "Let's go for a walk tomorrow morning. But how do you suggest I get rid of Primrose? She'll want to come too."

"I'd thought of that. I'll ask Stephen to suggest she keeps him company. She'll never refuse a request from her father."

This plan struck me as both simple and efficient. I thought: trust a German to plot like a machine! And in alarm I wondered if I had given the machine an oiling I would later regret. However a second later I had dismissed this suspicion as ridiculous. Eddie was hardly going to do more than talk about his osteopath, and besides . . . one could always rely on a clergyman to bust a gut to preserve the proprieties.

5

AT eleven o'clock the next morning we set off along the path which wound around the hillside at the back of the house and led into a long empty valley. The sun was shining. Huge clouds scudded across a pale sky. Stretching into the distance ahead of us the moors suggested both loneliness and freedom.

"It's a pity Wordsworth never had a go at this landscape," I remarked after we had been walking for some minutes in a silence which had become increasingly oppressive. "Plenty of scope for nature-mysticism."

"Gerard Manley Hopkins would have come closer to catching the atmosphere, I think. He'd have been starker and grittier."

"Don't you find Hopkins a bit difficult? Since English isn't your native tongue—"

"Like Stephen I enjoy a challenge."

Delighted to have the opportunity to talk about Aysgarth I said: "I suppose a self-made man like the Dean has to face continual challenges."

"It was certainly a challenge for him to make his way in the world after his father died bankrupt. He was lucky to have that uncle who egged him on."

"What uncle?"

"Oh, has he never mentioned him to you? But no, he wouldn't have bothered—Stephen never seems to talk about his extreme past nowadays . . . Well, he had this uncle who used to egg him on by urging: 'You've got to go chasing the prizes!' and the result was—"

"He married Dido. What a booby-prize!"

"Dido has immense wit and charm," said Eddie reproachfully.

"Oh God, I'm talking to a Dido-fan! I'm sorry, I quite forgot—temporary aberration—"

"She's always been very kind to me. Of course she has her problems—"

"Well done, Eddie, a superb example of a British understatement!"

"—but she's in a tough situation, isn't she? Thanks to Primrose she never has much chance to be on her own with her husband and children."

"I agree the Primrose situation is impossible," I conceded with reluctance. "Prim really ought to move right away from the Deanery—it's no good camping on the doorstep in that flatlet, it's much too close and she and Dido still wind up screaming at each other most of the time."

"The person I feel sorry for is Stephen, caught in the middle, but sometimes I feel he exacerbates the problem by never taking a firm line."

"Maybe taking the line of least resistance is the only way he can survive being married to Dido."

"I hardly think the marriage is that bad! He married her because she amused him—and I think she still does. He likes that smart life she provides, all the dinner-parties and the socialising—and why shouldn't he? After that poverty-stricken early life, isn't it only natural that he should now favour a little luxury and glamour?"

"Eddie, are you seriously trying to tell me they're well suited?"

"An attraction of opposites is by no means always a recipe for disaster. I think their personalities complement each other, hers so volatile, his so calm—"

"It's curious how we're all different people to different people," I interrupted, finally losing the patience to keep listening to this earnest opinion which struck me as being almost bizarrely wide of the mark. "Dido's obviously one person to you, another to me and Primrose and yet a third to the Dean."

"Stephen would say the apparent diversity is an illusion. 'It's all a unity!' he would say. 'It's all one!' One of Stephen's most marked theological traits is that he believes in unity, not duality, and that's why he gets so irritated with neo-orthodox men like the Bishop who employ the principles of dialectic to—"

"Oh God, Eddie, we're not going to discuss theology, are we?"

"I thought you liked it! I can remember you listening enrapt to Stephen when he talked about *Soundings*!"

"Well, I'm one person for the Dean," I said, "and I'm quite another for you. Let's go back to Gerard Manley Hopkins."

Eddie immediately began to discuss Hopkins' miserable life as a Roman Catholic priest.

We trudged drearily on across the moor.

"PRIMROSE mentioned that you were thinking of looking for a flat in Oxford," said Eddie as finally, to my profound relief, we returned within sight of the lodge. By that time I was so exhausted by our literary discussion that I feared I might fall into a coma at any moment. "When will you be leaving Starbridge?"

"I'm not leaving. I've changed my mind."

Eddie halted. I wandered on but eventually paused to wait for him. Beyond the house the dark, restless sea was swirling over the arc of sand.

"You're going to stay on in Starbridge?" He sounded stupefied.

"Yes, I'll start looking for a job when I get back. Any objections?"

"No. No, of course not. No, I was just so surprised—I thought Starbridge would be much too provincial for a sophisticated girl like you."

"I feel I need a complete change."

"I see . . . But that's tremendous! I'm so happy, I—" He somehow pulled himself together sufficiently to add in a casual voice: "Perhaps we could go to the theatre together sometime."

"Oh, is that old dump still operating?"

"It's no dump nowadays, I assure you! Last autumn there was an Ibsen season—and after Christmas they did an exceptionally good production of *Lady Windermere's Fan*—and this summer they'll be trying out a revival of one of the Noel Coward plays before it opens in London. I forget the title, but Martin Darrow will be playing the lead."

"In that case you can accompany me as I stampede through the streets to the theatre. I'm getting rather keen on the Darrow family."

I had made Eddie's day, his week, his month and possibly his entire year, but as we moved on once more along the path I began to regret my decision to be kind to him.

The road to hell, as we all know, is paved with good intentions.

IT seemed a great irony that now I at last had a man panting for my attention I could hardly have cared less, but I supposed I could at least regard this conquest as gratifying to my ego. Having reflected that my triumph would have been far more gratifying if Eddie had not been physically repulsive and mentally exhausting, I was inclined to conclude that I could have done without such a perverse development in my private life, but then I wondered if Eddie might have his uses as a smoke-screen. The thought of him playing Romeo certainly diverted Primrose.

"Did he jump on you?"

"Don't be absurd! There's no doubt he's a trifle smitten, but I'm sure he prefers to worship from afar."

"He might get bolder now he's broken the ice!"

"Not Eddie! No true masochist could pass up such a splendid chance to languish in frustration," I declared, and putting all thought of Eddie aside I began to make plans for my future.

I had already decided to look for a flat which was as near the Close as possible, but I knew it might take time to find the right place and meanwhile my need to escape from Primrose was urgent. I was terrified that she might soon see past the smoke-screen created by Eddie and sense I had been invading her territory.

I debated whether to beat a temporary retreat to Flaxton Pauncefoot, but that was miles away and besides, I had no wish for my parents to assume my will to be independent was wavering. To visit home, pick up my car and sort out my clothes was acceptable, but to roost at Flaxton Hall for days would create an impression of pusillanimity. Plainly I had to stay somewhere in Starbridge while I hunted for a flat, but where could I go? Primrose would be baffled and suspicious if I decamped abruptly to a hotel. I did know several of the inhabitants of the other houses in the Close, but I could think of no one—apart from Mrs. Ashworth—whom I could ask to put me up for more than a couple of nights, and the South Canonry, like Primrose's flat, was highly unsuitable for me in my present state; I could hardly live in close proximity to the Bishop while I was harbouring torrid thoughts about the Dean.

I was still wrestling with this apparently insoluble problem when Aysgarth, reading his daily letter from his wife, paused to observe to Primrose: "Dido may be in Leicestershire, but she's still tuned in to the Cathedral Close grapevine. Apparently Marina Markhampton's in Starbridge. She's looking after the Chantry while her grandparents are visiting the south of France."

Marina Markhampton was the youngest child of a wealthy gentleman of leisure who had married an equally wealthy wife and divided his time between Newmarket, where he kept racehorses, Monte Carlo, where he gambled away the money the horses won, and Camlott Edge in Dorset, where the Markhamptons had their ancestral home; in the hope of avoiding death duties his father, Sir William, had already ceded him the family estate.

Long ago in the 1930s Sir William's wife Enid had been a devoted fan of that legendary bishop of Starbridge, the port-swilling Dr. Alex Jardine, and she had never forgotten her amusing visits to the episcopal palace in those golden days before the war. Accordingly when her husband ceded the family estate to his son, Lady Markhampton had succumbed to a bout of nostalgia and demanded to spend her declining years in the Cathedral Close. The Chantry, a little six-bedroomed gem on Choristers' Green, happened to be vacant, and after a new lease had been extracted from the Dean and Chapter, Sir William and Lady Markhampton had lived there in bliss until one sad day in the 1950s when a burst pipe had ruined the priceless carpets. The Markhamptons had been in Cannes at the time and the naughty housekeeper had gone AWOL to some seaside resort in the north. As a result of this grisly experience, which had destroyed not only her carpets but her faith in housekeepers, Lady Markhampton had recruited her unmarried sister to house-sit when necessary, but the sister had recently died and now it appeared that Marina had accepted the invitation to replace her.

This was odd; Marina was not the sort of girl one pictured house-sitting in a provincial city. She was younger than I was, no more than twenty-one, and in addition to being beautiful and popular she had jet-setting tendencies. In the past I had occasionally encountered her at ghastly parties where I had been a wallflower and she had been pursued incessantly by panting young men. My brother Oliver said that the great debate about Marina Markhampton centred on whether she was *virgo intacta*. Apparently no debate was needed to establish the fact that she was the biggest cock-tease in town.

Having long since decided that Marina was someone who could never interest me, I now found myself revising my judgement. The Chantry would be wonderfully convenient. Choristers' Green, a square of lawn where the choristers had played before the Choir School had moved to the palace, lay at the north end of Canonry Drive, not far from the spot where the Deanery faced the west front of the Cathedral. Could I possibly cultivate this repulsive society stunner and wangle a bed while I looked for a flat? Before my days of ecstasy I would have dismissed the question as outrageous, but now, wafting along on my tidal wave of euphoria, I merely thought: hell, what have I got to lose?

I began to plot my cultivation of Marina Markhampton.

ON the last day of our holiday Primrose was felled by a malevolent attack of menstruation and decided to spend the morning in bed. I was delighted; her absence meant that at long last I had the opportunity to talk to Aysgarth on his own. Keen to make amends to her father for her kill-joy behaviour over Elvis she had insisted on joining us for our next record-session—with the result that I had soon replaced all the records in the hall cupboard. I could hardly go wild with the Dean while Primrose was supervising us like a schoolmistress. Aysgarth, I suspected, understood my feelings perfectly but said nothing for fear of upsetting his daughter. She really was the most colossal bore.

On that final morning at the lodge I waited until Eddie had trekked off to retrieve *The Times* and then headed for the drawing-room where Aysgarth was contemplating the sea. "Do you want to be alone, Mr. Dean?" I said tactfully. "Or can I sit with you and think beautiful thoughts?"

"What a good example you'd set me—yes, sit down at once! I was just plotting how I could murder Canon Fitzgerald and frame the Bishop for the crime."

"Are they driving you round the bend?"

"It's a wonder that I haven't grabbed a crozier from the Sacristy and committed mayhem long since! What with the Cathedral staff and the Chapter and the Greater Chapter all brawling away—"

The Chapter consisted of the three residentiary Canons, Fitzgerald, Dalton and Eddie, who all lived in the Close and helped the Dean run the Cathedral. The Greater Chapter consisted of the Prebendaries, or Honorary Canons, who were sprinkled through the diocese, many, though not all, with their own parishes to run. The title of prebendary was bestowed on the clergymen who had given exceptional service to the diocese.

"—and then that Archdeacon's always buzzing around like a wasp—"

The Archdeacon was the Bishop's henchman. The diocese was divided into two archdeaconries, and the Archdeacon of Starbridge, though not directly concerned with the running of the Cathedral, kept an eye on it from the diocesan office on Eternity Street.

"—and all the time the Bishop's breathing fire about the coach-park—"

"What coach-park?"

"I want to allocate that broad strip on the edge of Palace Lane to coaches. We really must cater for all these modern pilgrims, but of course Charles takes the snobbish line and says all vulgar charabancs must be left beyond the walls of the Close."

"How un-Christian!"

"Yes, isn't it? One day, I swear, I'll lose my temper and remind him that Jesus didn't go to public school—and talking of education, I've succeeded in locking horns with the Archdeacon over the Theological College."

"How on earth did you get drawn into that?"

"The Principal is a prebendary of the Cathedral and he's been asking my advice about the College finances, but every time I try to teach the bursar how to add two and two, someone tips off the Archdeacon who immediately accuses me of interference—"

"I'd murder the whole lot of them, if I were you, Mr. Dean. Why confine yourself to Canon Fitzgerald?"

"Why indeed?" said Aysgarth laughing, and then exclaimed impulsively: "How far away all that bickering seems, how unimportant! This holiday's done me so much good. I only wish I could stay here longer."

"So do I. It's hard to believe that tomorrow—"

"—I'll be back fighting the Bishop over the coach-park. But whatever happens I mustn't give way to the temptation to have a row with Charles over *Honest to God*. That really would be the last straw."

"I'm getting so interested in *Honest to God*!" I said. "Could you possibly explain it to me sometime?"

He reached out and playfully patted my hand. So close did I come to swooning as the result of this wholly asexual gesture of affection that I only dimly heard him say: "Eddie could probably explain the theological background better than I can. The three theologians Robinson extols are all German."

I was still trying to utter the words: "Forget Eddie!" when Primrose staggered downstairs to spoil our fun. I might have known she would stuff herself with aspirin and stage a spectacular recovery.

It occurred to me for the first time that it was going to be very difficult to see Aysgarth on his own after our return to Starbridge. A possessive daughter, a clinging wife, a time-consuming Cathedral, a waspish Archdeacon, a truculent Bishop and hordes of modern pilgrims were hardly going to leave much time for delicious little meetings *à deux*.

A faint shadow began to fall across my euphoria.

WHEN we arrived at Heathrow airport on the following afternoon we found Dido lying in wait for us. Aysgarth was pounced on, pawed and peppered with tearful kisses—"Disgusting!" muttered Primrose. "What a way to behave in public!"—and I had to try not to look as if I had unexpectedly encountered a full complement of the Spanish Inquisition. Even though I had no doubt that he had engineered their separate holidays in order to preserve his sanity, I hardly welcomed the reminder that he was legally yoked to a doting gorgon.

After Dido had flicked away her tears with a flap of her lace handkerchief, she found time to say brightly: "How pale you are, Primrose! Such a pity there's no sun in the Hebrides," and to me she added: "I'm so glad you didn't die of boredom, but my dear, you look extremely liverish— you should take a strong dose of salts as soon as you get home."

A chauffeur-driven limousine was waiting outside the terminal; Dido liked to make extravagant gestures with her private income. After Aysgarth had been whisked away, Eddie, Primrose and I rattled off in a bone-shaking bus to the long-term car-park. Depression crawled across my consciousness like a tarantula on the march. As I drove out of London all I could think was: that bloody Dido.

However in Starbridge I recovered my equilibrium, and by the time Primrose and I had dined off baked beans and Spam followed by tinned Ambrosia rice pudding, I had realised that since there was no hope of my passion being reciprocated it hardly mattered that Aysgarth had a wife. My destiny was to burn with unrequited love, and with a sigh of ecstasy I once more consigned myself to the flames.

We had returned on a Thursday, just over a week after our departure. The next morning I waited till Primrose had gone to work and then I strolled up Canonry Drive to Choristers' Green. The Chantry was wedged between a handsome Georgian house, formerly the Choir School but now a museum, and a dainty, early Victorian cottage; one of the best features of the Close was that its houses were all different and yet in their diversity they achieved a satisfying harmony. Studying the Chantry with care I noted that the curtains were still drawn across one of the bedroom windows. I moved on.

Five minutes later in Mitre Street I visited Boots, where I bought a few essential items such as toothpaste, and consulted a very well-informed girl at the cosmetics counter about eye make-up. Various experiments followed as I confirmed my suspicion that mere mascara was not enough to produce the glamour to which I now aspired, but eventually I emerged transformed and retired to a tea-shop called the Copper Kettle where I drank coffee and read the *Daily Mail*. More time passed. Then I padded back to the Close and once more eyed the Chantry. The bedroom curtains were now drawn back. For another minute I prowled around Choristers' Green in an agony of indecision, but at last I marched up to the Chantry and rang the bell.

"Is Miss Markhampton at home?" I said when the housekeeper opened the door. "I'm Miss Flaxton."

"Flaxton?" cried a disembodied voice in the distance.

"Hi, Marina—it's Venetia! Any chance of saying 'Welcome to Starbridge' or are you in the bath?"

"No, in shock! My God, Vinnie, what on earth are you doing in this gorgeous dump?" said Marina Markhampton, appearing at the top of the stairs in a white silk dressing-gown which looked as if it had been personally hand-stitched by Dior, and glided down to meet me as if I were one of her oldest friends.

VI

" 'It's love that makes the world go round.' That's what all
Christians have always said."

JOHN A. T. ROBINSON,
writing about Honest to God *in the*
Sunday Mirror, *7 April 1963*

I

SHE was shorter than I was, about five feet four, and had thick, smooth, natural blonde hair which cascaded to her shoulders as gracefully as if it had been arranged a minute earlier by some genius of a hairdresser. Beneath their heavy lids her eyes were a lazy, limpid blue. The cats-about-town used to say that her bone structure was reminiscent of a prize sheep, but in fact like many beautiful women her face was striking in its originality. She wore no make-up but looked radiant. If I had been feeling less nervous I might well have succumbed to the jealousy exhibited by all the cats-about-town.

"Let's have some coffee," she said after we had chatted about nothing for a couple of minutes. "Take a pew while I snap my fingers at the slave."

Still marvelling at my unexpectedly warm reception I sank gratefully onto the drawing-room sofa.

"It really is heavenly to see a familiar face," said Marina, wandering back into the room with a packet of chocolate biscuits. "Everyone in the Close appears to be either nine or ninety or simply impossible. Where are all the amusing people of our age?"

"In London, I suppose." I accepted a biscuit. "Which reminds me, Marina—"

"You want to know why I'm here, making sure the housekeeper doesn't sidle off to Blackpool amidst a salvo of bursting pipes. Well, it just so happened that I was being absolutely *persecuted* in London by two men at once, and the last straw came when my boss tried to play the *Moonlight Sonata* all over my left thigh."

"How hackneyed."

"Exactly what I thought. I was doing some temporary work—nothing strenuous, just answering the phone and pouring the champagne in one of those little art galleries in St. James's—and after the sonata I thought: hell, I've simply got to claw my way out of this *seething* sexual cesspit, I'll house-sit for Granny, gaze at the Cathedral and think pure thoughts about eternal life—but I've now reached the stage where quite frankly eternal life is wearing a bit thin, so I've decided to give an Orgy to resurrect this dump from the dead."

"Give a what?"

"An Orgy—with a capital O. Wouldn't it be madly way-out to dance semi-nude on the Cathedral lawn in the moonlight? Even better than last year during a May ball up at Cambridge when I wound up punting semi-nude on the Cam . . . But how frightful, I'm talking all about my boring old self—how are *you?*"

"Also in flight from the cesspits of London. I've just been on holiday in the Hebrides."

"The Hebrides?" said Marina intrigued as the housekeeper arrived with coffee. "How original! What inspired you to go there?"

"The Dean invited me. He'd been lent the Starmouths' hunting-lodge, and—"

"Oh yes, you're in cahoots with the Aysgarths, aren't you? I went out with James Aysgarth a couple of times in London when I was a deb—he's rather a dear but not terribly bright and I do like something with a high IQ. Norman Aysgarth's super but he's guarded night and day by Cynthia the Siren—who's actually quite fun when there are no men around—"

"I suppose the Aysgarth closest to you in age is Sandy. His IQ's high enough—"

"Yes, but he's got no sex-appeal. However the best Aysgarth, the crème-de-la-crème of the Aysgarths, the Aysgarth I'm simply passionate about is—"

"Christian," I said. "Welcome to the club. How do you get on with his wife?"

"Oh, I'm passionate about Katie too! In fact I was just deciding that they've simply got to be the guests of honour at my Orgy. And I shall invite Perry Palmer and Robert Welbeck and Katie's brother Simon— oh, and super old Norman too, I must have Norman because he's so like Christian, and that means Cynthia the Siren will have to come, but that's okay, I don't mind Cynthia. I shan't invite Sandy, though, because he's dull, and I shan't invite James because I'm not having anyone from the Guards. I've just about had it with all those Guardsmen trying to rape me in corners whenever they're not trying to rape each other."

"One must draw the line somewhere."

"Exactly. And I'm not inviting any floozies either—except Cynthia, and Cynthia'll be fine so long as no one tries to rape Norman—and no one will because my friends Holly and Emma-Louise are both so stylish, so absolutely trustworthy, and I do think it's important, don't you, to have girlfriends you can *trust*. I don't know what I'd do without Holly and Emma-Louise to soothe me whenever I've been pounced on by some wild-eyed Romeo—which reminds me, I'm going to invite Michael Ashworth, the Bishop's son. He's a real pouncer-de-luxe, but he deserves an invitation because of his first-class sex-appeal."

"How about Charley?"

"That ghastly prig? No fear!"

"By the way, is it true that Michael got kicked out of medical school for pouncing?"

"My dear, no nurse escaped."

"You mean he actually—"

"—broke every bed in sight. One of Emma-Louise's dearest friends is a nurse, and she told Emma-Louise—"

A long session of gossip followed.

"You don't happen to know why Charley Ashworth ran away from home when he was eighteen, do you?" I was tempted to ask eventually, much impressed by Marina's wide-ranging knowledge of our acquaintances.

"He inherited three thousand theology books from Granny's pal, dear old Bishop Jardine, and the shock sent him temporarily round the bend."

"But seriously, Marina—"

"Oh, I expect it was just a fit of adolescent pique. I know heaps of people who ran away from home for a weekend just to underline the fact that they were no longer in rompers. I did it myself as a matter of fact—flew off to Rome to see a performance of *Aida* in the Baths of Caracalla, cadged a lift on Banger Marsden's private plane . . . Do you know Banger?"

"Not exactly—"

"He was on his way to Naples, but after he'd dropped me off in Rome I linked up with Holly's brother—queer as a coot, absolutely safe—and off we toddled to *Aida*."

"But what on earth did your parents think?"

"Oh, my father doesn't think at all—he gave all that up years ago. And my mother just said: *'Darling!'* in despair as usual and began to paint another picture. Parents needn't be difficult, you know. It's all a matter of being kind but firm."

"Every time I try to be firm with my father he roars like a lion!"

"How exhausting! No wonder you've left London, although I must say, I do think you'd find Rome more amusing than Starbridge. You're obviously rather soignée nowadays, the sort of person who's been around."

"Well, by the time one's twenty-six, I suppose one *has* seen more or less everything—"

"Oh, of course!" She gazed at me with respect. "Yes, I can see that I completely misjudged you in the past—I thought you were a churchy blue-stocking like Primrose Aysgarth, the sort of person who's hopelessly square, yet now you're obviously a real trendsetter—imagine going to the Hebrides instead of to the boring old Riviera! I suppose the Hebrides will be the next 'in' place."

"The beaches were, I have to admit, quite stunning—"

"I bet. I say, I *am* glad you've wafted into my life just at the very moment when I need the assistance of someone really cool and with-it! Will you help me organise my Orgy?"

"Love to. Thanks."

"Where are you hanging out?"

"At the Deanery, but as a matter of fact, Marina, I've just had a brainstorm: there isn't enough room in Primrose's pad to swing a cat, so"—I took a deep breath—"is it at all possible—and of course you must be quite honest and say no straight away if the idea appals you—"

"If I'm on my own a day longer in this place I'll go crazy. How soon can you move in?"

I wanted to shout: "Whoopee!" in triumph but instead I said carelessly, as befitted the coolest of trendsetters: "Today?" and produced what I hoped was a grateful but sophisticated smile.

2

"IN my opinion," said Marina some hours later, "the best parties are the ones attended by a carefully picked handful of people, most of whom are known to one another. Those debutante balls with a cast of thousands were too dreary for words, weren't they?"

"Absolutely the bottom." I had rejoined her at four o'clock that afternoon after making a quick trip to Flaxton Pauncefoot to deposit my laundry and pick up some clean clothes. We were now drinking Earl Grey tea and nibbling slices of that delicious walnut cake from Fuller's. In between nibbles Marina chewed the end of her pencil as she contemplated her notepad and meditated on her guest-list.

"I want to have between eight and twelve of my favourite people— my basic coterie—plus between four to six outsiders—the wild-cards, as it were, in the pack," she was saying, "but accommodation could be a problem. We can't have too many bodies stacked up here or the slave might have hysterics and phone Granny in Monte Carlo."

"I'm sure we could devise a passable sardine arrangement for the girls. Then the Aysgarth crowd can cram themselves into the Deanery, and if Michael Ashworth comes that opens up the beds at the South Canonry—"

"The Bishop might have apoplexy at the thought of condoning an orgy."

"Well, of course we promote this to the older generation as just supper for a few friends with music afterwards."

"Oh, I see you know all the right moves!" said Marina. "Okay, assuming we neutralise Anti-Sex Ashworth, I think we've solved the accommodation problem—"

"If we're exploiting the beds at the South Canonry I don't see how you can invite Michael and not that prig Charley."

"Easy. Michael's in London but Charley will be in Cambridge by the time we give the Orgy, and Cambridge is so far away, almost in *terra incognita,* isn't it practically in the North Sea? No, we can't possibly ask anyone to trek down here from Cambridge—although . . . I say, I tell you who I'd like to invite! I was introduced to him last year during that May ball when I wound up punting semi-nude on the Cam. He's reading *Divinity*—of all subjects!—and he's not good-looking, all glasses and bones and mousey hair, but there's something about him which is absolutely mesmerising—"

"Does he by any chance tell fortunes?"

"Does he tell fortunes! I'll say he does. 'The Church is in your future,' he says, holding my hand so hard I nearly pass out. 'I see you moving in the shadow of a great cathedral!' "

"You're making this up, Marina!"

"No, I swear it—as soon as Granny asked me to house-sit, I remembered Nicky Darrow's prophecy! Listen, we simply must get hold of him—do you know if the new term's started up at Cambridge? Maybe he's still at home with the Holy One."

"The *who?"*

"Nicky's father's a holy hermit who lives in a wood and eats nothing but communion wafers. He's about a hundred years old and very wise, like the Delphic Oracle, and people come from all over England to see him, but very few make it into the holy presence because he's guarded day and night by his disciples, a savage band of Anglo-Catholic monks who—"

"Marina, this couldn't come within a hundred light-years of being true!"

"My dear, it's *gospel*. Old Mr. Darrow—or is it 'Father' Darrow—or is it possibly even 'Saint' Darrow—"

"No, that's too much, I baulk at sainthood—"

"Well, saint or no saint he's in tune with the music of the spheres and has a hot-line to God. Honestly! No kidding!"

"Talking of God," I said, glancing at my watch and scrambling to my feet, "it's time I popped over to the Cathedral for Evensong."

"Heavens above, Vinnie, you're not religious, are you?"

"Oh no!" I said. "But I like to pay my respects to God every now and then as a safety measure. After all, since the non-existence of God can't be scientifically proved, it seems only sensible to allow for the fact that He could be around." And leaving her boggling at my canny behaviour, I glided across Choristers' Green towards the Cathedral.

3

AFTER feasting my eyes on Aysgarth for half an hour I sped out of the Cathedral before Eddie could waylay me and headed for Primrose's flat. When I had removed my possessions earlier I had left a note of explanation, but nevertheless I thought I should call to smooth any feathers which might have been ruffled by my defection. On my arrival I found that Primrose had just returned from the diocesan office and was relaxing with the current edition of *The Church Gazette*.

". . . so don't take offence, Prim, because I really do think I'd be an ogre of exploitation if I cluttered up your space a day longer—I simply must give you back your privacy . . ."

Touched by such high-minded consideration, Primrose said how understanding I was and we parted good friends. My next task was to work out how I could avoid inviting her to the Orgy. The last person I wanted to see there was Primrose, looking down her nose as I launched myself into my new life as a member of Marina Markhampton's "basic coterie."

"Marina," I said as soon as I returned to the Chantry, "what the hell am I going to do about Primrose? I don't want to invite her to the Orgy but I don't see how I can ditch her. We've been friends too long."

"Has she a boyfriend whom we could coax to whisk her off to a champagne supper on the night in question?"

"Maurice Tait couldn't whisk off anything."

"Trust Primrose to fancy a non-whisker! But don't worry, we'll invite them both and make sure they're so appalled that they leave early. A basic coterie bash soon separates the wheat from the chaff—which reminds me, talking of the wheat, we must pick the rest of the wild-cards. I've chosen Nicky Darrow. Who do you fancy?"

I tried to look as if I were considering vast numbers of eligible males. "All the really interesting people are abroad," I mused mendaciously. "I'll leave the selecting to you."

"Okay, I'll give Dinkie Kauffman a whirl—she's an American girl who worked with me at the art gallery. Then I'll ask Christian to bring an interesting man—oh, and why don't we ask Michael Ashworth to produce a trendy male from the BBC?"

"But that means three out of the four wild-cards will be men!"

"So what? All the more fun for us girls!"

"Ah yes," I said, feeling that my mask of sophistication had slipped. "Silly of me."

"So much for the guests," said Marina, scribbling busily on her note-pad. "Now perhaps we should consider the really vital matter of drink. What shall we order?"

"Champagne, naturally," I said. "How about Veuve Clicquot '55?"

My mask of sophistication was instantly restored. "How marvellous!" said Marina admiringly. "You're a wine expert!" And I allowed myself a deprecating smile as I modestly examined my fingernails.

We were just trying to calculate the number of bottles which would be required when the telephone rang.

Marina picked up the receiver. "The Orgy Planning Office—may I help you?" she droned in the manner of a secretarial zombie, and then a second later her entire demeanor changed. "Christian!" she exclaimed. "So you got my message . . ." And as she talked on, telling him about her plans, it suddenly dawned on me not only that she was in love with him but that the unsupervised stay in a beautiful house, the placing of herself against the ravishing backdrop of the Cathedral, the exact nature of the social event which would inevitably lure him from Oxford—all had been planned long before she had left London. It seemed I had met yet another slave to a one-sided grand passion.

No wonder we had discovered we were soul-mates.

4

CHRISTIAN AYSGARTH was at that time nearly thirty-six and had been married for six years to the grand-daughter of a former Earl of Star-mouth, the ninth earl who had so interested himself in the affairs of the Church earlier in the century and whose wife—his second wife, Katie's grandmother—had prided herself on her collection of distinguished cleri-cal acquaintances; like Marina's grandmother she had been one of swash-buckling Bishop Jardine's "Lovely Ladies," happily married aristocratic women who could offer him a devoted platonic friendship in those fabled days before the war when bishops had apparently had no trouble combining a worldly glamour with the indestructible virtue required by their office.

Aysgarth—my Mr. Dean—had been Jardine's protégé. Inevitably he had gravitated into Lady Starmouth's benevolent orbit, but although Christian could remember being introduced to her during his adolescence, he had not met her grand-daughter Katherine until he was twenty-six, down from Oxford with his double-first and poised to be a "deb's delight," one of those eligible young males who were invited to adorn the debutante balls. Christian had been educated at Winchester and Balliol; he appeared every inch the gentleman, but nevertheless Lady Starmouth could probably never quite forget that his grandfather had been a draper. Katie, of course, cared only that Christian was tall, dark, handsome, brilliant and charming, an extraordinary specimen of masculine perfection, but like the rest of us who yearned for Christian she was obliged to yearn in vain—until he decided that the right wife could be a useful acquisition.

Katie was without doubt the right wife, perfectly equipped to play the heroine in the great romance which his life now demanded. Intelligent but not intellectual, beautiful, rich, well connected and well-bred, she was acquired in 1957. By that time the Starmouths had forgotten the grandfather who had been a draper. Christian had won such distinction up at Oxford that his pedigree had ceased to be important, and besides, his father had just been appointed Dean of Starbridge. The Aysgarths, as my father remarked at the time, had finally arrived.

My description of Christian may seem a trifle barbed but I have no wish to present him as a cardboard cut-out character, all surface and no depth, like the hero of a bad romantic novel. Let me now add that although he often seemed too perfect to be true, he was capable of exercising an unexpectedly cruel wit; he could also be arrogant and selfish. Katie adored him even when he was being monstrous, and I always thought this was a mistake. It might have been better if she had occasionally screamed abuse at him and slapped his face; it could have made the marriage more intriguing. However it was generally agreed that the marriage was a success, and although Christian never seemed much interested in the two little girls it had produced this may have been because he was not a demonstrative man and seemed to be repelled by any display of emotion. (On reflection perhaps Katie was right not to scream abuse at him and slap his face.)

Sometimes I wondered if he ever felt nervous because there was so little left for him to achieve. After leaving Winchester, where he had been a scholar, he had completed two suitably heroic years of National Service before going up to Oxford to read Greats. Having won his brilliant first he had then read Theology with equal success, but had afterwards refused to proceed to a theological college to train as a clergyman. No reason was ever given. "He just told Father he wasn't called to serve God in the Church," Primrose had told me at the time.

"But didn't your father want to know why?"

"Oh, he could never have asked. Father finds it difficult to talk to his sons—and the boys find it equally difficult to talk to him." Primrose had then paused as if searching for the appropriate words before adding obscurely: "I'm all right; Father has different standards for girls. I don't have to win scholarships or 'get on' in a first-class career because Father thinks I'm perfect just as I am. But it's much harder for the boys to be perfect. They live in terror of disappointing him."

"But why does he expect you all to be perfect?" I had said baffled. My father never expected his children to be anything but trouble.

"He sees us all as prizes—ultimate prizes—prizes awarded him by God—and of course those sorts of prizes could never be other than perfect."

"But nobody's perfect, Primrose!"

"No, but Father's such an idealist and he loves us all so much, so naturally we don't want to let him down. That's why the boys always do their best to hide their problems from him; they couldn't bear him to be upset."

"But that means they must all lead a double-life—the perfect life on the surface and the imperfect life underneath!"

"No, the boys all lead a single life; they simply bowdlerise their reports of it to Father. If anyone leads a double-life it's Father himself, living as the dynamic dean and the harassed husband. Probably the only way he can survive that awful woman is to divide himself into two in order to escape from her regularly."

I was to recall this conversation more than once in 1963, but I first recalled it on that April evening at the Chantry when I realised Marina was in love with Christian; I started to wonder if he too, like his father, was living a divided life. There was no denying his dynamic career at Oxford. Following up the medieval interests which he had acquired during his theological studies he was now coasting along towards the inevitable chair in medieval studies or medieval philosophy—or whatever the crucial professorship was in his rarefied field of endeavour. He had written two acclaimed books, both about the effect of Aristotle's influence on the medieval Church, and he was now working on a study of Averroës, the Arab philosopher. But how far did this distinguished career satisfy him? And how content was he with his apparently idyllic marriage? I had no idea, but the thought of Marina, hoving to on the horizon like some latter-day Helen of Troy, was vaguely worrying.

I have described Christian at length not merely because he was to be the star guest at the Orgy, but because it would have been obvious to someone more mature than I was then that the Aysgarth family was far more convoluted than was apparent during the jolly Sunday lunches which I occasionally attended at the Deanery. However, contrary to the sophisticated image I was so busily promoting to Marina, my experience of the world was still very limited.

The date of the Orgy depended on the state of Christian's engagement diary, but a blank space was uncovered beside Saturday, the eighteenth of May, and Christian said it would be a relief to escape briefly from Oxford while the undergraduates, tortured by examinations, were threatening to commit suicide en masse. Marina then spent much time worrying that her chosen guests might have other engagements, but in the end the Coterie proved quite unable to resist the magic combination of the Cathedral Close, Marina Markhampton and countless cases of Veuve Clicquot. In London imaginative excuses were produced to soothe various jilted hostesses. Only Nick Darrow in Cambridge said he was too busy with exams to accept the invitation, but Marina found out by chance from Michael Ashworth that Nick was planning to sneak back to the Starbridge diocese that weekend to see his father; apparently St. Darrow was about to celebrate his eighty-third birthday. Immediately Marina badgered Nick with a series of winning little notes until he wrote back and said he might be able to look in on the party for a short time after all.

"Imagine playing hard to get when one's only twenty," said Marina acidly. "He'll be a terror when he grows up."

"Maybe he genuinely doesn't want to come but doesn't have the experience to shake you off gracefully."

"But *everyone* wants to come to this party!" protested Marina outraged. "Everyone always wants to come to *all* my parties!"

"Maybe he's too young to know that."

I was somewhat perturbed by the guests' diverse ages, but Marina insisted that mixing age-groups created no problems for the Coterie. "Christian always likes to be with younger people," she said. "He missed so much fun when he was young because he had to study so hard, and now he says he'll be making up for lost time until he's at least forty. Anyway, apart from little Nicky, who's clearly very juvenile, the youngest man present will be Michael Ashworth and since he always carries on like a roué of thirty instead of an innocent of twenty-three, he'll fit in perfectly. The ages of the unmarried girls don't count, of course, so long as everyone's under twenty-eight. I've noticed that once unmarried girls get to that fatal age they become so nervous of winding up on the spinsters' scrap-heap that they set every man's teeth on edge."

I absorbed this information in silence as I realised that only two years separated me from the scrap-heap, but soon I was able to blot out this nightmare by ordering champagne by the case and arranging for the best firm of caterers in Starbridge to provide a sumptuous buffet supper. I did occasionally spare a thought for that sordid subject, money, but Marina was sublimely confident that her grandmother would foot the bills.

"Granny told me to have a lovely time while I was here," she said, "so I may as well take her at her word."

"Marina, I rather doubt that when Lady Markhampton made arrangements for you to buy food and drink on tick, she visualised you ordering umpteen cases of champagne."

"Well, if she gets cross Daddy can toss her a couple of hundred guineas next Christmas."

I decided to stop worrying about Lady Markhampton's potential cardiac arrest and start worrying about what on earth I was going to wear.

In those days one still dressed formally for parties—unless one was a student at some redbrick university or a freak at art school—so although Marina mused on the possibility of wearing nothing but a leopardskin bikini she was quick enough to whip a masterpiece of haute couture out of her wardrobe when the discussion became serious. As usual I looked frightful in all my evening dresses. Starbridge, typically provincial, was only good for tweeds and twin-sets. Making a quick dash to London I avoided Knightsbridge, where the snooty shop assistants made me feel like one of the Ugly Sisters in *Cinderella*, and waded through that Lethe of plebeian consumerism, Oxford Street. Since no one I knew ever went there except to buy underwear at Marks and Spencer's, I felt I could sink into a liberating anonymity and forget my inferiority complex.

I was just wandering past Richards—or was it C&A?—and thinking how grim life must be for the "lower orders," obliged through lack of money to buy their clothes in cheap shops, when I saw a greenish-golden slinky creation in the window and knew immediately that I was being offered the opportunity to convert myself into a sex-symbol. I sped across the threshold. The little assistant was charming and deferential. (Why *do* the upper classes confine themselves to ghastly, expensive shops? Why don't we *all* invade Richards and C&A?) The dress, which would have cost some astronomical sum in Bond Street, was mine at the drop of a ten-pound note. Then having saved myself so much money I decided I should celebrate my success by having a little flutter at Fortnum's. They do roast beef so well in the main restaurant, and a woman can lunch there on her own without being regarded as a freak.

At Waterloo Station I finally bought a copy of *Honest to God* but on the train I fell asleep before I had even reached page two. A half-bottle of Nuits St. Georges is probably not the ideal prelude to any serious study of theology.

When I awoke an hour later the guest-list for the Orgy was revolving in my mind, just as it so often did in those days in response to my eager anticipation. At the top of the list stood Christian and Katie, who would be leaving their two little girls behind with the *au pair* in order to make the lightning trip to Starbridge. Then came our second married couple, Christian's brother Norman, the barrister who lectured in law at London University, and man-eating Cynthia who had kept Norman from an academic appointment in Oxford by insisting that she was unable to live in the provinces. Their one child was also to be left at home, but unfortunately this always had to happen as there was something wrong with him; he was looked after by a full-time nurse. Whenever I saw Cynthia preening herself before the mirror in an ecstasy of vanity, I always reminded myself that she had a tragedy at the centre of her life and that allowances had to be made for her.

Chief among the unmarried guests was Peregrine Palmer, who had been at Winchester with Christian and who was reputed to have some secret job in the Foreign Office. (The word "spy" was never mentioned but everyone knew he spoke Russian.) Following Perry on the list was Katie's brother Simon, a handsome slab who was supposed to be "something in the City"—a euphemism which described the paid idleness of various upper-class males who were too brainless to do more than play polo—and after Simon came Robert Welbeck, who had been up at Oxford with Marina's brother Douglas some years ago and who was now employed by a merchant bank. The ranks of the bachelors were then boosted by Michael Ashworth, the Bishop's younger son, now learning to be a television producer after his hedonistic romps at medical school.

Next came the two girls who were due to join forces with Marina and me to keep the bachelors amused: Emma-Louise Hanson had become friends with Marina during their debutante days, and Holly Carr had been at school with Marina at Downe House. I don't think either girl did much. Holly was a *cordon bleu* cook and occasionally whipped up a chic boardroom lunch. Emma-Louise was supposed to be a secretary but was usually unemployed in order to attend to her social life.

These girls completed the list of the Coterie members. There followed the wild-cards, chosen to add spice to the party. Dinkie Kauffman, Marina's American friend from the art gallery, sounded promising; she was reputed to look like Jane Russell and talk like Philip Marlowe. Nick Darrow was too young to be seriously amusing but could nonetheless be relied upon to produce stimulating vibes. Don Latham, Michael's friend from the BBC, was an unknown quantity but since Michael had enthusiastically described him as "outta sight" one could hope for something original to materialise. Whom Christian intended to bring we had no idea, since he refused to tell us, but I was prepared to share Marina's confidence that this Mr. X would be fascinating.

At the bottom of the guest-list lurked Primrose and that drip Tait, but Marina and I had long since hatched a foolproof scheme for their speedy disposal.

I sighed, excitement pushing aside the inertia that so often follows an afternoon snooze, and at that moment realised that *Honest to God* was still lying in my lap. On an impulse I opened the book at random and read: "The words of St. Augustine, 'Love God and do what you like,' were never safe. But they constitute the heart of Christian prayer—as they do of Christian conduct."

So Bishop Robinson was dusting off those highly ambiguous words of St. Augustine's! No wonder Bishop Ashworth was having apoplexy at the South Canonry. Love God and do what you like. That seemed to imply . . . although of course St. Augustine hadn't meant . . . or had he? No, of course not. But what a potentially stupendous slogan for the sizzling 1960s!

Racing back to the Cathedral for Evensong I prepared to love God and dote on the Dean.

5

BY this time I had discovered that if one is violently in love the desire to talk constantly about the object of one's passion is very strong. I considered I was successfully maintaining a languid facade, but although I suppressed the urge to betray myself by addled chatter, Marina soon noticed my regular attendance at the Cathedral and finally I could no longer write off this behaviour as a metaphysical safety measure. In the belief that a half-truth is often more convincing than an outright lie I responded to her growing suspicion that I was a religious fanatic by confessing: "Well, the truth is I'm so fond of the Dean that I simply can't bear to disappoint him by not showing up regularly for services—he's been so kind to me ever since I was nine years old."

Marina was quite satisfied by this sentimental explanation but afterwards, with superhuman self-restraint, I confined myself to attending

Evensong no more than three times a week and entering the Cathedral on Sunday only for Matins. By loitering near the vestry after the service I often managed to bump into Aysgarth, but such golden moments were not guaranteed and indeed it would have looked odd if I had been perpetually encountering him. Soon I began to feel somewhat starved of his presence, but starvation, as anyone on a strict diet knows, can initially induce a powerful sense of well-being.

I was certainly overflowing with well-being when I returned to the Chantry after my quick trip to London and showed an admiring Marina my new dress. I was just rummaging in my bag for the receipt—of course Marina had refused to believe the dress had cost only ten pounds—when *Honest to God* fell out. At once Marina spotted the naked man on the cover and shrieked: "Super—pornography!"

"Down, Fido, down! It's a best-seller, available over the counter!"

"But what's it about?"

"God. He's the new 'in' thing. Everyone's mad about Him."

"Help! Maybe I should read a page or two. I'm actually quite keen on God, deep down, but the Church is so dreadfully square, isn't it?"

"No more!" I cried, brandishing *Honest to God* in triumph. "Bishop Robinson's making it trendy! He says that the heart of Christian conduct is loving God and then doing what you like!"

"No! You mean—"

"Of course. So long as you love God, everything's okay," I said, wondering idly if St. Augustine was turning far away in his unknown grave, and having poured myself into my new dress I began to practise various sultry poses in front of the looking-glass.

6

I REMEMBER the Orgy, that innocent affair; if it had been a real orgy we would have called it a party—or possibly, later in the sixties, a happening. How long ago it all seems now as I look back from the 1980s! It's hard to remember the exact quality of that lost era, but in 1963 if one was under thirty one lived in a world of untarnished dreams and ideals, unpolluted gaiety and adventure. Except for nicotine and alcohol drugs were seldom encountered—and who needed pot when one could get high on vintage Veuve Clicquot? Drugs were for riff-raff in those days, and we were the opposite of riff-raff; we were the *jeunesse dorée,* gathered by Marina Markhampton to celebrate life with style in ravishing surroundings, not to "turn on and drop out" in some sordid urban squat. Looking back at that magical evening I can see us all with such painful clarity, sophisticated yet innocent, fast but not corrupt—and above all so merci-fully blind to that terrible time ahead when the enchanting *communitas,* the group-spirit, of the early sixties fell apart and terminated in chaos.

"To the future!" cried Christian Aysgarth, raising his first glass of champagne, and at once my heart missed a beat because he was so attractive, his shining career seemingly stretching ahead of him into the distance, and when he spoke, his wife Katie gazed up at him as soulfully as if they were newly-weds while Marina, completing the triangle which I was later to find so mysterious, flung her arms around his neck and exclaimed what heaven it was to see him again. At that point Perry Palmer, Christian's old schoolfriend, said dryly: "You really should be a Moslem, Christian, in order to accommodate all these doting women in a respectable style!" whereupon Marina retorted: "Don't be a bitch, Perry!" and Christian drawled: "I'd like to see my bank manager's face if I were to tell him I intended to keep four wives!" Then Katie com-mented with unflawed serenity: "Think of the fun I could have gossiping with the other three whenever you were away!" and when they began to debate harems I lost the thread of the conversation until suddenly Christian caught my eye across the room as I held court with Norman Aysgarth and Robert Welbeck; I heard him declare: "If I have a harem I'm going to have Vinnie in it!" and when he winked at me I was reminded of his father.

I turned over the LP of Floyd Cramer, who had played the piano on so many of the Presley records, and as the party gathered speed time became displaced, just as it so often does when vintage champagne flows freely, and the exact sequence of events is now muddled in my memory, but I can recall wandering past the sofa some time later—had the buffet disappeared? No, there was still plenty left—and I can remember chang-ing the record again—we were on Cliff Richard by that time, but no, it couldn't have been Cliff because Marina didn't like him, so perhaps it was Adam Faith—or could it conceivably have been Eden Kane?—anyway, the record-player was drooling in the corner, but not too noisily, we didn't want to drown the conversation—and as I said, I was wander-ing past the sofa where Michael Ashworth was trying to grope two girls at once—I can't think who they were now, but I'm sure one was the American girl Dinkie Kauffman, who had a cleavage reminiscent of the Grand Canyon, while the other girl might have been Emma-Louise—and as I said, I was wandering past the sofa when I bumped into Katie's brother Simon, the handsome slab, who said: "Whoa there!" as if I were a horse—he always talked to women as if they were horses—and I had only just managed to stagger out of his way when I came face to face with Christian's friend Perry Palmer, who looked so ordinary, medium height, medium build, medium brown hair, medium plain face, but was supposed to be something rather extraordinary in the Foreign Office— although nobody knew for sure—and Perry lived in London at Albany, which was very grand and I couldn't help wondering how he'd wangled a flat there—a set, I mean, they call them sets in Albany—but perhaps the Foreign Office had some special pull.

Anyway, Perry said to me: "You seem to be the only intelligent girl here—you're the only one who's not swooning over Christian," and I said to him as I refilled our glasses: "Don't worry, darling—I'm not in love with him!"—which was a most peculiar thing to say, but fortunately Perry laughed and answered: "Didn't I say you were intelligent?" and it occurred to me that he was really rather entertaining and perhaps not a homosexual after all—although after the Burgess and Maclean scandal one could never be quite sure about anyone in that line—and certainly no one knew for certain that Perry was a homosexual, just as no one knew for certain he was a spy—in fact Marina said he was a eunuch, although when I asked her if she'd inspected his genitals she had to confess she hadn't—which just goes to show that no one ever tells the truth about sex, not really, it's all wishful thinking and fantasy tricked out with little flashes of romantic illusion.

"No one tells the truth about sex," I said to Perry in the kind of voice one uses to proclaim a profound truth after a couple of tankards of Veuve Clicquot—and Buddy Holly was playing on the gramophone which was strange because I could have sworn I put on Del Shannon—but Perry had been collared by Don Latham, the pal Michael Ashworth had brought down from the trendy division of dear old Auntie BBC, and I found myself facing Christian's wild-card, the mysterious Mr. X. And now I must go back to the beginning of the party when Floyd Cramer was playing the piano, because I have to record that when Christian walked in with Mr. X I couldn't believe it, I just *couldn't believe it,* because Mr. X turned out to be Eddie Hoffenberg—Eddie of all people!—and as soon as I could get Christian to myself—no mean feat—I hissed: "Chrissie, how dare you bring that Teutonic masochist!" Christian always hated being called anything but Christian, so he knew how cross I was, but to my fury he just laughed and said: "Eddie's one of the most interesting men I know—and I'm perpetually in his debt because he keeps Father happy by chatting about the Church. That's more than I can ever be bothered to do." And then he was snapped up by Marina before I could reply. I wanted to snap him back, but at that moment—it was still the Floyd Cramer era of the party—Primrose arrived with that drip Tait so Marina and I had to put our anti-Prim programme into action.

I shovelled some champagne down Primrose as quickly as possible while Marina replaced Floyd Cramer with Elvis Presley. Primrose turned pink, and when she was no more than halfway through her first glass—Elvis was panting "I Got Stung"—she said to me: "It's such a nuisance about this prior engagement but I'm afraid we simply have to go, don't we, Maurice?" Then Tait, who was goggling at Dinkie's cleavage, said obediently: "Yes, I suppose we do," but I thought nonetheless that he looked wistful as he was led firmly away by Miss P. Aysgarth, Girl Guide leader, and as I detected in him an embryonic inclination to lust after an exposed bosom I realised he was not quite the damp squib I had always thought he was.

"You look sensational, Venetia!" said Eddie, cornering me as soon as Primrose had departed with Tait in tow, and I was aware of Marina swapping Elvis for Jim Reeves now that our mission had been accomplished.

"You don't look so bad yourself, Canon," I said kindly, casting a vague glance at his well-cut suit and daringly striped shirt, and then I managed to escape from him by circulating with a plate of hors d'oeuvres. However instead of moping against a wall and wondering why he had come, Eddie circulated too, chatting away brightly to Norman's wife, man-eating Cynthia, who enjoyed talking to anything in trousers, even if it did look like Eddie, and then he had a long session with Marina's schoolfriend Holly Carr—Holly was nice, I liked her better than Dinkie or Emma-Louise—and finally as Christian, the beau of the ball, beckoned Eddie to his side I realised dimly that Eddie was being a social success—which seemed so unlikely that I had to have another glass of champagne to recover from the shock.

Then after I had declared to Perry Palmer that no one ever told the truth about sex—and now I'm jumping forward again and Buddy Holly was singing "Peggy Sue"—or was it "That'll Be the Day"?—I found myself confronting Eddie again and he was saying urgently: "I *must* talk to you," which seemed sinister, so I said to play for time: "You're in a peculiar state, Eddie—what's the matter?" and he was just beginning to tell me when Michael Ashworth, who had finished his double-grope on the sofa, slid his arm around my waist and purred: "Hullo, Gorgeous—how's life among the coronets?" That Michael was smooth enough to play host to a brigade of skates.

"Much the same as life among the mitres, I expect," I retorted, but Michael begged: *"Please!* Can't we leave the Church out of this?"—which made me realise what a problem it must be if one's father's known as Anti-Sex Ashworth and one's brother's famous as the biggest prig in town.

"But I'm mad about the Church!" I protested to Michael. "Wildly, passionately mad about it!" And at that moment, as if on cue, the Church entered the room in the form of a Divinity undergraduate—Marina's personal wild-card, hours late, floated into the party on a magic carpet of psychic vibrations and stared appalled at the riotous scene that confronted him.

"*Nicky!*" screamed Marina, halting in the act of dishing out chocolate mousse from the buffet. "You angel—you've arrived!"

"Who's this?" I heard Dinkie say intrigued.

I said: "It's my Talisman," but for some reason no one, not even Dinkie, took any notice of me. Then I realised this was because I had spoken the words in a whisper. Possibly it might be time to think about black coffee, but first of all I had to have a little more champagne to neutralise the shock brought on by the appearance of my very own Halley's Comet.

"Have a drink, Nick!" I cried, waving a bottle in his direction.

"Thanks," he said. "Just half a glass. I can't stay long. Sorry I'm late."

"I suppose you were treading your mystical paths so hard that you didn't notice the time!" said Marina, radiating indulgent charm.

"No, to be honest I just forgot about the party altogether." He accepted the full glass I offered him and looked hopefully at a dish of sausage-rolls. "Can I have one of those, please?"

"You *forgot?*" echoed Marina, hardly knowing whether to be amazed or outraged.

"Isn't he original?" I said, trying to galvanise her into displaying a sense of humour. "I bet no one's ever forgotten one of your parties before!"

There was much laughter and Marina sensibly decided to pass off the incredible faux-pas as a joke. "Ladies and gentlemen!" she declared to her guests. "This is the Coterie's soothsayer-in-residence—Nicholas Darrow!"

Nick gave her a most unfriendly look and devoured his sausage-roll in an agony of embarrassment.

"Brother of Martin Darrow the actor!" trilled Marina.

"Really?" exclaimed Holly.

"Gee whiz!" drawled Dinkie.

"Way-out!" breathed Emma-Louise.

"Idiot!" I muttered to Marina. "For God's sake put on another record and give the poor child a chance to merge with the crowd." I turned back to my Talisman. I felt I wanted to protect him. "Come over here, Nick," I said briskly, "and take no notice of all those asinine females. Do you know any of the Aysgarths? This is Christian—and his wife, Katie—" To my relief Elvis began to warble "It's Now or Never" and the Orgy picked up speed again as everyone finished boggling at the Infant Phenomenon.

The Aysgarths were kind to him but he was very shy and clearly out of his social depth. I wondered if he was embarrassed because he was casually dressed—I realised then that even the Oxbridge undergraduates had begun to display sartorial informality at parties—but after a while I came to the conclusion that he was oblivious of his blue shirt and jeans. It seemed far more likely that he hated parties and attended them only because someone had told him he ought to be more sociable. I was just wondering how I could alleviate his misery when he was kidnapped by Michael Ashworth, who knew him well, and borne off to amuse Dinkie and Emma-Louise.

I said to Christian: "We've got to save little Nicky from being mauled to pieces by those voracious floozies and then reassembled by Marina to perform parlour-tricks. Do something brilliant—instantly."

At once Christian rose to the challenge.

7

HE set down his glass. He swept to the record-player. He plucked the needle from the groove. Then adapting the famous Shakespearean technique for grabbing the attention of a crowd he declaimed: "Friends! Revellers! Companions! Lend me your ears!" And as soon as the raucous conversation ceased he declared: "It's time to propose a toast. Norman—draw back the curtains! And Perry—turn off the lights!"

The curtains skimmed on their rails, the switches clicked—and there beyond the window towered the Cathedral, floodlit and fantastic, a miracle of light erupting from the darkness, a stone vision that stunned the eye. I was not unfamiliar with this extraordinary sight, but at that moment the drama of the occasion was such that I felt as if I were seeing the nocturnal Cathedral for the first time. Like everyone else in the room I gasped, and suddenly the Orgy seemed trivial. I was reminded of Platonic philosophy. I had thought that reality had lain in the room around me, but that had been merely the shadow of the substance, and I now saw that ultimate reality, eternal and unchanging, lay elsewhere, beyond the pane.

"To Starbridge!" said Christian, raising his glass. "And to the Cathedral!"

There was a reverent silence as we all drank to the vision before our eyes, and then Dinkie—or was it Emma-Louise?—no, it was Dinkie, I remember the American accent—said: "Wouldn't it be just wonderful to go up on that roof and dance in the light of the moon?" and Katie's brother Simon shouted: "Whoopee!" in the manner of John Peel calling: "View halloo!" but Robert Welbeck said more rationally: "How could we ever get in?" Then Christian said to Norman: "Shall we nip down to the Deanery and filch the key from Father's study?" but Eddie interposed suddenly: "No need—I've got a key."

Dinkie's idle wish was at once brought out of the world of dreams and revealed as a practical possibility. Marina exclaimed gratefully to Eddie: "I'm *so* glad you came to my Orgy!" and Michael Ashworth (who I had just realised was very drunk) carolled: "A canon in the hand is worth a bishop in the bush!" but this clouded attempt at wit was greeted with howls from Dinkie and Emma-Louise, who pulled him down on the sofa and sat on him to keep him in order. Meanwhile Perry Palmer had switched on the lights again and Nick Darrow, who had been surreptitiously stuffing the last of the sausage-rolls into his pocket under cover of darkness, was saying politely to Marina: "I'm afraid I have to go now."

"But you can't!" wailed Marina. "I absolutely forbid it. Come up on the Cathedral roof and tell fortunes!"

"Sorry, I've got to get home to my father." He thanked her formally for the party and turned away as if there was no more to be said. At once Marina started to wail again but when Christian said lightly: "Where's my hostess with the mostest?" Nick was forgotten. I was just feeling grateful to Christian for preventing Marina from behaving like a spoilt child when I realised that Nick had paused by the door as if there was something he had forgotten. Then, very slowly, he turned to face me.

Around us everyone was shrieking and laughing again, but Nick and I seemed to be wrapped in a mysterious silence. Automatically we moved towards each other, and as we met in the centre of the room he said in a low, urgent voice: "Don't go to the Cathedral."

I stared, but before I could speak he had vanished, bolting from the room as if he had embarrassed himself.

So the Coterie's "soothsayer-in-residence" had been unable to resist delivering an enigmatic warning! Too radiant with Veuve Clicquot to be other than vastly entertained, I murmured indulgently: "Bless his little cotton socks!" (a favourite idiotic phrase of the time) and prepared for the assault on the Cathedral.

8

"I'LL have to run home and pick up the key," Eddie was saying to Christian, "but I'll meet you all by the Dean's door of the Cathedral in five minutes."

"Fine. I'll whip these Goths and Vandals into something that resembles a civilised order."

Eddie disappeared. Christian clapped his hands to recall everyone's attention and said laconically: "Let's keep the decibels low or the Constable of the Close will arrive frothing at the mouth. Are we ready?"

We weren't. The girls had to cover up their bare shoulders to protect themselves from the May night and various people found they had to go to the lavatory, but finally we all streamed out of the house across Choristers' Green and crossed the North Walk to the Cathedral churchyard.

I glanced at my watch. The time was almost eleven; Nick would only just have had time to escape from the Close before the Constable shut the gates for the night. I tried to picture my Talisman returning to his father, but I found I could not quite imagine the ancient St. Darrow who lived in a wood on communion wafers, and meanwhile we were all gliding and giggling across the sward, the girls' dresses glinting and the men's shirt-fronts gleaming in the darkness. Michael and Dinkie, prancing in front of the floodlights, began to jive silently together and vast shadows were cast on the huge walls ahead of us. In the distance the houses of the Close were almost all in darkness. The silence was profound.

"Here's Eddie," breathed Marina, who was holding Christian's hand. "Isn't he a pet?"

"I didn't know orang-utans could be classified as pets," I said tartly, whereupon Robert Welbeck, the merchant banker who had been up at Oxford with Marina's brother, linked his arm through mine, declared he worshipped glamour-girls who reminded him of Humphrey Bogart films and demanded to know why we had never met at a party in London.

"We did," I said, "but you were too busy worshipping elsewhere to prostrate yourself at my feet."

At that moment, which must have been eleven o'clock precisely, a time-switch flipped in the bowels of the Cathedral and all the floodlights went out.

Once again we gasped at the sight which met our eyes. The harsh glare of electricity was replaced by the soft glow of the moon. A delicate pale light bathed the ancient houses of the Close and conjured up images of the idyllic settings of countless fairy-tales, while the sward of the church-yard, shining eerily around us, suggested a magic garden full of lost echoes from the past. The black mountain of the Cathedral's north wall seemed to vibrate as if it were part of a huge animal—in fact so strong was this impression of life that I actually touched the stones as if I expected them to pulse beneath my fingers but of course the wall was cool, dank and still.

"What a sight!" I heard Perry say in awe as he stood hand in hand with Katie Aysgarth, while Norman, quoting from Macaulay with the confidence of a Winchester scholar, murmured: " 'Such night in England ne'er had been, nor e'er again shall be.' " Michael then tried to croon Presley's "Such a Night" but his pal Don Latham managed to cuff him while the girls—Dinkie and Emma-Louise but not Holly, who was spellbound—hissed: "Shhh!"

"No sacrilege, please, chaps," said Christian casually as Eddie unlocked the Dean's door, and Marina whispered to him: "It's a holy place, isn't it?"

"Well, what did you expect?" I muttered, irritated by this banal chatter which was marring the Cathedral's colossal vibes. "Brighton Pier on a bank holiday?"

"Hang on a minute," Eddie was saying, opening the door and switching on his torch. "I have to turn off the alarm before it summons the entire Starbridge police force and all three fire engines." He disappeared but returned in less than a minute to announce: "All clear!"

Drunken but awe-struck we tiptoed into the huge dark interior beyond.

9

"I WON'T switch on any lights," said Eddie, "or someone might see us and summon the Constable in panic, but I've brought two torches so if I lead the way—"

"Marina and I will bring up the rear and provide extra light," said Christian. "Well done, Eddie."

We set off in a hushed crocodile, crossing the Cathedral to the door at the tip of the south transept; the stairs beyond led not only to the tower below the spire but to the roof of the nave. Vast columns rose around us and disappeared into blackness. Long windows languished in the moonlight. Eerily the echo of our footfalls rebounded from the invisible ceiling. No one spoke until Eddie said, opening the door: "I think I can risk the light on the stairs—the windows overlook the cloisters, not the Close," and he flicked on the switch.

It was curious how the arrival of artificial light made us all relax. We staggered up the twisting staircase, various people making idiotic remarks, but once I paused to look down on the moonlit quadrangle of the cloisters and when I saw the seat donated by Lady Mary Calthrop-Ponsonby, I yearned for my Mr. Dean. In fact suddenly I was so overpowered by the wish that he could be with me that I had to lean for support against the wall.

"Get a move on, Vinnie," said Katie's brother Simon, addressing me as a horse as usual. I could have murdered him.

We reached the roof of the nave. I saw a dark velvet sky suffused with a pure white light. Below me the Bishop's palace, now the Choir School, rose in a flurry of Victorian gothic towers and turrets from its long garden, and beyond the silver gleam of the river the meadows, enchanted pastures, stretched to the distant mass of the hills. The sight was so beautiful that tears stung my eyes and again I found myself wishing with passion: if only he could be here!

Someone paused beside me. I looked up. It was Christian.

"Incomparable, isn't it?" he said.

"Stunning." The adjective seemed so inadequate that I wished I had remained silent.

"You're looking rather stunning yourself," Christian remarked idly. "In fact I've never seen you look better. Is the obvious explanation the true one?"

"What's the obvious explanation?"

"Are you in love?"

"Oh, good heavens!" I said languidly, but then in a moment of bravado I cast aside the mask of nonchalance and retorted: "Well, as a matter of fact yes, I am—but not with you, I promise!"

"And now, of course, I long to seduce you on the spot!"

Robert Welbeck, who had somehow become separated from me during the long haul up to the roof, chose that moment to lurch into us. "Venetia reminds me of Lauren Bacall," he said to Christian. "Venetia, any time you want me to play Humphrey Bogart—"

"Sweet of you, darling," I said, "but I wouldn't dream of stopping you running off to Casablanca with Ingrid Bergman."

"Save your energy, Robert!" advised Christian amused. "Venetia's in love with someone else."

"Oh God, why am I always last past the post in the race for the glamour-girls?"

Perry Palmer said behind him: "Let me give you a lesson in racing! Venetia, when you're next in London, have a drink with me at Albany and I'll show you my very curious Japanese prints."

"Fabulous—name the day!" I said promptly, and Christian laughed.

Marina, slinking up to our group, said with a commendably genuine affection: "What a *femme fatale* you are, Vinnie, luring these three gorgeous creatures into your net!" I suppose that if one has absolute confidence in one's ability to be the belle of every ball, one can afford to be generous, but I still admired Marina for not unsheathing her claws. My sister Arabella would have been scratching away furiously by that time.

In gratitude I said to Marina: "They're all yours, Helen of Troy. I'm off to the other side of the roof to contemplate eternity." I felt quite faint with euphoria. I had been called a glamour-girl—twice—and openly acknowledged as a *femme fatale.* My life as a social outcast was over. I had moved from the sidelines of life to the centre at last. I was madly in love. The world lay at my feet. I was in paradise.

At the west end of the roof I looked back and saw that Katie had joined the group I had abandoned. Christian was slipping his arm around her waist—and Marina perhaps found that too hard to watch; she was moving away, and although Perry held out his hand to her she ignored him. Robert Welbeck, in search of another glamour-girl, was prowling purposefully towards Dinkie, but Dinkie, in an unexpected twist, began to snog with the BBC's Don Latham. Norman and man-eating Cynthia were already locked in a voracious marital embrace as Cynthia settled down to her customary picnic, and out of the corner of my eye I saw Simon the horse-lover jump on Emma-Louise with such gusto that I could almost hear him thinking: tally-ho! Meanwhile Robert, balked of Dinkie, had sensibly decided to settle for that nice girl Holly Carr, and Marina, as if to show Christian she could survive well enough without him, was marching towards me with her head held high. But when she passed the door which led to the stairs Michael ambushed her and she surrendered with relief. Trust Michael Ashworth, I reflected not unamused, to wind up smooching with the belle of the ball.

Drifting away from them I reached the north side of the Cathedral and paused to stare at the city beyond the walls of the Close. At that point I could no longer see my companions, who were all on the south side; the vaulted roof of the nave towered between us as I stood on the north walkway and leaned against the parapet. I sighed, savouring my solitude, and gazing over the city I prepared to abandon myself to the most delicious luxury of dreaming about the man I loved.

A footfall sounded behind me. My solitude shattered. Too late I realised I was trapped. Then as a shadow fell across the parapet beside me the dreaded voice said hoarsely: "Venetia!" and Eddie Hoffenberg moved in for the kill.

10

"*VENETIA,* I must talk to you!"

"Oh God, Eddie, not now!"

"Yes, now, I must speak, I must—Venetia, you're the most tremendous girl I've ever met but I've never dared say so because I know you think I'm so ugly and I know how your father hates Germans—"

"Eddie, this is sheer masochism!"

"No, it isn't, it's sheer courage at last! Venetia, as soon as I saw you tonight I thought you were so beautiful, so radiant, so heroic—"

"Heroic? That makes me sound like a twenty-stone Wagnerian opera singer!"

"I'm sorry, heroic's the wrong word, I'm in such a state that my English has broken down—"

"Well, run away and mend it."

"Venetia—"

"I'm sorry, I know I'm being beastly, but I simply can't cope—"

"You don't have to cope. Just say you'll marry me. Venetia, I adore you, I'm demented with passion, I dream of you night and day—"

I tried to run away. He grabbed me. I shrieked: "Let me go!" and struggled violently, but his awful, flapping, great wet mouth descended on mine in a nightmare of revolting intimacy. I lashed out blindly with my foot. He recoiled with a yelp. Slapping him I wrenched myself free and dashed around the roof. All the snoggers looked up startled as I crashed by. Flinging wide the door I shot down the stairs and hurtled into the shadowy splendour of the transept. Moonlight was now pouring into the nave. Great sobs tore at my throat but somehow I managed to blunder across the transept and grope my way through the darkness of the northern aisle to the Dean's door. At last my fingers closed on the handle. I heaved the door open, I staggered outside—and I cannoned straight into a man who was about to enter the Cathedral.

But before I could even draw breath to scream he was grasping me reassuringly. "It's all right!" he said at high speed. "It's all right, it's all right—it's only me!"

I cried: "Oh, Mr. Dean!" and with all my defences utterly destroyed I collapsed sobbing against his chest.

II

"OH, Mr. Dean!" I cried again, controlling my sobs but not my desolation as he continued to clasp me firmly. "Why is life always so bloody unfair, why am I always getting kicked in the teeth, why does every attempt I make to be successful wind up in failure—no, don't tell me I'm so lucky, so rich, so privileged, don't talk to me about the starving millions in India, I don't want to know about the starving millions in India, I need all my strength to survive my own starvation, because what's the point of being rich and privileged if you're not loved, and I've never been loved, never, no one's ever really understood but I've been so lonely, I've felt as if I've been locked up in a prison on the edge of life, and I've tried

and tried to escape—and then tonight I really thought I'd done it, I thought I'd made it to freedom at last, and I was so happy, being accepted by a group of my sort of people, and it was all so wonderful, so perfect—and so beautiful up there on the roof—and I didn't even mind when everyone paired off and started snogging because I didn't actually want to smooch with anyone, it was enough that everyone accepted me as one of their set, and I was just thinking it was the happiest night of my entire life—except for that unforgettable night in the Hebrides, of course, when we danced to Elvis Presley—and in fact I was just wishing you could have been there on the roof with me when that *oaf* Eddie Hoffenberg crashed in and staged this ghastly love-scene which ended in his proposing marriage and slobbering all over me—and oh God, it was *foul* and worse still, *farcical,* I felt any audience would have passed out laughing because the scene was so bathetic—and although I didn't mean to be unkind to him, I was, I was beastly because it was just such a nightmare being slobbered over by someone who's physically repulsive, and I know you're thinking I should be grateful to be loved by anyone, even Eddie, but I'm not grateful, I'm not, I just want to scream with despair because no *real* man has ever found me attractive and I'm sure now no *real* man ever will, and I'm sorry, I do realise I shouldn't mind so much, but I do mind, Mr. Dean, I mind terribly because it seems so wrong that I should have so much love and no *real* man to give it to—"

Eddie burst panting through the door in an agony of anxiety and remorse.

12

"*VENETIA,* I—good heavens, Stephen!" He shied away in shock.

"Hullo, Eddie," said Aysgarth, very casual. "Having fun?"

"My God!" The expletive, forbidden for a clergyman, revealed the depth of Eddie's horror. "Has the Bishop been looking out of his bedroom window at the South Canonry?"

"No, fortunately for you I was telephoned by a star-gazing master at the Choir School."

"Stephen, I'm so sorry, I—I can't think why I let them all in, but it was just such a wonderful party and—"

"Quite. Now get them all out before the Bishop steams up here to defrock us both."

"Yes, Stephen. Yes, of course. Yes, straight away. Venetia—"

"Oh, don't you worry about Venetia," said Aysgarth. "I'll take care of her."

"Yes," said Eddie. "Yes. All right. Thanks." He stumbled back into the Cathedral and we listened to the sound of his footsteps as they receded into the distance.

At last the silence was absolute. It was too dark for me to see Aysgarth's face as we both stood in the shadow of the north wall. I could only wait in an agony of shame for him to pass judgement on my disgusting emotional outburst, but just as I was thinking hysterically that I could bear the silence no longer, he said in a tone of voice he had never used to me before: "My dearest Venetia," and then I knew he had moved through the looking-glass to join me in an utterly different world.

PART TWO

THE
SERPENT

"For nothing can of itself always be labelled as 'wrong.' One cannot, for instance, start from the position 'sex relations before marriage' or 'divorce' are wrong or sinful in themselves. They may be in 99 cases or even 100 cases out of 100, but they are not intrinsically so, for the only intrinsic evil is lack of love."

JOHN A. T. ROBINSON
HONEST TO GOD

VII

I

"MY dearest Venetia," said Aysgarth, setting aside the past, transforming the present and redesigning the future, "it does indeed seem very unfair that you should have to endure such unhappiness, but never think there isn't at least one person who understands exactly how you feel and who cares deeply what happens to you."

I tried to reply but speech proved impossible. I was now crying soundlessly, the tears streaming down my cheeks. Without thinking I rubbed my eyes with my hand, and then remembered—too late—that I was wearing eye make-up. Without doubt my face was now a mess. My tears welled faster than ever.

Then he gripped my hands. As he said: "I'll take you back to the Chantry," I was acutely aware that his fingers were very strong and very hot. They clasped mine so hard that I quite literally reeled, stumbling off balance, turning my ankle and snapping the heel of my shoe.

"Oh God—"

"It's all right, I've got you." He gathered me in his arms. I almost passed out.

"Sorry—tight as an owl—can't seem to keep upright—"

"Never mind, at least one of us is resolutely vertical!"

We laughed. My tears had stopped. The possibility of recovering my equilibrium no longer seemed fantastic.

"What's happened to your shoe?" he was saying.

"Accidental death." I stepped out of both shoes and he promptly released me in order to pick them up. I was now the same height as he was, and suddenly he seemed much closer.

Carrying my shoes in one hand he clasped my fingers again with the other and we began to walk out of the shadow of the Cathedral. The ground beneath my feet was cool and damp but of course I was walking on air so I barely noticed. With my free hand I tried to wipe the smudged eye make-up from my cheekbones. We said nothing. His fingers seemed hotter and stronger than ever.

We crossed the North Walk, we crossed Choristers' Green, we crossed the little lane which ran past the Chantry's front gate. The moonlight seemed blindingly white, and when we turned at last to face each other I could clearly see the downward curve of his sultry mouth. The expression in his eyes was inscrutable.

All he said was: "I think Lady Mary Calthrop-Ponsonby requests the pleasure of our company after Evensong tomorrow."

I nodded. He handed me my shoes. I took them and opened the gate.

"Are you all right now?"

"Oh yes," I said. "Very much so."

We smiled at each other. Then he began to walk briskly away towards the Deanery.

2

THE Orgy rolled on till dawn, but I barely noticed. I repaired my make-up, slipped into another pair of shoes, smoked a cigarette and savoured my euphoria. Eventually the Coterie floated back to the Chantry but to my relief there was no sign of Eddie.

"Gone home to do penance for permitting an orgy on consecrated ground," said Christian, giving me a penetrating look. "I must see Father tomorrow and claim full responsibility . . . Are you all right, Venetia?"

Before I could reply Marina cornered me. "Darling, do tell! Did Eddie try and rape you? What was going on? Why did you rush off the roof like a bat out of hell?"

"Eddie always drives me mad," I said with a yawn. "He just drove me madder than usual, that's all." And then driven by the urge to escape I tottered upstairs and passed out. God knows what happened as the Orgy drew to a close, but probably not very much. It was, after all, 1963, not that anarchic year 1968 and certainly not the year afterwards when everyone bucketed around burbling: "'69 is divine!" What a bore social life became—which is no doubt why I look back on Marina's Orgy with such uncharacteristically heavy nostalgia.

The next morning I rose early, my hangover soon negated by a potent combination of Alka-Seltzer and euphoria, and wondered if I was feeling energetic enough to buy a newspaper, but in the end I merely lay on my bed and thought of Aysgarth. At noon Marina appeared, looking fragile. Dinkie, Emma-Louise and Holly remained stacked in the spare-room for another hour but eventually they too emerged looking vanquished by Veuve Clicquot. I had to be careful not to appear too hale and hearty when I eventually gave them a lift to the station.

Time crawled on. The housekeeper and the charwoman, both heavily tipped, finished cleaning up the mess. At three o'clock I picked a flower and meditated on the ravishing symmetry of its petals. The sun shone. The birds sang. Drinking some tea I gazed in rapture at the Cathedral.

Sunday Evensong was at four o'clock, and never in my life had a church service seemed more meaningful. I listened to every note sung by the Choir, every word of the prayers and lessons. Phrase after phrase of the Collects, the Magnificat—even the Nunc Dimittis—seemed impregnated with a new and glorious meaning. As I tried not to look too often at Aysgarth I resolved recklessly to ignore the risk of being dubbed a religious maniac and to attend Evensong every day. Let everyone think I was experiencing a religious conversion! Why not? Other people experienced religious conversions. It happened all the time. Indeed perhaps I really was experiencing a religious conversion; I certainly felt God had decided to take some notice of me at last, and if God was now playing an active role in my life, surely I had a moral duty to be as devout as possible in order to express my gratitude?

I had just reached this virtuous conclusion when the service ended. The hour had come. Slipping away along the transept I heaved open the great door into the cloisters and skimmed down the north colonnade towards Lady Mary's seat on the edge of the lawn.

3

BIRDS were singing in the cedar tree. The sky had clouded over, though the air was still warm, and the colonnades were empty save for two tourists who were examining memorial tablets. Sitting on Lady Mary I watched them inch their way around the quadrangle. They were on the point of disappearing through the door into the nave when Aysgarth finally emerged from the transept.

He was looking exceptionally smart. His hair had been combed. He was wearing a well-pressed suit and highly polished shoes. His brisk, authoritative walk created an impression of power and confidence. He exuded a subtle air of distinction. As I repressed my desire to rush headlong into his arms a voice in my head was whispering in awe: this is the Dean of Starbridge, *the Dean of Starbridge,* and the Dean of Starbridge at present wants to see me more than anyone else in the world.

"Sorry to be so long," he said, rapidly covering the last yards that separated us. "I was button-holed by the Bishop in the vestry. That row over the coach-park is still going on."

"Are you winning?"

"Of course!" He smiled radiantly. Then he sat down, positioning himself so that his right thigh was at least six inches from my left, and folded his hands primly in his lap. "So!" he said, giving me a hot look with his steamy blue eyes. "How are you today?"

"Indescribably better." I too smiled radiantly, but he did not see me. He was too busy taking a quick look around the cloisters to make sure we were alone.

"Good." Reassured of our solitude he relaxed but for some reason refused to look at me. I supposed he wanted to ensure that the scene remained dignified and civilised. At once I resolved to be indestructibly nonchalant to signal to him that I was aware of his great eminence, that I understood his wish to remain unemotional in a public place and that I was not the kind of woman who indulged in embarrassing scenes.

"Have you heard from Eddie?" he said idly, flicking a speck of dust from his cuff.

"A pathetic little note of apology was pushed through the letter-box this morning. I felt lower than the lowliest worm."

"You can't help it if you don't love him." He gazed at the cedar tree as if it had developed an immense fascination for him. "And talking of love"—he clasped his hands together tightly—"Christian said you told him last night that you were keen on someone else. He wondered if the man might be Marina's brother, since that would explain your rather unlikely new friendship with Marina herself, and this seemed to me to be a plausible theory."

I managed to say: "Believe me, I'm not dying of unrequited love for Douglas Markhampton." I had suddenly realised that despite the hints I had dropped in my impassioned monologue he was still so unsure of my feelings that he felt driven to proceed with extreme caution. I wanted to shout: "It's you, *you,* YOU!" but of course I said nothing. I merely continued to loll on Lady Mary as if I hadn't a care in the world.

Meanwhile Aysgarth was savouring his relief that I was uninterested in Douglas Markhampton. As I watched, his clasped hands parted and his thick strong fingers uncurled themselves until they were resting lightly on his thighs. Then he said: "I don't see why you should die of unrequited love for anyone. Love should always be reciprocated in some form or another. It's too precious to waste."

"You mean," I said, wilfully obtuse in an effort to preserve my nonchalance, "I should somehow reciprocate Eddie's grand passion?"

"Oh, love can't be made to order, of course," said Aysgarth hastily. "All you can do there, I'm afraid, is be kind."

"I've certainly no wish to be unkind." I was watching his fingers curling and uncurling on his thighs. "But surely when people are plunging around in a sex-frenzy they're not interested in mere kindness?"

"Sex, I agree," said Aysgarth primly to the cedar tree, "presents enormous problems, but in the end it's love, not sex, that makes the world go round. I don't mean to denigrate sex, of course; God made the world and it was good, as the Bible says, and this means that sex is fundamentally good too, but love doesn't always require a sexual expression. Indeed love can transcend sex altogether."

"Honestly, Mr. Dean, I think Eddie's a long way from transcending sex!"

"He needs time to cool off, but perhaps later some form of friendship might be possible for you both. Of course there are those who declare that a true, loving friendship which transcends sex is impossible for any normal man or woman," said Aysgarth, interlocking his fingers again. "They say that in the garden of life sex is always the serpent lurking in the undergrowth to corrupt Beauty and Truth and Goodness, but I reject that kind of cynical, pessimistic view of the world. Even a serpent can be tamed and domesticated because with love nothing's impossible. In *Honest to God* Bishop Robinson says—"

"I've simply got to read this masterpiece!" I exclaimed, recklessly casting aside my nonchalance. "So far I've only read him quoting St. Augustine's slogan: 'Love God and do what you like.'"

"Ah yes, but laymen so often misunderstand that command—"

"It doesn't mean, does it, that you can jump into bed with whoever you like just so long as you turn up in church on Sunday?"

"Hardly!" He had at last relaxed; I thanked God for theology. "It means that if you love God—which is the purest, noblest sort of love—you should be able to love your fellow-men in the same way and then the love will both protect you from sin and steer you into the paths of righteousness. 'Love God and do what you will' thus becomes 'Love God and you'll automatically do the right thing'—and Robinson's relating that principle to what the Germans call *Situationethik:* he's saying that in moral dilemmas there are no hard and fast rules and that each situation should be regarded as unique; he's saying that love—the best kind of love—should be the only guiding light in seeking a resolution of moral problems."

"So love—the best kind of love—is the highest reality we can know?"

"Certainly, and it's there that we find God. God is Love—and Love, as Robinson points out so truthfully, can be found within the best human relationships. Therefore a truly loving relationship, whatever the context, can never be wrong."

"But supposing two people love each other," I said, "and one happens to be married to someone else?"

"Adultery," said Aysgarth, smoothing the material of his trousers over his thighs with strong sensual movements of his fingers, "is *prima facie* wrong. That we all know. But if, for example, a married man found himself in a *truly* loving relationship with a woman who was not his wife, there would be no adultery because he would love that woman enough to abstain from any behaviour which was morally wrong." Suddenly, quite without warning, he swivelled to face me and our thighs brushed. At once we gave galvanic starts and he glanced hastily around the colonnades, but we were still unobserved and a second later he was saying in his most urgent voice:

"Love's one of the ultimate prizes of life so it must never be torn up and chucked away. An illicit love must be transformed; a licit love must be exalted. Christians have always laid such emphasis on love. Tertullian tells us that in the days of the Early Church the pagans used to say: 'See how those Christians love one another!' Love's the key-note in Christianity, and Robinson's emphasising that fact in order to bring Christianity up to date so that it can speak afresh to modern man. God isn't out there in space, says Robinson. He's here, He's within the world, He's the very ground of our being. 'See how those Christians *love* one another!' says Tertullian, quoting the pagans. Christianity conquered that pagan world—and why? Because it was a religion based on love, the best kind of love, the love everyone needs in order to thrive and become whole. Sometimes it's possible for that love to have a sexual context, sometimes it isn't, but as I said just now, it's love, not sex, that makes the world go round. You told me last night how starved you were without love, and now I want more than anything else in the world to bring that starvation to an end. *'See how those Christians love one another!'* God's in every truly loving relationship. He's here now, with us."

He stopped abruptly and there was a pause before he exclaimed with an awkward laugh: "What a sermon! Forgive me—I didn't mean to behave as if I were in the pulpit." To my amazement he even began to blush, smoothing back his hair in an agony of embarrassment and staring furiously at his shoes as if he feared he had made a fool of himself.

"My darling Mr. Dean," I said, so touched by this wholly unexpected vulnerability that my eyes filled with tears, "you can preach to me as often as you wish for as long as you like, and I hope it'll be *very* often and for *very* long."

He finally dared to look at me again. Then overwhelmed by the unspoken message which must have been emanating from every line of my face, he dared to believe the unbelievable. Automatically he grabbed my hand and tried to speak but no words came. I found I was tongue-tied too. We could only sit clutching each other, my left hand locked in his right, but at last he managed to say: "You're a wonderful girl—and if Eddie's the only man under forty who can see that, I despair of the younger generation."

"Who cares about the younger generation?" I retorted, so racked by the urge to fling myself into his arms that I hardly knew what I was saying. "I certainly don't!"

He smiled. Then suddenly he began to radiate confidence. "If I write to you," he said, "will you write back?"

"Instantly. But Mr. Dean, don't tell me that our new friendship is to be solely confined to letters!"

"Perish the thought! But it won't be easy for us to meet on our own, and—"

He broke off. Far away in the north-east corner of the cloisters the transept door had closed with a thud and the next moment footsteps were ringing out in the colonnade. My view of the intruder was hidden by the pillars but Aysgarth, dropping my hand as if it had scalded him, signalled that danger was at hand. At once I assumed my most languid expression and pretended to examine a fingernail.

"Yes, well, to return to my earlier remarks," said Aysgarth as if we were engaged in an earnest intellectual discussion, "Bishop Robinson has studied the work of three German theologians, Tillich, Bultmann and—oh hullo, Charles! I thought you'd gone home."

Looking unexpectedly modern in a grey suit, the Bishop glided to a halt by Lady Mary. To indicate his episcopal rank he was wearing a purple stock and pectoral cross, but he seemed less intimidating without his old-fashioned uniform and I was surprised when I realised I was nervous.

"As a matter of fact I did set off for home," he was saying in response to Aysgarth's remark, "but then I remembered I wanted to look up a reference for a sermon. I've just paid a quick visit to the library."

There was a pause during which Aysgarth and I somehow restrained ourselves from staring in horror at the library windows which faced us above the east colonnade. Indeed I was still gazing at the Bishop as if driven to memorise every line on his face when he added in his pleasantest voice: "Did you enjoy your party last night, Venetia?"

"Oh, enormously!" I said, producing my best friendly smile as my heart began to thump. "I'm so glad Michael was able to come!"

"It was nice of you to invite him," said the Bishop, smooth as glass. "I was talking to someone at the Choir School this morning, and he seemed to think the party was really rather exceptional."

Aysgarth at once cleared his throat and made a great business of examining his watch. "Good heavens, look at the time! Venetia my dear—"

"Yes, of course, Mr. Dean," I said swiftly. "I'm sure you've got a thousand and one things to do. Thanks so much for sparing the time to talk to me about Bishop Robinson."

"How much longer will you be staying at the Chantry, Venetia?" said Dr. Ashworth suddenly as Aysgarth rose to his feet.

"Until Lady Markhampton returns in ten days' time."

"And then, I assume, you'll be heading back to London?"

"No." I was acutely aware of Aysgarth pausing, unable to resist the temptation to listen to my reply. "I'm going to get a flat."

"Here?" said the Bishop surprised. "In Starbridge? Does this mean you've been offered some exceptional secretarial post?"

"No, although naturally I hope—"

"Oh, you'll need an interesting job or you'll soon be very bored! There's not much in provincial old Starbridge, is there, Stephen, to keep a sophisticated young woman like Venetia amused!"

"I think Venetia might want rather more from life, Charles," said Aysgarth equably, "than mere sophisticated entertainment. Perhaps you could find her a job at the diocesan office?"

"Perhaps I could. If that's what she wants." With his most charming smile he added to me: "Come and see us again at the South Canonry! I'll ask my wife to phone you and fix a date." And before I could do more than murmur a conventional word of thanks he had gone, striding away from us without a backward glance and disappearing through the door which led into the churchyard.

"Glory!" I muttered. "Do you think he looked out of the library window and saw us holding hands?"

"Why shouldn't we hold hands?" retorted Aysgarth. "Aren't we old friends? *Honi soit qui mal y pense!*"

"But—"

"Personally I'm more worried about the star-gazing master at the Choir School who's apparently been unable to resist bleating to Charles about last night's rooftop revels. That could have a very adverse effect on the coach-park struggle."

"It could?"

"Yes, Charles could say to me: 'If you can't stop your own family running riot with their friends in the Cathedral, how can I trust you to control the occupants of ten coaches parked simultaneously in Palace Lane?' "

"Honestly, Mr. Dean, I can't think how you keep so sane amidst all these brawls and back-stabbings—"

"I've simply no time to go mad—which reminds me, I must dash home because a dozen people are coming for drinks. But when am I going to see you again?"

"I could attend Communion tomorrow. That would set the Bishop's mind at rest."

"I'd stop worrying about Charles, if I were you."

"But if he looked out of the window just now—"

"I'm sure he didn't. The last thing any dedicated academic does in a library is look out of a window."

"All the same it might be politic if—"

"My darling, you mustn't attend Communion merely to reassure the Bishop! That wouldn't be right."

After I had recovered from the delicious shock of being addressed as "my darling" I managed to mumble: "I want to attend Communion to try to be a better Christian. If Christianity's all about finding God in loving relationships, then I want to be a far better Christian than I've ever been before."

This pleased him. He gave my hand an approving squeeze before saying: "Stay on in St. Anselm's Chapel after the service tomorrow and I'll slip back from the vestry to meet you." In a burst of enthusiasm he added: "I can't tell you how much I enjoy talking to you—your destiny is obviously to be my Egeria!"

"The name rings a bell but I can't quite—"

"She was a great listener." He clasped both my hands as we faced each other. I had remembered to wear flat shoes so I was the perfect height to gaze into his eyes.

"St. Anselm's Chapel," he managed to say after an emotional silence. "Tomorrow morning at eight."

I nodded, once more beyond speech, and we went our separate ways.

4

I STAGGERED back to the Chantry where I found Marina reclining on the sofa in a dusty-pink negligée and indulging in one of her lengthy phone conversations; the faint squeak of a voice (male) was audible as I drifted past the receiver. When the squeak ceased Marina said: "Michael, how wonderful! I'd adore it," and stopped caressing a strand of her blonde hair in order to wave at me buoyantly. I deduced the Bishop's son was trying to line her up for another pounce. Vaguely I wondered if the Bishop himself had ever pounced around in his youth, but the thought of Dr. Ashworth behaving in a manner which could be described as sexually seamy was quite inconceivable.

The next thing I knew I was in my room and collapsing in a heap on my bed. I was in a stupor of ecstasy. The Dean of Starbridge—*the Dean of Starbridge*—had said I was wonderful. In other words—and I had to rephrase this sentence in order to savour its extraordinary content to the full—a brilliant, successful, attractive man had expressed a genuine admiration for me. Perhaps he even loved me, although of course I knew it would be unwise to assume this without further evidence that his feelings ran deeper than mere compassionate affection—and of course I knew I had no right to expect so much. But nevertheless he had said I was "wonderful" and called me "my darling." How intoxicating! I could still barely grasp the dimensions of my changed universe; I felt I could only gaze in amazement at the cosmic vista which had unfolded before my eyes.

Finding a sheet of writing-paper I printed: "N. N. Aysgarth. Norman Neville Aysgarth. Neville Aysgarth. Stephen Aysgarth." So many designations! For good measure I added all the titles he had had during his career. "The Reverend N. N. Aysgarth." (That described him when he had been a vicar.) "The Venerable N. N. Aysgarth." (That covered the years as Archdeacon.) "The Reverend Canon N. N. Aysgarth." (That dealt with Westminster Abbey.) "The Very Reverend the Dean of Starbridge"—

The Dean of Starbridge! And *me!* Carefully I drew a little heart, pierced it with a delicately etched arrow and wrote VENETIA at one end and NNA at the other. Never before had so trivial a doodle afforded me such immense satisfaction, and as I contemplated those magic initials my excitement reached new heights. Never mind that he had a wife. Never mind that he was a clergyman, a fact which prohibited anything so unspiritual as a full-scale adulterous love-affair. At least—thanks to Bishop Robinson—we could indulge in a high-minded love, a romantic self-denial and countless erotic meetings . . . However, it seemed unlikely that the Bishop of Woolwich had openly advocated eroticism when he had outlined his scheme for a new morality based on the noblest form of love. Picking up my copy of *Honest to God,* which had somehow become buried beneath the latest James Bond novel, the current copy of *New Musical Express* and *Lady Chatterley's Lover,* I opened the book and scanned the chapter on ethics. A heading announced: "Nothing Pre-scribed—Except Love." What a prescription! Enthralled I read on:

"This position, foreshadowed thirty years ago in Emil Brunner's great book *The Divine Imperative,* is given its most consistent statement I know in an article by Professor Joseph Fletcher in the *Harvard Divinity Bulletin,* entitled 'The New Look in Christian Ethics.' 'Christian Ethics,' he says, 'is not a scheme of codified conduct. It is a purposive effort to relate love to a world of relativities through a casuistry obedient to . . .' "

I lost interest. It was really amazing how those theologians could make even a subject like love seem boring. Tossing the book aside I paused only to burn my fevered jottings in the ash-tray and then I began to dream of a future in which nothing was prescribed except love.

5

THE Bishop was absent from Communion the next morning, but I knew that only Anglo-Catholics were in the habit of attending "mass," as they called it, every day. Aysgarth, being Low Church by inclination, pri-vately considered it quite unnecessary to attend Communion except on Sundays and special Holy Days, but since the Bishop always turned up at least twice during the week Aysgarth too, not to be outdone, appeared with a similar regularity in St. Anselm's Chapel for the weekday services of Matins at seven-thirty and Communion at eight. This spiritual one-upmanship would have been amusing if it had not reflected the antipathy between the two men, but in view of their strained relationship the situation could only seem unfortunate. I felt sorry for my Mr. Dean being burdened with a bishop he disliked, and I felt wary of Dr. Ashworth who I suspected might well harbour a ruthless streak behind his steel-plated charm. The desire to keep on the right side of such a formidable figure was strong, and I was sorry that I had no opportunity that morning to impress him by my presence at Communion.

I was also disappointed that the celebrant was not the Dean himself but the current canon in residence, Fitzgerald; Aysgarth merely assisted him. (Fortunately there was no sign of Eddie.) I did try to follow the service carefully in my Prayer Book, but I was feeling so exalted that I continu-ally lost my place and had a hard time keeping up with the other members of the small congregation, the retired clergy and withered old women who seemed to fill up so many nooks and crannies in the Cathedral Close. I must have been the youngest person present by at least thirty years.

I had never felt entirely comfortable with the Communion service. It had always conjured up for me images of cannibalism, and I had been accustomed to justifying my repulsion by arguing that we can't all find certain symbols equally meaningful. However, I was now so transformed by my new universe that I discovered even my attitude to Communion had changed. How could I have found that beautiful symbolism repulsive? How very far astray I must have been—in fact, how had I even dared to call myself a Christian? I resolved to turn over a new leaf. When my turn came to approach the altar-rail I remembered my confirmation classes, took the sacrament reverently and sank to my knees to pray as soon as I returned to my seat.

A shaft of sunlight penetrated the chapel and emphasised the delicate lines of the vaulted ceiling. Love, Truth, Beauty—the absolute values—all were present, Love represented by Aysgarth, Truth by the service which pointed to Christ, Beauty in the architecture of the chapel. How futile the Orgy seemed in retrospect, how meaningless and trivial! Eating too much, drinking too much, running around after men and thinking of nothing but sex—what an intolerable waste of time such pursuits were when there was this other world waiting to be explored! I could now clearly see that this other world was the true reality. Everything else was mere illusion.

I was still pondering on these radical thoughts when the service ended; Fitzgerald and Aysgarth padded off behind the verger to the vestry and all the old dears in the congregation tottered home to breakfast. I waited, watching the sunlight and mentally reciting religious poetry. I was just skimming through Blake's "Jerusalem" and had reached the line: "Bring me my arrows of desire!" when Aysgarth slipped back into the chapel.

"We'll go to the library," he said as I sprang to my feet. "The Librarian's never there before nine-thirty so we'll have the place to ourselves."

"Let's hope the Bishop isn't about to look up another reference!"

He laughed and we left the chapel together. There were two cleaning women at work, one flicking a duster in the nave and the other pushing a droning Hoover over the carpet by the high altar, but no one else was in sight as we crossed the transept to the door which opened onto the library staircase. On the landing above the first flight, the stairs continued upwards to the gallery which encircled the nave, but Aysgarth ignored them, advanced to the double-doors ahead of us and produced a key. The door swung wide. We entered the library.

It was a long room, very old, with a vaulted ceiling and that special musty smell of ancient paper and antiquated leather. Books lined the walls and beyond the Librarian's table I saw the chained manuscripts, treasures so precious that the pre-Reformation canons had tethered them to the reading-desks. On the west side of the room the long thin windows looked across the lawn of the cloisters to the wooden seat donated by Lady Mary.

"Have you been here before?" Aysgarth was saying as he closed the door.

"When you first became Dean you gave me and my parents a guided tour."

"So I did! But did I show you the cat?"

"Cat?"

"He's a doodle in our most famous manuscript, one of the earliest copies of St. Anselm's *Prayers and Meditations.* The first Bishop of Starbridge somehow managed to extort it from the monks at Canterbury." Moving to one of the chained treasures he opened the manuscript at a place which was already marked, and when I drew closer I saw illuminated capital letters, lines of pale brown unreadable script and, in the left margin, an exquisite little painting of a cat with a mouse in his mouth.

"He's been under discussion lately," said Aysgarth as I exclaimed in admiration. "I want to have coloured picture-postcards of him made to sell in the Cathedral shop, but I've met with opposition in Chapter. Fitzgerald said Puss-in-Boots here was neither a pertinent nor a reverent representation of St. Anselm's mighty work, and Dalton agreed with him."

"Honestly, Mr. Dean, how square—and how stupid!"

"My darling, you can't go on calling me Mr. Dean when we're alone together! Call me Stephen."

I said at once: "Oh no. Not Stephen. That's *her* name for you."

There was a silence. He looked away and lightly fingered the edge of the manuscript. My heart gave a massive thud.

"And anyway," I added rapidly, "don't you think it would be a mistake if I got into the habit of calling you by your Christian name? Supposing I slipped up in public. Primrose would say: 'Oh Venetia, why are you suddenly addressing Father as if he were someone of our generation?' And your wife would immediately deduce—"

"We mustn't talk of my wife," said Aysgarth. "The morality of the situation demands that we never discuss her."

With an enormous effort I managed to avoid a second deadly silence. In my most casual voice I said: "Okay, fine. If that's the way the cookie crumbles, so be it."

At once he laughed in delight and the tension vanished. "What a marvellous phrase!" he exclaimed. "Where did it come from?"

"It's one of Dinkie's gems. She's an American pal of Marina's and was one of the guests at the Orgy."

"I want to hear about this Orgy!" said Aysgarth, reaching out to clasp my hands. "Let's sit down on the window-seat and luxuriate in a long gossip!"

"How exciting that sounds, Mr. Dean!"

"Neville—please! I insist! It'll be such a change to become Neville again—but wait a minute, which Neville am I? I've been several Nevilles in my time."

"Well, now you can be a new one, specially for me."

I had spoken flippantly but I had enthralled him. "A new Neville!" he exclaimed, and gazed at me as if I had opened some indescribably alluring Pandora's box. Then tightening his grasp on my hands he declared buoyantly: "What a stimulating prospect—and now stimulate me further by telling me all about the Orgy!"

I laughed, unable to resist his high spirits, and firmly setting aside the queasiness which had assailed me when he had refused to discuss his wife, I began to describe the revels of Marina's Coterie.

6

HALF an hour later at a quarter past nine someone, thinking the double-doors were locked, inserted a key and tried to walk in.

"Quick!" whispered Aysgarth. "Puss-in-Boots!"

We raced silently to the reading-desk and by the time the Librarian had worked out that the doors were already unlocked we were gazing in rapture at the little painted cat.

"And the truth is," said Aysgarth in ringing tones, "the scribe almost certainly got bored with copying the manuscript, and—oh hullo, Gilbert! You're early this morning!"

"I have to leave early this evening to go to the dentist." The Librarian, a faded little wisp of a man wearing horn-rimmed spectacles and a suit which smelt of mothballs, was looking anxiously at me as if he feared he ought to remember who I was.

"Venetia, this is Mr. Pryce," said Aysgarth. "Gilbert—Miss Flaxton. I was just showing her our famous cat."

"Oh, I see," said the Librarian in the voice of one who was obviously baffled.

"Well, thank you so much, Mr. Dean," I said. "I mustn't take up any more of your valuable time."

"Not at all. I'll just escort you downstairs—"

"Oh, please don't trouble—"

"It's no trouble whatsoever!"

We escaped.

"That was bad luck," muttered Aysgarth on the stairs. "Let's step into the cloisters for a moment. He won't see us if we stay beneath the library in the east colonnade."

Seconds later we were gazing across the lawn to Lady Mary.

"Before we part," Aysgarth was saying, "we really must solve the problem of where we can meet without the Bishop, all three residentiary canons and the entire Cathedral staff tripping over us with remorseless regularity."

"There's an obvious solution," I said at once. "My time at the Chantry's running out, and when I get a flat—"

"Oh, I could never visit you there."

I was stunned. "You couldn't?"

"No, much too dangerous. I'm well-known in Starbridge, my visits might be noted, and besides . . . We have to remember that serpent, the one who's gliding alongside us in our beautiful garden and wearing a collar and leash like a well-behaved pet. If I really love you—and of course I do—I've no option but to keep that serpent under control."

"But if you can't come to my flat—"

"How I wish you could come to the Deanery as my secretary! But I don't see how I can fire dear old Miss Trotman. She's served under three deans, and . . . dear me, now improper that sounds!" He began to shake with laughter.

"But I don't see how I could possibly accept a job as your secretary . . ." I started to giggle. His laughter was very infectious.

"No, you couldn't. I'm fantasising. Now let me see—"

"Do you have a day off?"

"Certainly! Clergymen who work twenty-four hours a day seven days a week always wind up being no use to anyone."

"Well, in that case—"

"—we'll meet on Wednesday afternoons. Why don't I take you for a drive? Usually on Wednesdays I just eat a big lunch, quaff a bottle of wine and snooze the afternoon away, but now's obviously the time for radical reform!"

"But won't it seem odd if you revolutionise your day off so violently?"

"I'll say the doctor's advised me to lose weight by eating light lunches, cutting back on the drink and going on little excursions once a week!" He was excited. His eyes sparkled. He gave me a radiant smile. "Why don't we meet outside the Staro Arms at two next Wednesday?"

"Fine, but how do I communicate with you if something ghastly happens and I can't make it?"

"Ring the Deanery and say to whoever answers the phone: 'Please tell the Dean that Lady Mary wishes to speak to him about the memorial tablet.' "

"If only Lady Mary knew how useful she was being to us! Or at least

. . . Good heavens, Mr. Dean, we don't really think, do we, that Lady Mary's watching us from her own personal cloud in heaven?"

He laughed. "My dear, Christians no longer believe in the three-decker universe with heaven above the clouds, hell below the ground and the world in between! In the opening chapters of *Honest to God*—"

"I *must* read that book—"

"I'll tell you more about it on Wednesday."

Briefly our hands clasped. Above us the sky was a brilliant, cloudless blue, and as euphoria gripped me again I forgot about sex and marriage and all those other popular hobbies that human beings rated so highly. I remembered only that I was standing in the heart of a mighty cathedral, one of the greatest cathedrals ever built, while beside me stood its master, one of the most powerful churchmen in England, a man who had treated me as if I were truly exceptional and declared that he loved me. What more could I possibly want? Nothing. Indeed so great was my happiness that to have asked for more, I felt, could only have damned me as a monster of greed.

Skimming back to the Chantry I resolved to tackle *Honest to God* without delay.

7

MARINA was on the phone as usual. I heard her voice as soon as I entered the house, and glancing into the drawing-room I saw she was lounging on the sofa, the telephone receiver tucked casually between her left shoulder and ear as she varnished her nails. She was wearing skin-tight white trousers and a turquoise shirt and looked like an actress in one of those Hollywood films where Rock Hudson is always chasing Doris Day across massive sets with minimal results.

"But Don, of course I'm not interested in Michael!" she was saying. "Dinner? Well, perhaps when I'm back in London, but I may be going to stay in Oxford, so . . ."

I left her driving poor Don Latham round the bend, filched a glass of milk from the kitchen and retired to my room to wrestle once more with *Honest to God*. I had just read the sentence: "But he could use it to the spiritually sophisticated at Corinth with no consciousness that he must 'demythologise' if he were to make it acceptable," and I had just realised I had no idea either who "he" was or what "it" could possibly mean, when Marina, fresh from her telephonic dalliance, wafted into my room.

"I've now heard from everyone except Christian," she said fretfully. "I can't think why he doesn't ring."

"Marina," I said in my kindest voice, "if Christian were free to chase you as everyone else does, would you still be so anxious for him to phone?"

"But Christian's not like everyone else," she said earnestly. "He's special."

"In some ways, certainly. But perhaps not in others. Does he still love Katie, do you think?"

"He adores her. So do I. And she adores us—in fact we all adore each other, it's so blissful, so perfect—and so miraculous too that I've at last found a man who only wants to offer me a pure romantic love! If all the other men only knew how fed up to the back teeth I get with their pawing and pouncing and groping—"

The telephone rang. "Christian!" shrieked Marina and pounded away to her grandmother's bedroom to take the call on the extension.

I closed *Honest to God* and decided that Marina was either very ingenuous or else raving mad. What did Christian and Katie really think of this unsought third dimension to their marital life? Perhaps they thought Marina was a colossal bore but were too kind to say so. Surely any normal, happily married young couple would fight shy of an entanglement which converted them into two sides of an eternal triangle? Moreover although Marina might be happy with her pure romantic love, it seemed unlikely that Christian would be so easily satisfied; most men took one look at Marina and were overpowered by lust. Why wasn't Christian slavering at her feet? And why wasn't Katie offering her a poisoned chalice instead of an affectionate friendship? I was quite prepared to believe that idyllic eternal triangles could exist (usually in France) between very sophisticated middle-aged people who by their past sexual excesses had become anaesthetised to the primeval pangs of jealousy, but this triangle between a young Oxford don and two charming, well-brought-up young Englishwomen could only make the mind boggle.

I was still allowing my cynicism free rein when I remembered that I too was a member of an eternal triangle—although of course my triangle was straightforward with no mystery about it whatsoever. Dido was mad and bad. My Mr. Dean was privately sick and tired of her. The marriage was a mere formality. These facts had become obvious to me over the years and had been confirmed by my holiday in the Hebrides.

But the next moment I was recalling the queasiness which had assailed me that morning when Aysgarth had refused to talk about Dido. I knew the obvious explanation for his resolute silence was that as a devout Christian he was morally bound not to speak ill of his wife, but I knew too, as I looked back upon the incident with a cool, analytical eye, that

I had wondered for a split second whether he might still care for her. I had dismissed the notion at once as preposterous, but that, I now saw, had been a mere reflex action, the fobbing off of an unpalatable possibility. Supposing the marriage was a little more complicated than I had always assumed it was? Even though they no longer had sex he might still wish to keep silent not, as I had blithely supposed, out of Christian duty, but out of a genuine affection. And as in my memory I heard Eddie say: "He married her because she amused him—and I think she still does," I was aware of the queasiness sliding back into the pit of my stomach.

Dimly I became aware that I was no longer alone in my bedroom. Marina had returned and was saying exasperated: "Hey, wake up, Vinnie! Have you gone deaf? The call's for you!"

"Ah." I stood up automatically and then realised I had no idea what she was talking about. "How was Christian?" I said, trying to conceal my confusion.

"It wasn't Christian! *The call's for you!*"

The information finally registered. "Sorry!" I said, trying to look intelligent, but I still felt as dazed as if I had been slammed on the head—or as if Aysgarth's sedate little serpent, gliding along on his leash, had reared up to hiss straight in my face.

Outwardly casual but inwardly shattered by the twin demons of jealousy and doubt, I drifted past Marina to the telephone and discovered that my caller was none other than the Bishop's wife, Lyle Ashworth.

VIII

"Brought up with the bells of Canterbury ringing in his ears, never doubting what he believes to be the essential truth of Christianity, [Robinson] has been led to ask some radical questions about his faith . . . No question can be too radical, but one must ask whether the questions are rightly put, as well as whether they are rightly answered, and still more whether the answers are not incomplete."

JOHN LAWRENCE,
in The Honest to God Debate,
edited by John A. T. Robinson and David L. Edwards

I

"MRS. ASHWORTH —what a surprise!" I exclaimed, somehow pulling myself together. "How nice of you to phone!"

"I meant to phone long ago," said my heroine apologetically, "but social events multiplied at just the wrong moment and then to cap it all Charles, poor love, had to do his stint of reading the prayers in the House of Lords—which always puts him in such a bad mood because if he travels up to London daily the journey exhausts him and if he stays up in town he gets cross thinking of the work he could be doing at home. Anyway, he's recovered now, I'm glad to say, and we were wondering if by any chance you were free to have dinner with us tonight."

I was so intrigued by this glimpse of a rough edge to Dr. Ashworth's glass-smooth episcopal life that I was at last diverted from jealous speculation about Dido. I said promptly: "I'd love to come, Mrs. Ashworth! Thanks so much."

"Splendid! Seven-thirty for dinner at eight? We'll look forward to seeing you," said Mrs. Ashworth, perfectly sincere but now exuding the deft social manner of a successful "Mrs. Bishop," and with her mission accomplished she set down the receiver.

BY the time I returned to my room I could clearly see that my queasy plunge into the pit of doubt was an emotional vagary, perhaps some form of psychological reaction to my previous unflawed euphoria. It was, of course, quite inconceivable that my Mr. Dean could still care for the monster. A saintly toleration would be the most a woman like that could ever expect from her husband—who, out of sheer chivalrous good taste, would never complain about her to the woman he loved. How could I ever have succumbed to that degrading pang of jealousy? Only by first allowing myself to flirt with the notion that in an eternal triangle all might not be quite as it seemed, but I was sure now that I knew exactly where reality lay. I had him to myself; Dido was irrelevant; the serpent was under control again.

Feeling infinitely better I began to plan what I should wear that evening at the South Canonry.

I DRESSED with care in a plain green linen dress with cream-coloured accessories (belt, Italian shoes, bag, all matching) and spent half an hour applying my make-up in the hope that Mrs. Ashworth would be impressed by my progress in making the best of myself. My horrible hair was at that "in-between" stage, not short enough to be tidy, not long enough to be spectacular, but I curbed its yak-like tendencies by shoving it into a French roll and spearing it with an interesting metal object, somewhat like a miniature rake, which I had bought at Boots. Deciding that I could have looked better but that I could also have looked infinitely worse, I tottered off on my high heels to the South Canonry.

Mrs. Ashworth was wearing a severely tailored navy-blue dress with a touch of white at the lapels, no jewellery and her sphinx-like smile. Her smooth, flawlessly dyed hair was immaculate and her creamy skin was a perfect example of subtle make-up. Only the unusually dark shade of her nylons hinted that she might need to cover up varicose veins, but otherwise her appearance, as always, constituted a triumph of art over age.

It was she herself who answered my ring at the front door. The episcopal cook-housekeeper, charwoman and secretary all lived out and had gone home before my arrival; the chaplain and the lay-chaplain had retired to their cottages nearby; the Bishop and Mrs. Bishop were now free to pretend they were just like any other well-to-do elderly couple with two grown sons and a pleasant home in the provinces.

"How well you look, Venetia!" said my heroine, regarding me with approval. "Positively glowing—and how clever of you to choose cream accessories for that smart dress!"

My spirits soared. I felt as if I had been awarded high marks in a vital examination.

In the drawing-room the Bishop, evidently enjoying a day off, was wandering around in a dark suit, which seemed to shout *Savile Row* from every seam, a snow-white shirt and a dark tie adorned with a motif which I (through lack of acquaintance with Cambridge University, perhaps) failed to recognise. I suddenly realised Dr. Ashworth must have a private income. He looked much too glossy to be maintained on a clerical salary, even a clerical salary of episcopal dimensions, and his wife's clothes too had the kind of simplicity which can only be achieved by a generous expenditure.

"Venetia! How nice to see you!" As he exuded his famous charm it was impossible to imagine him sulking about the chore of reading the prayers in the House of Lords, and suddenly I was more acutely aware than I had ever been of the gap existing between a private individual and his public persona. "I'm so glad you were able to come at such short notice," he was saying. "May I pay you the compliment of saying how delightful you look?"

"Yes, please!" I said, thinking how odd it was that the Bishop's distinguished good looks should leave me unmoved while the Dean could reduce me to pulp by a mere twitch of his sultry mouth.

"Drink, Venetia?" said Mrs. Ashworth.

I requested a gin-and-tonic. Both the Ashworths were drinking sherry.

"I bumped into your father the other day in the House of Lords," said the Bishop, pouring out an austere measure of gin. "He very kindly gave me dinner."

I tried not to look too surprised. My father, loyal to Aysgarth, was not in the habit of showering Dr. Ashworth with impromptu hospitality at Westminster.

"He asked after you, of course," said the Bishop, creating a lavish waterfall of tonic before handing me my glass, "and I felt rather guilty that I couldn't give him more news."

"But I've written my parents a line every week since I've been at the Chantry!"

"Yes, he said he was grateful to know you were still alive but he was anxious for more details."

"Parents are so inquisitive," said Mrs. Ashworth casually, offering me a cigarette. "They simply can't help themselves. Michael says it's a terrible failing."

"Oh, but my parents aren't normally inquisitive at all!" I said, very suspicious now of my father's uncharacteristic behaviour and wondering in alarm if he was on the brink of interfering in my affairs. "As I'm the youngest of six, they'd exhausted their capacity for being inquisitive long before I was born."

"Heavens, Lyle!" said the Bishop, giving me a light for my cigarette. "Where would we be now if we'd had six children?"

"In the grave," said Mrs. Ashworth, exercising a dead-pan humour, and added without a pause: "Charles did his best to reassure your father, Venetia. I don't think you need worry too much."

"Perhaps not, but I'd better pour a little oil on the troubled waters." Obviously my father, having concluded I was drifting along aimlessly as usual, was revving himself up to intervene on a grand scale. "I'll ring my mother. I suppose I should have phoned before but I was waiting until I had some interesting news to impart."

"Maybe I can provide it!" said Dr. Ashworth, finally sitting down. "I was very struck by your disclosure yesterday that you're looking for a job in Starbridge. Would you by any chance be interested in working for me on a part-time basis?"

I nearly dropped my glass.

"Charles is anxious to write a book," said Mrs. Ashworth, following on from her husband with such effortless fluency that I was reminded of a pair of acrobats pirouetting together on the high wire, "and since his secretary's seriously overworked he feels he can't ask her to take on such a substantial new project."

"I'd pay the top rate, of course," the Bishop chimed in with such perfect timing that I even began to wonder if the dialogue had been rehearsed. However, I came to the conclusion that it was not the dialogue but the stylish marital double-act which had been rehearsed, time and again, in the past whenever the Bishop and his wife had worked together on a scheme dear to both their hearts. "I can't say for certain how long the job would last," Dr. Ashworth was adding, "but I'd estimate a minimum of three months."

"How very exciting!" I said, finally finding my tongue. "Am I allowed to ask what the book will be about?"

"I intend to demolish *Honest to God* by John Robinson, the Bishop of Woolwich."

I nearly dropped my glass again.

"Charles adores demolition work," said his wife serenely. "His first book demolished the Arian heresy. He's never looked back since."

"Super!" I said. It seemed the safest banality to utter.

"The biggest difficulty about this job from your point of view," resumed the Bishop, conveying moderate anxiety by a slight furrowing of the brow, "is that as I'll be dictating the book in my spare time your hours will be somewhat irregular, but my wife tells me you dislike the conventional nine-to-five routine so perhaps you'll take this snag in your stride. It would be easier if I could dictate into a Dictaphone, but I've never been able to establish a satisfactory working relationship with a machine."

"So like a clergyman!" murmured his wife. "Always has to have an audience when he holds forth."

"Nonsense!" said the Bishop good-humouredly. "The truth is machines encourage verbosity, whereas if one talks to human beings one has to stick to the point or else they fall asleep. I shall depend very much on the quality of your reaction," he added to me with a smile, "in order to gauge how accurately I'm hitting the nail on the head."

"Robinson's supposed to be writing for the intelligent layman, benign to the Church and interested in theology," said Mrs. Ashworth, "and Charles wants to do the same. Then he remembered you'd heard of *Soundings* and knew the meaning of 'metanoia,' so—"

"—so I realised you'd be ideal for the job," said the Bishop, turning on the full force of his charm as the Ashworth double-act pirouetted gracefully to its finale on the high wire. "Do say you'll take it on!"

I had a quick think. At least episcopal employment would stop my father barging into my new life and accusing me of drifting. And the job would without doubt give me the best possible reason for remaining in Starbridge; any embryonic suspicions would be instantly annihilated. I had a brief vision of Aysgarth, listening with avid amusement as I recounted every detail of the Bishop's fulminations against *Honest to God,* and the next moment my mind was made up. Returning Dr. Ashworth's smile I said with sincerity: "Thanks so much, Bishop—I'm immensely flattered. When would you like me to start work?"

4

THE Bishop declared he wanted to start work as soon as possible but was then reminded gently by his wife of his numerous engagements for the coming week. Finally we agreed that I would present myself at the South Canonry on the following Monday at nine o'clock; since he took his day off on Mondays he would have the leisure to make an early start, but on Tuesdays, Wednesdays, Thursdays and Fridays he would be obliged to postpone me until five and might even be obliged to cancel me altogether if he had a long afternoon engagement. At these set times he would dictate for an hour and afterwards I could type up my notes whenever I wished. What kind of a typewriter would I like? He would hire any machine I fancied. He quite realised that a smart London secretary would expect only the best equipment.

"I'd like an IBM Electric," I said, deciding to play up to this glamorous image he was imposing on me. In 1963 only the most favoured super-secretaries in London were blessed with this great dream-machine. "But I don't know whether you'd be able to hire one in Starbridge."

The Bishop said he was sure the biggest office equipment firm would be delighted to track down an IBM Electric especially for him. What a treat it would be to have a secretary who was young and up-to-date! He would have to take care that Miss Peabody didn't become jealous; he foresaw he was going to wind up delectably pampered.

"Yes, darling," said Mrs. Ashworth, "but before you get carried away by your luscious masculine pipe-dream, try pampering Venetia by offering her another drink."

I surrendered my glass with relief. I had in fact been feeling thirsty for some time.

"You must order all the stationery you need from Paige's in Chasuble Lane," said the Bishop to me as he flashed the gin bottle at my glass and again drowned the result ruthlessly with tonic. "Miss Peabody will give you a letter of authorisation. Incidentally, thinking of Miss Peabody, I hope I don't dictate too fast for you. She sometimes has trouble keeping up with me."

"I have a certificate for a hundred and forty words a minute," I said reassuringly, playing the super-secretary for all I was worth, but in fact God only knew what my shorthand speed was by that time. It was some years since I had sweated blood scribbling hieroglyphics at a breakneck pace in the classroom, and I had never bothered to sweat much blood since.

"A hundred and forty words a minute!" marvelled the Bishop. "A real Rolls-Royce of a secretary! I doubt if Miss Peabody can even reach ninety."

"Well, darling," said Mrs. Ashworth, rising to her feet, "if you'll excuse me I'll leave you for a moment with your Rolls-Royce while I toss off a few miracles in the kitchen."

Immediately the Bishop began to ask me about my past jobs. His sympathetic interest was very appealing and I had no doubt he was sincere, in the sense that he genuinely wanted to find out more about me, but nevertheless I found it quite impossible to tell whether this desire sprang from a detached curiosity or a Christian concern or a mixture of the two. I came to the conclusion that he was fundamentally unreadable. His professional persona was so strong that he resembled a book cast in bronze.

However, no sooner had I reached this sinister conclusion than his elder son telephoned from Cambridge and at once the Bishop's manner changed. The professional charm and well-oiled pastoral skills were discarded. The suave prelate vanished. In his place appeared a friendly father, relaxed, affable and unaffected. Evidently with Charley the Bishop could be himself.

"Can't wait to see you again, old chap," he said at the end of the conversation. "There'll be so much to talk about."

I tried to imagine either of my parents saying such words to me but my imagination was unequal to the challenge. I could only comment lamely after the Bishop had replaced the receiver: "I suppose that since Charley's going into the Church you have a lot in common with him."

"That's true," said Dr. Ashworth with unexpected simplicity. "I'm so lucky to have Charley. He's a very great blessing to me." And then as he looked past me I glanced over my shoulder and saw Mrs. Ashworth was standing in the doorway.

"So that was Charley," she said, moving back into the room to join us. "I was hoping it was Michael." She smiled at me. "Michael's like you," she said. "Saddled with elderly parents whom he finds incurably 'square.' "

"My dear Lyle!" exclaimed the Bishop, effortlessly concealing himself again behind the mask of his formidable charm. "I'm sure Michael would remain devoted to us even if we were hexagonal! How are the miracles going in the kitchen?"

"All performed. 'Dinner, my lord,' as the butlers used to say to bishops in the old days, 'is served.' "

I knocked back my gin-flavoured tonic and wondered anxiously if there would be wine to accompany the meal.

5

TO my relief the Bishop offered me a decent claret to accompany the delicious *boeuf bourguignon* which, so Mrs. Ashworth told me without shame, had been produced earlier by the cook-housekeeper. There were fresh vegetables and some crusty French bread. I had been indifferent to food since the onset of my grand passion, but landing a job with the Bishop had made me hungry and I now settled down to indulge in the sin of gluttony with the necessary civilised restraint.

The conversation soon began to bounce along at a brisk pace. I found myself engaged in discussing John Freeman's television programme *Face to Face,* speculating about the play based on C. P. Snow's *The Masters* (due to open in London at the end of the month), debating how far *Lord of the Flies* reflected the truth about British schoolboys, damning the architecture of the new Guildford Cathedral, analysing the brand of existentialism currently being purveyed by Jean-Paul Sartre and reflecting on Dr. Ashworth's assertion that theologians should fight the impulse to hitch their wagons to the philosophy which was currently in favour among the intelligentsia.

"If I may repeat the immortal opinion held by Dean Inge," concluded Dr. Ashworth, "he who marries the spirit of the age will quickly find himself a widower."

"So you don't approve of Dr. Robinson embracing Tillich's existentialism?" I enquired boldly, remembering a comment made by Eddie in the Hebrides. By this time I had downed two glasses of claret and staged a fighting recovery from my ethereal gin-and-tonics.

"A bishop who is apparently ignorant of various basic theological concepts—who misuses, for instance, the word 'supernatural'—is most unlikely to grasp the complexities of a theologian like Tillich. What Robinson has done is to pluck some quotations from the Tillich canon and declare them to be in some way magically relevant to the 1960s. But that's not serious scholarship. That's journalism."

"But I thought Dr. Robinson *was* a serious scholar!"

"He's done some sound work on the New Testament," conceded Dr. Ashworth graciously, "but in writing *Honest to God* he's moved right out of his depth."

"The moral of the whole story," said Mrs. Ashworth, "is never read avant-garde theology when you're confined to bed, as Robinson was, with a slipped disc; it can produce a fatal craving to write a scandalous book. More vegetables, Venetia?"

"No, thanks. But Bishop, surely Robinson's right to try to restate Christianity for modern man?"

"Who *is* this modern man Robinson keeps talking about?" said the Bishop. "And more interesting still, why is Robinson so obsessed with him? In my opinion he feels obliged to make amends for his privileged clerical background by being sentimental about the unchurched masses, but if he'd actually grown up among the unchurched masses—as I did, coming not from the Cathedral Close at Canterbury but from Surrey's outstandingly secular 'stockbrokers' belt'—he'd regard them far more realistically, I assure you."

"But are you saying modern man doesn't exist?" I pursued, determined not to be diverted by speculation about Dr. Robinson's psychology. By this time my tongue was almost hanging out for a third glass of claret.

"Modern times exist," said the Bishop, replacing the stopper in the claret decanter, "but modern man, I fear, remains his ancient, sinful self. Darling, is there pudding or do we graduate straight to cheese?"

"There's a rather extraordinary syllabub. Are you brave enough to sample it, Venetia?"

I said I was feeling brave enough for anything, and for a while the conversation veered towards cookery, but eventually as I dug into some Stilton and pined—fruitlessly—for a glass of port, I was able to return to the Bishop's subtle attempt to undermine Robinson's credibility.

"Dr. Ashworth, is it really your thesis that the driving force behind the writing of *Honest to God* was Robinson's inverted ecclesiastical snobbery?"

"Not entirely, of course," the Bishop had to admit, "but I think I'm making a valid comment on the origins of his compulsion to slate the Church, pander to atheists and attempt to redesign God to suit some mythical variety of *Homo sapiens* which he's pleased to describe as 'modern man.' I'm afraid his current antics only remind me of those young people who rebel against their conventional middle-class families by becoming rabid Marxists."

"Heavens, I hope Michael doesn't go red!" said Mrs. Ashworth, much struck by this parallel. "That really would be the last straw."

"My dear," said the Bishop, "this family may be middle-class, but I don't think I'd call it conventional."

"Surely no one who's entitled to be addressed as 'my Lord Bishop' can seriously continue to consider himself middle-class," I said, reluctantly abandoning all hope of a glass of port.

"Oh, that's just window-dressing," said the Bishop airily. "Just part of my current worldly trappings. It doesn't alter my basic ingredients at all."

"Darling, you sound like a recipe in need of a good cook," said Mrs. Ashworth, "but I'm going to leave you to simmer on the stove while I whisk Venetia away to my sitting-room. Give me a shout if you need stirring."

We withdrew first to the kitchen, where coffee had percolated for us. Apparently the Bishop never drank coffee in the evening, but Mrs. Ashworth produced two large mugs, each adorned with a painting of the Cathedral, and we prepared to overdose on caffeine. I liked the idea of drinking post-prandial coffee out of mugs; the rejection of the conventional *demi-tasse* struck me as being both pragmatic and adventurous.

"I wanted to talk to you on your own anyway," Mrs. Ashworth was saying as we settled ourselves in her plant-less, flower-less sitting-room, "but I also felt I had to remove you before Charles lost control and embarked on another *Honest to God* sermon. What on earth did clergy-men talk about before that book appeared? I honestly find it hard to remember."

"Have you read it, Mrs. Ashworth?"

"Yes—in bed, so that Charles could nudge me whenever I dozed off."

"Thank heavens—I thought I was the only one who found it tough going!"

"I think a lot of laymen find it tough going but nobody dares say so."

We smiled at each other. After the effort of sustaining such an intellec-tual conversation at the dinner-table without benefit of a substantial infusion of alcohol, I was finding it a relief to relax with my sympathetic hostess.

"Have a chocolate," said Mrs. Ashworth, opening a box of Cadbury's Milk Tray, "and tell me everything. How are you getting on with that charming little glamour-puss Marina Markhampton?"

"Amazingly well," I said, selecting an orange cream. "You mightn't think it, but she's not the usual cat-about-town at all. She puts a high value on friendship with girls and she's not stupid."

"I think Michael's wishing she could put a higher value on friendship with men!"

"I bet he does! He's madly attractive," I added generously, "although of course much too young for me."

Mrs. Ashworth smiled and said: "What did you think of the other men at the party?"

"Oh, they were all fabulous, Mrs. Ashworth—except for Katie's brother Simon who insists on treating women as if they were horses."

"All whips and lumps of sugar?"

"All slaps on the rump and hearty laughter. I reeled with relief into the orbit of Christian's Winchester chum Perry Palmer who lives at Albany and keeps curious Japanese prints in a room he refuses to specify."

"Sounds more intriguing. Is Perry the one who's attracted you?"

I sipped my coffee and said: "What makes you think I'm attracted by anyone?"

"Oh, my dear! A little while ago this interesting but dowdy girl tells me with deep gloom that she's on the sidelines of life because no man has ever found her attractive. Tonight this same interesting girl, now transformed into a radiant young woman coruscating with charm and glamour, appears in my drawing-room and inspires my normally level-headed husband to burble about secretarial Rolls-Royces! Of course I'm just a clergyman's wife," said Mrs. Ashworth, as if she were the unworldly partner of an innocent curate in some country parish far from the fleshpots of Mammon, "but it does occur even to me, in my ancient respectability, that this particular Rolls-Royce is currently running on some very high-quality petrol indeed. But I don't want to pry. Would you rather talk of something else?"

"Not before I've thanked you for all those compliments! And I really am very excited about being the Bishop's Rolls-Royce. May I ask . . . was it you who suggested the idea to him?"

"No, he thought of it all by himself," said Mrs. Ashworth, as if the Bishop were an exceptionally clever small child. "I simply egged him on. By the way, have you found a flat yet?"

"No, I must have a blitz on the estate agents tomorrow."

"Well, before you start blitzing perhaps you'd like to consider an idea of mine. Do you know Archdeacon Lindsay?"

"Only by reputation. Primrose is mad about him."

"Then you'll probably know that the Archdeaconry of Starbridge is attached to the benefice of St. Martin's-in-Cripplegate—which means, among other things, that the Lindsays live in the centre of Starbridge at St. Martin's vicarage. At the bottom of the vicarage garden are the old stables, and on the first floor of these stables there's currently a vacant flat. The building has its own entrance on Butchers' Alley, so you wouldn't have to worry about Mr. and Mrs. Archdeacon spying on all your comings and goings, and on the ground floor, which Mr. Lindsay uses as a garage, I'm sure there'd be room for your car. Michael was telling me that you have this snazzy little MG—"

"And I was worried about finding parking once I'd left the Close! Mrs. Ashworth, you're a genius. How big is this place?"

"Small bedroom, large living-room, kitchen and bathroom. The previous archdeacon had the flat made to house his mother-in-law, who was an awful old fusspot, so I'd imagine it's reasonably comfortable."

"It's quite obviously paradise. How do I get an appointment to view?"

"Shall I phone Mrs. Lindsay now? She's a nice woman, I think you'll like her—and she's trying so hard to marry off her four daughters that I guarantee she'll be much too busy to breathe down your neck."

"The ideal landlady presiding over the ideal flat where I shall live while I work at the ideal job! Do you realise, Mrs. Ashworth, that you and your husband have just redesigned to perfection my entire life in Starbridge?" I said, radiant with gratitude, and it was only when she gave her sphinx-like smile that it occurred to me to wonder why she and the Bishop had decided to take so much trouble over a young woman they hardly knew.

IX

"God, Tillich was saying, is not a projection 'out there,' an Other beyond the skies, of whose existence we have to convince ourselves, but the Ground of our very being . . ."

"For assertions about God are in the last analysis assertions about Love—about the ultimate ground and meaning of personal relationships."

JOHN A. T. ROBINSON
HONEST TO GOD

I

WHEN I arrived back at the Chantry I stumbled across a large envelope which was lying on the hall floor by the front door. It was marked: "The Hon. Venetia Flaxton," and in one corner Aysgarth had printed "BY HAND."

"Coo-ee!" shouted Marina, who was watching television in the drawing-room. "How was Anti-Sex Ashworth?"

"Thundering about the sinfulness of man!"

The telephone rang. As I hesitated in the hall with the envelope in my hands I heard Marina say: "Robert! What a lovely surprise! I was afraid you might be Michael or Don . . ."

I sped upstairs, shut myself in my room, ripped open the envelope and pulled out the contents. In addition to the May issue of the Cathedral magazine there were two letters. The first read:

My dear Venetia,

I was delighted to see you at Holy Communion this morning, and I thought you might like to see the latest edition of our magazine. My leading article, dealing with the importance of art in connection with religion, may remind you of my recent attempt to have the beautiful painting of the cat in the St. Anselm manuscript made available to a wider public in the form of a picture-postcard. In sending you my blessings, I remain your affectionate friend,

N.N.A.

The second letter read:

My darling Venetia—my Egeria!

I felt I must write and tell you how wonderful it was to see you this morning—I could have murdered that old stick Gilbert for tottering into the library just as your narrative describing the Orgy was becoming delectably racy! How I wish *I* could have gone to a party like that when I was young, but I never did, not even up at Oxford; I was the wrong class, didn't know the right people, had no money, etc., etc., and anyway I had to work so hard to "get on" that I could ill afford to take time off for pleasure. Never mind, I can now enjoy youthful orgies vicariously, through you!

You looked quite ravishing in your party gown—and equally ravishing in that striped frock you were wearing this morning, and how I managed to avoid "pouncing" on you (as you would say) in the manner of young Michael Ashworth as we stood side by side gazing at Puss-in-Boots I can't imagine. Incidentally I was quite shocked by your description of Michael, and I'm sure none of *my* boys would ever carry on in that tasteless fashion. I'm sure—indeed I hope!—they've done some hard chasing in their time, but young drunks who "grope" (as you put it) in public are most definitely not amusing, and I've always impressed on my boys—though by example, not by sermons, I hasten to add—that women should be put on pedestals and reverenced.

Dear me, how strait-laced that sounds! And as you know I'm not a bit strait-laced, I pride myself on my liberal outlook, but although I passionately believe that sexual love is good and right, I utterly disapprove of behaviour which is self-centred and lacking in respect for the opposite sex—and thus uncivilised to the point of vulgarity. Someone once remarked that the biggest argument against immorality is that it's in such bad taste. (Could this have been Oscar Wilde? But no, Wilde would surely have turned the comment inside out and declared: "The biggest argument against immorality is that it's in such *good* taste!") Of course the remark about bad taste is an exaggeration, but there's an element of truth in it because man was made to reach for the stars, not to roll around in the mud—and now we're definitely in Wilde's territory; do you remember that line from *Lady Winder-*

mere's Fan: "We're all in the gutter but some of us are looking up at the stars"? Maybe I'll preach on that theme soon and stress that we should *all* be star-gazing. How I'd love to see the Bishop's face if I took Oscar Wilde for my text!

I'm enclosing the Cathedral magazine because I need an excuse for delivering this missive by hand—and I also enclose a fake letter for you to show Marina in case she sees me pop the envelope through the letter-box. I intend to entrust my letters to the post in future, but I was so bursting to communicate with you that I thought I must just take one little risk! Now darling, remember your promise and write back *instantly.* Our rendez-vous on Wednesday afternoon is still (as I write this) forty-two hours away and I can't wait till then to hear from you. Much, *much* love,

NEVILLE.

2

"MY darling Mr. Dean," I wrote later after Marina had retired yawning to bed.

I adored both your letters, even the fake one, and thought your article about art was fabulous. Do keep on with your crusade to get Puss-in-Boots on a postcard!

So glad you wanted to pounce on me in the library—I bet your pounces are everything pounces should be (private and paradisiacal) and not ghastly plunges made in an alcoholic fog (public and puke-worthy). But I'm not sure I really want to be put on a pedestal and reverenced—unless, of course, the reverence came in the form of regular dusting of the most stimulating variety.

But before you produce your duster, "get a load of this!" (as Dinkie would say). There have been sensational goings-on at the South Canonry where I've just dined off an extraordinary syllabub and a measure of claret so small that all I could do was inhale it. That famous double-act, Dr. and Mrs. A., kidnapped Yours Truly, and as the result of my incarceration beneath the episcopal roof I'm on the point of winding up in the Archdeacon's lap! I'm also on the point of winding up on the episcopal pay-roll, as my Lord Bishop has bribed me to work for him by offering me an immense salary and an IBM dream-machine.

He vows—wait for it!—to demolish the divine Dr. Robinson in a new book (to be dictated at odd hours to the Hon. V. Flaxton, super-secretary) and his wife implies this will be his biggest demolition job since he took an axe to the Arian heresy in his gilded youth. He's a little nervous of his secretary, an item called Peabody (I didn't dare ask how many bishops she'd served under!) but he fancies he can get away with taking me on as a luxury and he's already referring to me as a secretarial Rolls-Royce.

This letter, designed to form part of a lurid best-seller entitled *How to Get On in the Church of England: A Guide for Single Girls under Thirty,* comes to you with best love from your devoted

EGERIA.

P.S. Why on *earth* have I been so suddenly marked out for this extraordinary episcopal attention? Did Dr. A. play Peeping Tom after all as we sat on Lady Mary? Could he conceivably regard me as a "lost girl" who has to be "redeemed"? (I seem to remember that Gladstone underwent similar behavioural problems when he kept bringing prostitutes home to tea.) Any light you can throw on this bizarre situation would be greatly appreciated.

The next morning, on my journey to the newsagent's shop beyond St. Anne's Gate to buy the *Daily Mail,* I dropped the letter in the pillar-box on the North Walk and had the satisfaction of knowing it would catch the first post. To my amazement it reached the Deanery by the second post that morning. (The post then was not nearly so bad as it is now, but even in 1963 such extraordinary speed was a notable occurrence.) Aysgarth wrote back that afternoon, and the following morning, the day of our rendez-vous, I was ripping open the envelope.

"My darling Venetia," I read.

I'm truly appalled by this episcopal skulduggery which is driving you into the Archdeacon's lap—does Mrs. Lindsay know you intend to use this singularly unattractive archidiaconal feature as a resting-place?—and I'm *very worried indeed* about this "dream-machine" you mentioned. It sounds exceedingly improper. The initials IBM are, of course, quite unknown to me since clergymen should have better things to do with their time than read articles in *The Times* about American corporations, but in my opinion all single girls under thirty who aspire to "get on" in the Church of England should regard such questionable modern devices, labelled IBM or otherwise, with suspicion.

My Lord Bishop's daring in risking the wrath of Miss Peabody is second only to his nerve in engaging my Egeria to string his pearls of wisdom—or, as would seem more likely, his fake-pearls of folly. If he were to spend more time reconstructing the Christian faith for our day and age, as our hero Robinson is doing, and less time demolishing what he's pleased to call heresy, the level of church attendance in the diocese of Starbridge might conceivably rise from its present all-time low! My dearest, must you really indulge in esoteric rites with your dream-machine in the company of this over-educated reactionary? How can I save you from such a sinister fate at the South Canonry, and how, for goodness' sake, can I prevent you winding up in the Archdeacon's lap? This letter comes to you with best love from your devoted but deeply concerned MR. DEAN, now to be addressed by you *(please!)* as

NEVILLE.

P.S. No need to worry about the Ashworths. To me the explanation of the unprecedented benevolence is simple: (1) The Bishop's reached the age when he'd far rather dictate his rubbish to a gorgeous young creature like you than to a hideous old hag like Peabody; (2) Mrs. Bishop has reached the age when she wants to compensate herself for her absent sons by acquiring a substitute daughter, and (3) they may well be engaged in a conspiracy to capture you as a girlfriend—perhaps even as a wife—for Charley, whose continuing lack of interest in girls would be enough to worry any parents who want a normal life for their son.

P.P.S. As soon as we meet in the courtyard of the Staro Arms I shall demand an explanation of the Archdeacon's lap!

Longing to see you,

N.

3

"I THOUGHT this moment would never come!" said Aysgarth as I scrambled into the front seat of his dusty Humber that afternoon. "My darling, you're looking like a pre-Raphaelite Guinevere, radiating mysterious allure, and how Lyle Ashworth dares to leave you alone with a sex-obsessed Bishop and a dream-machine I can't think. What's the news from the Archdeacon's lap?"

The Humber had halted seconds earlier in the courtyard of Starbridge's oldest hotel, a former medieval hostelry rumoured to have been patronised by Chaucer. No native of Starbridge seriously believed this fable, but it made fine fodder for the tourists and had spawned a cottage-industry which produced cheap mugs adorned with pictures of Chaucer fondling a quill pen.

As Aysgarth enquired about the Archdeacon's lap he spun the car into a three-point turn and with an anguished squeal of tires the Humber shot out of the courtyard into Eternity Street. I had long suspected that Aysgarth was a racing-driver manqué; whenever he was behind the wheel of a car he seemed to be celebrating an escape from his life as an eminent churchman. That afternoon he was wearing an ancient pair of grey flannel trousers, a faded blue shirt which was stretched tightly across his midriff, no tie and a shabby tweed jacket which looked as if it had been rescued from a jumble sale. His white hair was bedraggled, suggesting that he had repeatedly run his fingers through it in a fever of romantic impatience, and as he smiled at me he revealed his square, raffish teeth, proved indisputably genuine by the fact that they were out of alignment. (I suspected the Bishop possessed dentures; his teeth were far too even to be true.) As soon as I had entered the car I had been aware of a fascinating odour of cigarettes and Lux soap overlaid with a faint, tantalising whiff of whisky.

"My darling Mr. Dean!" I exclaimed impulsively. "How exciting you are! Just like an English version of James Cagney!"

He laughed and laughed. At the hump-backed bridge which spanned the river, the car swooped up and down so wildly that my stomach seemed to hit the soles of my feet, but all he gasped as I shrieked was: "Isn't life fun?"

We drove on in ecstasy out of the city.

4

"... SO I'm all set to take up residence in the Archdeacon's lap next week," I said, concluding my report on the flat in Butchers' Alley as the city rapidly vanished into the distance behind us. "My own home at last! The moment I move in I shall put a rose between my teeth, open a bottle of champagne and loll naked on a tiger-skin rug beneath a poster of Elvis Presley!"

"I must lurk beneath the window with a periscope! Do you really have a tiger-skin rug?"

"No. I don't approve of skinning cats."

"Neither do I. By the way, talking of cats," said Aysgarth as the car roared down the valley towards the hills which marked the beginning of Starbury Plain, "I was all set to fight for Puss-in-Boots again at yesterday's Chapter meeting, but I never got the chance. That fatuous ass Fitzgerald, who's long been seduced by the Parish and People Movement, started nagging me to make the Sung Communion the main service on Sunday mornings and call it a Eucharist, and by the time I'd beaten him off—"

"But isn't that just a High Church fad?"

"Yes, but now we've got an Archbishop of Canterbury who runs around in a purple cassock instead of a decent pair of gaiters the Catholic wing of the Church of England thinks it can get away with anything."

"No Popery!"

"Well, one mustn't be bigoted. Certainly as a liberal I favour ecumenism—unity for all Christians—even though it's no good expecting the Roman Catholics to do anything except kick us in the teeth. The first move towards unity will have to come from them."

"So while you wait you amuse yourself by beating up the Anglo-Catholics whenever they get too Romish!"

He laughed. "Oh, I can be charitable towards the Anglo-Catholics—with an effort! That's the point of the Church of England—Catholics and Protestants are united under one umbrella. But no one's going to catch *me* tinkering with the Communion service and destroying the basic pattern of Sunday worship in the name of some half-baked liturgical fashion which seduces every High Churchman in sight! Low Church by inclination I may be, having been brought up by evangelical Non-Conformists, but in worship I've always tried to follow the Church of England's famous 'Middle Way,' the road between the extremes of Catholic and Protestant practice, and it's in the name of that 'Middle Way' that I absolutely refuse to downgrade Sunday Matins. 'Over my dead body,' I said to Fitzgerald—"

"What bad luck that you should be saddled with an Anglo-Catholic canon!"

"Oh, there'll be murder done in our Chapter meetings yet, I swear it! No good looking to the Bishop for support, of course; you've only got to mention the word 'Eucharist' to him and he's off on some outstandingly boring dissertation on the Early Church—"

"But the Bishop's not an Anglo-Catholic, is he?"

"No, but he has Catholic leanings. He's keen on confession and retreats—and he's always saying that every clergyman should have a spiritual director—"

"Have you got one?"

"Certainly not! Using an intermediary in dealing with God is a very Catholic concept, and anyway my soul's my own business; I don't want some stranger messing around with it, and in my opinion agonising over one's spiritual life simply encourages morbid introspection. God helps those who help themselves—although of course," said Aysgarth, becoming cautious as if he had suddenly realised he was being too dogmatic, "sometimes in very difficult situations one's unable to help oneself. Then one does indeed need the help of an older clergyman of great spiritual wisdom. But usually such occasions are rare." He paused before adding: "I used to talk to Bishop Bell occasionally about various private problems. I've missed him since he died in '58."

"You don't feel tempted to unburden yourself to your current father-in-God Bishop Ashworth?"

"What an appalling thought! No, I'll leave that sort of charade to Fitzgerald. What a bishop! What a canon! Or as Cicero would have said—"

"*O tempora!*" I quoted. "*O mores!*"

"My darling!" He turned his head to smile at me in delight and the car nearly plunged into the ditch. I screamed lightly but I was enjoying myself too much to care whether or not we veered off the road. I was enthralled by his frank talk about the Chapter, and I felt as privileged as if I had been listening to the Prime Minister describing the private feuds of his publicly united cabinet.

By this time we had left the main road and were zipping along a country lane. A wandering cow bellowed in horror as we shot past within inches of its flank. The occasional pot-hole tested the durability of the back axle. The car panted uphill with all the zest of a bloodhound pounding across wide open spaces. We were now climbing onto Starbury Plain, and as we left the trees of the valley behind, the bare hills began to level out around us to form a vast, undulating plain.

"Can't you get rid of Fitzgerald, Mr. Dean?"

"No cause, I assure you, is dearer to my heart, but unfortunately removal isn't so easy . . . Darling, do stop calling me 'Mr. Dean' now that we're alone together! I—heavens above, here's the car-park! I nearly missed it."

The brakes squealed, the tires screeched and the car behind us gave a blast on the horn. Cutting our speed violently in a few hair-raising seconds, Aysgarth swung the Humber off the road into the parking area laid out by the National Trust when it had acquired the acres surrounding the famous ancient monument, Starbury Ring. This megalithic stone circle, reached by a twenty-minute walk along a bridle-path, was fortunately unpopular with the majority of modern tourists, most of whom preferred to avoid exercise. On that afternoon there were no coaches in the parking area and only a couple of cars. No one was in sight. The cars' occupants had all disappeared over the brow of the hill on their way to the Ring.

"What shall we do?" said Aysgarth, switching off the engine. "Walk or luxuriate?"

"Oh, luxuriate—much more fun!" I said at once, remembering that he too, like most tourists, shied away from exercise.

He sighed and gazed without enthusiasm at the bridle-path. "I really should walk," he said. "It would be good for me."

"It would be even better for you if you relaxed here in the car and told me all about *Honest to God*!"

He laughed and quoted: " 'I can resist everything except temptation!' " Then he reached out and clasped my hand.

5

BUT in fact he resisted temptation well. Apart from clasping and squeezing my hands he attempted no other torrid activity; he seemed far more interested in indulging in stimulating conversation. At the end of our interlude he said with a sigh: "This has been such fun—what a pity we can't stay longer!" And he gave me a peck on the cheek. Back in Starbridge he dropped me in Eternity Street so that we could return separately to the Close, blew me a kiss, breathed some passionate parting words and disappeared in a cloud of exhaust fumes.

Staring after him I tried to work out why I felt not merely disappointed but confused.

6

"*MY* darling Neville," I wrote that night at the Chantry.

It was marvellous to see you today without everyone breathing down our necks, and many thanks for explaining the first part of *Honest to God*.

I paused. I was sitting at the table in the dining-room and across the hall in the drawing-room Marina was engaged in a telephone conversation with Katie Aysgarth. Christian had finally sent Marina a note of thanks for the Orgy and she had used this communication as an excuse to ring him up, but Katie had soon followed her husband to the phone, and as I listened I realised Marina was being invited to Oxford as soon as Lady Markhampton had returned home. Marina's expressions of gratitude were numerous and ecstatic; she appeared to give no thought to the masculine groans which would erupt when she cancelled her London dates, and soon she was gossiping away to Katie on the theme of how awful all men were except Christian. I was now more convinced than ever that their eternal triangle was very odd indeed.

Meanwhile that other odd person, Perry Palmer, had phoned me to confess that the curious Japanese prints were a fiction but that he would be delighted to show me instead another great curiosity, his full coal-cellar, whenever I returned to London; it was an old joke among Christian's friends that Perry, whose set in Albany had hardly been altered since Victorian days, had absent-mindedly ordered a vast quantity of coal for his fireplaces shortly before London had been declared a smokeless zone. Amused by the flaunting of this legendary museum-piece I promised to phone him when I was next up in town; I had already decided that Perry could replace Eddie as my smoke-screen, deflecting the world's attention from the real object of my passion.

The thought of the object of my passion prompted me to turn back to my letter. "Of course Robinson's absolutely right," I wrote fluently.

We can't go on thinking of God as an old man in the sky who made a space-trip to Bethlehem two thousand years ago, dressed up as Christ, and left the universe untended. Much better to chuck away all those obsolete old myths and throw the whole Christian tradition in the melting-pot in order to recast the faith in terms that are intelligible to the secular mid-twentieth century! That's exactly what people of my generation want. We want to move forward from our parents' world, the world the war rendered obsolete, and create a world that's *new.* No more dead-wood, no more hidebound tradition that's meaningless, no more risible fairy-tales. Everything must be hard, cool, clear and unsentimental.

So no more talk of God as an old man in the sky who carries on like some irascible father-figure! People of my generation have quite enough trouble with their fathers without wanting a father-figure God! I think it was quite brilliant of Paul Tillich to say instead that God is the "Ground of Our Being," and I think it's even more brilliant of Robinson to pick up this definition and develop it. To think of God as being present throughout the whole world, present in some mysterious way deep down inside us, is much more meaningful than thinking of him as "out there," high up in some corner of the universe that the scientists can never quite find. How clever of Robinson to see that the concept of depth has so much more meaning for us today—after all the talk of "depth psychology"—than the concept of height!

Next time we meet you must move on from Tillich and tell me

about those other German theologians Robinson likes so much. I want to hear more about Bonhoeffer's "religionless Christianity" and Bultmann's "demythologising." (Does Bultmann really say that the only thing that matters is the message? How modern that sounds! Do you suppose he's ever worked in an advertising agency?)

It's agonising to think we have to wait a whole week to resume such a riveting conversation—please write *soon* to ease my torment!

Lashings of love,
EGERIA.

I had just tucked this letter in an envelope and was sealing the flap when Marina arrived in high spirits after her stimulating phone call. "Writing to the mysterious Mr. X?" she said. "I told Christian just now that I suspected you were on the brink of a mad affair with Perry, but Christian just said: 'Whoever the lucky man is, it certainly isn't my friend Peregrine'—which rather suggests, doesn't it, that he knows something about Perry that we don't. I wonder what went on when they were at school together . . . Do they swim in the nude at Winchester?"

"I should think they do a lot of things in the nude at Winchester."

"I was wondering about Perry's possible lack of genitalia."

"Perhaps all—or nothing, as the case may be—will be revealed to me when I inspect his coal-cellar."

"But seriously, Vinnie, who *is* this secret man in your life?"

"Jesus Christ. Everyone and no one. God—who's to be found in loving relationships. God's the Ground of Our Being. He's not up there in the sky—he's down here, deep down inside every one of us—"

"Darling, have you been hitting the gin?"

The telephone rang. Marina flitted away to answer it but flitted back to report: "It's churchy old Primrose—are you in or out?"

"Oh God! I'd better be in, but what a bore." Still clutching my unaddressed envelope I slunk to the phone. "Primrose! How thrilling to hear from you—how's life with the Archdeacon?"

"Well, that's just it," said Primrose, very cool. "The Archdeacon and I were just going over the minutes of the last meeting of the diocesan Board of Finance when he happened to mention—"

Mr. Lindsay had revealed I was about to move into his lap and work for the Bishop.

"Oh, didn't I tell you?" I said glibly. "Really, I'm getting so old that I'm forgetting what I said to who!"

"Rubbish!" said Primrose. "You've simply dropped me with such a bang that everyone in Starbridge must be deafened. Now look here,

Venetia. Is it anything I've said? Because if I've done something to offend you, I want to know so that I can put things right. You're my best friend, and—"

"Oh, Primrose . . ." I felt a complete heel. "No, it's nothing you've done, I promise—"

"Then I simply can't understand what you see in Marina Markhampton. She's so absolutely trivial, not worthy of someone with your brains. You're not having some ghastly lesbian affair with her, are you?"

"Honestly, Primrose! What a suggestion!"

"Dido says she's sure Marina's a lesbian."

"I'm surprised to find you listening to Dido!"

"Dido's very shrewd about who's carrying on with who. For instance, do you remember that alto-tenor with the long blond hair who sang in the Cathedral choir last year? Tommy Fitzgerald said Father ought to make the alto-tenor cut his hair to disguise the fact that he was obviously queer as a coot, but Dido just looked Fitzgerald straight in the eyes and said: 'My dear, he only pretends he's queer because he wants to cover up the fact that he's having an affair with the organist's wife.' The alto-tenor ran off with her a week later. Fitzgerald was livid—not with the alto-tenor, of course, but with Dido for being right."

"Well, if Dido thinks I'm having a lesbian wing-ding with Marina—"

"I didn't say Dido thinks that. Dido just thinks Marina's a lesbian. Dido's only comment on *you* is: 'If dear Venetia's lingering in Starbridge just for the thrill of working for the Bishop, I'd be very much surprised.' "

There was a silence.

"Hullo? Venetia?"

"Sorry, just trying to figure out what on earth Dido's getting at. Does she think I'm about to run off with the new alto-tenor?"

"Well, there's a rumor going around that you're madly in love—"

"Oh, my God! I make one drunken joke to Christian and for some perverse reason he chooses to broadcast it as gospel truth to all and sundry! There's no one, Prim, honestly—except perhaps Perry Palmer. He's just invited me to see his coal-cellar."

"Perry's a eunuch."

"Have you cast-iron evidence of that fact?"

"Well, no, but . . . I say, Venetia, you haven't finally discovered a mad passion for Eddie, have you?"

"Don't be revolting! Look, come and see me on Monday after I've moved into the Archdeacon's flat, and we'll knock back a bottle of champagne together to celebrate my acquisition of the new pad."

"I'll bring a bottle of sherry," said Primrose. "If I drink more than two glasses of champagne I get a headache."

"Oh, for God's sake, Prim, you drink your two glasses and I'll toss off the rest! You talk like an old maid sometimes!"

There was a pause. Then: "Sorry," I mumbled. "I didn't mean that. How's Maurice Tait?"

"Very well, thank you," said Primrose politely. "What time shall I come on Monday?"

"Oh, just roll along when you've finished work. It'll be fabulous to meet again!"

"Fabulous," said Primrose.

We said goodbye and hung up.

7

AFTER the conversation I spent several unpleasant seconds thinking of Dido's talent for discerning who was sleeping with whom, but then I dismissed her from my mind by recalling that in fact I was sleeping with no one and that there was no logical reason why she should regard me with suspicion. My episcopal job, socially glamorous and intellectually stimulating, was quite sufficient to justify my stay in Starbridge to all but the neurotically suspicious.

I then remembered that I had not yet summoned the energy to inform my parents of my great coup in landing a job with the Bishop, and it occurred to me that before they, like Dido, succumbed to the neurotic suspicion that I was on the brink of behaving like a decadent member of the aristocracy, I should pen the required letter without delay. Accordingly, having returned to my writing-case in the dining-room, I found a fresh sheet of paper and wrote:

Dear Mama,

I've rented a flat (12 Butchers' Alley) and intend to live in Starbridge for at least three months as from next Monday, in order to help Bishop Ashworth write his new book. My landlord is Archdeacon Lindsay. I don't anticipate being in London in the immediate future, but I might look in at Pauncefoot some time if you happen to be around. Meanwhile please try and stop Papa rampaging around the House of Lords, collaring prelates and badgering them with questions about me. I hope you and your plants are thriving.

Love,
VENETIA.

I spent five minutes trying to decide whether to provide my new telephone number but finally wrote it down as a postscript. I had realised that if one of my parents died I would feel guilty if the survivor was unable to contact me immediately.

"Writing letters again?" said Marina, nursing a cup of hot chocolate as she drifted into the room to say good night. "You write more letters than any girl I've ever met."

"Just keeping the parents happy." I began to address the envelope.

"Oh, parents!" said Marina. She spoke as if referring to a rare species of animal which existed only on the far side of the globe. On an impulse she sat down opposite me at the table and gave her hot chocolate a stir. "I've trained my mother never to expect a letter from me, but if you can keep your parents at bay with letters, maybe I've made a mistake. That weekly phone call I have to make is really a fearful bind."

I had by this time had ample experience of the weekly Markhampton phone call. Marina would sigh and moan beforehand, but the conversations with her mother always sounded happy enough. "Why don't you try talking to your father occasionally?" I said, folding the sheet of writing-paper in half. "It might provide a welcome variation in the routine."

"Oh, my father barely talks at all," said Marina. "Not to me anyway."

"What bliss." I began to slip the letter into the envelope and the silence that followed was broken only by the rustle of paper, but at last Marina said nonchalantly, so nonchalantly that I hardly realised what she was saying: "Well, I don't care. What the hell? He's not my real father anyway."

My tongue halted in its progress down the envelope's flap. Then I completed the lick and very carefully pressed down the seal. "No?" I murmured so vaguely that I sounded as if I were barely concentrating on the conversation. "I don't think I knew that."

"Oh, good. Sometimes one imagines the whole world's twittering about it behind one's back, so it's nice to know you weren't keeping quiet out of an urge to be tactful . . . I never quite know what you're thinking, Venetia. You're a bit of a mystery in some ways."

"Well, at the moment my thoughts are utterly predictable and completely mundane. I was wondering when you found out about this tiresome little kink in the family tree."

I had struck the right casual note. As she relaxed, stirring her hot chocolate, I realised she wanted neither sympathy nor a prurient curiosity but a detached interest which bordered on the clinical. All emotion had to be kept ruthlessly at bay.

"It happened last year," she said. "I was at that restaurant off Berkeley

Square—you know the one, all fish and dim lighting—and someone in the party said to me: 'Of course your real father's the art critic Walter Forrest, isn't he?' and I said: 'Of course, who else?' and then I didn't hear anything for five minutes—at which point I had to rush to the lavatory to be sick."

"I hope there wasn't some quizzy dragon on duty."

"I don't know what was on duty. All I remember now is the revolting pink carpet. Anyway, after that I decided to ask my mother about Walter Forrest—I was actually rather excited to think I'd been fathered by something intelligent—so eventually I cornered Mummy in her studio. She was painting the most sensational picture, lots of naked legs and pubic hair and stray breasts floating all over the place, and I don't think she really wanted to be interrupted but I stood my ground and said: 'So I'm Walter Forrest's bastard—how thrilling!' For a moment she just went on mixing her paints. Then she said: 'Don't worry, darling, Daddy and I both adore you and Walter's never been in the least interested in children. I'd forget all about him, if I were you.' I asked why I hadn't been told and she just said: 'I honestly didn't think it would make you happy.' I tried to explain that I felt a bit of a fool since obviously everyone knew except me, but she never batted an eyelid. 'Oh no!' she said. 'No one knows anything for certain, but you do have a great look of Walter and of course it's well-known that among our sort of people the last child in the family is often a cuckoo in the nest.' Then she went on painting. I wanted to ask her more but then I realised I had to find a lavatory and vomit again . . . Well, I mean, the scene really was rather pukeworthy, wasn't it?"

"Terribly dreary," I said. "What a drag." I suddenly realised I was creasing my mother's envelope at one corner with small, furtive movements of my fingers.

"Sorry to waffle on about something so sordid," said Marina, taking a sip of her hot chocolate. "I've never told any of my other girlfriends, but perhaps I was lured on this time because you're so much more soignée than they are. For instance, I'm sure you know all about what goes on among our sort of people, and anyway you're the last child in a family yourself, aren't you? I suppose I knew subconsciously that you'd understand."

"Uh-huh." I smoothed the crease out of the envelope. "Did you ever confront Walter Forrest?"

"Why do you think I got that job in the art gallery? When he turned up at one of the exhibitions, I marched straight up to him and said: 'I'm Marina, Alice Markhampton's daughter.' And he said: 'Oh yes? It's years since I've seen Alice. I hope she's well.' Then he turned his back on me and began to talk to someone else."

"Brute. I'd have clobbered him."

"It *was* a bit much, wasn't it? Oh, how I hated all men at that moment, *hated* them—in fact I still do sometimes, it comes over me in waves . . . although never when I'm with Christian, of course."

"I like Christian," I said. "I always have. But I don't know what goes on there."

"Then I'll tell you. He's good and decent and kind. That's why I love him. On that ghastly evening at the restaurant after I'd vomited in the pink-carpeted lavatory, it was Christian who took care of me. I couldn't tell him what was wrong and he didn't ask. He just got a taxi and brought me home and we drank tea together while he held my hand and told me all about how awful life was in the Middle Ages. Wasn't that nice of him? By the time he'd finished I'd almost forgotten how awful London was in 1962."

"Good old Christian," I said. "Does he ever kiss you?"

"Oh, just the occasional peck on the cheek. But he holds hands beautifully."

"You don't think he might ever try and do more?"

"Why should he?" said Marina, finishing her hot chocolate. "He's got Katie." She stood up. "I'd better totter off to bed before my eyes close. Thanks so much for listening, Vinnie. I hope I didn't bore you."

But I was unable to reply. My entire world had suddenly gone pitch black. Horror had paralysed every muscle in my body.

"Venetia?"

In the nick of time the instinct to dissimulate in order to survive came to my rescue and will-power triumphed over paralysis. I managed to say casually: "Sorry. Still thinking of Christian. No, of course you didn't bore me, Marina."

"You won't tell anyone about Walter Forrest, will you?"

"Never."

She smiled gratefully and wandered away.

8

I HAD already tortured myself with the notion that Aysgarth's silence on the subject of Dido might indicate he still retained a trace of asexual affection for her, but the possibility that now assailed me was infinitely more pulverising. Later, sleep proved impossible. I was quite unable to forget Christian, able to indulge in a chaste romantic friendship with Marina because his sexual appetite was satisfied by his wife. Their triangle now seemed uncomplicated; I felt I could understand not only Katie's serenity and Christian's restraint but the ambivalence towards men which made Marina no threat to either of them at the profoundest level of their relationship.

But my own triangle, previously so straightforward, was now distorted by doubt.

I tried to pull myself together. No matter what Christian was doing with Katie, it was unthinkable that my Mr. Dean might still be having sex with Dido.

So why was I thinking the unthinkable?

At two o'clock I went downstairs and mixed myself a whisky-and-soda, a drink I normally avoided because it had a soporific effect on me, but twenty minutes later my eyelids showed no inclination to droop. I began to pace around the drawing-room.

If I refused to believe that my Mr. Dean was continuing to have sexual intercourse with his wife, what were the implications? I tried to survey the facts with detachment. Of course our grand passion was as yet at an early stage, but I could not deny I had been puzzled by his failure to express his feelings more hotly in the car-park of Starbury Ring. But perhaps he had been shy. I had not forgotten his unexpected shyness on Lady Mary when we had met after the Orgy. On the other hand, he had appeared to be unafflicted by shyness in the car-park. So if he wasn't having sex with his wife and if he wasn't overwhelmed by his inhibitions, what was the explanation for the marked absence of passion which had left me feeling bewildered and dissatisfied?

I toyed with the appalling possibility of impotence, but discarded it. It was true that Aysgarth was sixty-one, but plenty of men skipped around at that age and he had often boasted he had the constitution of an ox. Certainly I could never remember him being ill. While eavesdropping long ago on a conversation of Arabella's I had gleaned the information that impotence could be caused by indulging too heavily in alcohol, but surely an ox-like constitution could absorb generous doses of alcohol without disastrous side-effects? And anyway, Aysgarth had always seemed to have this risky pastime well in control.

I applied myself afresh to the mystery. Then suddenly I realised I had quite overlooked the fact that he had powerful moral reasons for restraining himself with me. I hadn't exactly forgotten that he was a clergyman, but I had been so carried away by my desire for a strong physical response from him that I had reacted like an ignorant layman and underestimated the spiritual force of his beliefs. The most obvious solution to the mystery of his non-passionate behavior, as I now realised, was that he was being compulsively high-minded and noble.

It was also time I remembered that clergymen had no choice but to be high-minded and noble; that was what was expected of them and if they frolicked around committing adultery they were defrocked—although that, of course, applied only if they committed the ultimate sin of being found out. How often did clergymen stray from the moral path? It was bound to happen occasionally, since they were human beings and not robots, but I doubted that it happened often, and I found it hard to believe it happened to anyone who got beyond the rank of vicar. A clergyman able enough to progress to the upper reaches of his profession would be able enough to know how to ensure his survival. Aysgarth had evidently worked out (with the aid of Bishop Robinson) that he could allow himself a warm, flirtatious friendship with me, but his moral beliefs, which I had no doubt were strong, and his instinct for survival, which I had no doubt was well developed, would ensure he carried the affair no further.

That all made sense. And that indeed was the situation I had been prepared to accept after the Orgy when, riding high on a tidal wave of euphoria, I had decided it would be greedy to want more than a chaste romantic friendship. But no matter how valid these rational deductions were, they didn't tell me what I was to do now that greed had triumphed—and they didn't tell me either what Aysgarth was currently doing about sex. According to Arabella, men had to have sexual intercourse of some kind regularly (unless, I assumed, they were like Perry Palmer—and no one knew for sure about Perry anyway) but I had apparently argued myself into believing Aysgarth was at present a complete sexual abstainer. Was this abstinence possible? Was it likely? Arabella would without doubt have answered no to both questions, but Arabella had never been mixed up with a high-minded clergyman. I thought abstinence was possible but I had a terrible feeling it was not very likely—and if Aysgarth was keeping me at a chaste distance, there was only one other woman to whom he was likely to turn for sexual satisfaction.

I had a second whisky-and-soda.

I then tried to tell myself that I didn't care what he was doing about sex so long as he loved me, but I knew this assertion bore no relation to reality. I did care. I cared passionately. I didn't want to share him with anyone. I wanted him all to myself. In fact, as I could now acknowledge, recklessly embracing my mounting greed, I wanted to be his mistress. Marriage, unfortunately, was out of the question, since I could never ruin his career by involving him in a divorce, but I was sure that a consummated grand passion would at least give me peace of mind; never again did I want to swill whisky and pace the floor in the early hours of the morning while I tormented myself with revolting thoughts about his relationship with that appalling woman.

Of course it was impossible that he should still be sleeping with her. But I could see I had to make it more than impossible; I had to make it inconceivable.

Then alongside me in the world of allegory, the demure little serpent, gliding along on his leash, slipped his collar at last and slithered away beyond my control into the garden.

X

I

"LET me tell you what I plan to do," said the Bishop, resplendent in his old-fashioned uniform, his episcopal ring glinting in the light as he toyed with his pectoral cross.

It was Monday, the first day of my new job, and we were closeted together in the South Canonry's morning-room which had been turned into an office for me. My hired IBM Electric typewriter gleamed on its table by the window. I myself was arranged nearby in the classic secretarial position, one leg crossed over the other and my shorthand notebook resting on my uppermost knee. I wore an austere white blouse and a black skirt and looked (I hoped) vaguely religious, as befitted an office-serf in attendance on a prelate. My horrible hair, now growing wildly towards a pre-Raphaelite length after its tiresome "in-between" stage, was scraped off my face and stuffed into a sort of net which I had speared with another interesting metal object from Boots. I could feel the hair weighing on the nape of my neck like an enormous doughnut as I held my pencil lightly above the blank page.

"First of all," said the Bishop, lounging elegantly against the chimney-piece, "I shall simply be dictating random observations. These may seem quite disconnected. Then after I've studied these opening remarks on paper I shall arrange them under various headings so that they form an outline of the book. It's possible that I might keep Robinson's structure of God, Christ, worship, ethics and so on, but his writing is so emotional, his theology so vapid and his conclusions so wild that I fear any attempt to mimic his structure can only have unfortunate results. However, we shall see. Now Venetia, do stop me if I go too fast. When I'm in full theological spate I tend to get carried away."

"Yes, Bishop." I felt as if I were attending some famous general who was surveying the battlefield before a world-shattering military engagement.

"Very well, off we go. Number one: the Bishop of Woolwich, whose fame hitherto has rested on his New Testament scholarship, has with great courage ventured into fresh woods and pastures new. Unfortunately he has chosen to plunge into the woods of doctrine and the pastures of ethics. Since it is clear that his grounding in both is slender—to put it kindly— his brave little book cannot in truth be described as a work of scholarly importance. It would be more accurate, I think, as well as more charitable to classify this latest addition to the Robinson *oeuvre*—that's O-E-U—"

"*Oeuvre*. I've got it, Bishop."

"—latest addition to the Robinson *oeuvre* as a devotional work. Dr. Robinson is clearly devoted to God, to Jesus Christ and to the Christian religion. This is admirable. The only trouble is that his God is not the Christian God, his Jesus is not, as the doctrine of the Church upholds, God incarnate, and his Christian religion is merely an exotic amalgamation of various Christian heresies which have long since been discredited. End of paragraph. Can you read that back to me, please?"

I read it back.

"By Jove, you're good!" said the Bishop. "Well done. All right, on we go. Number two: Dr. Robinson is zealous in proclaiming that the metaphor of height, so long used in descriptions of God, can no longer be meaningful to—quote—modern man—unquote. He insists that we can abolish the metaphor by speaking of God as something which exists 'deep down' in every individual, and he validates this proposition by declaring that it will be more easily understood by 'modern man' because of his familiarity with the concept of depth psychology. However, since all talk of God can only be in terms of symbols, depth is just as much a metaphor as height. In the name of depth psychology—which is probably only fully understood by a very small number of so-called modern men—Dr. Robinson has fatally limited the doctrine of God by abolishing the concept of transcendence. Note: I shall deal later with his wholly inadequate attempt to give transcendence a new definition.

"New paragraph. Number three: the Bishop appears to have fallen wildly in love with the writings of three German theologians: Rudolf Bultmann, Dietrich Bonhoeffer and Paul Tillich. The latter has described God as the 'Ground of Our Being,' an appellation which the Bishop seems to find peculiarly intoxicating. Wrenching this phrase from the context of Tillich's interesting though questionable existentialist theology, Dr. Robinson expands his depth metaphor to declare that since God is the Ground of Our Being we can find Him, regardless of whether we go to church or not, by gazing down into our inmost depths. This, of course, as any student of the Early Church will know, was the attitude of the philosopher Valentinus in the second century—see my book *Valentinus, Scourge of Orthodoxy,* published by Cambridge University Press in 1954. In other words," said the Bishop with a gleam in his eye, "what we have here is a brand-new version of the heresy of the Christian Gnostics who nearly destroyed the Church in the first centuries after Christ. Venetia, Gnostic is spelt—"

"G-N-O-S-T-I-C."

"This is wonderful!" said the Bishop. "You're the first secretary I've met who could spell Gnostic! But I mustn't forget, must I, that I'm writing for lesser laymen who won't know what that word means, so I think I'd better now dictate a paragraph on the Gnostics—or shall I leave it till later? No, let's strike while the iron's hot. Before I go on to enquire why Robinson, in his passion for the work of German theologians, has chosen to fall in love with Bultmann, Bonhoeffer and Tillich instead of with Barth and Niebuhr, I shall just pause to demolish the heresy of Christian Gnosticism."

Dr. Ashworth was enjoying himself hugely. Feeling quite overwhelmed by the devastating confidence of his scholarly authority I began to feel far more confused than I had ever anticipated.

2

WHEN I arrived back at the Chantry for a sandwich lunch I found a letter had arrived for me by the second post.

"My darling," I read.

I must see you—can't wait till Wednesday to find out what went on at the South Canonry during your first encounter with the dream-machine! Lady Mary post-Evensong Monday? Hope this catches you before you move into the Archdeacon's lap. In great haste, all love,

N.

This was very satisfactory, and I phoned Primrose at the diocesan office to postpone our house-warming drink. Then I gathered up my possessions, said a genuinely fond farewell to Marina and bucketed away in my MG to my new flat overlooking Butchers' Alley.

3

ABOUT half a dozen tourists were wandering around the cloisters as I took possession of Lady Mary, but there was no sign of any member of the Cathedral staff. It was a clouded evening and after a wet morning Lady Mary was somewhat damp. Adjusting my raincoat carefully under my bottom I resigned myself to rheumatism and waited.

"Phew!" said Aysgarth, hurrying up to me five minutes later. "Sorry about the delay but I got mixed up with one of the vergers who reports a sinister smell emanating from St. Anselm's Chapel—there's been a recurring drainage problem there ever since my predecessor Dean Carter built a lavatory on the cheap at the back of the Sacristy. What a life! But my darling, don't keep me in suspense—what happened at the South Canonry?"

"The Bishop demolished the Gnostic heresy."

"Oh good heavens, not that old rubbish again!"

"You may laugh, but it was pretty powerful stuff! Is there any possibility he might wind up Archbishop of Canterbury?"

"No, he wasted too much time turning down those earlier bishoprics in order to write about Church history—and talking of Church history, what on earth's the Gnostic heresy got to do with poor old John Robinson?"

"Well, apparently there was a Christian Gnostic called Valentinus—"

"Never heard of him. No, wait a minute—"

"The Bishop—Ashworth not Robinson—wrote a book—"

"So he did, yes, I do dimly remember skimming through a review years ago, but what's the point in raking up people like Valentinus who lived in a completely different world and whose thought-forms in consequence are wholly irrelevant to the 1960s?"

"Dr. Ashworth seems to operate on the theory that the more things change the more they remain the same. He thinks that when Robinson substitutes the depth metaphor for the height metaphor he's just as much a heretic as Valentinus was."

"What utter nonsense! To say that God is the Ground of Our Being and that we can find him by looking deep into our consciousness is entirely consonant with the Bible. Think of the quotation: 'The kingdom of God is within you!'"

"Ah yes, of course. Yes, I see. But how amazingly complicated theology becomes once you scratch below the surface—"

"That's exactly why it has to be kept simple for laymen and expressed in fresh up-to-date terms which are instantly meaningful to them. God is within the world and God is Love; therefore God is to be found in one's deepest, most loving relationships. That's how one translates the technical term 'the immanence of God' for modern man."

"Yes, I see. Gosh, thanks for reasserting Robinson's thesis for me—I was beginning to feel quite—" I broke off as I saw that drip Maurice Tait trickling down the colonnade towards our corner of the lawn.

"Oh hullo, Mr. Dean—hullo, Venetia—"

"Hullo, Maurice!" said Aysgarth. "I caught Venetia meditating here and we've somehow wound up discussing heresy. Am I seeing you at the Deanery for dinner tonight?"

"No, that's tomorrow. Tonight Primrose and I have our Bible study group."

"Ah yes, of course. I remember now." He waited till Tait had trickled away before adding under his breath. "We really mustn't meet here too often. It's too public."

"Never mind, the day after tomorrow's Wednesday, and—"

"—and you can bring me the latest report on the Bishop's heresy-hunt!" He gave me a sparkling smile. "Two o'clock at the Staro Arms?"

"Can't wait!"

We parted with a torrid squeeze of the hands.

4

"... AND the truth is," said the Bishop, pausing in his prowls around the morning-room to adjust one of the buttons on his gaiters, "that if one denies God's transcendence by reducing Him to some all-pervasive presence within the world, one sails in very dangerous waters indeed. God is Love, says Dr. Robinson—correctly. But he writes as if what he really believes is that Love is God, a pagan concept resulting—at its best—in the notion that God is scattered throughout the world in a sentimental *esprit de corps,* and—at its worst—in the notion that God can be evoked by orgiastic sexual rites. The reduction, dilution and downright perversion of the doctrine of the immanence of God in this manner should not be countenanced by any responsible Christian theologian. To indulge in such slipshod thinking," said the Bishop, the gleam returning to his eye, "is to succumb to the age-old heresy of pantheism."

He prowled on, glossy, distinguished and formidable, around the austere morning-room of the South Canonry. "Dr. Robinson declares," resumed Dr. Ashworth dreamily, pausing by the window to gaze into the far distance, "that he is not a pantheist, but this declaration, I fear, cannot alter the fact that much of what he says is pure pantheism. God is much greater, more infinitely Other, more mysteriously transcendent than Dr. Robinson's puny vision of a disseminated love ethic can ever suggest, and no matter how often the Bishop claims to be preaching panentheism—"

"Hang on," I said. "You've finally floored me. Pan—"

"Pan*en*theism. That's what pantheists claim to believe when they're trying to pass their beliefs off as orthodox. Perhaps I'd better dictate a note explaining—"

The Bishop demolished the heresy of pantheism.

5

"*CHARLES* has wilfully misunderstood Robinson," said Aysgarth as his car roared around a rural corner at fifty miles an hour on Wednesday afternoon. "Robinson clearly rejects pantheism and there's no reason why he shouldn't support panentheism, the theory that the world is only part of God. Charles is getting all steamed up because he thinks Robinson's abolished God's transcendence, but in fact he hasn't abolished it at all; he's simply redefined it. He says the transcendent is the Beyond in our midst."

"But what on earth does that mean?"

"It relates to the numinous, those moments when one becomes aware that there's something greater than ourselves all around us. It's a well-documented anthropological phenomenon."

"Oh, I see. But—"

"If you ask me, Charles just isn't in touch with the ordinary worshipper in the pew. Modern man wants to be told in plain language what God's like and where he can find Him."

"Does he?" I said, as we took another corner too fast and an oncoming car hooted at us. "It seems to me that all modern man wants to know is: (1) what can God do for me, (2) why should I bother to believe in Him when I'm doing very nicely, thank you, and (3) what are the odds on life after death?"

"Oh yes, yes, yes!" said Aysgarth indulgently, slamming the car into a lower gear in order to roar up a steep hill. "All people who are undeveloped spiritually get stuck on those sort of questions, but that's only because they've got completely the wrong idea about God and think of Him as a tyrannical old man up in the sky. Once you show them that God is the Ground of their Being and that He can be found in loving relationships, then their whole self-centred, self-seeking perspective on life will change and the way will be paved for spiritual progress."

"Ah!" I said intelligently, but in fact I was no longer thinking of God.

I was much too busy watching Aysgarth, much too occupied with fantasies about his short, thick, sexy fingers as they idly caressed the wheel.

6

"SHOULD we make amends for last Wednesday's sloth and walk up to the Ring?" he suggested reluctantly when he parked the car ten minutes later.

"No, it looks like rain—let's play safe and stay here," I said at once, and he laughed as he switched off the engine.

After we had spent some time gossiping about a variety of subjects, he told me about his latest problem, a dispute over a modern sculpture which he had commissioned for the Cathedral churchyard. I was always surprised by Aysgarth's interest in art, but apparently his impoverishment as a London schoolboy had prompted many retreats on wet winter weekends to the picture galleries where no charge was made for admission, and years later when he had become a dean his interest in art, long dormant, had revived. Many deans believed they had a duty to reflect the art of their times in their cathedrals, and Aysgarth had soon decided he was called to leave an aesthetic mark on Starbridge.

He had started by commissioning a stained-glass window from the Frenchman Chagall (then almost unknown in England except by the cognoscenti) and when this had been received with startled enthusiasm, he had formed his ambition to acquire a modern sculpture. However, photographs of the semi-completed work had now been greeted with horror by Fitzgerald and Dalton, and even Eddie, the Chapter's third canon, had been dubious.

"But what's wrong with this great work of art?" I demanded.

"Nothing—it's 'fab,' as Pip would say!" Aysgarth became enthusiastic. "It's red, white and blue, and consists of a matchstick-type of man rising up a climbing frame from an open box of cigars. The climbing frame represents the spiritual life and the seven cigars represent the temptations of the material world—although of course they're not really cigars; they're a purely abstract representation of the seven deadly sins. Harriet's calling the work 'Modern Man in Search of God.' "

"Who's Harriet?"

"The sculptress. Harriet March, the widow of Captain Donald March who was killed on Everest. Surely you've heard of her?"

"Trust you to have a beautiful girlfriend panting to offer you a symbolic representation of the seven deadly sins!"

"My darling!" said Aysgarth, greatly entertained. "So long as I have you, the beautiful Harriet can pant in vain!"

"Quite right—why bother with symbolic representations when you can have the real thing?" I retorted, and as he laughed, my right hand, which had apparently acquired a will of its own, came gently to rest on his left thigh.

I heard his sharp intake of breath and saw his mouth curve downwards in its sultriest line as the laughter died. The next moment he had grabbed my left shoulder with his right hand and was wrenching me closer to him. I was startled to discover that a passionate embrace in the front seat of a car requires a considerable degree of bodily contortion. It always looks so easy in films.

But if the embrace was passionate, the kiss was not. After grazing my cheek with his lips he stopped short of my mouth.

"No, no, no," he said abruptly, slumping back behind the wheel. "That won't do at all." He shoved open the door. "Let's walk up to the Ring."

"Do we have time?"

Glancing at his watch he grimaced and pulled the door shut. "No." Glowering through the windscreen at the bare sensuous lines of the landscape he gripped the steering-wheel so hard that the brown age-spots on the back of his hands stood out starkly against the pale skin.

A long silence ensued.

Eventually I felt driven to mutter: "Sorry. My fault," but he answered in his curtest voice: "Don't be absurd."

As we continued to sit in the car a gust of wind hurled some drops of rain at the windscreen, and I was about to venture a comment on our wisdom in avoiding a walk when he said suddenly, not looking at me: "If it's anyone's fault it's mine for permitting this friendship, but I can't believe it's wrong. I've been granted a unique opportunity to practise what I preach, and what I believe in is the primacy of love; I believe that if you really love someone you'll love them enough not to damage them in any way. One must be self-denying, not selfish; protective, not destruc-tive; reaching up always towards the light, not stooping to grovel in the dark. And when our friendship's over—when you marry a man of your own generation who's utterly right for you—then I want you to be able to look back without regret and think with affection: *there* was a man who really loved me."

"My darling Mr. Dean—"

"Neville. Of course, being only human, I do find myself wishing . . . But that's no good, is it? One can drive oneself mad by wishing. What is, is. One must accept it and do the best one can, serving God according to one's conscience—and it would go against my conscience to destroy what we've found together. It's a sin to destroy love, a *sin*. A genuinely loving relationship such as this . . . well, Robinson says it all, doesn't he?

Let the conservative churchmen thunder away about absolute moral rules that can never be altered! The only ethic that matters is to act with love and compassion." Reaching out blindly he turned the key in the ignition but the engine stalled. He was in such a state that he could only stare afterwards at the dashboard as if he had forgotten how to drive.

Hesitantly my voice said: "Neville, this may seem a very silly question in the light of all you've just said, but . . . well, if you love me—"

"If!" He looked at me as if amazed that I should be so tentative. "Of course I love you!"

"So does that mean . . . that's to say, do you . . . oh God, I can't quite put this into words—"

"Do I what?"

"Have other romantic friendships. I mean, do I have to share you with anyone else? I mean—"

He was appalled. "My darling, you're the most marvellous girl in the world and I love you so much I hardly know what to do with myself— how could I look at anyone else?"

"Oh, Neville—" I broke off, sick with relief, but then doubt smote me again. "But if there's no one else," said my voice rapidly, "what do you do about . . . oh God, I'm sorry to be so ignorant and unspiritual, but . . . well, unless a man's called to celibacy, doesn't he go mad unless he has sex regularly?"

There was a pause. For a split second his eyes went blank but then the next moment he was responding in the way I had least expected: he laughed.

"So that's the reason for my Chapter's erratic behaviour!" he exclaimed amused. "Maybe I could solve my entire problems as Dean by prescribing mass-fornication!"

"But seriously, Neville—"

"Seriously, my dear, not only can the sexual drive vary enormously from individual to individual but it can also vary enormously within each individual. There are no hard and fast rules, I assure you, about the sexual behaviour of human beings." And he added helpfully: "Take my Chapter, for example. Fitzgerald professes to be called to celibacy. He's probably a repressed homosexual, but whatever he is it's plain that sex is low on his list of interests. Dalton's a widower who would like to marry again. I suspect he's becoming fed up with his enforced celibacy, but on the other hand he seems to get by all right—he usually manages to present an equable facade. Eddie's probably got the strongest sex-drive of the lot, but unfortunately he has problems which have so far prevented him marrying. Possibly his enforced celibacy exacerbates his tendency towards hypochondria and morbid introspection, but one can't be certain; maybe an active sex-life would in fact make very little difference to the neurotic side of his personality. The point to note, of course, is that none of my three celibate canons is either raving or dying from lack of sex, and contrary to all the male moanings you may have heard, no one has ever yet expired from chastity."

I felt sick with relief again. Obviously he was implying that it was possible for him to do without sex.

Or was he? I remembered that split second when his eyes had gone blank. But probably the blankness had reflected a mere bourgeois frisson arising from the fact that an unmarried girl had asked him a blunt sexual question.

"Gosh, Neville, thanks for talking so frankly—you must be thinking me a complete ignoramus, but—"

"My darling, I'd be rather shocked if you weren't!"

Yes, that, of course, was a typically bourgeois response and the split-second blankness of the eyes was now explained. At last I could relax. Without doubt he was undergoing a period of chastity, unwilling to sleep with the neurotic wife who was too paralysed by her fear of pregnancy to want to sleep with him.

I resolved to think no more of Dido.

7

I WAS just manicuring my nails on the following afternoon and thinking that I might potter along to the South Canonry to do a little typing, when the front doorbell rang at the foot of the stairs which led up to my flat. Marina had gone to Oxford and Primrose would almost certainly be at work in Eternity Street. I decided it was probably my landlady Mrs. Lindsay—or possibly one of her four jolly-hockey-sticks daughters with whom I had nothing in common. I was still trying to devise a plan which would enable me to repel their friendly overtures without being rude, but fortunately I suspected that they already regarded me as an aloof freak and were anxious to leave me alone.

With reluctance I descended the stairs and opened the front door.

"Ah, there you are, my dear," said Dido, streaming past me across the threshold and skimming up the stairs. "I'm sure you don't mind if I come in, do you, but I was just passing down Butchers' Alley on my way to Mitre Street to buy a wedding present for that dreadfully plain daughter of Mrs. Pinn—such a mercy some man wants to marry her, it just shows one should never give up hope—when I remembered you, tucked away in the Lindsays' flat above their garage—and my dear, I must tell you that a couple were burnt to death in a flat over a garage only the other day when the car underneath them blew up, I read it in *The Times* so it must be true. However, you're not going to be here for long, are you, so I doubt if you'll be burnt to death, but nevertheless you should be very careful of exhaust fumes and always keep your window open.

"Anyway, my dear, Maurice Tait came to dinner the other night and mentioned that he'd seen you loitering with Stephen in the cloisters and I thought: Venetia! How dreadful, I've quite forgotten her—and I'm famous for remembering all my acquaintances, from the Bishop right down to that poor Cathedral cleaner with the cleft palate—so *immediately* I said to Stephen: 'Darling,' I said, 'we must have Venetia to dinner—it's ages since she's been here!' and Stephen looked pleased because he's so fond of you, Venetia dear, along with Harriet March and half a dozen other young women—Stephen always has to have his little harem!—and as my entire life is devoted to making Stephen happy I'm all for encouraging these harmless friendships by including the girls in my guest-lists—why, I even post his letters to his female correspondents when I find them lying on the hall table! I've never been able to understand wives who can't take a generous, tolerant attitude to all their husbands' friends, and indeed, as I've so often told Primrose, I'm firmly convinced that possessiveness is the mark of an inferior nature—good heavens, look at this! What a dingy little room, no light, and the carpet needs replacing and what a pity the walls are such a sickly shade of cream, but never mind, at least you must be saving money as the Lindsays would surely never dare charge much for such a run-down little garret.

"Now, Venetia my dear, I've been examining my diary, and it's a *little* difficult to slip you in at present, but how about the Saturday after next, eight o'clock for eight-thirty? I shan't invite Eddie, I know things are delicate there—and never let it be said that I'm not a supremely tactful hostess—but I'll try to lure Perry down from London for the weekend.

"Well, I really must rush off to Mitre Street, but it's been lovely to see you and I'm glad you've at least got some sort of a roof over your head—although if you'll take my advice you'll remove those vulgar posters from the walls and put up something more dignified. After all, we mustn't forget, must we, that you're now nearer thirty than twenty and really too old to behave like a teenager over Elvis Presley. Well, goodbye, my dear, it'll be lovely to see you on Saturday week, I'm so glad you're working for the Bishop, living on top of the Archdeacon and having little chats after Evensong with the Dean—I mean, it's all so terribly *seemly,* isn't it, and I'm sure it's such a relief for your parents who must have been wondering where on earth you were going to drift to next—no, don't worry, don't bother to come down, I'll see myself out . . ."

She flew away like the evil witch in a fairy-tale.

I WAS literally shaking with rage. Collapsing on the sofa in my beautiful flat, the first home I had ever had of my very own, I stared in the dim light, which I found so restful, at my glorious posters of Elvis celebrating the joy of life. The posters, offset by the rich, Cornish-cream shade of the walls, looked stunningly vivid, an inspired stroke of off-beat interior decoration. The threadbare brown carpet, so arrestingly different from all the priceless rugs I had had to endure in my parents' houses, blended perfectly with the Cornish-cream paint and the flowery, yellow-green pattern of the curtains. My record-player sat snugly in a corner. My current selection of books, ranging from *Honest to God* to *Lady Chatterley's Lover,* stood proudly on a shelf. There was not a plant in sight. The room was *mine,* and I loved it fiercely.

I spent some time wishing that Dido would fall under a bus in Mitre Street, but eventually my rage was superseded by fright. That drip Maurice Tait! I might have known he'd go bleating to Dido that he'd seen me loitering with Aysgarth on Lady Mary. But on the other hand, why shouldn't I loiter occasionally with Aysgarth after Evensong? Considering my long acquaintance with him, most people would judge my behaviour unremarkable, and surely Dido couldn't be thinking . . . But God alone knew what Dido thought. And when a woman was as neurotic as she was, what did her thoughts matter anyway?

But the more I recalled her words, the more uneasy I became. That reference to Harriet March had been unwelcome. And did Dido really post her husband's letters to a variety of youthful ladyfriends? That sounded like fantasy—or perhaps a memory of the days when Aysgarth had occasionally penned a line to members of Primrose's "Gang," now defunct. Aysgarth had told me plainly that he loved me too much to look at anyone else. So why was I experiencing these twinges of anxiety? Of course Harriet March was a woman of exceptional charm and glamour, but my Mr. Dean only had one day off a week and the vital afternoon away from home was spent with me. That was undeniable. I supposed he was in correspondence with her about the sculpture, but nonetheless I was sure no letter to her ever began "My darling." So much for Harriet March.

I relaxed but I felt worn out. I had had no idea jealousy could be so exhausting. "Possessiveness is the mark of an inferior nature," Dido had said, but that statement was soaked in irony because she herself was possessiveness personified. I thought of the ghastly scene she had staged before Aysgarth had departed for the Hebrides, and suddenly, before I could stop myself, I was feeling uneasy again. Surely when a woman was as possessive as Dido she would want to possess the object of her adoration? But if she was frightened of conceiving . . . if she was neurotic enough to have what Dinkie called "hang-ups" . . . No, sexual intercourse was out of the question and I had been mad to allow myself to be tormented by doubt again.

Concluding that her appalling visit had made me thoroughly overwrought, I pulled myself together and headed for the South Canonry to resume my typing.

9

I DECIDED not to describe Dido's visit in detail when I wrote to Aysgarth, but I did mention that she had called as the result of Tait's betrayal. Aysgarth was unperturbed; he wrote back that there was no need to worry about Tait's gaffe since Dido had not thought the episode in the least suspicious and was indeed genuinely remorseful that she had not invited me to dinner earlier. I doubted the remorse but was glad to be reminded that Dido often did have good intentions. I even saw that she had probably descended on my flat with no prior intention to reduce me to pulp and might even have thought she was doing me a favour by reminding me that I was nearer thirty than twenty. Dido's devotion to what she was pleased to describe as her "candour" arose from the belief that one had a moral duty to help others towards self-improvement by pointing out their faults and mistakes. It was quite possible that in making her criticisms she had had only my welfare in mind.

Usually I managed to avoid mentioning Dido when I replied to Aysgarth's letters which soon began to arrive every day. Our correspondence ranged over a broad number of subjects—literature, art, current events, television, Church gossip—but before long I realised that what he enjoyed most was telling me about his work. It seemed to be a relief to him to complain not only about the bickering in Chapter but about the many minor crises which occurred regularly among the community of over a hundred people who worked at the Cathedral. When it dawned on me that he was very much alone, poised at the top of the Cathedral's organisational pyramid, I had a fresh insight into Eddie's role in his life. In the absence of a friendly relationship with the Bishop, Aysgarth relied heavily for support on the one Cathedral executive whom he could trust to be loyal under any circumstances.

"At least I can always rely on Eddie never to stab me in the back," Aysgarth wrote,

> but nevertheless I feel I can never fully confide in him—and this isn't just because we've always had a relationship in which he pours out his troubles and I do the listening. It's because I feel that with men I have to "put up a front"—show no weakness, be tough, appear successful at all times. That's the result of my upbringing, when I was browbeaten into "getting on" in the world, and attitudes acquired in childhood are sometimes not so easy to slough off in later life. Bearing this idiosyncrasy of mine in mind you'll be able to understand why it's such a luxury for me to have a female confidante; I can relax at last, stop "putting up a front," be myself—*my new self*—THE NEW NEVILLE! Darling, I can't tell you what a psychological liberation I experience not only when I see you but when I pick up the pen to write you a letter . . .

I was just wishing yet again that Aysgarth's liberation would be less psychological and more physical when I received a communication from Eddie, the first I had received since his pathetic note apologising for his behaviour on the Cathedral roof. Having written a one-line reply to suggest that we should treat the fiasco as if it had never happened, I had not expected to hear from him again, and I unfolded his new letter with considerable reluctance.

"Dear Venetia," I read.

> I hope you didn't tear this up as soon as you saw my writing on the envelope. Let me say straight away that I won't refer to the episode on the Cathedral roof again, but I wonder nevertheless if something of value might yet be salvaged from the debacle. Stephen is always adamant in insisting that love should never be just chucked in the nearest wastepaper basket and forgotten, so perhaps my love could eventually be recycled in a more acceptable form. Certainly it's purely in the spirit of Platonic friendship that I write to remind you that Martin Darrow will be appearing soon in Coward's *Present Laughter* at the Starbridge Playhouse as part of a trial run in the provinces before the show opens in the West End. If you'd still like to see him, then I'd still like to take you. No fuss, no mess, I promise. Think it over.
>
> Yours,
> EDDIE.

Feeling faintly nauseated I tossed off a note which read:

Dear Eddie:

Better not. It's a bit early yet, I think, to talk in terms of Platonic friendship.

I gritted my teeth before forcing myself to add:

But maybe one day.

Yours,

VENETIA.

Then I began to prepare for my next expedition to Starbury Plain with the Dean.

10

IT was a wet afternoon so once again we failed to reach the Ring. We sat in the car and smoked and gossiped and laughed while he squeezed my hand in a dozen different ways amidst countless sultry looks and frequent observations about how wonderful I was. How I stopped myself plastering him with kisses I shall never know, but I had made up my mind that the affair should proceed at his own pace. My brush with his thigh last week had only upset him, and besides, never having been romantically involved with anyone before, I was in fact reluctant to take the lead in making advances; the thigh-brush had merely resulted from a mindless spontaneity. So although I was longing for a passionate kiss I endured without complaint the agonising frustration generated by the hand-squeezing, and told myself sternly that deep moral convictions in a clergyman could never be rapidly overcome.

I eventually received another peck on the cheek when we parted. Making an enormous effort I convinced myself I admired him more than ever for his devotion to the high ideals implicit in Robinson's New Morality, and made a new resolution to be patient.

11

THREE days later I went to dinner at the Deanery.

When I arrived I found to my dismay that I had been included in one of Dido's notorious "little dinner-parties for sixteen," evenings of social carnage during which she threw together some ill-assorted guests, mixed them ruthlessly with her family and interrupted every conversation until everyone was either silenced or outraged. On that evening little Pip escaped the lethal frivolities; he was considered young enough to have an early supper and listen in tranquil bliss to Radio Luxemburg, but Dido's daughter Elizabeth was present, flexing her intellect and competing not unsuccessfully with her half-sister Primrose as the female brainbox of the family. But Elizabeth, even at fourteen, was far sexier than Primrose and batted her eyelashes precociously at some sixteen-year-old male infant who had been roped in to keep her amused.

The other guests consisted entirely of residents of the Close, the boring ones who enjoyed reading the obituaries in *The Times* and discussing who had just had a stroke. Evidently Dido was swiping a bunch of unwanted people off her party-list in one fell swoop. None of Aysgarth's sons by his first marriage was present, and there was no sign of Perry, who had obviously had the brains to elude Dido's attempt to kidnap him. The nadir of the dinner arrived when I caught the attention of a retired general who kept squeezing my knee under the table until I managed to tread on his toe. His wife said with mild interest: "Is your gout troubling you again, dear?" as he turned purple and yelped with rage.

At the head of the table Aysgarth, looking serene, caressed his glass of claret but drank little. I never once caught him looking in my direction.

In the drawing-room after the meal he did manage to say to me pleasantly: "And how's your new flat, Venetia?" but before I could tell him what he already knew the witch descended on her broomstick, slipped her arm through his and declared: "Venetia's looking a trifle wan, don't you think, Stephen? But then working for the Bishop must be so exhausting—which reminds me, do tell Stephen, Venetia, what the Bishop's putting in his book because it's certain to be something about sex—we all know dear Charles can't think of anything else—and Stephen always adores it, don't you, my love, when the Bishop is simply too puritanical to be true."

"Do I?" said Aysgarth vaguely, but he was smiling at her, his bright eyes crinkling at the corners, and she was leaning hard enough against him to ensure he slipped an arm around her waist to prop her up.

"Darling Stephen!" exclaimed Dido as I glanced at the ceiling, the fireplace, the door, the windows—at any object except her adoring dark eyes. "Always so wonderfully discreet!"

I managed to say: "If you'll excuse me for a moment . . ." Then I escaped, dived into the cloakroom and collapsed shuddering on the lavatory seat. Some time passed. Eventually I dragged myself back to the fray. Aysgarth had his arm around his daughter Elizabeth by this time and was talking to a couple so old I felt they ought to be dead. Meanwhile

Primrose was chatting about the Girl Guides to some battle-axe whose sex was denoted only by a long skirt, and Dido was still swooping around on her invisible broomstick. As I re-entered the room I saw with dread that I had once again caught her attention.

"Venetia"—I braced myself for another pulverising assault—"I'm so sorry I couldn't lure Perry here tonight but he was going sailing with a crowd of friends—did you know Perry kept a boat at Bosham?—and although he swore he was devastated to miss you, he couldn't alter his plans."

"That's all right, Mrs. Aysgarth. I can live without Perry."

"Then who's the one you can't live without? I'm sure we're all agog to know! Christian said—"

"Christian got it wrong. There's no one in my life at present except God."

"God?"

"Uh-huh. You told me to find Him. So I did."

"You mean you've had a religious conversion?"

"Thanks to you, yes. I've just read Bishop Robinson's book."

"Oh?" said Dido, and added in a not unfriendly voice: "What did you think of it?"

"I was terribly impressed. It's wonderful to find a bishop who speaks for our day and age."

"I think it's a load of codswallop," said Dido, "and I don't think he speaks for our day and age at all. How can anyone think that's a relevant book for modern man when the author never mentions what kind of world modern man has to live in? He spends enough time quoting Bonhoeffer and Tillich, but he never mentions that Bonhoeffer was hanged by the Nazis and Tillich was driven into exile. What does he have to tell us about sin and evil? Damn all! It's all airy-fairy liberal optimism about how God's really down here on earth, but Robinson, it seems, is firmly wedged up there in the clouds! Darling Stephen—who of course is quite the most romantic idealist who ever lived—may choose to fall in love with *Honest to God,* but that's only because he's so high-minded that he'd stagger through a sewer and still manage to keep his eyes on the stars." As if allowing me time to digest this Wildean metaphor she turned aside to survey the progress of the party and bawled in a stage-whisper to her step-daughter: "Primrose, do pass round the cigarettes!"

"Mrs. Aysgarth," I said, unable to help wondering where she had picked up this withering critique of Bishop Robinson, "have you actually read *Honest to God?*"

"My dear, at a sitting! Doesn't everyone? I always like to keep up with Stephen's interests so that I can discuss them intelligently with him, and no matter how busy we are during the day, we always make time to meet at night for a cosy chat *à deux*. He comes to my bedroom and—Primrose dear! *Primrose!* My God, there's none so deaf as those that refuse to hear—excuse me a moment, Venetia."

I looked wildly around for any object which might have contained alcohol but saw only coffee-pots.

"And as I was saying," said Dido, swooping back after a mini-slanging match with Primrose who had refused to pass around the cigarettes, "Stephen comes to my room every night and we talk about everything—really, I always feel so sorry for couples who say they can't communicate with each other because I'm convinced that communication is the secret of a really successful marriage—and having been married successfully for eighteen years I should know what I'm talking about. Indeed I honestly feel that where Stephen's concerned I'm practically psychic, but I suppose that's what happens when you know someone through and through—and God knows, no one knows Stephen as well as I do—except possibly Jon Darrow, but unfortunately he's senile now and sees no one, poor old man. Well, my dear, my duty as a hostess calls and I must run off and ask the general about his gout—but do help yourself to something from the decanters over there behind the admiral. Perhaps a little Rémy Martin might be appropriate? Brandy's always so useful if one's feeling as peaky as one looks."

She swooped away.

I drank two triple brandies. Then having made my escape I drove erratically back to my flat and lay awake in torment until dawn.

XI

"Chastity is the expression of charity—of caring, enough. And this is the criterion for every form of behaviour, inside marriage or out of it, in sexual ethics or in any other field. For nothing else makes a thing right or wrong."

JOHN A. T. ROBINSON
HONEST TO GOD

I

I OVERSLEPT and missed not only the early service but Sunday Matins. I did rush to the Cathedral in time for the Sung Communion, but the Dean glided away afterwards without once looking in my direction. In despair I retired to the cloisters and waited on Lady Mary but no one came. I felt demented.

Back at the flat I wrote:

Darling Neville,

I really was rather demolished by dinner last night. Any chance of seeing you before Wednesday? All love,

V.

Then I returned to the Cathedral with the idea of leaving the letter in the Dean's stall to await his arrival for Evensong, but the eagle-eyed Cathedral guides were everywhere and a stout lady arranging flowers by the lectern made any attempt to sidle unobserved to the stall impossible.

Stumbling home I tore up the letter and phoned the Deanery.

Dido answered.

I hung up and mixed myself a dry martini which would have stopped even James Bond dead in his tracks. Then I slumped down on the sofa beneath the Elvis posters and began to cry.

"...AND when Bonhoeffer states that mankind has come of age," dictated the Bishop, "and implies that man—modern man—can get along without God, he is clearly flirting with nothing less than the Pelagian heresy. Or in other words, Dr. Robinson follows Bonhoeffer on this point *at his peril.*

"However," added Dr. Ashworth kindly, stroking his pectoral cross as if it were a domestic pet, "the Bishop tries hard to redeem himself by stressing the importance to modern man of Christ, and indeed his view of Jesus is not entirely without merit. His statement, for instance, that Christ is the window through which we see God is well in line with orthodox thinking. Nevertheless I fear that when he mocks the traditional concept of the Incarnation in various facetious sentences, he not only diminishes the doctrine of God; he puts himself squarely in line with those who followed Arius in the days of the Early Church. What we are dealing with here," concluded Dr. Ashworth, blissfully happy, "is yet another resurgence in a brand-new form of an age-old challenge to orthodoxy."

And he proceeded to demolish both the Pelagian and the Arian heresies.

3

"MY darling, I'm desperately sorry—I got your letter yesterday, but I couldn't meet you on Lady Mary because—oh hullo, General! Fancy seeing you here!"

"Just had a spot of lunch, Dean." The general gazed at me with his protuberant, gooseberry-coloured eyes as I paused by the open door of Aysgarth's car in the courtyard of the Staro Arms. "Good afternoon, Miss Flaxton."

"Good afternoon, General." I slid uneasily into the passenger seat.

"Well, Venetia," said Aysgarth. "We mustn't keep Lady Mary waiting, must we?"

"It's so kind of you to give me a lift," I said to him in ringing tones. The general was slightly deaf. "I do hope I'm not taking you too far out of your way."

"Were you in the dining-room, Miss Flaxton?" said the general, now exhibiting a marked curiosity. "I didn't see you."

"No, I was in the river-garden."

Aysgarth said firmly: "If you'll excuse us, General—"

"Of course, of course . . ."

As the car shot forward across the courtyard, Aysgarth muttered: "We'll have to arrange a different rendez-vous—we can't risk that old buffer seeing us again."

"Never mind, we're finally alone together. That's all that matters."

The car roared with a screech of the tires into Eternity Street and rocketed away towards the river and the suburbs.

4

"MY darling, why were you so upset in your letter? Why did you want to meet me last night on Lady Mary?"

"It was that dinner-party."

"I knew you'd find it dull, but—"

"Dull! Do you think I simply wanted to whine that I was bored? I tell you it was vile—vile, vile, *vile!*"

He was very shocked. "But what happened?"

"Let's wait till we get to the car-park. I can't possibly discuss this unless I have your full attention."

In response he promptly trod on the brakes, pulled the car round the corner into a side-road and halted beneath the branches of a chestnut tree. We had crossed the river by that time and were in one of the quiet, dignified residential streets of the suburb called Parson's Mill.

Switching off the engine he demanded: "What did Dido say?"

I tried without success to speak.

"You shouldn't take any notice of her," he said. "Just let all those words pour off you like water off a duck's back."

"Unfortunately," I said, "her words aren't water and I'm no duck." I stared fiercely out of the window at the flower-filled front garden of the nearest house as I added: "I'm sorry—I know you don't want to talk about her—"

"I'll talk about her till the cows come home if that'll put things right. Tell me exactly what she said."

"It wasn't so much what she said as what she implied."

"And what was that?"

But I was silent. In the end all I could say was: "I had this horrible feeling that she knows everything about us."

"Impossible."

"She said you discuss everything together—"

"Hardly! Do you think I tell her about my Wednesday excursions?"

"But what do you say to explain your absences?"

"Nothing. She's out playing bridge with her girlfriends. It's a regular four. Next week, when she's the hostess at the Deanery, I shall have to take a little more care when I slip out, but she'll be much too busy to notice me."

"But if she suspects we meet, she'll watch you more closely and—"

"She suspects nothing. It sounds to me as if you've completely misread her. The trouble with reading Dido is that she shoots innumerable arrows at the target of truth and just because she scores a certain number of bull's-eyes one can easily be fooled into thinking not only that she hits the mark every time but that she knows much more than she actually does. Now listen to me and I'll set your mind at rest by explaining exactly what's going on. You're female, under thirty and congenial to me so Dido's going to be lukewarm towards you. Nothing new there, of course; that's been the situation for years and from Dido's point of view little has changed. But from your point of view everything's changed—which explains why you're now ultra-sensitive to every arrow Dido shoots from her bow. But what you should remember is that from Dido's point of view the only change in the situation is your mysterious decision to stay in Starbridge and live in a déclassé flat when you could be bobbing around London and living somewhere smart."

"Exactly. Dido probably thinks—"

"No, she doesn't. I've pointed out that this is the 1960s and upper-class girls are no longer as hidebound by convention as they were twenty— even ten—years ago. You've always been intrigued by the ecclesiastical— what could be more natural than that you should be unable to say no when the Bishop, very flatteringly, offers you a job? And since you've finally made the break with your parents, what could be more natural than that you should rebel against your upbringing in a stately home by living in a small flat? Dido, I assure you, quite saw the logic of that argument, and as soon as you pushed your religious conversion claim on Saturday night she was fully prepared to concede that your continuing presence in Starbridge was no longer a mystery. She was actually very benign towards you, said how greatly you'd improved—"

"You discussed me, then," I said, "after the party."

"Oh, we discussed everyone! We always have a post-mortem on our social events!"

"Yes. She did in fact say that you go to her bedroom every night for a cosy little chat."

There was a silence while I stared fiercely at the flowers again, but at last I heard him say: "Darling, you don't have to be jealous of Dido."

"Why not?" I swung to face him. "She's your wife, isn't she?"

"Yes, but . . ." Now it was his turn to stare at the flowers. Then he said: "Try to understand. She's a sad person in many ways. She has many difficulties. She needs someone to look after her and I'm the one who's been called to do it. But all that has absolutely no bearing on the strength of my love for you."

"You mean—what you're really saying is—"

"Dido's Stephen's responsibility," he said. "But neither of them has anything to do with us."

I stared at him but he was smiling as if he had not compounded the mystery but elucidated it. "Feeling better?" he said lightly. "Shall we go on?"

I nodded. I felt I needed time to think. Reaching out he gave my hand a comforting squeeze and then started the engine to resume our journey.

5

WE really must walk up to the Ring today," said Aysgarth, parking the Humber. "I feel we need to be wary of too many delicious incarcerations in the car."

We set off along the bridle-path which led upwards over the ridge, and soon vast views of the Plain began to unfold in every direction. Aysgarth's was the only car in the parking area, but ahead of us some hikers were moving steadily towards the brow of the hill.

"Are you all right?" he said, reaching for my hand. "You're very quiet."

"I was just thinking that although I've known you for so many years, I don't really know you at all. This Stephen whom you now talk of as a separate person—when did he come into being?"

"1946."

"But you married Dido in 1945 and I thought she'd always called you Stephen!"

"Yes, but it took me a while to grow into him, and I was still Neville in 1945. That was Neville Three," he added placidly, apparently unaware that the conversation was in any way bizarre. "Now, of course, I'm Neville Four." Pausing for breath he turned to survey the landscape. The hill was steeper than it looked from the car-park. "My goodness, what splendid views!" he exclaimed. "But I don't like the look of those black clouds over there."

"Never mind the black clouds. Tell me about the first three Nevilles."

Without a second's hesitation he said: "Oh, they wouldn't interest you at all."

"Everything about you interests me, Neville. I love you so I want to know you through and through."

"My darling!" He gave me his sexiest smile. "How very sweet you are, but I think we've wasted quite enough of our precious time together talking about matters which just aren't relevant to our wonderful love here and now in the summer of '63. I want to talk about *you!* Tell me everything you've been doing—how's life at the South Canonry?"

I gave up and began to describe the Bishop's continuing demolition of heresy.

6

"*CHARLES* has got it entirely wrong as usual," said Aysgarth. "He's misunderstood the Bonhoeffer dictum and he's perverted Robinson's views on the Incarnation. The truth is Robinson's remarks on kenotic Christology clearly indicate—whoops! Here comes the rain! What an unjust reward for my virtuous attempt to exercise!"

Haring downhill hand in hand as the heavens opened, we reached the car and hurled ourselves inside.

"How out of training I am!" gasped Aysgarth as he subsided behind the steering-wheel. "Darling, if I drop dead, abandon me at once, I implore you, and thumb a lift back to Starbridge. I'd hate to embarrass everyone by dying in scandalous circumstances . . . Good heavens, look at this!" he added as the rain began to pound more heavily than ever against the windscreen.

"There was a very erotic song in the hit parade some time ago," I said, watching him smooth back his wet hair. "It was called 'The Day That the Rains Came.' "

"Did it conjure up images of wet earth and steaming grass and people plunging naked through the undergrowth?"

"You're thinking of D. H. Lawrence!"

We laughed, and suddenly the expression in his eyes changed. For a moment I thought he would do no more than look at me, but I was wrong. He leant forward to kiss me on the mouth.

Then I ceased to hear the rain drumming on the roof, ceased to see the water streaming down the glass, ceased to think of anything except the man I wanted—and alongside us in the land of allegory the powerful, predatory serpent, no longer sedate and domesticated, surged forth from the undergrowth to encircle us both at last.

"IT can't be wrong," said Aysgarth. "I just don't believe it's wrong. Love makes everything right. It must do. It must."

I was unable to reply. I was aware of a variety of physical reactions which I have no intention of describing in clinical detail, but my awareness was dim because I was almost unconscious with ecstasy. I could only stay glued to his wet shirt-front and pray not to weep with frustration when the embrace inevitably ended.

Then I heard him whisper: "You're such a prize, Venetia, *such a prize!* So of course," he added with a sigh as he finally released me, "I must never win you."

At first I thought I had misheard him. "Never win me?"

"No, I must keep you perfect. All prizes are perfect, naturally, or they wouldn't be prizes, but winning them can be dangerous. One can win a prize, discover its imperfections and then realise one doesn't want it any more."

I stared at him. Yet again he seemed quite unaware that the conversation had become bizarre. "Are you implying," I said incredulously, "that if you won me you'd soon get bored and toss me aside?"

"No, I'm merely reminding myself that if I won you I'd be winning a flesh-and-blood person, not a fantasy, and we might well fail to live happily ever after—or in other words, I was reminding myself that chasing the prizes can lead one into a world of illusion. It's always vital that I remember that."

"Neville, all this talk of prizes—"

"Yes, it's absurd, isn't it? It used to be a fixation of mine, the result of my impoverished youth and an uncle who urged me to go 'chasing the prizes of life' in order to make the best of myself. But I've got a more balanced outlook on life now." He fumbled in the pocket of his jacket and produced a packet of cigarettes. "Shall we smoke?"

I waited until our cigarettes were alight before I said: "Eddie mentioned that uncle of yours."

"Uncle Willoughby—a marvellous old boy he was, took care of us all in the difficult days after my father died. No doubt it was because my life was so far from perfect then that I used to dream of perfection—to dream, as Uncle Willoughby would have put it, of the ultimate prizes: a perfect home, a perfect career, a perfect wife, perfect children—"

"But Neville," I said, "no one's really perfect, are they?" I was remembering Primrose telling me long ago of her brothers' unflagging efforts to acquire flawless masks.

"No, of course true perfection can't exist in this world," he agreed willingly enough, "but one should still dream of perfection, cherish ideals, aim for the finest prizes—goals, I mean—"

"There you go again!"

He laughed. "I'm incorrigible, aren't I? Let's talk of something else."

"No, I want to talk more about you."

"But there's nothing to say! You know it all."

"Do I? I know you were born in Yorkshire and that your father died bankrupt when you were seven. I know you and your brother were then boarded out in London in order to go to a good school while your mother's poor health forced her to live by the sea in Sussex with your sister. I know you won a scholarship to Oxford where you took a first in Greats and received your call to be a clergyman. I know you married at twenty-four and had five children. I know you were Rector of Willowmead, Archdeacon of Starbridge and a Canon of Westminster. I know that after your first wife died you married again and had five more children, only two of whom survived. I know you're now Dean of Starbridge. Yes, it's quite true—I do know all about you. So why do I increasingly feel you're a complete stranger?"

"My darling, I can't imagine why you're so keen to wrap me in mystery! I'm just a Yorkshire draper's son who's made good. What could be more simple than that?"

"I'll tell you: all the Yorkshire drapers' sons who haven't made good. They're the simple ones. I now realise that you must be quite extraordinary and tremendously complex, but I don't see how I'm ever going to know you through and through when you resolutely refuse to talk about yourself."

"But you understand me perfectly! You're so sympathetic, so intuitive, so clever, so—"

"Thank you, I hope I'm all those things, but—"

"You're all those things and much, much more," he said, stubbing out his cigarette and switching on the ignition, "so can't you see how unnecessary it is to delve into my utterly irrelevant past? Neville Four doesn't have a past, that's the truth of it. He just has this glorious present with you."

I took the hint and pursued my cross-examination no further, but as the Humber descended from the hills into the valley, I began to wonder if I understood even less than I had imagined.

WE were more than halfway to Starbridge before I summoned the nerve to ask: "Neville, what exactly is your connection with Nicholas Darrow's father, that clergyman who ran the Theological College back in the forties?"

The car swerved slightly, but to my relief he seemed more astonished than annoyed by this new attempt to probe the past. "Jon Darrow?" he exclaimed. "Why on earth should you want to know about him?"

"I've been told he knows you through and through."

At once he said sharply: "Who said that?"

"I'm sorry, I really don't want to mention her name again, but—"

"Why in heaven's name should Dido have been talking to you about old Darrow?"

"Well, she was boasting about how well she knew you, and—"

"Ah, now I understand this new obsession of yours to know me through and through! Darling, you must stop seeing Dido as a rival—and you must stop believing every word she says. She doesn't know me well at all. She only knows Stephen."

Dimly it occurred to me that in order to participate intelligently in these extraordinary conversations I needed a wisdom which I had not lived long enough to acquire.

"And who does Darrow know?" I said cautiously.

"The first three Nevilles."

"Not Stephen?"

"No, I haven't seen much of the old pirate since Stephen evolved." He tried to overtake the car in front, thought better of it and dropped back. The oncoming car hooted furiously as it skimmed past our wing-mirror.

"Why do you call the old boy a pirate?" I said when the sound of the horn had died away. "I thought he was a holy hermit who lived in a wood on communion wafers."

Aysgarth laughed so hard that he nearly drove through a red light. We were now re-entering the suburb of Parson's Mill. "It's really amazing," he exclaimed, "how myths form around that buccaneer! My dear, Father Jonathan Darrow is an eccentric Anglo-Catholic priest who used to perform charismatic wonders, flirt with scandal and make strong archdeacons weep. His years at the Theological College constituted his respectable phase. Before that he'd done more or less everything—he was even a monk in the Anglican Fordite Order during the twenties and thirties! Young Nicholas, of course, was fathered later. Martin the actor was fathered long before."

"But is the old boy really living in a wood as a hermit?"

"I think it would be more accurate—though less amusing—to say he lives as a recluse twelve miles from Starbridge; he had a cottage built for him in the grounds of the Manor House which his second wife owned at Starrington Magna. She's dead now, I'm sorry to say—a nice woman she was, I liked her—and the Manor itself is run by a religious community of about eight men and women who keep an eye on the old boy to make sure he's all right."

"You mean he's capable of living alone in his cottage? Someone told me he was senile."

"There was a rumour he was unhinged for a time by his wife's death, but I suspect the people who say he's senile are the people who can't imagine why anyone should want to live as a recluse."

"But Neville," I said as we approached the bridge over the river, "how did this clerical eccentric, whom you don't seem to like much, come to know you so well?"

"Ah," said Aysgarth. He paused. Then he said: "Well, as a matter of fact he gave me a helping hand once. Very decent of him and I appreciated it. I was going through a bit of a spiritual crisis at the time."

"You mean you'd lost your faith?"

"Good heavens, no!" said Aysgarth shocked. "Who do you think I am—one of Graham Greene's whisky-priests? No, life just became a trifle awkward for a few days, that's all. However, I survived. I'm a born survivor," said Aysgarth, hands resting lightly on the wheel as the car shot over the bridge, "and so's that old pirate Jon Darrow. Incidentally, what do you think of that boy of his? I haven't seen him since he was a child."

"He's a psychic. He gives the impression of never travelling without his crystal ball."

"That sounds like a chip off the old block! There was some wild talk about how his father foresaw Pearl Harbor but I never believed a word of it. Dear old Darrow, he used to drive me mad when I was an archdeacon, but he was a great character. I shall feel sorry when he's finally called to meet his maker."

That remark gave me a jolt. St. Darrow, Nick had told me, was eighty-three. The old boy could be borne off by the angels at any minute. I had to act fast.

After parting from Aysgarth outside the Staro Arms amidst the usual torrid hand-squeezes and smouldering looks, I retired to my flat and tried to work out how I could gain access to this ancient recluse who had once known my Mr. Dean so well.

FROM the telephone operator I obtained the number of Laud's College in Cambridge, but when I put through the call I was told term had ended. I then looked up the number of Starrington Manor where one of St. Darrow's disciples managed to produce my Talisman after a three-minute hunt.

"Sorry to bother you, Nick," I said, determined not to make Marina's mistake of drowning him in cloying enthusiasm, "but I was hoping you could give me some advice about your brother. I've been invited to see *Present Laughter* and"—I paused with thespian skill to convey the impression that a casual thought had just drifted into my mind—"oh, by the way, I assume you'll be heading for the Starbridge Playhouse too some time that week?"

"On the Friday, yes."

"Ah, I think Eddie—Eddie Hoffenberg, my escort—can only manage the Saturday, so I doubt if I'll see you, but I must just ask this: as I told you once, my mother's a huge Martin Darrow fan—would he think me a colossal bore if I went backstage and asked for his autograph for her?"

"Actors never mind being asked for autographs," said Nick in a tone of voice which suggested he considered all actors far beneath him. It occurred to me then to wonder if he might be jealous of his handsome, successful brother.

"But do I have to mention your name in order to win admittance to the august presence?" I pursued, craftily signalling to him by my facetious tone that I too thought actors were a race apart.

"I shouldn't think so. But mention it if you like," said Nick, picking up my signal and becoming gracious.

"Lovely, thanks so much. I say . . . will your father be going to see the play?"

"Yes."

"How exciting for him! I hope he likes it. Older people often find Coward quite shocking, I believe."

"My father isn't that sort of old person," said Nick, becoming austere, "and since my mother was a Coward fan, he's familiar with the text of *Present Laughter.*"

"Super! Okay, Nick, mustn't delay you any longer—see you around some time. 'Bye."

I hung up, found pen and paper and wrote:

Dear Eddie,

After that mean-spirited, un-Christian little note I sent in response to your last letter, am I allowed to change my mind about *Present Laughter*? I've decided I'd like to go, although for various reasons the only evening I can manage is the Friday. However, if you'd prefer not to escort me—indeed if you'd prefer to tear up this note and jump on it—I shall quite understand.

Yours,
VENETIA.

I posted this missive five minutes later in the Chasuble Lane pillar-box. Then feeling confident that I would eventually come face to face with St. Darrow, I congratulated myself on my Machiavellian skills and began to speculate again—fruitlessly—on the mysterious multiple personalities of my extraordinary Mr. Dean.

I O

AN hour later I was just goggling at the television news (the Profumo scandal was now in full flower) and spooning baked beans into my mouth when the telephone rang. It was my mother, who had discovered that Martin Darrow was to appear at the Starbridge Playhouse. Enthralled by the thought of seeing her hero in the flesh she was already planning her visit to Flaxton Hall which could be used as a base for her assault on the theatre.

". . . and I was wondering if we could go to *Present Laughter* together, darling," she added. "I'd so like to see your flat—perhaps we could have an egg or something before the play. Can you boil an egg yet?"

"Oh yes, but it's so messy—all that steam—"

"Well, never mind, a sandwich would do—"

"Will Papa be with you?"

"Oh no, he'd never go near anything by Coward. That's why I thought that perhaps you and I—"

"Mama, it's terribly unfortunate but I've just agreed to go to the play with Canon Hoffenberg. Could you arrange to go with one of your Starbridge pals instead? You could come here for a drink first, of course—"

"Canon Hoffenberg!"

"Yes, but don't tell Papa—he'll ring up and start bawling away about the damned Huns, and frankly I'm not in a mood to take it."

"Oh, I know, darling, I know, so exhausting, and personally I've always rather liked Canon Hoffenberg—"

"Just let me know when you're coming, Mama, and I'll go out and buy some gin."

"No, no, don't buy any gin—your father will be so relieved when I tell him with a clear conscience that you don't keep spirits in your flat. A glass of sherry would be quite sufficient for me."

We parted amicably. Eyeing the gin bottle nearby I made a mental note to hide it in the airing cupboard before my mother arrived. Then I returned to the apparently endless television report on the Profumo scandal (distinguished married man ruined by ravishing young floozie) and began munching away once more on my baked beans.

I I

"DEAR Venetia," wrote Eddie in a letter which was delivered by hand.

I've got two tickets for the front row of the circle for the Friday performance. I shall be having dinner first at that new restaurant, the Quill Pen, in Wheat Street and if you'd like to join me, just let me know. Otherwise I'll pick you up at your flat at 7.40. The restaurant column of *The Starbridge Weekly News* said that on the Quill Pen's wine-list there was a very bold sparkling Mosel (which one seldom encounters in this country), but perhaps you'd prefer champagne, which I've no doubt the Quill Pen can also supply in abundance.

Yours,
EDDIE.

I wrote back:

Dear Eddie:

Congratulations on the front row of the circle! I thought the best seats would already have been nabbed, but maybe the Cathedral clergy have a special pull at the box office. I'll drink anything that sparkles—in fact I'll drink anything—but I'm on a diet so I'll say no to the Quill Pen. See you at 7.40 as you suggest. Many thanks.

Yours,
VENETIA.

Then I picked up Aysgarth's daily report, read it through yet again and wrote:

My darling Neville,

Thanks so much for your letter, but honestly, there's no need to work yourself into such a frenzy of remorse—it wasn't *your* fault that I was demolished at the Deanery! In fact I can see now (thanks to you) that I overreacted to all D's remarks and made a mountain out of a molehill, so really I can blame no one for the demolition but myself. Sorry I got so fixated on your past and tried to turn you into a mystery-man. I'm sure you really are terribly simple and that I really am being terribly stupid. It's just that I find you so enthralling that I tend to go into an overheated feminine flat-spin unless I understand every single thing you do. Such a drag for you! I promise to behave more rationally in future.

Apart from my idiotic behaviour (as specified above) I adored every minute of our meeting, especially the bit where we stuck together so torridly that steam rose from our wet clothes. But I think you're right and we should change the rendez-vous from the Staro Arms. How about the car-park of the Starbridge Playhouse? Which reminds me, I decided to make my peace with Eddie by agreeing to go with him to see *Present Laughter*. Eddie suggested this outing some time ago and I thought it might be a painless way of compensating him for my beastliness on the Cathedral roof. Then I shan't have to go out with him again.

Darling, what a *bore* about Fitzgerald taking a phallic view of the sculpture's "box of cigars"! He must have a mind like a sink—in fact I'm really quite shocked. As for him saying that the sculpture displays no Christian message but only symbols of the old earth-mother type of religion, all I can say is that I think he's behaving like a Freudian case-book.

Longing to see you again and *panting* for your next letter. By the way, I suppose it's a bit late in the day to start worrying, but are you sure it's safe for me to write as frankly as this? Wouldn't it be wiser if I addressed you as "Dear Mr. Dean," signed off "Love, Venetia," and cut out all references to generating steam? Whenever I think of the Profumo scandal (can't wait for the House of Commons debate!) I get very nervous of taking any potentially scandalous risk. Much, *much* love from your devoted

EGERIA.

Aysgarth wrote back by return:

My darling,

Don't worry about our letters. I always get up early to put in an hour's work before breakfast, and D always has breakfast in bed as compensation for the fact that she seldom manages to sleep before three in the morning. My study, as you know, is next to the front door and I see the postman come up the garden path—usually around seven. There's absolutely no possibility that D would ever be up at that hour, and by the time the second post arrives Miss Trotman's here to pounce on it (though she would never, of course, open an envelope marked "Private and Confidential"). The only tricky time is on weekends but I'm very vigilant and D's really much too absorbed in her own affairs to bother to ambush the postman. All your letters I keep under lock and key, and the key itself is always in my pocket. So say whatever you wish when you write to me—there's no scandalous risk involved!

As for John Profumo, I'm sorry for him, of course—I'd be sorry for any man who wrecked a successful career—but I fear my sympathy is limited. Any distinguished man who's fool enough to mess around with the demi-monde as represented by Christine Keeler is taking not merely a scandalous risk but a suicidal one.

I've thought a lot about our last meeting (the steam in the front seat!) and I'm sure everything's all right. You have such a benign influence on me; I'm feeling more energetic, drinking less, losing weight—even praying better! (And like John Robinson I confess I always found schematic teaching about prayer rather a dead loss—there! I've never told anyone that before.) Robinson is right, of course, in saying that prayer shouldn't mean a withdrawal from the world but a wholly committed engagement with it. Praying is working, relating to other people and above all *loving*. How clearly I can see that now, and you're the one who's helped me to see it. So I'm sure our love is right, sent by God to help me become a better clergyman. The gifts of the Spirit, as the famous saying goes, can be recognised by their fruits.

How very good of you to be so kind to poor old Eddie. I think this is admirable. Well done! I too shall be going to see *Present Laughter* but not until the Saturday—D plans to give a farewell party for the cast afterwards at the Deanery. I must say, I'm looking forward to comparing Martin Darrow's stage-skills with his father's—that old ecclesiastical adventurer used to act like mad whenever he donned a cassock and glided around performing his Anglo-Catholic rituals! No wonder he spent seventeen years being a monk; the urge to dress up in medieval costume and play the holy man would have been far too delectable to resist, and as for his faith-healing phase later—when he tried to play Svengali, Rasputin and Our Lord Jesus Christ all rolled into one—well! Poor old Dr. Ottershaw (Bishop of Starbridge 1937–1947) nearly had a heart-attack.

If it hadn't been war-time Darrow would never have been recruited to teach at the Theological College, but the situation was desperate and he did have the right academic background. But look what his invasion produced! A perfectly respectable college, known for its middle-of-the-road churchmanship, was turned into a hotbed of Anglo-Catholicism laced with periodic outbreaks of charismatic wonders! I admit the College became a huge success, but as soon as Darrow retired in 1950 it collapsed like a pricked balloon and became rather nasty. There was a terrible scandal in the '50s when . . . but no, I must be loyal to the Church and preserve a discreet silence! Charles Ashworth mopped up the mess when he became Bishop. I'll say this for Charles: he doesn't stand any nonsense when it comes to clerical behaviour which is really quite unacceptable.

Must stop now, darling, but I send my best love as always,

N.

P.S. Let's have a quick tryst on Lady Mary—how about Sunday post-Evensong?

Drinking a cup of black coffee I wondered how much longer I could tolerate a diet of occasional quick trysts on Lady Mary and a weekly steamy kiss on Starbury Plain.

12

"AND now," said the Bishop, gorgeous in the yellow sports-shirt and snow-white slacks which he had elected to wear for his morning's round of golf, "having demonstrated that Dr. Robinson is ill-advised to ignore all the great mystics of the Church who throughout the centuries have withdrawn from the world in order to pray—having demonstrated, in other words, that prayer is *not* solely a matter of engaging with the world and exuding love from every pore—we will turn to assess what Dr. Robinson is pleased to call the New Morality. We're going to examine the spectacle of a well-meaning, fatally idealistic middle-aged cleric who proposes to grapple with the increasing problem of sexual license by tearing up all the old rules and merely urging people to love one another. What sort of a world, I ask myself, does the good Bishop think he's living in?"

Dr. Ashworth paused, reaching upwards to stroke that domestic pet, his pectoral cross, but encountered instead only the glossy grey hairs which were exposed by the open neck of his sports-shirt; he had forgotten that the cross had been discarded for his round of golf. "I'll have to rephrase all that later, of course," he said to me. "The tone is much too withering for publication, but while I'm getting my ideas down on paper I shan't bother to apply a coating of sugar. Now let me think. Ethics has many aspects and I'm not sure which one I should tackle first." So absorbed was he in his thoughts that he was unaware of his wife opening the door of the morning-room. "Shall we have sex straight away?" he mused to me as she peeped in. "Or shall we save it for later?"

The point of my pencil snapped.

"Darling," said Mrs. Ashworth serenely from the threshold, "that remark deserves to go straight into the Oxford Book of Quotations."

The Bishop gave a galvanic start and then, to his great credit, laughed with genuine amusement. I promptly giggled in sympathy and Mrs. Ashworth produced her sphinx-like smile.

"Dear me!" exclaimed Dr. Ashworth. "What an extraordinary clanger! I really didn't think I was capable of such a performance—"

" '—as the bishop said to the actress,' " droned Mrs. Ashworth, successfully giving the famous old joke another whirl.

This time no one made any attempt not to laugh, and it was some seconds before Mrs. Ashworth managed to say: "Charles, I came to tell you that your brother's on the phone. Can you possibly tear yourself away from Venetia to speak to him?"

"I'm sure Venetia would welcome a break from my inanities!" gasped Dr. Ashworth, and disappeared, still laughing, to his study.

"If he's going to dictate about sex," said Mrs. Ashworth, "you'd better have a drink. Gin-and-tonic?"

"I'd love one, but no—it might have a fatal effect on my shorthand."

"In that case stay and have a drink afterwards. Since he switched you today from nine to five in order to trek over that awful golf course, I think the least I can do is provide a gin-and-tonic in compensation."

I agreed to a drink at six. Dr. Ashworth returned from his study but was soon recalled by another phone call which was promptly succeeded by a third.

"Sorry, Venetia," he said afterwards, "but I'm going to have to call off this session. The Archdeacon's coming round to discuss an emergency."

Was I disappointed or was I relieved that the Bishop had been obliged to postpone his demolition of the New Morality? I had no idea. Then I realised that this was because I wanted to have no idea. For one long moment I saw myself marooned amidst an array of mirrors which tilted up and down so rapidly that I could no longer distinguish between reality and illusion in their shifting reflections, but then I pushed this unnerving image from my mind, pulled myself together and prepared to enjoy a drink with my heroine.

XII

"The chapter on 'The New Morality,' for example, is particularly disquieting. One feels that a careful study of the troubles that befell St. Paul in Corinth . . . would be profitable to the Bishop. It is likely that the Apostle would prove a far better guide than D. H. Lawrence, that devotee of a religion far older than Christianity and still one of its principal rivals."

GLYN SIMON,
in The Honest to God Debate

I

"HOW'S the love-life?" said Mrs. Ashworth after we had been chatting for a while in her sitting-room.

"Promising. I may be going sailing soon with Perry Palmer. He keeps a boat at Bosham."

"That's Christian's friend, isn't it—the young man you mentioned to me the other day."

"Yes, that's the one." I suddenly wondered if she had heard the rumour that Perry was a eunuch, but since the Aysgarths and the Ashworths had never lived in each other's pockets I felt there was a good chance the story had failed to reach the South Canonry.

"What does he do for a living?"

"No one knows for sure but he's reputed to be a spy."

"How fashionable!"

"Oh, he's hardly the James Bond type—"

"Just as well, perhaps. Michael adores the James Bond novels," added Mrs. Ashworth as an afterthought, "and Charles gets so cross, says they're decadent. Of course he's read them all." Casually she flicked ash from her cigarette into the nearest tray. "Well, congratulations on landing an old Wykhamist who lives in Albany and keeps a boat at Bosham! But why aren't you living up in London so that you can see him more often?"

"Oh, that wouldn't do at all, Mrs. Ashworth!" I said glibly at once. "He might think he was being chased. I've made up my mind to play this very cool."

"How sensible," said Mrs. Ashworth, blowing some smoke languidly towards the ceiling.

I realized it was time I displayed some passion. "Of course we do write a lot—"

"Write! I thought your generation only used the phone!"

"Well, naturally we phone each other as well—"

"It sounds as if you've got yourself very well organised," said my heroine kindly. "I'm so glad."

Without warning I heard myself blurt out: "Yes, I'm very lucky compared with Dinkie—that's Dinkie Kauffman, an American friend of Marina's. She's got herself mixed up with a married man, and it all sounds desperately frustrating because they can only meet once a week and since he won't go to her flat the meetings always have to take place in his car."

"How intriguing. I've never before heard of a married man who wouldn't snap up the chance to go to his mistress's flat."

"Oh, she's not his mistress, Mrs. Ashworth! It's all rather peculiar. You see, he keeps insisting that he doesn't want an affair but he also swears he's madly in love with her—which is all so confusing to poor Dinkie, who can't figure out what's really going on—and I couldn't figure it out either when she asked my advice."

"Maybe he wants to do the right thing and marry her first. Is there a divorce in the offing?"

"Oh, there's no question of a divorce! And the wife could live for ever, according to Dinkie."

"It sounds to me," said Mrs. Ashworth, "as if Dinkie's wasting her time."

"But Mrs. Ashworth, surely an affair is always a strong possibility when two people are madly in love? I mean, *I* know, of course, that an affair would be morally wrong, but poor Dinkie—who's not religious—is in such a state over her grand passion that she's nearly being driven mad by all this high-minded abstaining. She feels that if only she could have a little bit of bed now and then—"

"The trouble with grand passions is that the lovers are never content with just a little bit of bed now and then."

"But half a loaf's better than none, surely? And she does absolutely accept that she can't marry him—"

"That's purely a temporary phenomenon, the result of lack of experience and wishful thinking. Once she was his mistress she'd soon start to wonder how long the wife was going to go on."

"Dinkie already wishes the wife was dead, I know—and oh, Mrs. Ashworth, the most ghastly part of the whole situation, the part that's driving Dinkie up the wall, is that she thinks he may still be sleeping with his wife. He says he's not—or rather, he implies he's not—I mean, he's never actually said to Dinkie: '*I do not sleep with my wife,*' but he obviously wants to give the impression that he—"

"Of course. No married man in his right mind is going to say cheerfully to his potential mistress: 'Oh, by the way, I'm still sleeping with the old girl, but you don't mind, do you?'"

"You mean . . . you think the likelihood is—"

"Oh yes. Have another gin."

I accepted another gin. I had to concentrate very hard to make sure that my hand was steady when she returned my glass. Then I said evenly: "I don't know how you can be so certain, Mrs. Ashworth. Surely it's fairly common for couples who have been married for years not to sleep together? In fact I thought this was always the main reason why husbands strayed."

"A straying husband would certainly indicate that the marriage has its difficulties, but those difficulties needn't necessarily be sexual. If this man's content to breathe passion over Dinkie but take the affair no further, I'd guess the marriage has its private compensations which aren't apparent to the outsider."

"But surely there must be another explanation! If the man's a romantic—or an eccentric—"

"Oh, anything's possible, certainly. I suppose the next most likely explanation for his abstinence is that he's impotent: he'd get his thrills out of passionate kisses and he'd make some excuse—a moral objection to adultery would do nicely—to ensure he stayed out of the bedroom."

"As a matter of fact, Dinkie says he *has* voiced a strong moral objection to adultery—"

"Ah well, there you are."

"But Mrs. Ashworth, couldn't he be genuinely held back by his moral beliefs?"

"My dear," said Mrs. Ashworth, "I know it's quite wrong for a bishop's wife to be so cynical, but at least I'm being entirely honest when I say that in my opinion a man in the grip of a grand passion can always work out a way to circumvent his moral beliefs. He'd still hold those particular beliefs, of course, but he'd decide his case wasn't covered by the rules. There's nothing like a grand passion for encouraging self-deception on an epic scale."

"So you think that eventually he'll work his way around his moral beliefs and sleep with Dinkie after all?"

"Goodness only knows what he'll do, but tell Dinkie that if she paddles in the pool of adultery she could well wake up one morning and find that the waters have closed over her head. I knew a young woman once," said Mrs. Ashworth, sipping her gin, "who got in a fearful mess with a married man—a very respectable married man—really most eminent—someone who had absolutely no hope of a divorce—and at first she thought she'd be satisfied with just a passionate kiss now and then but she wasn't, she wasn't satisfied at all, she was soon so jealous of the wife that she became bitter and miserable—even in the end unbalanced—yes, in the end she became quite mad, so mad that she was almost destroyed—*almost destroyed*—and even when by some undeserved miracle she was rescued by a good man who married her, she wasn't right, not for years, and that was so terrible for the husband . . . although I'm glad to say that in the end everything came right and they were happy. But at what cost! And after such suffering! It was an appalling case and I'll never forget it. Never."

After a pause I managed to say: "What happened to her married lover?"

"Oh, he was ruined, of course," said Mrs. Ashworth in the manner of a pathologist dictating a report from the morgue. "He resigned his job. He never worked again. He died before his time of cancer." And she ground out her cigarette in the ash-tray as if to symbolise the life that had been so inexorably extinguished.

There followed a silence which I was unable to break. Then she said with an effortless resumption of her relaxed, friendly manner: "Charley's making a quick visit home this weekend—are you free for Sunday lunch? I'm sure he'd enjoy seeing you."

"I don't think he would, Mrs. Ashworth. When we met on the train before Easter we had rather a slanging match."

"That sounds promising! Charley loves to be combative. Do come!"

Unable to think of an excuse more compelling than sheer incompatibility I gave way and accepted the invitation. Then feeling deeply disturbed I returned home and watched television without comprehension in the dusk.

2

AT three o'clock in the morning I was finally able to think: he's undeniably healthy and so the likelihood is he's sexually unimpaired; therefore if he's not sleeping with his wife, the chances are that he'll eventually work his way around his moral convictions and wind up sleeping with me. Then I was able to doze off, but when I awoke four hours later my resolution to be patient withered in seconds and I felt overpowered by the longing to see him.

Recalling his spiritual timetable I realised he would be absent that morning from the early services in St. Anselm's Chapel so I made no effort to go to the Cathedral, but soon after nine I telephoned the Deanery.

Aysgarth's secretary Miss Trotman took the call.

"Good morning," I said. "Could you remind the Dean, please, that Lady Mary wishes to speak to him this evening about the memorial tablet? Thank you so much." But as I hung up I realised I would now have to devise a new telephone message; Lady Mary could hardly go on wanting to speak to the Dean about a memorial tablet.

The difficulties of communication suddenly seemed intolerable. For a moment I sank deep into depression, but then pulling myself together I began to look forward to seeing him later in the cloisters.

3

HE called back at noon. "Can't talk now," he said. "Just wanted to say 'message received.' See you on Lady Mary after Evensong," and he hung up.

Some hours later I was just rising to my feet at the start of the service when I noticed that Dido was present in the congregation. She appeared unaware of me, but I found myself unable to stop looking at her and eventually, inevitably, our glances met. At once she gave me a bright smile. Not to be outdone I gave her a bright smile in return, but when I stared fiercely at the high altar afterwards I could only see the cross through a haze of tears. At the end of the service Aysgarth walked past without looking at me and Dido zipped across to the vestry door to wait for him.

Abandoning all hope of a tryst on Lady Mary I went home and drank three double-gins.

4

"MY darling," wrote Aysgarth in a letter which caught the last post and arrived at my flat early on Wednesday morning.

I'm devastated that I shan't be able to get to Lady Mary after all this evening—D, who hasn't been to Evensong for ages, has just announced that she feels spiritual and knows she's being called to attend. (This is a very typical D-remark and is probably more or less true, so you needn't worry that she suspects anything.) Thank God tomorrow's Wednesday and we can have plenty of time to talk. I'm just praying the Lady Mary signal doesn't indicate some dire emergency.

Life certainly seems to be increasingly fraught on the ecclesiastical front, and Harriet March's magnificent sculpture is fast becoming too hot to handle. The traitor Fitzgerald, hatching a fiendish anti-sculpture conspiracy with all the reactionary philistines in Starbridge, has roped in Archdeacon Lindsay who now informs me that I have to seek a faculty (that's a form of ecclesiastical permission) before I instal any structure in the Cathedral churchyard. Now, this would seem to be nonsense as deans are autonomous and neither their cathedrals nor their churchyards are subject to the Chancellor (chief legal eagle) of the diocese who sits in the Consistory Court and grants faculties. But Lindsay informs me that legally the magnificent sward which surrounds Starbridge Cathedral is not in fact a consecrated churchyard (used for burials) but unconsecrated curtilage (mere adjacent land), and all unconsecrated curtilages require a faculty before alteration. Again, this would appear to be rubbish, because although the sward is no longer used for burials it certainly was in the old days, but Lindsay declares that all the burials were irregular since under a Cathedral statute the only consecrated burial ground is the lawn of the cloisters.

Well, of course it's easy to see what happened: once the cloisters' lawn was full up they started burying people out on the sward—and since no one in the old days would have dreamed of having themselves laid to rest in unconsecrated ground, this must mean that at some time or other the place was consecrated. I pointed this out to Lindsay, but he only said stuffily: "In the absence of evidence of consecration, the statute must prevail." That was more than I could take. *"Evidence?"* I said. "The evidence lies in the few tombstones you can still find embedded in the churchyard's turf! They prove consecration beyond any shadow of doubt!" But Lindsay dug in his toes, announced that the Chancellor would have to rule where the burden of proof lay, and stalked off.

So the fight is on, and what I have to prove is that no one has power over that sward except me. I shall collar Gilbert (the Librarian) and get him (1) to look up the appropriate statute in the original Latin (Lindsay only has an English translation), and (2) if no mistake's been made in interpreting the statute, to start tracking down the inevitable later consecration. There *must* be a record of it somewhere! I just can't believe that any past Dean of Starbridge would be so unfamiliar with the Cathedral statutes as to permit burials on unconsecrated curtilage.

I need hardly remind you that Lindsay is the Bishop's henchman and

I need hardly add that this whole devious episcopal attempt to cut back my power makes me absolutely *furious.*

To cap it all—as if I needed more trouble!—our guest preacher for Sunday Matins has been knocked over by a motorbike so I'll have to deliver a sermon in his stead. Dalton's preaching at Evensong, so I can't ask him, and Fitzgerald insists that he has to go to see his widowed mother that weekend. *(Typical!)* Eddie's volunteered, always the masochist, but I had to ask him to do an awful job only the other day (chairing the Cathedral guides' meeting—i.e. presiding over a mass manifestation of verbal diarrhoea) and I really can't always be exploiting poor Eddie.

My darling, forgive this grim catalogue of debilitating anxieties—I can't tell you how I long to see you again, you're my life-line and I know that when I see you I'll be able to dredge up some new strength. Next week looks as if it'll be even more frightful than this week— three diocesan committee meetings, two big funerals and one of those stupefyingly dull special regimental services stuffed with field-marshals, generals and other prize asses, and mitigated only by a touch of royalty. D, needless to say, has long been planning the buffet-lunch for sixty, and has acquired a fantastically expensive new outfit in order to dazzle the Duke and Duchess. How I remain solvent God only knows, since even D's substantial private income can hardly be expected to stretch from here to eternity, but so far my bank manager hasn't cut me dead in Mitre Street.

Occasionally, very occasionally I think how nice it would be not to have to worry about money, but I suppose I'm so used to living on a financial knife-edge that I'm now well past the sleepless-nights stage. One can get used to anything in the end, but oh, how *tired* I get of all the strain sometimes, how utterly fed up and exhausted—yet when I see you, so young, such fun, so full of life, then not only does my weariness vanish as if it had never existed but I can remember what it's like to be happy.

Darling, I love you and I can't wait, *can't wait,* till tomorrow—2.00 in the Playhouse car-park—do you think this time we'll finally make it to Starbury Ring?

All my love,

N.

Refolding the letter I thought: he can't stand her; I'm the one he wants. And all doubt was once more wiped from my mind.

"STARBURY Ring!" I exclaimed. "At last!"

We laughed and clutched each other, still breathless from our climb over the ridge from the car-park. Then we staggered forward in search of a suitable place to recover from our uncharacteristic exertion.

Starbury Ring, a mysterious circle of standing stones, was usually described as resembling Stonehenge, but I always thought it was more like Avebury; each stone stood by itself and no three had been placed together to form an arch. On that afternoon the sun shone strongly from a sky dotted with large white clouds, and the view to the horizon, usually misty, was as clear as if it had been drawn by a fine-nibbed pen. A few hikers were wandering around flapping their guidebooks, and there were one or two prone hippies soaking up the vibes, but as usual the site was underpopulated. Retreating into the shade of one of the stones we were easily able to tuck ourselves out of sight of our fellow-visitors.

"It's wonderfully phallic, isn't it?" I said, gazing at a tall slim stone nearby.

"Wonderfully!" he said smiling, and when he took me in his arms nothing mattered, neither the separations, nor the frustrations, nor the suspicions, nor the bewilderment, nor the anguish, nor the tears—nothing mattered except that we were together. I kissed him and hugged him and gasped when he rolled over on top of me and laughed when he rolled all the way over to the other side by mistake, and when he laughed too we clutched each other in an ecstasy of happiness and I heard him whisper: "Isn't this fun?" But once he released me the fun was wiped out and the frustration was so agonising that my eyes filled with tears. Much humiliated by my weakness but determined not to make a nauseating exhibition of myself, I covered my face with my hands.

"My darling . . ." Realising how upset I was he tried to take me in his arms again, but at that moment some people walked past and I knew he immediately thought, just as I did, how appalling it would have been if one of those casual passers-by had been known to him.

I began to struggle to my feet. "I can't stand this lack of privacy any longer. Let's go to my flat."

Without a second's hesitation he said: "I can't."

"Oh yes, you could!" I said fiercely, demented enough to abandon my waiting game and hammer at the mystery of his abstinence. "You'd take the slight risk involved, but you won't because you don't love me enough!"

"That's not true!" He seemed genuinely appalled.

"Then I don't understand anything here." In exhaustion I slumped against the standing stone.

"But I've explained in great detail! If I don't come to your flat, it's not because I don't love you but because I love you too much to use you for my own selfish purposes when I'm quite unable to offer you marriage. According to John Robinson—"

"Dr. Ashworth thinks John Robinson's up the creek."

"Ah well!" said Aysgarth at once, all scorn. "What else can you expect from a reactionary like Charles?"

The last shreds of my self-control were destroyed. Stepping forward until my face was only inches from his I said rapidly in a voice which shook with emotion: "I like that Bishop. I admire him. I think he's a very clever man with a good sense of humour who talks a lot of sense. All those 'Anti-Sex Ashworth' slurs are rubbish. I don't believe he's anti-sex at all. He's obviously got a happy, successful relationship with that wife of his—and she's *really* fabulous, so intelligent and sensible and sympathetic and unchurchy, in fact I think she's a truly *Christian* person. So who are you to criticise the Ashworths—you with your unhappy marriage and your neurotic wife who manages to drive everyone up the wall? Who are you to look down your nose at Charles Ashworth just because he has the brains and the training and the guts to swim against the John Robinson tide and stand up for what he believes to be right? Dr. Ashworth's battling away in the *real* world and Mrs. Ashworth's right there alongside him, but we don't live in the real world, neither of us does when we're together like this, it's all a fantasy, all just an unconsummated dream!"

If I had thought I would shock him into silence, I was wrong. Immediately he answered: "You're the most real thing in my life. This *is* reality," and as he kissed me I knew he was right; we were living in the real world, we truly were, and the Ashworths were just a dream-couple I had idealised when I was in a disturbed state of mind. And in my sinister hall of mirrors all the glass abruptly tilted to reflect clear, dazzling images once more instead of a horrific assembly of distortions.

"My darling Mr. Dean," I whispered, the hated tears streaming down my face, "forgive me, I didn't mean what I said, I didn't mean it—"

"It's all right," he said gently, holding me close. "I do understand. The Ashworths have been very kind to you—why shouldn't you stand up for them if you wish? That's admirable. But never think they have some God-given monopoly on reality because I'm just as capable, I assure you, of being absolutely down-to-earth and realistic."

"Then Neville, what exactly's going on? I accept that your religious beliefs are very strong and entirely genuine, but—"

"They are, yes. Do I need another reason for abstaining from adultery?"

"No, of course not, but—"

"I can't quite see why you're so anxious to shroud me in mystery all the time."

"I suppose I'm afraid that you've got some sort of peculiar hang-up—"

"What on earth's a hang-up?"

"A psychological block which results in abnormal behaviour."

"My darling, you're the one who seems to be behaving abnormally, suspecting me of lunatic tendencies! How could I hold down a top job in a major organisation unless I was exceptionally sane and well balanced?"

"I'm not talking about sanity exactly. I'm talking about—"

"Why should you think I have one of these hang-up things?"

"Well, when you were talking about prizes—"

"Oh good heavens, I got that old *idée fixe* under control years ago! Now listen to me. Since you rate realism so highly I suggest you forget the fantastic explanations and focus on the rational thinking which buttresses the moral beliefs which you apparently find so implausible. The rational thinking goes like this: Dido's thirteen years younger than I am, and the odds are she'll outlive me. That means I can never offer you marriage, and in the end it'll be marriage you'll want. Moreover in a few years' time you won't want to be married to a man who's pushing seventy. You'll want to be married to a man of your own generation— and so, no doubt, you shall be. Some great paragon will come riding along on his white horse, and—"

"How loathsome! And even if you're right, why should that affect us now? While we wait for this big bore to arrive, why can't we—"

"Because if you got too involved with me, you'd never even see the great paragon, let alone recognise him as a potential husband."

"Thank God—a merciful escape!"

"No, my dear, that wouldn't be a merciful escape. That would be a great tragedy—and I'd be responsible. I'd have destroyed your best chance of happiness and probably ruined your life." He shuddered so violently that I at last realised how serious he was. "To take a woman's love," he said, "and then to destroy her—no, I couldn't do that. I couldn't live with myself afterwards. It would destroy me too."

"Oh darling, surely that sort of melodrama only happens in nineteenth-century novels!"

"You think so?" He turned away abruptly, and because he then had his back to me I barely heard him add: "Women should be preserved from destroyers. Whatever I do I'm going to avoid putting you through hell."

Before I could stop myself I said: "Sometimes when you keep rejecting me like this I feel I'm in hell already."

When he spun back to face me I saw he was appalled. "My darling—" He broke off, then exclaimed in despair: "Maybe I've got this all wrong and I should give you up."

"Oh no!" I said at once. "I'd be in a far worse hell if you did that!"

He gave me a long kiss before saying: "I'll never give you up, never— at least, not until the great paragon rides out of the mist on his shining white horse!" And at last he managed to smile at me.

"But even then—supposing I were to marry just for the social convenience—couldn't we—"

"Oh, you aristocrats!" he said laughing. "What a bunch of pagans you are!"

"But seriously, Neville—"

"My dear, I don't share my prizes, and besides . . . if you lose a prize it ceases to be a prize any more, doesn't it?"

"Here comes that *idée fixe* again—"

"Yes, but it's not an *idée fixe* any more, it's just a little quirk in my personality. My darling, if you married of course our friendship would have to end. It would be quite immoral if I cast any kind of a shadow over your married life, and anyway you must never, never marry just for convenience."

"But if I can't marry you—"

"Don't let's think of the future," he interrupted. "Let's make it a taboo subject, like the past." And as he began to kiss me again I knew that juxtaposed to us in the land of allegory the serpent was tightening the grip of his coils.

6

"I'VE made a decision," said the Bishop, sleek in his Savile Row suit, as he absent-mindedly moved his pectoral cross to the exact centre of his purple stock. "I'm going to postpone my comments on the New Morality until I can gauge approximately how much space I can afford to give it. Otherwise I shall get carried away and dictate enough material to give my publishers heart failure at the thought of the production costs."

"Okay, Bishop." I could now clearly identify as relief the emotion which seeped through me as this new postponement was announced.

"I want to make a stab at the opening chapter," Dr. Ashworth was saying, "but before I start, could you just make a note that the depth metaphor which Robinson finds so startlingly original has of course been used by the mystics for centuries? I think I ought to point out that it doesn't necessarily lead straight to Valentinus' Gnostic heresy."

I scribbled away busily.

"Oh, and remind me to stress the role of the Devil in the propagation of heresy, would you? These starry-eyed liberal churchmen who peddle heretical theories are always so anxious to gloss over him."

I somehow managed to scribble on without batting an eyelid.

"The Devil," mused Dr. Ashworth, "is a symbol representing an aspect of absolute reality. He's not a mere fable which 'modern man' can water down and redesign, and any churchman who gives the impression that the Devil's no longer important deserves a stern rap across the knuckles . . . All right, let's make a stab at the opening chapter. Are you ready? Good, then off we go. 'Chapter One: The Doctrine of God' . . ."

7

"MY darling," wrote Aysgarth.

Do please forgive me for upsetting you so much up at Starbury Ring. What I was really saying, as I believe you understood in the end, was that it's not merely preferable but *vital* that we should love each other in the right way. Then we'll both survive. The truth is I feel I've driven a very special bargain with God. If I keep our love within acceptable bounds it'll remain a blessing; it'll continue to give me the strength to survive what is at present a tough professional and domestic life, and it will even (as I mentioned to you before) inspire me to be a better clergyman. But if I let my love stray beyond the pale, God will withdraw His blessing and (as the old-fashioned churchmen used to thunder) the Devil will move in. Of course no one seriously believes in the Devil any more—he's just a childish image from a bygone era, like the picture of God as an old man in the sky—but one can "demythologise" the Devil by talking of him in psychological terms (alienation, dissociation) and literary metaphors (dereliction in the wasteland).

My darling, I want to ensure your happiness, not drive you into the wasteland of a breakdown, and you're so special, so precious, so perfect, that I'm determined to put aside all my selfish desires in order to preserve you from harm.

I suspect I'm now sounding turgid in my earnestness, so let me hastily move on to another subject. The Bishop at once springs to mind, and I must confess straight away how startled I was when you leapt so loyally to his defence! Charles has, of course, a superb intellect and is without doubt a most devout Christian, but he's a typical product of a privileged public school/Oxbridge background: all charm on top, all reactionary attitudes and snobbery and stab-you-in-the-back ruthlessness underneath. Perhaps it's because I'm just a Yorkshire draper's son, but the older I get the less patience I have with these pillars of the Establishment. It's all dinner at the Athenaeum and gossip at the House of Lords and let's-keep-everything-(especially-the-Church)-exactly-as-it-is. Well, time will deal with them all in due course! *Honest to God* is a watershed. In twenty-five years' time all the conservative elements in the Church will have been swept away and we'll be living with the triumph of liberalism in the form of a dynamic radical theology.

As for Lyle Ashworth, I was even more startled that you should have adopted her as a heroine! She's not the sort of woman other women usually like. Men always get on with her all right, of course (although personally I've never found her in the least attractive), and in fact I've sometimes wondered if she was faithful to Charles during those three years he spent as a prisoner of war. She used to slink around in a little black dress and very high-heeled shoes and look like a cross between Greta Garbo and Marlene Dietrich. However, that's all a long time ago now and I can't deny she's transformed herself into an irreproachably seemly "Mrs. Bishop."

Darling, I hardly know how I'm going to endure the agonising wait for our next meeting! I can't exaggerate how utterly renewed you make me feel; when I returned from our outing to the Ring I tossed off that Sunday sermon with no trouble at all and it's turned out to be a stunner. (Excuse the boasting but I wanted to leave you in no doubt of your amazingly beneficial effect on me!) Always remember that I'm *passionate* about you and that you're the most vital thing in my life. All my love,

N.

P.S. *(Later)* Fitzgerald has just denied he ever mentioned the sculpture's phallic cigars to the Archdeacon and says Lindsay's only concerned about the legal status of the churchyard. What a liar Fitzgerald is! Of course he's deliberately roped in the Bishop's henchman in order to involve Charles in the fight against the sculpture!
P.P.S. *(Later still)* Gilbert's just phoned after a fearful intellectual session in the library with a professor whose speciality is medieval Latin. There seems to be no doubt that the Cathedral statute refers only to the cloisters' lawn as the Cathedral's consecrated burial ground.

Gilbert says the reasoning behind this rather curious state of affairs almost certainly arose from the fact that while the Cathedral was being built, the deceased of Starbridge were buried at St. Martin's-in-Cripplegate which in those days had a far more extensive burial ground than it has now. As you probably know, St. Martin's church preceded the Cathedral; it was originally built for the spiritual benefit of the Cathedral workmen, and soon afterwards it became the parish church, replacing the Saxon round church which had been destroyed by fire. According to Gilbert's theory, the first bishop probably reckoned that the hoi-polloi could go on being buried at St. Martin's while the Cathedral could be reserved for the nobs—and since the graveyard at St. Martin's was already the official parish burial ground, he wouldn't even have had to issue an edict; all he would have needed to do was acquiesce in the status quo.

So the evidence so far certainly supports Lindsay's claim that the Cathedral churchyard is unconsecrated curtilage, but I'm going to assure him that the hunt is now on in earnest for evidence of the later consecration which I feel sure must exist. That'll make Lindsay sweat blood! Meanwhile little Gilbert is almost hysterical with excitement and has plunged back into the library to comb the archives. Join the Church for an action-packed career liberally seasoned with suspense! But seriously—what a life . . .

8

"*I THINK* it's terrific that you've chucked up your vapid society life in order to live in a small flat in a provincial town and work for a clergyman," said my fiery contemporary Charley Ashworth, pale brown eyes almost golden as he regarded me with whole-hearted approval. "I wouldn't have thought you had it in you."

His mother groaned lightly, laying down her knife and fork in protest, but I was enjoying my food too much to follow her example. It was Sunday, and in accordance with Mrs. Ashworth's invitation I had presented myself at the South Canonry for lunch. The roast beef was succulent. The Yorkshire pudding had already melted in my mouth. The roast potatoes and the peas were sublime enough to qualify the South Canonry for three stars in the Guide Michelin. Having recently suffered from a surfeit of solitary encounters with tins of baked beans, I had already decided that this perfectly cooked meal represented gourmet cuisine in its most triumphant form.

"What have I said now?" demanded Charley in response to his mother's quiet moan of despair.

"Darling, Venetia may not like to hear her respectable past described as a 'vapid society life,' nor may she be very happy to hear that you didn't think she had it in her to live differently. When are you ever going to learn that this mania of yours for being outspoken is often tactless, offensive and just plain wrong?"

"Come, Lyle, that's a bit stiff, isn't it?" said the Bishop good-humouredly, spearing his last slice of Yorkshire pudding. "Charley's merely anxious to be truthful, and one should always seek to discern the truth, whatever the truth is."

"Not if it means getting everything wrong and being downright rude," said Mrs. Ashworth.

"I don't get everything wrong!" said Charley indignantly. "Of course we all make mistakes, but most of the time I think the truth's blindingly obvious."

"That remark just shows you've reached the age of twenty-five without growing up," I said, finally giving way to the urge to have a bash at his bumptiousness. "Most of the time the truth's a complete mystery—in fact sometimes I think it's a miracle that anyone ever has an inkling about what's really going on."

"Well spoken, Venetia!" said my heroine.

"Over to you, Charley!" said the Bishop, effortlessly neutralising the friction between his wife and son by adopting an amused, affectionate tone. "How are you going to respond to that 'palpable hit'?"

"Venetia has obviously been too greatly influenced by the philosophical idiocies of Berkeley," retorted Charley, "but I stand by the absolute values of Plato and hold that the fully real is fully knowable!"

"But surely," I said, moving in for the kill with my verbal rapier, "Platonic philosophy has been exploded by the logical positivists?"

"Plato will be remembered when A. J. Ayer is forgotten!" said Charley, furiously parrying the blow. "Logical positivism is just a temporary aberration from the truth, like the theology of John Robinson!"

"Rubbish!" I said, fighting bravely on although my rapier was now shuddering in my hand. "In twenty-five years' time the conservative wing of the Church will be extinct and we'll be living with liberalism in the form of a dynamic radical theology!"

Charley snorted with contempt. His remarkable eyes seemed to blaze with golden sparks, and his wide, mobile mouth was set in a passionate snarl. He looked like an outraged Pekingese.

"In twenty-five years' time," he declared, "John Robinson will be a back-number, radical theology will have reached a dead end and the

Evangelicals will be on the march again to set the Church back on course after the mid-century decades of decadence and debility!"

"Phew!" said the Bishop. "That was a real scorcher! Lyle, is there any more of that sensational Yorkshire pudding?"

My rapier had shattered. Aysgarth's bold prophecy was in shreds. Automatically I turned to the Bishop for the final word of authority. "And you, Dr. Ashworth," I said, "what do you think?"

"I think," said the Bishop, "that the gifts of the Spirit can be recognised by their fruits, and that 'Truth,' as the old saying goes, 'is the Daughter of Time.' "

"Seconds, Venetia?" I suddenly realised Mrs. Ashworth was hovering at my elbow with a plate of sliced roast beef.

"No, thank you." I felt unable to face another mouthful; the mere thought of food made me recoil.

"I hope I haven't upset you," said Charley, dropping his abrasive manner as he saw my leaden expression. His naive concern was curiously appealing. "It's so nice to talk to a girl who can actually talk back. I just love having a good slanging match."

In the ensuing silence the Bishop tried to smother a smile, Mrs. Ashworth assumed her most inscrutable expression and Charley, who had turned red after paying me this extraordinary compliment, furiously attacked his last roast potato.

I came to the unexpected conclusion that although he was now too juvenile to take seriously he might well evolve into the most stimulating man. However, I could hardly afford to waste my energy visualising Charley in the 1970s; I needed all my strength to face the approaching treacle-tart and custard.

It really was the most superb Sunday lunch.

9

"*. . . AND* grim news has emerged from the library," wrote Aysgarth.

Gilbert, twittering with horror, has unearthed some most unwanted evidence in the papers of Josiah Samuel Hawkyns, Bishop of Starbridge 1703–1716. Apparently the Cathedral statutes were lost during the Civil War—the clergy thought Cromwell might burn the library, so as many books and documents as possible were removed and hidden when the Roundheads were reported to be closing in on Royalist Starbridge. As it turned out, the Roundheads only rampaged through the Cathedral smashing up all the side-chapels, but the Bishop died of shock and later it was realised that no one knew where he had hidden the statutes. Cromwell hanged the Dean *en passant* and so Starbridge later had a new bishop and a new dean, neither of whom had any idea of the exact rules laid down for the governing of the Cathedral. Inevitably, within a generation, people were being buried on the sward as a result of their belief that they would be committing their mortal remains to consecrated ground.

And now we come to Bishop Josiah Samuel Hawkyns. In 1707 he found the statutes hidden behind a secret panel in the dining-room of the old episcopal palace and to his delight he discovered—here we go!—that the Cathedral churchyard was not a consecrated burial ground in the power of the Dean and Chapter but unconsecrated curtilage to which he as Bishop could stake a claim. Accordingly he dispossessed the Dean and Chapter, banned all future burials from the churchyard and used the sward for grazing his horses. Dean Augustus St. John Merrivale is reported to have drunk three bottles of claret and died of apoplexy—and I'm not in the least surprised.

However, unlike poor Augustus St. J. M., I shall somehow restrain myself from knocking back a vat of St. Estèphe and survive to fight the next battle—which, of course, will now centre directly on the sculpture. I have to apply for a faculty in order to place it in the churchyard, and Charles, through Lindsay, is bound to oppose my application, but by heavens I'll get that faculty even if I have to extract it by shaking the Chancellor until his teeth rattle!

Meanwhile Fitzgerald was seen by my spy Eddie lunching in the Quill Pen with the Archdeacon—the whole issue reeks of conspiracy, but I'll fight these philistines to the last ditch. Fitzgerald even had the nerve to say to me in Chapter that it was impossible for a phallic symbol to be aesthetically pleasing. "My dear Tommy," I said, "what could be more phallic than our unique and ravishing spire?" Fitzgerald went purple, as if I'd uttered a string of four-letter words, and Dalton said primly: "Isn't that going a little far, Stephen?" I'd like to shoot the pair of them—and the Bishop and the Archdeacon too!

Talking of Charles, I'm now convinced the Ashworths want to marry you off to Charley, so I'm most relieved to hear you think he's too juvenile to take seriously. He has a volatile temperament, and volatile temperaments, as I know full well, can make married life very exhausting. However, despite this handicap I'm sure he's a good boy; I've always taken an interest in him ever since he told me when he was very small that he wanted to be a clergyman, but because Charles and I were never exactly the best of friends I haven't seen as much of either Charley or Michael as I might have done. My mentor Bishop Jardine

(Lyle's former employer) was very partial to them both and even asked me on his deathbed to keep an eye on them while they were growing up, but that, of course, was when we thought Charles wouldn't come home from the war.

You didn't tell me anything about your conversation during this culinary dream of a Sunday lunch, but I assume Charles was too busy demolishing roast beef to demolish heresy!

Now, darling, as I've already told you this is the most frightful week for me, and although I thought I'd be able to escape on Wednesday afternoon as usual, the vast funeral allocated to Wednesday morning has acquired a sting in its tail in the form of a lunch for the most important mourners, and to my rage I shall be unable to get away. Thursday is this ghastly regimental service followed by a buffet-lunch for sixty. Friday afternoon would have been possible—the morning's no good as I shall be kidnapped by Miss Trotman for dictation—but now I have to go and see the Cathedral's solicitors about my application for a faculty. Saturday's useless as both James and Sandy are coming down for the weekend, while Sunday—ah yes! On Sunday I'm supposed to be worshipping God in the Cathedral! I knew there was something I wanted to do if only I could find the time! But seriously . . . what a life.

All I can suggest is Lady Mary on Wednesday evening. Darling, I'm sorry, sorry, *sorry* to be so inaccessible, but I'll make it up to you on Wednesday week, I promise—if I'm not dead with frustration as the result of being unable to swamp you with kisses this week among all those superbly phallic standing stones. Write soon—only the thought of receiving your letters makes the prospect of this week bearable, all love,

N.

10

". . . AND that concludes my account of the drama of regiment and royalty," wrote Aysgarth after describing Thursday's special service so wittily that I laughed out loud.

Let me now pass to a different form of drama and remark how amazing it is that *Present Laughter* opens next week—time seems to have flown lately, although it now seems an eternity since I last saw you (I don't count our rendez-vous yesterday on Lady Mary—that was just a crumb to keep me from starving). How I rely on your letters to ease the agony of waiting for next Wednesday—and talking of your letters, thank you so very much for the understanding you displayed when you commiserated with me about that **** Fitzgerald. As an eminent cleric I shouldn't even think this word, let alone hint at it in a letter to a lady, but since it's not a blasphemy and since I know you supported the use of four-letter words in *Lady Chatterley's Lover,* I think I can at least be permitted an explosion of asterisks! If *only* I could get Fitzgerald promoted out of the diocese! I'll have to renew my machinations at Church House.

I'm toying with the idea of writing a survival manual for deans, and the chapter headings are forming effortlessly in my mind's eye. (1) How to survive your bishop. (2) How to box with your archdeacon. (3) How to kick a canon upstairs. (4) How to outwit a conspiracy to grab your churchyard. (5) . . . oh, the possibilities are endless! Isn't it amazing that the Church should give the impression to laymen of being a stagnant pool? What a masterly exercise in public relations! But no, on second thoughts, perhaps the image isn't so wide of the mark after all. Any biologist will tell you that a stagnant pond is always teeming with life—and that the life can take very unattractive forms. All my love, darling, longing, absolutely *longing* for Wednesday,

N.

P.S. *(Later)* Lindsay's just phoned to ask when I'm seeing Trumpet (senior partner in the Cathedral's firm of solicitors). "Tomorrow," I said, "and I'm sending the bill for the consultation to the diocesan office." There was a strangulated gasp. I waited for the thud which would indicate that his body had hit the floor, but he somehow kept upright and said in a voice which quivered with rage: "I think that's a somewhat inappropriate remark. The Chancellor will, of course, make an order later in respect of costs." Well, I couldn't resist it; that snooty upper-middle-class tone was like a red rag to a bull, and I wanted to scare him out of his wits. "Fine," I said, "but let me warn you that by the time I've won this case by fighting it through the Consistory Court to the Court of Arches and the Privy Council—with the aid of the best ecclesiastical lawyers in London—the Chancellor's going to award me costs so large that you'll need a thumbscrew and a rack to extort the money from the parishes." Then I hung up and had a triple-whisky to calm me down! Heaven only knows what Lindsay had, but I only wish it was three bottles of claret and apoplexy. The plot thickens! Be sure to tune in tomorrow for the next instalment of *The Aysgarths,* an everyday story of clerical folk . . .

"NEVILLE," I said on the following Wednesday after we had been embracing for some minutes in the car-park on Starbury Plain, "don't you think the front seat of a car is entirely the wrong place to demonstrate one's white-hot passion? I always seem to wind up being much too intimate with the hand-brake."

He laughed, resuming the embrace, but he soon became wedged, as before, between the seat and the steering-wheel. He kept the driver's seat placed well forward in order to accommodate his short legs and the result was that the wheel allowed him little room to manoeuvre. "We must look on the front seats," he said humorously, pausing for air, "as a modern version of the chastity belt!"

"But I'm so tired of these contortions! Why don't we transfer to the back seat?"

"Passers-by might think——"

"I'm tired of passers-by. In fact I'm tired of this car-park. If you don't want to walk up to the Ring, let's go down to Chancton Wood and romp naked through the undergrowth!"

We both rocked with laughter at the ridiculous picture the proposal evoked. "You, of course, have the figure for earnest, earthy Lawrentian romps!" he gasped at last. "I'm keeping my clothes on!"

But he drove to Chancton Wood.

"I'M sorry," I said after we had wound up far off the beaten track in a grove of beech trees, "I know I've dragooned you here against your better judgement and you're probably wondering what on earth I'm going to suggest next, but I do accept that we can't 'go all the way,' as my American friend Dinkie would put it. I just got so tired of other people milling around us, that's all."

"So did I. And there's been no dragooning. I drove here of my own free will." Suddenly he exclaimed in despair: "How little I can offer you! No wonder you became so angry up at the Ring two weeks ago—and no wonder you became so discontented today. I so much wish——" But he stopped.

At once I said: "It's all right. You're utterly convinced it would be disastrous as well as morally wrong. I do understand." But as I spoke my mouth was dry with excitement. It had occurred to me that his despair might drive him towards some form of capitulation.

"I know John Robinson's right," he was saying unevenly. "I know he is." But the next moment he was scrambling away from me out of the car as if he were unable to endure the emotional dilemma which Dr. Robinson had so serenely sketched.

Flinging open the passenger door I joined him as he slumped against the side of the car and shoved his hands deep into his pockets. His misery was evident in every line of his bowed head, drooping shoulders, down-cast eyes and downturned mouth, and suddenly all my longings seemed intolerably immature and self-centred; I wanted only that he should be happy again, secure in his indestructible idealism.

"My darling Mr. Dean," I said, "of course John Robinson's right! And I'm more than willing to cope with the demands of the New Morality. What I couldn't have coped with would have been some peculiar hang-up about being too terrified to win a prize in case you later found you didn't want it—or perhaps some peculiar mania for preserving women from destruction. Do you remember how you once wrote to me and said quaintly that women should be put on pedestals and reverenced? That really made me very nervous! But of course I can see now that you were just expressing your romantic idealism and your high moral principles. And they're the reason, aren't they, why you're unable to discuss your marriage. It's not because you're still sleeping with Dido, still emotionally involved with her. It really is because your high moral principles demand that you don't talk about her behind her back."

He froze. "You didn't seriously think—"

"Yes, I did, as a matter of fact. I was convinced that the only reason you were able to take a high moral line with me was because you were still sleeping with her."

He was ashen. He opened his mouth, shut it again and ran his fingers wildly through his hair. At last he managed to say: "I'm going to explode that theory once and for all," and then he pulled me violently into his arms.

During the embrace that followed I became aware—as indeed I had been aware two weeks before at the Ring—that he was a long way from being impotent. He kissed me so hard my tongue hurt. Then without looking at the door of the car's back seat, he reached out and pulled down the handle.

13

"OF course," he whispered, "we won't go far. But I want to go far enough to prove . . . and it would be just such a luxury to . . ." Words finally failed him.

I said: "I always did think it was the little luxuries that made life worthwhile," and we both laughed, hugging each other.

Then he began to fumble clumsily with his trousers.

A LONG time later as we were lighting cigarettes he said in a low voice: "Be honest with me—did you find all that unspeakably sordid?"

"Sordid? For God's sake, what kind of a Victorian middle-class chump do you think I am?"

"I'd have thought any girl, no matter what her class, might react adversely to an unfettered display of male carnality."

"Unfettered display of . . ." I dissolved into helpless laughter. "Darling, you're talking exactly like a character in one of the Victorian pornographic novels that Arabella found in Great-Uncle Frederick's library! But no, on second thoughts the seducer would have talked about his 'member,' not about his male carnality. Must you really be quite so bourgeois and old-fashioned?"

He winced. Instantly I was stricken. "Oh darling, I'm sorry, I'm sorry—"

"I'm the wrong class, the wrong age, the wrong everything as far as you're concerned!" he cried in despair.

"So what? I'd love you even if you were a working-class navvy of ninety. Now stop worrying that I found that delicious groping sordid because the truth is I thought it was complete and utter bliss—in fact I'm quite sure the full sex-act could only have been an anti-climax," I added in my firmest voice, and as he smiled shyly—he even blushed—I had a glimpse of the passionate but strait-laced young man he must have been long ago in a remote era which I could not quite imagine.

I kissed him. "Have I really shocked you so much?" I said amused. "What happened to that bold, freewheeling dean who supported the publication of *Lady Chatterley's Lover* and who's now fighting tooth and nail for the right to instal a box of phallic cigars in the Cathedral churchyard?"

To my relief he laughed and relaxed. "He was temporarily elbowed aside by Neville One who was brought up by Primitive Methodists!"

"And when do Nevilles Two and Three make their appearance?"

"Never, they're dead. Good heavens, look at the time! My darling, I must drive back to Starbridge as fast as if I were Juan Fangio chasing the world championship!"

We rocketed out of Chancton Wood and roared down the main road to the city. I think I only screamed three times. At least we didn't kill anyone. As we soared over the river into Eternity Street I gasped: "Don't forget to drop me by the Staro Arms!"

"No, can't stop—there's a hulking great monster pawing the back bumper—"

"Then turn into the Close!"

"No, someone might see us"—we shot off at a tangent towards the market-place—"but don't worry, I'll go round by St. Martin's and drop you at the top of Butchers' Alley."

We zipped around the market-place, dived up Wheat Street, zoomed down Barley Road and bounced to a halt in Chasuble Lane behind a parked van. "Bother!" said Juan Fangio's impersonator with commendable control of his language, and gamely nosed the car around the van's right wing. Brakes screeched as a lorry coming the other way successfully avoided a head-on collision, and in the distance the screaming abuse of the appalled driver wafted towards us on the summer air. "They really should make more one-way streets in this city," said Aysgarth placidly, trying to reverse back behind the van but finding that the car following us was blocking his path. "Now, I wonder what I ought to do next?"

"Perhaps I'd better nip out and vanish," I said as an intrigued policeman began to cruise in our direction.

"That might be a good idea. Juan Fangio's temporarily stuck. Goodbye, darling—all my love—write soon . . . "

The last thing I heard as I headed for Butchers' Alley was the policeman saying genially: "Well, well, well, Mr. Dean! You seem to be causing a little bit of chaos here . . ."

I thought: that's the understatement of the century.

Then I fell into my flat, sank into a delicious hot bath and reflected that even though I might still die *virgo intacta* I at least knew all there was to know about orgasms.

15

"*I'VE* brought you a plant," said my mother an hour later as I opened the front door and found her standing with a nasty-looking potted object in her arms. Behind her the uniformed chauffeur languished at the wheel of the Daimler which was slumbering, with superb insolence, beneath a sign which declared NO PARKING. *Present Laughter* had opened that week at the Starbridge Playhouse, and my mother was now on her way to worship Martin Darrow. "Plants are such nice house-warming presents, I always think," she was adding, "and that's a particularly superior one because it does well with little light—it occurred to me that if you overlooked a narrow street like Butchers' Alley the absence of light might create difficulties. All you need to do is water the plant until the soil is moist, *but not sodden,* and never let it stand in a pool."

"Thanks so much, Mama . . . Sorry these stairs are so steep."

"They're no steeper than the servants' stairs at Flaxton Hall . . . Oh, what a dear little attic! I like it *very* much—how charming! But I do think Mrs. Lindsay might have put up more suitable pictures—it looks as if those teenage daughters of hers made the selection! Next time you're at the Hall, darling, do help yourself to a couple of old masters from the attics."

"Yes, Mama. Sherry?"

"Lovely—yes, please! I must say, Venetia, you're looking very well, really most striking—and so much more dignified than Arabella who's suddenly gone ash-blonde and was photographed at Pompadour's (always a fatal sign) with Archie Blenham's ex-brother-in-law who's now on his third divorce. I don't *think* she's sleeping with him, but of course it's quite impossible to be sure."

There was a pause. Then my voice said: "I'm sorry, Mama, but could you just say that last sentence again?"

"I said I don't think she's sleeping with him but of course it's quite impossible to be sure. She absolutely swore to your father last week that she'd never committed adultery in her life—so sweet of her to want to protect him from unpleasantness!—but a woman with dyed ash-blonde hair is surely *capable de tout.* Oh, and by the way, darling, while I'm on the subject of your father, I do wish you'd drop him just a *tiny* line so that he stops complaining about being neglected. It would make my life so much easier—and talking of letters I must tell you that Enid Mark-hampton wrote the other day and said how delighted she was to meet you again when she returned to the Chantry—she said what a charming

girl you'd become! There! Isn't that nice? I always believe in passing on
'dew-drops.' Apparently Marina had mentioned to her that you went
regularly to the Cathedral—well, naturally I didn't tell your father
because he would have worried that you might be 'getting religion' and
becoming unbalanced, but believe me, as the worn-out mother of four
lively daughters, I was *delighted* to think of you surrounded by clergymen
and thinking noble thoughts! And talking of clergymen, how's that nice
Canon Hoffenberg?"

I began to talk about Eddie and tried hard not to think of my Mr.
Dean in Chancton Wood.

16

LATER when I was alone I thought: he still never said directly that he
wasn't having sex with Dido, he still refused to consummate our affair,
and he was still evasive about his past. We had appeared to progress in
Chancton Wood but in fact the progression had been an illusion. Nothing
had changed because none of the mysteries had been solved.

My mother's fatal words echoed in my ears. "I don't think she's
sleeping with him but of course it's quite impossible to be sure . . ."
However in my case it was indeed possible to be sure. If my Mr. Dean
had looked me straight in the eyes and said: "I don't have sex with my
wife," I would have believed him. But instead he had only said: "I'm
going to explode that theory," as if a sexual blitz-krieg was more convincing than a clergyman's simple denial.

I mixed myself a dry martini and sat sipping it as the twilight
thickened.

After a while a new truth dawned. I saw it had now been proved that
moral convictions alone could not be responsible for his refusal to have
full sexual intercourse with me, because if he could overcome those
convictions sufficiently to ensure we were both sexually satisfied in
Chancton Wood, there was no reason why he shouldn't satisfy us both
in the conventional manner. What kind of a tortuous casuistry was
responsible for his decision that one route to sexual satisfaction was
permitted while another was taboo? It made no sense at all, but I now
had a horrible suspicion that his behaviour was somehow connected—in
the most intimate way imaginable—with Dido.

Yet I couldn't be certain. The rock-bottom truth was that I still had
no idea what was going on in Aysgarth's mind, and that, of course, was
why it was still so vital that I should succeed in milking Father Darrow
for information.

In forty-eight hours' time I would come face to face with him in the Starbridge Playhouse.

But I had no idea how I could ever contrive to see him on his own.

17

"THAT'S odd," I said to Eddie in the front row of the circle on Friday evening. "I know Nick Darrow's going to be here with his father, but I can't see them."

"I didn't think Father Darrow went anywhere nowadays," said Eddie, looking up from his programme in surprise.

"The opportunity to see his famous son tread the boards was obviously too potent to resist." I cast a quick look around the circle again but there was still no sign of Nick. The Starbridge Playhouse, an art-deco lump built to replace a decayed Edwardian gem, was a miniature version of the palatial cinemas of the 1930s. The facilities it offered were excellent, a fact which explained why Starbridge was so often favoured by West End producers who wanted to try out their work in the provinces, and the audience, seated on only two levels, had been shamelessly pampered by the architect; in addition to the first-class acoustics and comfortable seats there was a bar on each floor. Nevertheless, in the perverse manner of human beings, the older inhabitants of Starbridge were united in pining for their rat-and-rot-infested Edwardian gem and regarded the modern theatre as "characterless."

"Why are you so anxious to see Nick?" Eddie was asking curiously.

"He's my Talisman and whenever I see him something extraordinary happens. I met him in the spring and was whisked away to the Hebrides, I met him in May and was whirled into the Orgy—" But before I could say more the lights began to dim. Casting one last fruitless glance around the auditorium for the Darrows, I prayed fiercely that they were both present and then made up my mind not to let my acute anxiety ruin the play.

18

MARTIN DARROW, seemingly tailor-made for the part of Gary Essendine, was given a rapturous welcome by the audience as soon as he made his entrance and with the aid of an able supporting cast transformed Coward's dated play into a sparkling entertainment for the 1960s. Taller than I had thought he would be but looking younger now that he was not subjected to television close-ups, he moved with effortless grace around the stage, spoke his lines with masterly skill and somehow resisted the awful temptation to "go over the top" once he had the audience in the palm of his hand.

"He's very good, isn't he?" said Eddie with genuine admiration as the curtain descended amidst thunderous applause for the first interval, but I was already saying: "Excuse me—must find Nick," and dashing up the gangway to the exit.

I hung around the foyer as people gushed out of the stalls, but no Darrow of any kind emerged.

"I should think the old man's staying put," said Eddie as he joined me.

"Then they've got to be in the seats underneath the circle," I muttered. "There's nowhere else they can possibly be." I charged into the auditorium and to my vast relief saw Nick straight away. He was sitting in a row near the back, and beside him was a very, very ancient item indeed, an apparition which displayed the almost translucent skin of extreme old age. I thought vaguely how good it was of him to come and was sure he was hating every moment of it. Poor old man! No doubt he wished he were tucked up in an armchair in front of the television. In panic I wondered if I had made a colossal mistake in believing that St. Darrow could be a source of enlightenment; he looked much too old to be a source of anything, and perhaps Dido had been right in dismissing him as senile.

"Venetia!" Nick had risen to his feet and was gaping at me. "I thought you were coming to the play tomorrow!"

"Change of plan!" I said brightly, moving down the row in front of him where all the seats had been temporarily vacated. "And how's my Halley's Comet? Is something extraordinary just about to happen?"

Nick smiled and turned to his father. I heard him say: "This is Venetia Flaxton."

The very, very ancient item moved. It rose to a vast height, gave me an enigmatic, fascinating smile and offered me a thin, beautiful, elegant hand which achieved an astonishingly firm, positive, compelling grip. Grey eyes, immensely steady, looked not only at my face but deep into my soul. My jaw sagged. My eyes widened. I was speechless.

"How do you do, Miss Flaxton," said Father Jonathan Darrow.

PART THREE

THE
GREAT
POLLUTANT

"Where, one must ask, will the ravages of liberal theology end? The Devil and Hell went long ago; the position of the Blessed Virgin has been seriously undermined; God, who until last week was invulnerable, is now distinctly on the defensive. What will ultimately be left except a belief in the need for bishops, if only to give evidence in trials about obscenity and to talk to pop singers on television?"

T. E. UTLEY,
in The Honest to God Debate

"The fact that the old land-marks are disappearing is not something to be deplored. If we have the courage, it is something to be welcomed . . . "

JOHN A. T. ROBINSON
HONEST TO GOD

XIII

" . . . it seems to be assumed throughout [Honest to God] that what 'modern
man' can or cannot believe is the test of truth. Yet the problems of 'modern man'
are not always as new as they are made out to be. Christianity is not easy
for the natural man to accept in any age. Nor is mid—twentieth century man of necessity
the type of the future. In the next century man may be astonished at the confidence
of some of our disbeliefs."

JOHN LAWRENCE,
in The Honest to God Debate

I

DID I manage to utter the formal words of introduction as I shook hands
with Father Darrow? I have no idea. I was in a trance. All I could think
was that this was no pathetic old man but a magic seer who could tell
me everything I wanted to know. Immediately the stakes in the complicated game I was playing seemed to increase tenfold. Now it was not
merely important but vital that I should see him on his own.

". . . and you know Canon Hoffenberg, don't you, Father?" Nick was
saying.

"We met when I attended the Theological College after the war,"
Eddie said. "How nice to see you again, Father Darrow! I hope you're
well?"

"Well enough, thanks." He smiled thinly as if he felt a man deserved
a more austere expression of good will than the fascinating greeting he
had produced for me.

I finally managed to recover my poise. "You must be so proud of your
son!" I said. "I'm hoping to go backstage afterwards to get his autograph
for my mother." And I added brightly to Nick: "Will you be going
backstage too?"

Nick obviously felt such adulatory behaviour was far beneath him.
"No, we're meeting Martin at the Staro Arms."

"What a coincidence!" I exclaimed wide-eyed. "We'd planned to have
a drink there, hadn't we, Eddie?"

"Oh yes!" said Eddie, playing up with unexpected resourcefulness. "Perhaps you can get your autograph there instead, Venetia—it would save you fighting your way backstage!"

"What a brilliant idea! Although of course," I added smoothly to Nick, "we wouldn't want to intrude on any family reunion."

"There'd be no intrusion," said Father Darrow before Nick could speak. "The reunion's already taken place."

"And Martin's spending Sunday with us anyway," said Nick, taking his cue from his father but not looking particularly enthralled at the prospect of seeing us later.

"Marvellous!" I said gaily, smiling at him. Then I stole a glance at Father Darrow. With shock I found he was looking straight at me and at once I was aware of the irrational conviction that he was reading my mind, skimming through it in the manner of someone obliged to absorb the main story of a newspaper in seconds. Again I felt as if I had plunged to the ground in a lift; I was reminded of my first meeting with Nick on the Starbridge train at Waterloo.

"Well!" said my voice with a dreadful false heartiness. "We'll look forward to seeing you both later! Come along, Eddie."

The next thing I knew I was reeling into the foyer.

"Shall I fight for a gin?" offered Eddie, eyeing the bar where a dense multitude was screaming in a haze of cigarette smoke.

"Please." I felt I had to get rid of him in order to concentrate on my recovery.

He battled back with a couple of gin-and-tonics just as the bell rang to signal the end of the interval.

"Eddie, you're heroic." I knocked back my drink. "And thanks for playing along with my performance in the stalls."

"Am I allowed to ask what's going on?"

"No. Just keep on being heroic."

The bell started to ring again.

We returned to our seats in the circle.

2

"*IS* this my family I see before me?" mused Martin Darrow, half in and half out of the character of Gary Essendine as he made a grand entrance into the main reception room of the Staro Arms. "It is! But who's the lovely lady with the tiger-eyes, the pre-Raphaelite locks and the exquisitely dressed companion?"

Eddie boggled at this histrionic approach and I was aware of Nick fidgeting in an agony of embarrassment, but I sprang up, captivated by such uninhibited charm, and replied promptly: "I'm Venetia Flaxton and this is Canon Eddie Hoffenberg of the Cathedral. Congratulations—we enjoyed your performance enormously!"

"Now if this were a Hollywood musical," said Martin amused, "a dozen singing waiters would immediately appear with champagne! Thank you, Venetia. How do you do, Canon. Well, in the absence of the singing waiters, what are we all going to drink?"

"The bar's closed," said Nick austerely.

"Well, of course it is! This is spiritual downtown Starbridge, not wicked old Sunset Strip! But as I'm a resident I can still terrorise the lounge-waiter. What would you like, Miss Tiger-Eyes?"

"I'd adore a brandy," I said. "Rémy Martin would do."

"I'm mad about this girl," said Martin. "What a throwaway line! Like saying: 'I'd adore a car—I think I could just about stand a Rolls-Royce!'"

We all laughed. Eddie settled for a whisky-and-soda, Nick for a Coca-Cola and the old man, after a fractional hesitation, requested a glass of port.

". . . and my usual orange juice, please, Bill," said Martin to the waiter as he offered me a cigarette. "Now Dad, let's hear your verdict—were you appalled?"

"Not in the least," said the old man serenely. "It was a most entertaining and well-constructed play and I'm sure it was most difficult to write. It occurred to me that Mr. Coward is probably underrated by the serious critics despite—or perhaps because of—his popular success."

If I had had any lingering doubts about his mental faculties these shrewd remarks would have destroyed them. I was delighted by this tribute to Coward's craftsmanship, but before I could say so Nick muttered in an urgent voice to his father: "What Martin wants to know is not what you thought of the play but what you thought of him."

This amused Martin very much. "You funny boy!" he exclaimed indulgently as if Nick were a child who had made a precocious remark. "Do you really think Dad isn't aware of that?"

Nick shot him a furious look but the old man said in a soothing voice: "He only wanted me to put you out of your suspense—and of course I should have congratulated you straight away, just as Miss Flaxton did. Most of the time I quite forgot you were Martin, and on the rare occasions when I did remember I was always so thankful that you weren't like Mr. Essendine in real life."

This was evidently the right thing to say. Martin laughed and commented to Eddie: "There speaks the ex-monk and the priest!"

"Of course Gary Essendine was very naughty," I said, "but so were the girls. I loved it when Joanna said she'd lost her latch-key—I laughed like a drain."

We were still deep in our discussion of the play when the drinks arrived, but as Martin raised his glass to me with a smile I summoned my nerve, produced my programme and asked him to autograph it for my mother.

". . . and she's Lady Flaxton, not Mrs.," I added hastily after he had declared he would produce a personal dedication.

"I'm wild about the aristocracy," said Martin, scribbling busily. "I always think 'All Men Are Equal' is quite the most boring lie ever invented."

The conversation, sustained almost entirely by Eddie, Martin and me, continued to bowl along at a smart pace while I racked my brains to devise a scheme for separating Father Darrow from his family so that I could beg him for a private audience at a later date. Nick, out of his social depth again, gazed into his glass of Coke as if he were seeing mystical images in the depths, but was probably only longing to go home. The old man sat very still and said little but appeared quite content to sip his port and listen to us. However, as soon as I had swallowed my last mouthful of Rémy Martin he said to his younger son: "We must be going—can you bring the car to the door?" and Nick jumped up with alacrity.

"I hope you won't be offended if I offer to pay for the drinks," said Eddie to Martin. "We actually came here with the intention of playing host—if the bar had been open—"

The futile argument began over who was to foot the bill. I write "futile" because it was quite obvious that Martin intended to pay and equally obvious that Eddie could not bring himself to accept this generosity without making a lengthy protest.

I looked at Father Darrow and Father Darrow looked at me. We were still seated. Martin and Eddie were drifting, like boats turned loose from their moorings, towards the centre of the long, low-ceilinged room. Nick had by this time vanished to retrieve the car.

Father Darrow said quietly but distinctly: "You want to see me, don't you?" and somehow I managed to utter the syllable: "Yes."

"Come to my cottage at Starrington Manor at eleven o'clock tomorrow morning."

"Okay." I could barely speak.

Martin, having won the argument, drifted back to attend to the aged parent. "Want a hand, Dad?"

"No, thank you." The old man rose carefully to his feet. Although he stooped he was still taller than either of his sons. Taking his time he moved across the room as if he were a great actor making a supremely dignified exit, and Eddie hurried ahead to hold the swing door open for him. Beyond the main entrance of the hotel Nick was waiting beside a small black car.

"I was glad to see you again, Canon," said Father Darrow, offering Eddie his hand. "May God bless you. And please remember me, if you will, to your friend the Dean." Then he turned to me. "Goodbye, Miss Flaxton."

"Goodbye, Mr. Darrow—Father Darrow, I mean," I said, so jolted by his unexpected reference to Aysgarth that I made a mess of the farewell, but he smiled at me before disappearing into the night.

Afterwards as Eddie and I walked down Eternity Street I realized it was time I provided some explanation, no matter how fantastic, of my peculiar behaviour, so I said with fervour: "Martin's fabulous, isn't he? Much better-looking than either Nick or the old man. I suppose he's on his third or fourth wife by this time and keeps a glamorous mistress in some thrillingly seamy place like Pimlico."

Eddie heaved the windy sigh of the dedicated masochist. Too late it occurred to me that by pretending I had a crush on Martin I was being brutally tactless.

"Such a pity he's so old!" I said hastily. "Of course I could never be really serious about anything over fifty."

Eddie sighed again as if he had decided it would be more fun to disbelieve me. All he said was: "I think I must make another appointment with my osteopath. My back's taken a turn for the worse."

I could have slapped him.

In silence we walked on down Eternity Street.

3

STARRINGTON MAGNA, a sprawling village which stood twelve miles from Starbridge, was surrounded by farms owned by wealthy London business-men who liked to play in the country at weekends. However, Nick told me that Starrington Manor's Home Farm was run by a local man while the Community cared for the Manor's extensive grounds. The house itself, I discovered, was not a Georgian mansion like my home but a rambling old pile which reminded me of a gingerbread house designed by a talented cook. It sat placidly in the sunshine amidst daisy-strewn lawns and looked hospitable. I found it a marked but not unattractive contrast to the glacial symmetry and manicured swards of Flaxton Hall.

"It's most peculiar of Father to see you like this," said Nick, leading me across the back lawn towards a wood. "I can't understand it. He never sees women. In fact he seldom sees anyone. You must be careful not to stay more than ten minutes, and please don't stage an emotional scene because he wouldn't like it. He's too old now for all that sort of thing."

"Who do you think you are?" I said. "A Norland nanny, complete with pram and nappies?"

Nick said obstinately: "He's got to be looked after."

"I thought the Community did that."

"Huh!" said Nick in contempt and fell silent.

Before we entered the wood we passed a long, tangled herbaceous border bright with blooms. I thought how my mother would have rushed to tidy it up and ruin it.

"I like this place," I said impulsively. "It's got a good atmosphere."

Nick stopped mooching along like an overgrown James Dean and decided to be gracious. "Father keeps the atmosphere clear," he said mysteriously, "and not even the Community can pollute it."

"What's wrong with the Community?"

"Bunch of silly neurotics playing at the religious life. Father only keeps them around for my sake so that I don't have to worry about either him or the house when I'm away."

Having entered the wood we were now following a well-marked path. The light, filtering through the leaves, was green and dim and cool.

"How did your father find these nut-cases?"

"They found him. Weak people are drawn to him because his psyche's so strong," said Nick proudly, as if his father were an extra-sensory Tarzan. "He started with a couple of ex-monks—Anglican Benedictines from the Fordite Order—who needed a home while they readjusted to life in the world. They eventually married but, thank God, haven't reproduced. Probably don't know how. Then we've got an ex-mission-ary, an ex–Naval chaplain, an ex–theological student and an ex–pop singer, all with various terminal hang-ups. The pop singer's writing an opera about God."

I was much intrigued, but before I could ask more questions the bushes parted on my left and I saw below me in a fairy-tale dell, framed by beautiful trees and magical shafts of sunlight, a vision of architectural perfection. It was a little chapel, exquisitely proportioned, a miniature variation on the classical themes expressed so sublimely by St. Paul's church in Covent Garden.

"My God!" I said, stopping dead to gape in admiration.

"Nice, isn't it?" said Nick, now very friendly.

"Celestial. What's that ruin in the background?"

"A chantry destroyed by religious thugs at the time of the Reformation."

Dreamily we wandered on down the path towards the glade on the floor of the dell. Birds sang. Beyond the intricate pattern of motionless green leaves the sky was a pure, misty blue. The sense of peace was overpowering.

On reaching the glade I noticed that beyond the chapel stood a little house with a slate roof and walls of golden stone. Flowers grew in the window-boxes which flanked the open front door, and a tough-looking tabby-cat, guarding the threshold, watched our approach with a knowing expression before disappearing nimbly into the interior.

Nick paused. "I'll hang around out here," he said, becoming bossy again. "Father might need me. And remember: no more than ten minutes. I don't want him tired."

"Anyone would think *you* were the parent here! Incidentally, why do you call him Father while Martin addresses him as Dad?"

"He doesn't like being called Dad but Martin doesn't know because Father never liked to tell him for fear of hurting his feelings." Nick sounded pleased by this, as if he had scored in some important way over his famous half-brother.

I was about to say frankly: "You Darrows are the oddest bunch!" when a shadow moved in the doorway and I realised that Father Darrow was now standing watching us, the tough tabby-cat curled neatly in his arms.

4

"COME in, Miss Flaxton," he said. "Off you go, Nicholas."

"But Father—"

"Quite unnecessary for you to stay, thank you."

Reconverted into an overgrown James Dean, Nick slouched off across the glade with his fists shoved deep in his pockets.

"It's very difficult for Nicholas that I'm so old," said Father Darrow, setting down the cat before ushering me across the threshold. "Old people can seem so fragile to the young and he's become over-protective, but as you see, I'm quite capable of looking after myself."

I stared around. The room was perhaps fifteen feet square and contained a bunk bed with drawers underneath, a small wardrobe, a table with two chairs, an easy chair with a footstool and numerous shelves of books on either side of a stone fireplace. There were no pictures, no photographs, only a crucifix hanging over the bed. Everywhere was fanatically tidy and spotlessly clean. The old man was spotlessly clean too, just like the room, and neat as a new pin. In contrast to the previous evening, when he had been dressed as a layman for his outing to the theatre, he had now chosen to appear as a clergyman; he wore a black suit, a black stock and a snow-white clerical collar. He also, unlike most ordinary Anglican clergymen, wore a small pectoral cross, representative, I supposed, of the Anglo-Catholic churchmanship which made him prefer to be addressed as "Father" rather than "Mr." His beautiful hands gestured that I should sit down at the table. He offered me tea.

"Well, if it's not too much trouble . . ."

But the kettle had already been boiled in the little galley-kitchen. "They were able to bring electricity to the cottage without much trouble," he said, as if he felt obliged to explain the presence of modern conveniences. "The main road runs close to here beyond the wall of the grounds. However, I chose not to have electric radiators. I prefer an open fire, even if it does mean a little extra work."

The tabby-cat was washing its paws on the hearth but when Father Darrow sat down opposite me the animal padded over to us. The old man poured out the tea and nodded to the cat. Instantly it leapt into his lap and began to purr.

"It's very good of you to see me like this," I said, watching his hands stroke the stripey fur, "especially when you never see women."

"What a nasty old misogynist that makes me sound!" He gave me his most fascinating smile. "It's true that in the old days my ministry was to men, but that wasn't because I disliked women; it was because I liked women too well. However, at the advanced age of eighty-three . . . Well, nowadays I see just whom I want to see, that's the truth of it. Most people I don't want to see. Nothing to say. But occasionally I come across a person who screams silently: *Help! Help!*—and then, I assure you, I'm the most sociable creature you could imagine."

I was entranced. "You really heard me screaming for help?"

"A young woman," said Father Darrow, "attractive, delightful and obviously well-to-do, sits down at a table with four men. But she has no eyes for her escort, no eyes for the famous actor who's being so charming to her and no eyes for the young man who's too shy to be more than conventionally civil. Again and again she steals glances at this very decrepit old party who's quite clearly, as they say, 'past it.' And again and again, whenever the decrepit old party meets her fascinated gaze she looks away as if she's been caught in a fearful indiscretion. Now what can be the meaning of this curious behaviour? In addition it's clear that the young lady's in a state of profound agitation. She twists the strap of her bag; she drinks her brandy too fast; she talks with great style but little content. Adding two and two together I make an unlikely four: the young lady has heard about me and for some reason believes that I can ease her agitation. I take a gamble, I suggest an interview and she almost collapses with relief. So! Here you are, and all I now have to do is ask how I can help you."

"Why, you fabulous old pet!" I cried, but then realised in embarrassment that this was hardly the most respectful way to address a clergyman. "Sorry," I muttered. "Demented with relief. Slip of the tongue."

But Father Darrow looked delighted that a young woman should be calling him a fabulous old pet, and as he smiled at me again he seemed so sympathetic, so kind and above all so immensely approachable that I felt I could talk to him without pause for hour after hour while I bared my soul for his inspection. Having been obliged in recent weeks to keep my own counsel and dissemble endlessly in order to preserve my great secret, I found that the impact of meeting someone to whom I could open my heart was so great that I had a wild desire to weep. But I controlled myself. No emotional scenes, Nick had said. I didn't want the old pet regretting his decision to give me an audience.

"Well, you see, it's like this," I said, dry-eyed but not, unfortunately, very coherent. "I seem to have got myself into rather a peculiar situation with a clergyman—I mean, don't get me wrong, I'm not his mistress, at least not exactly, but nevertheless . . . well, it's just rather a peculiar situation." Gulping some air I tried not to panic.

"Oh, I'm very used to clergymen in peculiar situations," said Father Darrow, mercifully unshocked and still exuding his bewitching sympathy from every pore. "Have a little sip of tea."

I had a little sip of tea. Then I managed to add: "We're madly in love but it's all very confusing."

"There's a wife, I daresay, in the background," suggested Father Darrow helpfully, stroking the cat behind the ears.

"Yes, but we've both accepted that there can be no divorce." Suddenly the words began to stream out of me. "The real problem," I said, "is what sort of relationship we can have. You see, he believes—and he's terribly modern in his outlook—he believes there are no hard and fast rules any more when it comes to dealing with ethical situations; all you have to do is act with love—which sounds like an invitation to a sexual free-for-all but it's not. The catch is that you have to act with the very best kind of love, pure and noble. So if a man loves a girl and says to himself: 'Do I take her to bed?' the answer's not yes, it's no, because if he really loves her he won't want to use her to satisfy himself in that way."

"This sounds like the New Morality outlined by Bishop Robinson in *Honest to God.*"

"So you know all about that!" I had thought an ancient recluse would hardly bother to keep abreast of modern theology. "What do you think of it?"

"The important question is what *you* think of it."

"I just don't know any more, I'm so confused. My clergyman, following the New Morality, says that even though he's married we're allowed a romantic friendship so long as we truly love each other, because so long as we *truly* love each other we'll be high-minded enough to abstain from anything that's wrong—wrong in the sense that it would hurt either us or other people. Well, that's fine, so heroic, but the trouble is, the deeper I get into this relationship the less sense that seems to make. I mean, if you love someone you do want to go to bed with them, you can't stop yourself, sex becomes like a tank, crushing all the noble thoughts into the dust."

"You're saying that the gap between Dr. Robinson's idealism and your experience of reality has now become intolerably wide. And what about our clergyman? Is he experiencing this gap too?"

"Yes, but . . . Honestly, Father Darrow, I just don't know what's going on in his mind. There's no doubt he's a deeply moral man—I mean, this is not, repeat *not,* your typical runaway vicar who periodically features in a *News of the World* scandal—but sometimes I think he's making the New Morality an excuse for not going further with me; I've begun to suspect he's held back not by his moral beliefs, genuine though they are, but by some sort of psychological block which arises out of his past."

Father Darrow was deeply interested. "Have you any idea what this could be?"

"In my worst moments I suspect it's all connected with his wife, and in my very worst moments I get obsessed with the thought that he's still sleeping with her, but the truth is I just don't know. All I do know is that occasionally he seems very mixed up—some of his conversations are really bizarre—yet at the same time he must be extremely sane and well balanced."

"What makes you so sure of that?"

"Well, I wasn't exaggerating a moment ago when I said he's not your typical runaway vicar. He's not a vicar at all. He's terribly distinguished, he's one of the most important men in the diocese, and he simply couldn't hold down such a job unless he was sanity personified."

"Ah yes," said Father Darrow, "I see it all now." He set down the cat. "You wanted to see me because I know him well and you think I can unlock the mystery of his personality for you."

"That's it." I sagged with relief. "His wife says you know more about him than anyone else except her, so I thought that if only you could explain him to me I'd at last be able to understand what's going on."

"What's going on," said Father Darrow, "is adultery, Miss Flaxton."

"Oh no!" I said at once. "Didn't I make myself clear? We haven't had sex. I mean, we haven't had complete sex. I mean—"

"How often do you see this man?"

"Once a week on his afternoon off, when we go for a drive in his car, and sometimes we're able to see each other for a few minutes in between, but he writes every day and I write back so we're in close touch."

"He likes your letters, does he?"

"Oh, he adores them! And he adores me—he says I'm the greatest prize he's ever encountered—"

"Yes, of course. He would. I recognise him now."

I stared. "You do?"

"Oh, he's quite unmistakable. Tell me, has he perhaps encouraged you to call him by another name, a name he doesn't normally use?"

Shock locked itself in a lump in my throat as the mounting strain of the interview finally took its toll on me. I was unable to speak.

"It's the Dean, isn't it?" said Father Darrow.

I covered my face with my hands and began to tremble.

5

"DON'T be afraid," said Father Darrow instantly. "I'm sorry I sounded tough. Men often prefer compassion laced with toughness—it helps them maintain their self-control when such things are still important to them, but of course women aren't confined in that kind of emotional strait-jacket."

"Too bad they're not," I said. "I can't stand either sex when they're slobbering all over the place. Disgusting." I looked away as my eyes filled with tears.

"Let me pour you some more tea," said Father Darrow.

"Oh, please don't now bend over backwards to be gentle and kind!" I said. "That would finish me off altogether. Go on being tough. I'd prefer it." A tear rolled down my cheek. Loathing myself for being so feeble I made a mighty effort, dashed the tear aside and commented with a meticulous logic: "Since you recognised Aysgarth from the way he's conducting this affair, I can only assume that this has all happened before."

Father Darrow only said: "What name's he using now?"

"He's gone back to Neville."

"No, he's gone on. This would be Neville Four."

I suddenly realised I was terrified. I forgot my desire to cry. I could only stare at him transfixed as he so casually conjured up the vision of a Dr. Jekyll accompanied by a gang of Mr. Hydes, but at last I managed to stammer: "Father Darrow, you've just got to explain—what in God's name is going on?"

"What's going on, as I've already told you, is adultery, Miss Flaxton."

"Yes, yes, yes, but what's *really* going on?"

"That *is* what's really going on. That's reality. Aysgarth's psychology is in fact very unimportant in this context."

"But—"

"You think that if you understand his psychology you'll be able to discern where the affair is going and what you may reasonably expect from it in the way of emotional satisfaction. But Miss Flaxton, fortunately you don't need to know anything more about Aysgarth in order to make this crucial discernment. It's quite obvious that the situation's leading to catastrophe and that you should escape from it at once."

I whispered: "Catastrophe?"

"You both stand in very great danger."

"You mean in danger of being found out?"

"No, in danger of spiritual destruction. Can't you feel the Devil caressing the hair at the nape of your neck?"

Instantly my scalp prickled. In fact so powerful was the impact of his suggestion that my hand automatically sped to the nape of my neck to clamp down on the hairs which I felt sure were standing on end. Then reason reclaimed me. Withdrawing my hand I wiped my sweating palm on the skirt of my dress and said in fury: "You can't frighten me like that! No one believes in the Devil any more!"

"Don't connive at your own destruction, Miss Flaxton. To pretend the Devil doesn't exist is to invite him to annexe your soul."

"But this is 1963! We don't believe in a three-decker universe any more! We don't believe in God as an old man up in the sky! We don't believe—"

"We don't believe the Devil is a charming little imp with horns. That's true. The symbol's outdated. But that doesn't mean the Devil doesn't exist, and that doesn't mean the 1960s can do without symbols in their attempt to express ultimate reality. Believe me, Miss Flaxton, there's nothing so very special about the 1960s—although future historians may well look back in wonder that so much was disbelieved so irrationally by so many."

"But Bishop Robinson says—"

"The Bishop's reaching for new ways to speak about God, but two can play at that game—let me reach for a new way of speaking about the Devil. Forget the little imp with horns! Throw him in the melting-pot, as Dr. Robinson would say! But now think of Hiroshima, Miss

Flaxton. When the atomic bomb was dropped many were killed but some people did survive apparently unscathed. Yet they were not unscathed. They had been contaminated by a great pollutant. It was invisible, but it entered the flesh of those unfortunate victims and settled in their bones and is to this very day busy destroying them. That was a very great pollutant, Miss Flaxton, one of the greatest mankind has ever known. But there's another pollutant, the greatest pollutant of them all, and it attacks not men's bodies, like radioactivity, but their souls. The attack is launched through the human consciousness, which, as any psychiatrist will tell you, is a dense and often impenetrable mystery. Human consciousness is like a well, and into that well, through every little crack in the brickwork, the Great Pollutant will seep unless rigorous efforts are made to keep it out. But if no efforts are made or if the efforts made are too feeble to be effective, the shaft will be fatally contaminated; a scum will form upon the water and in the end the entire well will be rank and putrid. Then the well, that source of life, will be dead, and the Great Pollutant will have triumphed over the miracle that was once clear and shining and beautiful in God's sight."

There was a silence. I smoothed the nape of my neck again with shaking fingers and stared blindly down at the table.

"You may think you stand in the light, Miss Flaxton, but it's a false light, and wherever the false light exists *it* will be there, the Great Pollutant, pouring darkness into the well of consciousness in order to lay waste the human soul."

"But I love Neville! And since love is good—"

"As I said, you may think you stand in the light but the light is false. Now let me abandon the language of mysticism and talk directly of hard facts. I believe you when you say you love this man. But since he belongs to another woman, there's no place for your love to exist. This truth is symbolised, of course, by the fact that you can only meet for any considerable time in that transient object, his motor car. To create a place where your love can exist in any satisfactory way is in fact impossible, and indeed any attempt to create such a place is to dabble in the dangerous delusion that your love can bring you anything other than the most destructive suffering. I beg you, Miss Flaxton, face reality. Don't be beguiled by Aysgarth's fantasies—or by your own."

"But I *am* trying to face reality! If you could only explain his psychology to me—"

"That's beyond my power. I'm a priest. I can't betray the secrets of the confessional."

For a moment I was dumbfounded. Then I was furious with myself for not foreseeing this impasse, and my fury combined with my disappointment to form an overwhelming despair. Again I found myself struggling to suppress my tears.

"I'm very sorry," said Father Darrow, "but what I can and will do is list the facts which—unlike Aysgarth's psychology—are absolutely crucial here. One: Aysgarth is obviously living in a state of very great illusion. Two: this is probably, though not necessarily, generated by a desire to escape from profound problems either in his private life or in his professional life or in both. Three: because he's in such severe difficulties he needs spiritual counselling without delay. Four: you're in a position to wreck both his public and private life, and five: he's in a position to destroy you. That's reality, Miss Flaxton, and in consequence the only realistic advice I can possibly give you is to end the affair immediately."

I sat shaking, shocked and shattered in my chair as the tears rolled silently down my cheeks.

"Now let me warn you against the pitfalls you'll be tempted to rush into as you automatically try to resist this advice," said Father Darrow. "One: don't write me off as a senile old codger who's forgotten what it's like to be in love. I was about Aysgarth's age when I fell violently in love with my second wife, who was then a woman not much older than you are now, and that's a memory that can never die. Two: don't write me off as an old-fashioned priest who's mindlessly committed to supporting a conventional moral line. My support is rational, not mindless, because conventional morals actually evolved to deal with realities; they weren't invented by a gang of old buffers who sat down one afternoon and decided to flex their imaginations in order to cause the greatest possible inconvenience to the greatest number of people—indeed if morals were invented in that way I wouldn't be interested in them; my business is entirely concerned with reality, not fantasy. Three: don't deceive yourself with the thought that Mrs. Aysgarth might suddenly die. It's true any of us can die at any time, but if you spend your life waiting for her to die you'll wind up wanting to murder her—which will mean you've gone out of your mind. Four: don't deceive yourself with the thought that this marriage could break up. Clerical marriages do break up, sad to say, but this one won't. It's not in my power to say why he's bound to that wife of his, but believe me, he's tied with ropes of steel. Whether he's still intimate with her—a question you obviously find of deep interest—I have no idea, but in fact that's not important. All that's important is that by making love to you—in whatever sense—he's doing you nothing but harm."

"But he's not! He couldn't! He's so good, so kind, so—" I choked on my words, lost control, started sobbing. "He hasn't harmed me!" I shouted hysterically. "He hasn't done anything to me!"

Father Darrow rose to his feet and said simply: "Follow me."

I stumbled after him as he led the way to a door on the other side of the room. When he opened the door I saw a bath, lavatory and basin beyond.

"Come along," he ordered as I hesitated. "Come here."

I staggered over the threshold and instantly he gripped my shoulders and spun me to face the mirror over the basin.

"There," he said. "*Look* what he's done to you."

I stared into the glass. A bleary, blotched, blighted face, haggard with sleeplessness and drawn with grief, stared back. All my eye make-up had smudged. My chalk-white cheeks had a greenish tinge. Tears were everywhere.

Wrenching myself from Father Darrow's grip I hurtled back to the table and collapsed in a heap on my chair.

"And that's just the beginning," said Father Darrow. "That's just a little preview of the inexorable horrors to come. Now tell me"—unexpectedly his voice softened as he altered his approach—"are your parents alive?"

I nodded dumbly.

"Could you not go and visit them? They might be able to offer support to you in this very difficult time."

"Well . . ."

"But perhaps they're not particularly sympathetic."

"They're okay." I groped on the floor for my bag and began a long search for a handkerchief. "But they're old, you see, so old, and I couldn't bother them with my problems. It wouldn't be right."

"How considerate. That sounds as if you're fond of them."

"Oh yes," I said, "very fond."

"Are you an only child?"

"No, I'm the last of six children." Quite without warning my voice added dully: "Sort of an accident, I expect." I was astonished. It was as if my voice had acquired a will of its own.

"Oh yes?" said Father Darrow, exuding his bewitching sympathy again and mentally wrapping it around me as if it were a rug.

"Yes . . . At least, that's the impression one gets."

"Does one?" said Father Darrow, metaphorically tucking me up in the rug and adjusting each fold to make sure I was cosy.

"Well," said my voice, responding to the cosiness by becoming confidential, "when I was conceived my parents were visiting Venice—which was a very peculiar thing for them to do as Papa hates Abroad—and since they were both over forty and since it's hard to imagine them being much interested in sex even when they were young, one can only suppose that Venice went to Mama's head with extraordinary results."

"What about your father?"

"Oh, nothing goes to his head except Latin and Greek. I can just imagine him sulking in Venice while Mama yearned to have a fling with some gorgeous Venetian . . . In fact ever since I saw the film *Summer Madness* in which Katharine Hepburn falls in love with Rossano Brazzi in Venice, I've wondered . . ." But my voice trailed away.

"Yes?" said Father Darrow, very, very gentle now, his tough manner utterly abandoned. "What have you wondered?"

"I've wondered if Mama had a similar fling . . . but I don't suppose she did."

There was a silence. Father Darrow was uncannily still. I was reminded of a cat waiting with infinite patience and extreme cunning outside a promising mousehole.

"My friend Marina Markhampton's father isn't her father at all," said my voice vaguely after a while. "They say it happens quite often among our sort of people. But of course I don't really believe it happened in our family."

Another silence fell. The cat continued to wait outside the mousehole and at last my voice remarked idly: "My father's a frightful bore, but I'll say this for him: he always does his moral duty. He's taken a most conscientious interest in my welfare, and considering that I'm a freak, not like any of the others, and haven't even been able to get myself married, I think he's heroic to take any interest in me at all. In fact when we drive each other up the wall—which is most of the time—I almost wish he'd stop being so heroic and disown me altogether. But of course he never would. That wouldn't be doing his moral duty."

I looked around the room. The cat was snoozing on the hearth. A clock was ticking somewhere, and on the wall above the bed the crucifix hung in shadow.

"My father's a very moral man," said my voice. "He's always crusading for some worthy, enlightened cause in the House of Lords—yet he's not demonstrative with people, only with causes. The last time he kissed me, for instance, was at my sister Sylvia's wedding—he kisses people at weddings for some reason—but that doesn't matter, does it? I don't mind him not slobbering over me. What I mind is being treated like a worthy cause which has to be hammered into shape. I don't want to be hammered into shape. I want to be me. But he doesn't see *me* at all, doesn't care, doesn't want to know, doesn't understand . . . Yet he's brilliantly clever—I don't want to give the impression he's a fool, and I don't want to give the impression he's a monster either. When he's in a good mood no one can be more charming and amusing—except his playmate Aysgarth, of course. But wait a minute—you don't know, do you? I was forgetting. Now this is *really* bizarre. Aysgarth and my father are devoted to each other, have been for years. Isn't it the most extraordinary coincidence that I should have fallen so violently in love with my father's best friend?"

"Extraordinary," said Father Darrow without expression.

6

AT that point I noticed that my handkerchief was stained black with my ruined eye make-up and I asked his permission to retire to the bathroom for repairs. Glancing in the mirror again I had a fleeting vision of myself as a hag past fifty.

"Sorry I waffled on like that," I said as I returned to the table and collapsed once more in my chair. "I'm afraid I digressed from the main problem. If we can get back to Aysgarth—"

"I can well imagine him enjoying *Honest to God.*"

"Yes, he adores it, but on the other hand Bishop Ashworth thinks it's absolutely the bottom—which is so confusing, because they can't both be right, can they?"

Father Darrow merely smiled and said: "They're creating a paradox but the real truth lies beyond."

"And what's the real truth?"

"*Honest to God* is more than one book. It's one book for the Bishop, another for the Dean—and no doubt it's yet another for someone else. This has happened because the work is written with the most passionate emotion, and it's this emotion which is striking all the different chords in people's hearts as they watch a bishop, who is supposed to be all-knowing in spiritual matters, grappling with the faith like an ordinary pilgrim. Some people admire him for his honesty and humility but others cannot forgive him for it. Some commend his attempt to frame original opinions, but others merely despise him for his lack of scholarship. Poor Dr. Robinson is a beleaguered man at present and deserves, if nothing else, our prayers."

"But you, Father Darrow—where do *you* stand in the *Honest to God* debate?"

"Beyond it. I think that beyond all the words lies the Word which dwarfs them all. 'In the beginning was the Word . . .' How well do you know St. John's Gospel? It's the greatest mystical tract ever written and deals, as mysticism always does, with matters which can't in truth be translated accurately into ordinary language at all. God is very much greater than a little book like *Honest to God,* Miss Flaxton, and *Honest to God* in fact reflects not God at all but twentieth-century man, bewildered and alienated, freed from witchcraft but enslaved by the dogmas of science, liberated by the Enlightenment but imprisoned by rationality, blessed with the power of improving his material world but knowing too that one push of a button could bring it all to an end. Dr. Robinson is wrestling with the tragedy of modern man, and as a modern man himself he conducts his fight within the wrestling-ring of modern times, but the whole truth, of course, can never be confined to a mere wrestling-ring. Our bodies may be obliged to exist in such a confined environment, but our real selves," said Father Darrow, regarding me with his clear grey eyes, "are not confined by the prison of space and time."

I suddenly realised, as I had a split-second vision of the vast mysteries which enfolded mankind, that he had folded up the Church of England into the size of a handkerchief and tucked it neatly away in his pocket. I said, groping for words: "You're beyond all formal religious structures, aren't you, as well as being beyond all fashions in religious thought," but he answered at once: "Mysticism is certainly beyond fashions in religious thought, but all mystics need a formal religious framework in order to achieve a proper balance in their spiritual life."

"And you've chosen Christianity."

"No, Christ chose me. Are you too a Christian, Miss Flaxton, or are you merely an interested observer?"

"I'm a Christian, but no one did any choosing. It was simply dished out to me, like a British passport, because I was born in a certain time and a certain place."

"Perhaps the choosing's now about to begin. Have you thought much about your faith?"

"Well, off and on, I suppose, the way one does occasionally . . . I mean, yes, I have, of course I have." I hesitated but then said impulsively: "It's all true, isn't it? It must be. St. Paul talked to the eyewitnesses. You can't get around that. And then there's the transformed behaviour of the apostles. You can't get around that either. Something happened, although we'll never know for sure what it was, and now we're sitting here talking together and the whole great circus of the Christian Church is lumbering merrily on its way because two thousand years ago in an obscure Roman province a carpenter conducted an itinerant ministry, wrote nothing and was executed. That's so unlikely that one couldn't possibly believe it except that it happens to be true."

Father Darrow smiled and commented: "Tertullian said: 'It must be believed, because it is absurd!' "

"My father says Tertullian was a fool. My father's got a psychological block about Christianity—he can't discuss it rationally at all."

Father Darrow said: "Go home and see your father. Talk to your mother. Perhaps she can act as a bridge between the two of you."

"Why do you keep going on about my parents?"

"There's something there that needs healing, and once the healing's been achieved you may see your present situation in a different light."

"But my father's not a problem at present! My real problem——"

"Tell Aysgarth," said Father Darrow, "that last night at the Staro Arms Jon Darrow sent his compliments to him and invited him to call any time at Starrington Manor. Now kneel down, please, and we'll pray that the power of the Holy Spirit may heal you of your sickness and grant you the strength to survive the times which lie ahead."

I was a little startled by this suggestion and more than a little appalled by the implication that I was ill, but I told myself strength was well worth praying for and that I really did have a moral obligation to be polite to the old pet. Trying not to feel too self-conscious I knelt down, clasped my hands together and closed my eyes. He was silent for so long that I glanced up but when I saw his lips were moving I shut my eyes again and waited. Eventually he said a prayer aloud. I recognised it. It was one of the Collects which were recited at Evensong.

"Lighten our darkness, we beseech thee, O Lord . . ."

I thought of the Great Pollutant, spreading through my life like a lethal poison, and I was just beginning to pray very earnestly indeed for an antidote when Father Darrow, quite without warning, laid his hands on my head and pressed down so strongly that I nearly collapsed. My mind went blank. I felt as if I had been given an electric shock, although of course that must have been an illusion created by the power of his personality. But the most shattering part of all was that I felt sexually excited. In fact I thought I was going to have an orgasm. For a moment I was transfixed, too appalled and repulsed to move, but as he himself faltered, knowing something had gone wrong, I ducked away from his hands, grabbed the rim of the table and hauled myself to my feet. I was shuddering from head to toe.

He said in great distress: "My dear child, I——" but he was interrupted by a thunderous knocking at the door.

"It's all right, I'm okay, don't worry . . ." But I hardly knew what I was saying. The whole incident was so unspeakably sinister that I could only batten down my horror by pretending I was unscathed, but he barely heard my reassurance. He said stricken: "Forgive me—I should have realised the state you'd be in as the result of your association with that man—I shouldn't have tried any healing which involved physical contact——" But again he was interrupted by a thunderous knocking on the door and this time Nick burst in without waiting for an invitation to enter.

His father was livid. "Nicholas, go outside this instant!"

"But I only came back because——"

"*Out!*" shouted the old man, now very distressed.

"No, wait!" I cried, seizing the chance to escape, and to Father Darrow I added at high speed: "I've got to go now, thanks for seeing me, please don't worry, I'm all right, everything's fine, it doesn't matter." I grabbed my bag and stumbled to the door.

"I only came back," Nick said soothingly to his father, "because I was sure you'd be getting tired and needing to be rescued."

"Ah, Nicholas, Nicholas . . ." But the old man's anger was spent, and as I glanced back from the doorway I saw him sink down exhausted upon the nearest chair. "Very well, take Miss Flaxton away."

Nick promptly hustled me past the threshold and closed the front door. Since I was too shattered to speak and he was too furious, we walked in silence out of the dell, but when we finally emerged from the woods he said, still outraged: "You shouldn't have seen him. His psychic judgement's not as sound as it used to be, that's the trouble. A year ago he'd never have dreamed of seeing a woman alone for a consultation which involved healing."

"How did you know he——"

"I looked through the window. Of course I could see it had gone wrong. Imagine chucking up his golden rule like that at the age of eighty-three—what an absolutely idiotic risk for a clever old priest to take!"

"Oh, for God's sake, Nick, why shouldn't the fabulous old pet have some fun while there's still time?"

"You've simply no idea what I'm talking about."

We stalked on without speaking across the daisy-studded lawn but when we at last reached my car he did manage to mutter apologetically: "I'm sorry you're so upset."

"How do you know I'm upset?"

"I can feel. If only I could help you . . . but I don't know how."

"Some day, baby," I said, mimicking Dinkie's New York twang. "Some day. Now run off and play with your crystal ball." By this time I was as exhausted as Father Darrow. Slumping into the driver's seat I drove raggedly away, but as I glanced in the mirror and saw Nick was still staring after me, I felt the nape of my neck tingle with fright again.

In horror I wondered if he had been not only spying at the window but eavesdropping at the door.

I SOMEHOW succeeded in convincing myself that Nick would never have been so naughty as to eavesdrop; a quick glance through a window was pardonable, particularly since he had been worried about his father's stamina, but listening at the keyhole would have been impossible to justify under any circumstances. However, this conclusion only made his parting expression more sinister. He had looked as if he was watching me drive to my doom, but of course that statement was mere fanciful nonsense and indicated that the closing moments of the interview with Father Darrow had put me in a thoroughly neurotic frame of mind. Obviously it was now time to make a supreme effort, face the incident with all the calmness and rationality at my disposal, and defuse the horror by working out exactly what had happened.

I shuddered but pulled myself together. I had no doubt that Father Darrow had acted in good faith and had had no salacious designs on me whatsoever; the old pet wasn't an old monster. Yet sex had been present in that fiasco somehow and it hadn't been a normal kind of sex. It was as if the sex, dark and distorted, had been a mere marker, an indication that another far more dangerous force had been on the loose in that room, and suddenly I heard Father Darrow saying: "I should have realized the state you'd be in as the result of your association with that man." He had spoken as if my state, whatever that was, had adversely reacted with his psychic healing in the manner of two chemicals frothing and hissing when they were mixed in the same test-tube. It was as if Father Darrow had produced a clear, unpolluted essence, and I had produced—

I suddenly realised I was going to be sick. I had to stop the car so that I could vomit into the ditch which ran alongside the country lane, and afterwards I sat shivering for a long time in the driving-seat before I was able to light a cigarette.

But I could now put into words what had happened. Father Darrow had tried to cast out my polluted essence, but because his psychic judgement had been impaired (as Nick had put it) he had tackled the task in the wrong way. The exorcist had slipped up. Game, set and match to the—

But of course we didn't talk about the Devil, not now, not in 1963. And we didn't talk of polluted essences either, or psychic healing, or two chemicals snarling at each other in a test-tube as if they were people. I was going off my rocker. I had to calm down. Where was my intellect, my rationality, my comforting mid–twentieth-century scepticism? The paranormal was great fun, of course, but once one started taking it seriously one wound up in a loony-bin.

Everyone knew that.

The cigarette continued to shake in my hand.

I thought: what I need's a drink. So I stopped at the nearest pub and downed two gin-and-Frenches. That fixed me up. The world stopped looking as if it had been painted by Hieronymus Bosch and began to look like a landscape by Constable again. Very pretty country around Starbridge. Lovely part of the world.

As I drove on I thought: I just got overwrought. The old pet battered home the morality message with a hammer the size of a croquet mallet and destroyed my defences. Then I compounded my weak emotional state by drivelling on and on about my father, and finally I was so debilitated that when the old pet pressed me on the head I lit out in the craziest possible way. Not the old pet's fault, of course. It was a mere reflex action stemming from the fact that I'd recently discovered the joys of sex. Obviously any male touch at present had the power to send me bananas. All rather amusing really.

I stopped at the Staro Arms and had another couple of gin-and-Frenches, just to make sure I stayed madly amused and the world stayed like a Constable landscape. I decided I adored the Staro Arms. So picturesque. Such fun. Super.

Guiding my car with light-hearted flair through the streets to Butchers' Alley I reached my flat and after several attempts succeeded in fitting my latch-key in the lock. The front door swung open—and there on the mat lay a letter which had arrived in the second post.

At once all thought of the old pet was wiped from my mind. Riding high on my tidal wave of euphoria I ripped open the envelope and feverishly started to read.

8

". . . AND there was Charles," wrote Aysgarth,

dressed to kill in full episcopal uniform and playing the Boss with a capital B. "Sit down, please, Stephen," he says in the creamy voice prosecuting counsel use when they aim to destroy a leading witness for the defence. "Malcolm Lindsay's told me you're a trifle worried about the potential cost of your application for a faculty, and it occurred to me that both the diocese and the Cathedral could save money on legal bills if you and I got together for a little chat." Which, translated from Ashworth-speak, meant: "The Archdeacon's run screaming to me about your threat to bankrupt the diocese but I'm here to tell you that I'm not standing any nonsense over that blank-blank sculpture and you'd better pull yourself together pretty blank quick."

Well, I sit myself down, very cool, calm and collected, and I cross one leg over the other so that I look wholly relaxed—these little gestures are very important in any power-struggle—and then Charles idly starts fingering his pectoral cross, underlining the fact that he's the Bishop—a cunning counter-play—and he even has the nerve to angle it so that it flashes in the sunlight. First round to him. Then he says: "I must be quite frank and tell you that the most extraordinary rumours have reached me about this sculpture. According to Tommy Fitzgerald it may well be a fine work of art, suitable for display in a museum, but in his opinion it's quite unsuitable for display in a churchyard. He says it'll cry out to be vandalised by the hooligan element in Starbridge's teenage population."

This was certainly a new approach from the traitor Fitzgerald. I said, mild as milk: "Why does Tommy think it'll attract vandals?" and Charles answered: "He says part of the sculpture looks like a bunch of used condoms." To which I instantly replied: "I rather doubt if Tommy would known an unused condom if he saw one, let alone a used one." That hit the target all right. Second round to me. Charles said: "The fact that Tommy's been called to lead a celibate life doesn't automatically mean he has no knowledge of contraceptives." At once I riposted: "Well, if it doesn't mean that it certainly ought to." Third round to me. Charles said: "I can't help thinking that Tommy's sexual history is entirely irrelevant to this discussion, but while we're on the subject of sex perhaps this might be the moment to inform you of the rumour that you know Harriet March rather better than would be prudent for a man in your situation."

That really jolted me. I managed to say: "That's a slander!" and Charles, I think, realised that I was speaking the truth. He said: "Yes, I was sure it was, but people have noted the fact that you've commissioned this work from a youthful and attractive woman, and they wonder what prompted you to select her." I answered reasonably enough: "The Cathedral can't afford Henry Moore. Mrs. March was recommended to me by a friend at the Tate." Charles at once backed down on that subject (another round to me) but then plunged back into the attack. He said: "Very well, I accept that she's a reputable artist, but the fact remains that we can't have anything which can be mistaken for either condoms or male genitalia—or both—lying around in the Cathedral churchyard. Think of the inevitable blown-up photographs in the gutter-press!"

Sometimes I really do wonder about Charles. I'm very keen on sex, but it's never occurred to me to imagine blown-up photographs of those cigars—what a pornographic imagination he must have! However I refrained from any barbed remark and said politely: "I think it would set your mind at rest if you visited Mrs. March's studio and saw the work as a whole instead of relying solely for information on photographs of isolated details." (I should explain that after I had the idea of commissioning Harriet, she produced some rough sketches so that the matter could be discussed by the Chapter, and everyone, even Fitzgerald, backed me in approving the commission. It was only when Harriet very kindly sent along some photos of the work in progress that Fitzgerald started getting hysterical.)

Charles said coolly: "The photographs I was shown were very explicit," but of course he knew I was right in principle so he's agreed to visit Harriet's studio. The most ironic part about the whole brouhaha is that I honestly believe the sculpture will be a brilliant work of modern art. It's not as if I'm deliberately trying to be outrageous.

Well, I won that particular skirmish but I can see there's an almighty battle approaching because Charles is obviously dead set against the sculpture and I don't think for one moment that this visit to the studio will change his mind. He'll try and strong-arm me into backing down—and if I were him I'd do it before my application for a faculty reaches the Consistory Court. He won't want the whole diocese twittering over the fact that the Bishop and the Dean are locked in mortal combat over a bunch of phallic cigars.

My darling, I must just see you for a few minutes so that we can exchange views on *Present Laughter*—Lady Mary after Sunday Evensong? (D's attending Matins and won't turn up twice.)

All my best, best love,

N.

I thought vaguely of Father Darrow talking of the Great Pollutant, but that seemed a mere fantasy from the realms of science fiction.

I began to count the hours that separated me from Lady Mary.

9

". . . AND there, sitting beside Nick in the stalls, was this ancient sage, ghost-pale and quietly vibrating in time to the music of the spheres. I thought he was a fabulous old pet."

"*Darrow?*" exclaimed Aysgarth, vastly amused. "That ecclesiastical buccaneer?"

"I thought he was adorable. And afterwards at the Staro Arms—"

"—he asked to be remembered to me. Yes, Eddie told me that yesterday."

"Oh, that was only half the message! While Eddie and Martin were haggling over the bill the old pet said to me: 'Next time you're visiting your friends the Aysgarths, tell the Dean that Jon Darrow sends him an invitation to call at Starrington Manor at any time.' "

Aysgarth looked startled. "The sinister old magician! Why did he say that to you and not to Eddie?"

"It was only an afterthought—"

"The old pirate doesn't have afterthoughts. He has psychic intuitions—which of course I don't believe in." But he looked rattled.

After a pause I said uncertainly: "Will you go?"

"To see Darrow? Well, I suppose I might drop in around Christmas, just to be friendly."

I suddenly started to feel confused. "You won't go now?"

"Darling, I'm a very busy man and to tell the truth I just don't have time for him at present. Old pet indeed! However, I suppose I shouldn't be surprised you were mesmerised. The naughty old charlatan was always a dab hand at hypnosis."

My heart began to beat rapidly. "What do you mean?"

"Oh, those psychics are capable of hypnotising anyone—it's all part of the stock-in-trade! You remember I told you how he bounced around my archdeaconry trying to be Svengali, Rasputin and Our Lord Jesus Christ all rolled into one?"

"Yes, but—"

"He called it a ministry of healing. I called it a shameless use of hypnosis combined with an appalling psychic parlour-trick which he had the nerve to call the laying-on of hands. The whole episode ended scandalously, of course, but then that sort of sinister quackery always does." Glancing at his watch he sprang to his feet. "I must fly. Two o'clock on Wednesday in the car-park of . . . shall we say the Crusader Hotel?"

"I'll be there."

Turning his sexy mouth well down at the corners he gave me a smouldering look, told me he loved me and vanished.

After a while I realised the glass had tilted again in my hall of mirrors. Father Darrow was no longer a gifted sage whom Aysgarth in his guilt was trying to avoid. I had been deceived after succumbing to hypnosis, and the gifted sage was in reality a senile eccentric whom Aysgarth very sensibly wanted to forget.

Embracing this rational conclusion with profound relief, I was finally able to write the old pet off as a back-number.

XIV

*"Bonhoeffer's theory, much admired by the Bishop of Woolwich,
that man has now 'come of age' seems to be a silly and unprofitable one
. . . Has man, having come of age, ceased to be a sinner? Has he
ceased to be limited and mortal?"*

R. P. C. HANSON,
in The Honest to God Debate

I

"MY darling," wrote Aysgarth later that week after another scorching
session in Chancton Wood.

> *Horrors!* Jack Ryder, who's the editor of *The Church Gazette,* rang me
> up this morning and said the rumour's reached London that I'm
> planning to instal a machine for French-letters in the Cathedral church-
> yard! I said: "I know I defended the publication of *Lady Chatterley's
> Lover* but this accusation's ridiculous—and what's more, you know
> it!" Jack brayed with laughter and said: "Okay, spill the beans and I'll
> try to print a report which doesn't teeter into pornography." So I
> explained that I was in the process of applying for a faculty to instal
> a work of art in the churchyard, and then I dictated a dignified
> paragraph about how the Dean and Chapter had commissioned from
> the celebrated sculptress Harriet March a work entitled "Modern Man
> in Search of God." Jack then demanded baffled: "But what's all that
> got to do with condoms?" and I was at last able to declare roundly:
> "Absolutely nothing!"
>
> I was just thinking that I'd successfully trounced *The Church Gazette*
> when my spy there, a very nice young woman called Flora MacBain
> who edits the Children's Column, rang to make sure I'd remembered
> that Jack Ryder was bosom-friends with Charles Ashworth when they
> were up at Cambridge together in the '20s. "If you're not levelling
> with Jack he'll find out!" warned Flora, who was clearly reluctant to

stop believing in the fable of the ecclesiastical condom dispenser. My first reaction was: Charles won't gossip about the cigars to any news-hound, even if the hound's the distinguished editor of *The Church Gazette* and even if the hound's a Cambridge chum. Then I thought: wait a minute. Who else but Charles could have ensured that Jack Ryder was so well primed with the latest gossip from the Cathedral Close at Starbridge? And I realised that this was almost certainly the beginning of Charles's attempt to strong-arm me—he was using Jack to drive me into a corner.

Five minutes later the phone rings. It's Charles. Could he possibly drop in at the Deanery? "Certainly—come over straight away!" I exclaim, radiating Christian hospitality. Then I mop the sweat from my brow, gird my loins for battle and somehow manage to abstain from swilling a triple-whisky to calm my nerves.

"Finally in walks Charles in one of those show-off Savile Row suits that make him look like a tailor's dummy. However, I note that he's not in episcopal uniform (apart from the purple stock and pectoral cross) and I've already noted that he's calling on me instead of sum-moning me to the South Canonry. Deduction: he wants to soften me up before he tries to twist my arm out of its socket.

"My dear fellow, have a sherry!" I say at once with a welcoming smile, but he declines. He's just heard, he says mildly, from Jack Ryder that the condom rumour's reached London and in his opinion it was imperative to act before the *News of the World* moved in for the kill. What did I propose to do?

I said I couldn't see the need for immediate panic, since the *News of the World* reporters were hardly about to storm Harriet's studio, and I suggested that the best course was for Jack to run a piece to defuse Fleet Street's fire—a responsible article which stressed the symbolic meaning of every feature of the sculpture. Then Charles began to twist my arm. He said: "The gutter-press aren't going to be deterred by any high-minded piece in *The Church Gazette*. As soon as this matter's aired in the Consistory Court, we're in for banner headlines."

I took a deep breath, looked him straight in the eyes and declared: "Let me disabuse you of any notion that I'll withdraw my application for a faculty just because there's a possibility that this superb work of art might be mocked by a gang of Fleet Street philistines. It would be against my liberal principles to submit to such censorship."

I thought I'd rocked him but he snapped back: "No one's asking you to submit to censorship. I'm merely asking you to exercise your common sense. Do you really want to make a laughing-stock of our Cathedral?"

"It's *my* Cathedral," I said, "and in any other diocese in England it would be *my* churchyard. If you hadn't hit on the idea of raking up all that rubbish about unconsecrated curtilage, we wouldn't now be heading for the Consistory Court and banner headlines in the *News of the World*."

"And if you hadn't commissioned a wholly unsuitable sculpture from an attractive young woman you met by chance at a party," said Charles, hitting well below the belt, "I wouldn't have been obliged to rake up the rubbish about unconsecrated curtilage in order to preserve the dignity of the Cathedral churchyard." Then before I could reply he stood up and added in his plummiest public-school voice: "I confess I find this conversation singularly unedifying so I shall now terminate it with the suggestion that we both pray for guidance." And off he stalked to the South Canonry.

Very tricky. The awful part is that there's a lot of truth in what he says; Fleet Street could go to town over those cigars. I honestly didn't think anyone would take much notice of proceedings in a Church court, but maybe I wasn't thinking too clearly. It only needs some bright spark on *The Starbridge Weekly News* to flash the news to a London hack and then the whole tinder-box of Fleet Street will be ablaze—with the result that the Consistory Court will be turned into a circus and the sculpture will become as much a *cause célèbre* as *Lady Chatterley's Lover.* But what am I to do? As I see it, I've no choice; I've got to defend good art from the onslaught of the philistines and I've got to oppose any attempt at censorship by arm-twisting. To back down at this point would be a craven act of cowardice and I refuse even to consider that such an option could be open to me.

What maddens me most of all is to reflect that if that fatuous ass Fitzgerald hadn't gone around Starbridge bleating about used contraceptives, this whole disaster would never have happened! Sometimes I think that widowed mother of his really does have a lot to answer for . . .

2

"MY darling, I absolutely mustn't go any further—"

"Are you worried in case I get pregnant?"

"There's no question of me ever putting you in a position where you might get pregnant."

"How can you say that when we're so obviously on the brink of—"

"But we're not. I'm reining myself in." Drawing back from me he began to rearrange his clothes.

"Who's reining himself in?" I burst out, overpowered by my frustration. "Neville One, who was brought up by puritan Non-Conformists? Nevilles Two and Three, who are supposed to be dead? Stephen, who's supposed to be left at home with Dido? I know it can't be Neville Four—he loves me and wants to go on!"

"For heaven's sake!" he said irritably. "Stop treating a mere metaphor as a concrete fact!"

"Your behaviour *is* a concrete fact, and I've come to suspect this whole mystery's somehow bound up with your multiple personality—"

"I have no multiple personality. What mystery?"

I ignored him. "If Neville One can be subjugated," I persisted recklessly, "and Nevilles Two and Three are dead, then it must be Stephen who's holding you back—which in turn must mean that your behaviour's all connected with Dido. Look, Neville, just what the hell is your relationship with that woman?"

He got out, slammed the door so violently that the whole car shuddered, and strode off into the woods.

I stifled a sob. Then I hared after him.

3

"HOW dare you talk to me like that!" he shouted. "How *dare* you!" His short, powerfully built figure was now exuding an anger so violent that I recoiled from him in terror. Nothing had prepared me for such rage because never had I seen him so transformed. My Mr. Dean had vanished and in his place stood a monster who looked murderous. I nearly fainted with fear.

Then the horror ended. The stranger vanished. My Mr. Dean, white with fright, stammered: "Forgive me, forgive me, forgive me—" and hugged me so tightly that I could hardly breathe. "How could I have lost my temper like that?" he said appalled. "And with you—the most precious thing in my whole life! How vile, how wicked, how—"

I sobbed no, no, no, it was all my fault and I'd never mention Dido again as long as I lived and please, *please* could he say he forgave me for making him so angry.

The dialogue eventually reached its foregone conclusion when we embraced, but afterwards he was unable to let the matter rest. He said urgently: "That wasn't Neville Four. I promise you that wasn't Neville Four."

"No, of course not." I dried my eyes.

"That was Neville Two," he said, fathoms deep in mystified anxiety, "Neville Two when Neville Three was too weak to contain him. But how could he possibly have staged a resurrection?" Catching sight of my expression he added hastily: "It's all right, you'll never see him again, I promise. Neville Four's reburied him and covered the grave with cement."

Unable to frame anything which could resemble a reply, I clasped his hand and we walked slowly back to the car. Above us in the trees of Chancton Wood the beech leaves were a vivid, sunlit green.

When we were sitting in the car again he said rapidly: "I'm under such stress at the moment. That's no excuse for what happened, of course, but at least it's an explanation for such a horrific failure of self-control."

"Honestly, Neville, let's just forget it."

"I can't. Supposing I'd hit you?"

"But you didn't."

He seemed not to hear me. It was as if he were immersed in some private nightmare and was flailing around trying to wake up. "I have this horror," he said, gripping the steering-wheel, "this absolute horror of hurting women. They have to be kept safe, cherished, put on pedestals, worshipped, preserved from destruction." He was now gripping the wheel so hard his entire hands shone white. "If I ever wound up destroying a woman I couldn't live with myself—I've told you that before, I've told you that I'm afraid of destroying you. And now I'll tell you that I'm afraid of destroying *her*. A wife must always be able to believe with confidence that there's one act her husband would never do with another woman. Then she won't be destroyed."

After a while I managed to say: "Darling, I do understand."

But of course I didn't. I could now see the "ropes of steel" that bound him to Dido and prevented him from consummating our affair, but where those ropes had been forged and how they had come to bind him I had no idea.

He remained, as before, a mystery.

4

THE phone rang as I was drinking a deluxe dry martini, smoking my umpteenth cigarette of the day and feeling light-headed with relief. I had just worked out that Aysgarth, terrified of destroying Dido with another pregnancy, could not possibly be having sex with her; the very thought of such destruction would be sufficient to render him instantly impotent.

"Hullo, darling," said my mother as I answered the phone. "It's me. How's the plant?"

"Oh, doing wonderfully well!" I had thrown out the corpse that morning.

"Do remember what I said about not watering it too much—"

"Yes, Mama. Any news?"

"Well, we're coming down to Pauncefoot the weekend after next—I have to judge the flowers at the village fete and your father's decided to come too, which is a good thing as he's been working so hard in London (*endless* committees) that I really feel it's time he had a rest. Anyway, darling, we'd love to see you—why don't you come for the weekend and bring some young people?"

"Will anyone else be there?"

"Only the Dean," said my mother satisfied, and added as I nearly knocked over my martini: "By a tremendous stroke of luck we discovered Dido was going to be away that weekend—she's taking the children to visit her sister in Leicestershire—so as soon as he heard the good news your father rang the Dean to issue the invitation."

"Splendid—I'll cadge a lift. Is he arriving on Saturday morning?"

"No, Friday night. That'll give him a little extra time because he has to leave early on Sunday morning in order to get back for Matins. We were hoping he could give the Cathedral a miss that weekend, but apparently that's not possible."

"What a bore. Okay, Mama, expect me to turn up with him on Friday week."

"You wouldn't like to bring a friend? Perhaps Primrose—"

"No, Primrose is fearfully busy at the moment," I said, "and as I've seen so little of you recently I'd rather come on my own."

That pleased her. She asked after the Bishop, my work, the Lindsay family and my flat. Then she maundered on about Arabella's marital problems, but when I at last succeeded in terminating the call I yodelled: "Yippee!" at the top of my voice and mixed myself another jumbo martini.

5

"... *AND* it's certainly very exciting that we can be together for a weekend," Aysgarth wrote,

> although I daresay your father will stick to me like glue. However, no doubt we can wangle some time together in your little sitting-room! Do you remember how we read Browning together there once when you were seventeen? You said (knowing everything, of course, just as one always does at that age) that Browning was hopelessly passé, but I persuaded you to change your mind! How my mother loved

Browning's poetry. In some ways you remind me of her. She was an exceptionally clever, charming woman who—wait for it!—wrote the most delightful letters! I was her favourite. We always got on famously.

But I shall hastily terminate that Freudian digression—how tiresome it is that nowadays a man can't even make an innocent remark about his mother without being suspected of all manner of complexes!—and pass on to my current ecclesiastical nightmare. A diocesan committee which will advise the Chancellor on the artistic merit and general suitability of the sculpture is now being assembled, but I've no faith that the members will do anything except fling up their hands in horror. Meanwhile I'm still recovering from the spectacle of my bishop throwing his weight around like a *mafioso*. But why should I be so shocked? Power-mania is an occupational hazard for big-time executives in large corporations, and no doubt I was being naive in supposing that a man who wears a flashy gold cross is somehow miraculously uncontaminated from all the seamier aspects of corporate life at the top. Fancy Charles trying to strong-arm me out of a hearing in the Consistory Court like that! Disgraceful.

To further complicate my life—as if it needed further complications—a thoroughly ridiculous storm-in-a-teacup has erupted and threatens to turn into a hurricane-force gale. Lady Bone-Pelham, widow of the very recently deceased Sir George Bone-Pelham who did something so secret in the war that nobody ever discovered what it was, telephoned me this morning to say that Sir George made a deal with my predecessor to ensure he'd be buried in the cloisters. The preposterous sum of £3,000 is reported to have changed hands. My predecessor Dean Carter, who is even now, no doubt, shaking hands with Sir George in some unimaginable realm of the hereafter, is not available for questioning but I'm prepared to bet heavy money that he'd never have taken a bribe. I explained to Lady Bone-Pelham that for hygienic reasons we no longer buried people within the Cathedral but I offered her space on the cloisters' wall for a memorial tablet and earnestly assured her that Sir George could be laid to rest in the very best part of the cemetery. "Over my dead body!" was Lady B-P's retort. Unable to cope with the thought of two Bone-Pelham corpses on my hands, I then told her I'd have to consult the Chapter. Eddie thinks she's almost certainly certifiable. Fitzgerald and Dalton, loyal to their former boss Dean Carter, are outraged by the bribery slur and say they don't even want to sanction a memorial tablet. But meanwhile how on earth do I convince a senile old lady that I can't dig up the cloisters' lawn to receive her distinguished husband? All my love, darling, from your demented but devoted

N.

6

"WELL, Venetia," said my father a week later at Flaxton Hall, "so you've finally deigned to visit us! You look, I may say, quite remarkably well, which is very perverse of you since young girls who storm off to lead independent lives are supposed to be rapidly wrecked by numerous unspeakable adventures . . . My dear Aysgarth, how delightful to see you again! What did you think of that article I sent you on Mithraism?"

Aysgarth and I had been unable to enjoy ourselves in Chancton Wood that week because he had been obliged to attend an important meeting, but fortified by the knowledge that we would be spending the weekend under the same roof we had faced the loss of our Wednesday outing with equanimity. Leaving Starbridge on Friday afternoon in his car we had paused among the ruins of Flaxmundham Priory, but our hope of a romantic interlude had been terminated by a coachload of trippers. Undaunted, confident that there would be better opportunities later, we had pressed on to Flaxton Pauncefoot and had arrived at the Hall in time for tea.

"What a lot of weight you've lost, Mr. Dean!" said my mother admiringly as soon as she saw him. This observation was true but although Aysgarth should now have appeared smart and streamlined he still contrived to look scruffy. On that day he wore his best suit and a new white shirt, but both were the wrong size for his new figure; moreover his tie was carelessly knotted and he had forgotten to have his shoes cleaned. In contrast my father, lounging around in his shabbiest country clothes, contrived to look not only distinguished but elegant. It was a great sartorial mystery.

Dinner was a success. Aysgarth's dinner-jacket was well-worn and his trousers were a fraction too long, but he was in such sparkling form that I was sure no one cared that he looked as if he were wearing hired clothes. He and my father spent some time discussing the resemblance between the Kennedy brothers of America and the Gracchi brothers of Ancient Rome. (This conversation took place before either of the Kennedy assassinations, a fact which no doubt explains why I remember it as a prophetic debate.) I slung in a controversial comment now and then and enjoyed the conversation immensely. My mother made a valiant effort to conceal her boredom and was once allowed to murmur what fun it must be for the Americans to have a young couple in the White House, but everyone was much too busy arguing about the Gracchi to reply.

Eventually I was obliged to leave the men to their port and retire to the drawing-room where my mother droned on and on about Absolutely-the-Bottom Arabella and whether or not Sylvia was pregnant again. I yawned and flicked through *Country Life* and wished I could be swilling port with the men.

They joined us for coffee but afterwards my father was unable to resist the temptation to monopolise his favourite playmate and Aysgarth was borne away to the library for further delicious intellectual debate. I was so livid that I had to have a bath to calm myself down. Then I hung around my little sitting-room upstairs for hours but no one came. Finally I was once more in such a state of frustrated rage that I sneaked down to the dining-room to filch some brandy from the sideboard, but as I passed the library door and heard my father's animated voice I knew I could give up all hope of seeing Aysgarth that night. I fell asleep on my sitting-room sofa at one o'clock in the morning and woke in a filthy mood with a crick in my neck some time after four.

However my spirits revived at breakfast when my father said: "It's a damn nuisance, Aysgarth, but I'll have to put in an appearance at the village fete this afternoon. Would you mind pottering around here on your own for a couple of hours?" and Aysgarth answered that he wouldn't mind in the least and perhaps Venetia could take him for a little stroll on the grounds.

I gave him a chaste smile and instantly began to wonder if against all the odds and despite all the hang-ups I could lure him from my sitting-room sofa to my bed in the room next door.

7

IT began to rain but I never noticed. It was Aysgarth who remarked: "Why are village fetes always so unlucky with the weather?" but I barely heard him because I was gripped with the hope that I might finally lose my virginity. We had started off sitting on my sofa with a battered volume of Browning but the book had soon fallen to the floor. So much for Browning. No buttons had been undone but I had slipped out of my shoes and we were just pausing while I began to undo his tie. He had one hand on my thigh, I remember—under my skirt, of course—and the other hand was playing sensuously with my hair.

Then the catastrophe happened.

Without warning the door swung open and my father walked into the room.

8

HE stopped dead.

Fortunately the sofa faced the fireplace, not the door, so it was impossible for him to know that Aysgarth's hand was beneath my skirt. All he could see was Aysgarth stroking my hair—a gesture which could have been dismissed as a casual manifestation of affection—and I apparently fidgeting with Aysgarth's tie. This was certainly curious behaviour but not necessarily either suggestive or compromising. In fact in that appalling moment after my father's entrance I saw that the scene was not beyond redemption. All we had to do to survive the disaster was remain cool, behave casually and laugh off the apparent intimacy as mere asexual playfulness between old friends.

But Aysgarth leapt to his feet as if he had been caught *in flagrante,* and to my horror I saw him begin to blush.

My father quietly closed the door.

Still no one spoke. I was now so shattered that I could only act instinctively and my instinct was to protect Aysgarth by calling attention to myself. Slipping back into my shoes I wandered to the window, peered vaguely out at the rain and enquired: "Was the fete washed out?"

"The diehards adjourned to the marquee but I thought I'd come home." My father's voice was as idle and untroubled as my own. Pleasantly he added: "You'll excuse us, Aysgarth, but I'd like a word with Venetia in private."

"Yes, of course, my lord," said Aysgarth fatally, and walked out. He had not called my father "my lord" since the accession to the Deanery six years before.

The door closed again. I went on watching the teeming rain and at last I became aware that my father was watching it too. He was standing beside me with his hands in his pockets. We were about four feet apart.

"I wanted to have a word with you," he said, "about your mother's seventieth birthday next month. I've decided to give a little family dinner-party for her at Lord North Street. I did think of having it down here—much nicer to be in the country in August—but Harold and Amanda can only stop in London for twenty-four hours en route from Turkey to America. Apparently Harold has to go to Washington that weekend. I can't imagine why."

"Curious."

"Very. Anyway, the big question is: what will you children give her as a present? Oliver's organising the matter—you'd better have a word with him. There's been talk of a silver rose-bowl."

"Super! Asprey's or Garrard's?"

"I doubt if Oliver's got that far yet. But the point's this, Venetia: make sure you're up in town on Saturday the twenty-fourth of August or I'll be very cross."

"Wild horses wouldn't keep me away."

"Good. By that time, of course," said my father as we continued to gaze at the rain, "you may well have become a little tired of Starbridge. The city has its charms, I quite see that, but when all's said and done . . . well, it really is a trifle provincial."

I said nothing.

The rain drummed on and on against the long slim Georgian window.

"Nevertheless," said my father mildly, "I'm sure it's been an interesting interlude for you. I admit I was cross when you left home, but now I see it's been all for the best."

After a moment I said cautiously: "Oh?"

"Yes, I was stupid not to see that straight away. In fact I can see now I behaved very stupidly, throwing scenes and taking umbrage. Only the other day your mother called me a very stupid man and said I had only myself to blame if you didn't write to me."

"Mama said that?"

"I can understand your surprise. That was, of course, most uncharacteristic behaviour on your mother's part as she's renowned for her placid nature and affectionate disposition. But the other day she spoke her mind. About you. Most interesting. Made me think a bit, I can tell you. Felt quite chastened afterwards."

"Good heavens. How very remarkable."

"Yes, wasn't it? 'You stupid man!' she stormed at me. Me! *Stupid!* I nearly had apoplexy. Then I had to face the ghastly truth: she was right. I've been very, very stupid all my life about women. Never understood them. Closed book. My mother died young and I had no sisters. Eton—Oxford—all-male establishments . . . Emerged brilliantly accomplished and a complete fool. Most extraordinary paradox. Suppose it must happen quite often. Very hard for the wives, though. And the daughters."

He began to roam around the room and after a moment he exclaimed: "What a wonderful stroke of luck it was that your mother agreed to marry me! I wasn't even heir to the title then, just a younger son and so very stupid—how brave it was of her to take me on! I knew nothing about women, nothing at all. My father—all that drink—all those mistresses—disgusting! I was so ashamed . . . And then my brother dying of—well, I can't tell you what that was like, no words could describe the horror, particularly at the end when his brain rotted. So I always said to myself: bloody women, do without them, live like a monk. But then I met your mother, so comfortable, so ordinary, so nice-natured, so *safe,* and it occurred to me I was really very miserable living like a monk, so . . .

"How your mother put up with me I don't know. Miracle. Anyway, we wound up very happy and the boys came and then the girls and our family was complete. It was complete after Arabella, as a matter of fact—two boys and two girls, that was exactly what we wanted—but then Sylvia turned up unexpectedly. Not that I minded. I liked my girls, nice little bits of fluff, pat them on the head regularly, tell them how pretty they were—easy. But your mother was much put out by a fifth pregnancy and said afterwards: *'No more.'* Well, I quite understood. 'Don't want any more,' I said. 'I'm quite happy. Two sons and three little bits of fluff. Marvellous.' But you know, Venetia, it wasn't so marvellous. In fact as time passed it really wasn't so marvellous at all."

My father had paused by my writing-table and as I slowly turned to look at him I saw him start to fidget with the edge of the blotter. "Of course," he said, not looking at me, "I was proud of my boys, fine little fellows, and I was devoted to my three bits of fluff, pretty little things, but as they all grew older none of them shared my interests and I still had no one to talk to. I didn't admit to myself that I was disappointed, but your mother knew, and when I finally went through an exceptionally glum patch—the forties can be a very depressing time—she said to me: 'I can't stand you mooching around like this—take me somewhere beautiful like Venice for a holiday!' I said: 'I don't like Abroad.' That maddened her. 'You beastly, selfish man, thinking of no one but yourself!' she cried. 'What about me? I'd love to see Venice!' So off we went and at first I sulked but soon I found it all most interesting and in the end we had a whale of a time, the best time we'd had since our honeymoon, and when I returned to London I felt fit to burst with high spirits. And then . . .

"Well, you know what happened. I said aghast to your mother when she told me: 'I'm dreadfully sorry—I know you didn't want any more,' and she laughed and laughed—oh, how she laughed! Then she said: 'You silly man, do you think I didn't plan it all right down to the special four-poster bed?'

"What a woman! I was so grateful to her and so excited and I kept thinking: this'll be the one, this'll be it, Latin and Greek prizes galore, intelligent conversation, the comfort of my old age. Then you came.

"Well, I was disappointed, wasn't I? I was such a very stupid man, and the stupidest part of all was that I didn't realise how stupid I was being.

All I could see was that there you were, just like me, but the wrong sex. No good. First of all I wanted to write you off. Then I found I couldn't write you off, I couldn't bear it, it seemed such a waste, so I decided to overlook the fact that you were a girl, pretend you weren't, and push you towards the best possible education—you couldn't go to Eton but at least you could go up to Oxford and be a pseudo-boy following in my footsteps. And that, incidentally, was when I got interested in promoting the cause of higher education for women; what I was actually interested in was converting women into pseudo-boys.

"I never stopped to think, did I? I never stopped to say to myself: Venetia's not a pseudo-boy, she's a girl. Such a mistake, because as your mother pointed out to me the other day, you've always resented me for not accepting you as you are. Very wrong of me, not fair to you, but now, thanks to your mother screaming out all those home-truths when I moaned about you not writing to me, I finally understand what's going on. You're a girl and you want to get married; you want to have a husband, children, a nice home, all that sort of thing. Not much good having brains if you wind up an old maid. The way of the world. Not the way things ought to be, perhaps, but when one gets down to the hard facts of life, that's the way things really are.

"So," said my father, having mangled the top sheet of the blotter into a crumpled heap, "I now hear from various reliable sources—your mother and her Starbridge grapevine—that Canon Hoffenberg has been paying his respects, and perhaps this is the moment when I should state unequivocally that I've recovered from the First and Second World Wars. Can't keep hating Germans for ever. The Christians always behave as if they have a monopoly on forgiveness, but they haven't—there are times when forgiveness is a moral duty for everyone, and although I'm not religious," said my father, finally abandoning the writing-desk and wandering back to the window to inspect the rain, "let no one say that I'm not a deeply moral man."

He paused to gaze at the sodden garden before adding: "I like Hoffenberg. Good brain. Pleasant fellow. Successful in his field. Nothing much to look at, of course, but then neither was your mother—by which I mean that if you're like me (and you are) you'll want to feel *safe* with a good companion, not tormented by a thorough bad lot. So what I'm saying is, Venetia, to put the matter in a nutshell, if you wanted to go ahead with Hoffenberg, I wouldn't stand in your way, quite the reverse, I'd be very pleased. I shouldn't have been so prejudiced against him earlier, I can see that now. I should have said to myself: if Aysgarth rates him a capital fellow, he's got to be all right."

There was a pause while he fingered the hem of the faded velvet curtain. Then he said vaguely: "I worry about Aysgarth sometimes, stuck with that bloody awful wife. If he were a layman there'd be no difficulty; he'd keep a nice little bit of fluff somewhere and everyone would live happily ever after, but clergymen can't afford to keep little bits of fluff. Clergymen can't afford to keep anything except their heads. Very dangerous, losing your head if you're a clergyman. Aysgarth's a clever man, one of the cleverest men I've ever met, but unfortunately even clever men have their blind spots, as your mother knows all too well." He hesitated. The rain continued to drum against the pane. Then as he peered down at the velvet hem in his hand I heard him say indistinctly: "Sorry I've always been such a bloody fool, Venetia. Damn stupid. But I swear all I want now is your happiness. Remember that."

In the long silence that followed he stopped inspecting the curtain and very slowly turned to face me, but when he saw the tears streaming down my face he was quick to act. He exclaimed surprised: "Silly little thing! What's all that for?" and gathered me clumsily in his arms.

9

MAKING an enormous effort I pulled myself together. There are some things which one just should not do in the presence of an elderly parent devoted to the art of maintaining a stiff upper lip, and my father was already intensely flustered. He was muttering: "There, there!" and patting me gingerly on the back as if I were a baby suffering from a troublesome case of indigestion. His tweed jacket smelled of tobacco and mothballs and that vague aroma of sketchily washed male which is so pervasive among Englishmen brought up in the days when bathrooms were uncomfortable ice-boxes. His body, ramrod stiff, exuded an agonised fright. He really was, as he had so bravely confessed, quite hopeless with women.

"So sorry," I said at last, using the cuff of my cardigan to wipe my eyes. "Slightly overcome. Temporary aberration. Nothing to worry about."

We parted.

"You'd better go and wash your face," said my father. "It looks an awful mess and I don't like that black stuff around your eyes at all. Oh, and deal with Aysgarth, would you? I know the poor fellow can't help being a draper's son, but sometimes these self-made men really have no idea how to behave."

"Leave him to me."

The conversation closed. My father collapsed on the sofa to recover while I staggered away to the bathroom to wash my face. I spent some time re-applying my make-up. Then I went to Aysgarth's room and knocked on the door.

It flew open. "Venetia—" He was distraught. His hair swooped wildly over his ears as if he had raked it over and over again with his fingers. His bright eyes were clouded with anxiety, anguish, even terror. He could barely speak.

"Yes, yes, yes," I said soothingly, setting him aside so that I could slip into the room and close the door. "It's all right. It never happened."

He stared at me without comprehension.

"Just act as if it never happened," I said patiently as if I were instructing a small child, "and everything will be fine."

"But I don't understand—what on earth did he say?"

"He rambled on about Mama's coming birthday and indulged in a long sentimental reminiscence about how wonderful she was."

"But what did he say about me?"

"Oh, he implied you were wonderful too. He said you were one of the cleverest men he'd ever met."

"But my dear Venetia—"

"Oh, can't you see it doesn't matter? You're his friend and he'll stand by you! All you have to do now is chat about the classics to him as usual—and for God's sake stop calling him 'my lord.'"

He stood there, as baffled as if I had spoken in a foreign language, and groped for the words to express his feelings. "But if I'd been him—and if you'd been Primrose—"

"But that's the whole point," I said exasperated. "He's Ranulph Flaxton and I'm Venetia. We're different."

Light finally dawned. "Ah yes," he said. "Yes, I see." And he looked around the room as if he were trying to work out how he had arrived there after his long, long journey from the small town in Yorkshire where his father had kept a shop.

"Here," I said, trying to help him along. I picked up his hair-brush from the dresser. "Tidy yourself up a bit. You look like an eccentric scientist."

He accepted the brush without a word, smoothed his hair and straightened his tie.

"Fabulous!" I said encouragingly. "Now off you go. We can't talk in private again this weekend, of course. Everything will have to wait."

"But when I drive you back to Starbridge—"

"Oh, that's impossible now. I'll have to stay on and get the train back on Monday."

Again he seemed nonplussed. "But you'll still meet me," he said painfully, "on Wednesday?"

"Of course!"

"And you'll keep writing?"

"Reams. Oh Neville, do stop asking these idiotic questions! Just go and have a nice bright chat with my father about Livy or Plutarch or Xenophon or Tacitus or—"

He nodded and stumbled away.

I 0

I SAT for a long time on the sofa in my sitting-room and stared at the unlit fireplace. Outside the rain eventually stopped. The room was very quiet. The serenity of Flaxton Hall enfolded me like a womb.

Having made the decision to skip tea I went out, wandering through the dank Italian garden and ploughing in my Wellington boots along the muddy path which encircled the lake. From the far side I looked back at the Hall. Its ruthless Georgian symmetry seemed peculiarly satisfying, a dream from the brain of a classicist devoted to geometry, a vision from which all the mess and muddle of the world, all the anomalies and contradictions, had been magically eliminated. I suddenly realised how devoted I was to Georgian architecture and how partial I was to the classics. I began to wish I had gone up to Oxford after all.

Squelching back around the lake I reached the floral garden designed by my mother where huge blooms reeked and flashed in artificial chaos among vast curving borders. I was still faintly revolted by such horticultural excess, but now I could see how well that riotous extravaganza of colour complemented the austere lines of the house. I paused to stare at the Hall again. Some people would have said it was as repellent as the garden, as lifeless in its perfection as the over-manicured mausoleums which the National Trust propped up for tourists, but I knew it could never be lifeless for me. It was home. It was where I belonged, and when I thought of my little nest in Starbridge I could see that although it was wonderfully original the originality would one day wear thin. Starbridge, as my father had said, was really just an interlude for me, and later when I was married I would have a large house of my own, another geometrical dream, with a huge garden, all lawns and trees, no flowers in sight, and there would be a lake, not necessarily an artificial lake designed by Capability Brown, but nevertheless a serene stretch of water where I could lie in a boat and gaze at the sky and think beautiful thoughts.

The best part about being married would be that I'd have the chance to achieve an idyllic life as a chatelaine. All the Coterie would roar down for weekends, and what fun we'd have, celebrating life with lashings of champagne! In fact I now realised I could hardly wait to acquire my own little corner of England because once I was a chatelaine with a husband to prove I was no pitiable freak I could become *me* at last, lying on a couch like Madame Récamier, smoking a cigar like George Sand, talking philosophy like George Eliot, tossing off witticisms like Dorothy Parker and hipping and thighing around like Mae West. I would be faithful to my husband, of course; it would be my moral duty to reward him as lavishly as possible for transforming me from a pathetic spinster into a married sizzler, but nevertheless I thought I might amuse myself—just occasionally—by dallying with a little bit of masculine fluff during my leisure hours . . .

Returning to the house as well as to earth after this mesmerising fantasy, I left my Wellingtons in the flower-room, slipped back into my shoes and padded upstairs. On reaching my bedroom I found that a letter had been pushed under the door. It read:

Darling,

I'm so sorry about the mess. Your father's been wonderful, and we've just finished mulling over his new monograph on the Battle of Actium. He thinks it was entirely Cleopatra's fault that she and Antony were defeated but I think this view hardly does justice to Cleopatra—or indeed to young Octavian who, as history subsequently showed, was a far more formidable man than either of his rivals in the Triumvirate. I must say, it was pleasant to forget all about Harriet's sculpture—and Sir George Bone-Pelham's corpse! But I confess I remain rather bothered by the scene between you and your father. I can't visualise it at all. Surely *something* must have been said? I can't believe he would have condoned our new intimate relationship. I daresay I'm being very lower-middle-class, but I just don't "get it," as the younger generation say. Do please explain!

All my love,
N.

I wrote back:

Darling Neville,

You can't talk about your wife. And I can't talk about my father. Let's leave it like that, shall we?

Masses of love,
V.

P.S. Glad you survived the monograph on the Battle of Actium. Papa's such a bore about Cleopatra—I think he honestly believes all her troubles stemmed from the fact that she wasn't educated at Cheltenham Ladies' College.

I shoved this note under his door and slipped away without attempting to talk to him.

Some people from Flaxfield joined us for dinner. Mr. Wharton, an old friend of my father's, talked incessantly of politics, Mrs. Wharton discussed gardening with my mother, and Margaret Wharton and I reminisced fitfully about the schooldays we had shared at Cheltenham. Halfway through the meal old Wharton remarked brightly that he had seen a book on sale at W. H. Smith's and it appeared to be about theology even though it had been placed among the best-sellers; there was a naked man on the cover and the book had some sort of catchy title—had the Dean ever come across it?

I had a sudden glimpse of a vast, indifferent world which Dr. Robinson's theological H-bomb had never reached, and it was then, as my imaginary mirrors tilted to reflect yet another reality, that I began to be fatally disorientated.

I I

IN bed that night I asked myself which scenes represented reality and which scenes represented a dream. Then it occurred to me that all the scenes were real but that they took place in different worlds which existed alongside one another in parallel strips of time. All I had to do in order to sort myself out was to perceive which world I belonged in, but perception was no longer easy; I seemed to be living in more than one strip. I still thought that Starbridge was intensely real and that the interpretation of *Honest to God* was the most crucially important intellectual question of my life at that moment, but the other world was now equally real, the world of geometric houses and sensible marriages and agnostic indifference to theology, the world where my father, stupid man, had had the brains and the cunning and the sheer bloody guts to bare his soul and thus prove, without ever mentioning the word love, exactly how much I meant to him.

I thought: *that* was real.

But Aysgarth was real too, my darling Mr. Dean, so vital, so amusing, so clever, so passionate, so adoring . . . and such a mystery. *He* refused to bare his soul, but what did his silence actually mean? Did it mean he didn't care for me sufficiently to be honest? Or did it mean he was so mixed up that he could find no words to express his secrets? How could I know? How could I ever know? All I knew was that I didn't want to give him up . . .

And that, I had no doubt, was the greatest reality of all.

12

"MY darling," wrote Aysgarth early the next morning.

You looked quite lovely at dinner last night, much the most attractive woman in the room. How amusing that Wharton had barely heard of *Honest to God*! But if he was abroad when it was published and reads only the secular press, all is at once explained. I was impressed by your father's summary of the book! I always feel he would have made a good theologian if only the tragedies which overtook his father and brother had not resulted in him rejecting God in order to come to terms with his pain.

While on the subject of your father I must tell you that I shall not, of course, press you further about your interview with him; I can quite see this may well have been upsetting and best forgotten. But darling, when I refused to talk about Dido, it wasn't because I didn't want to share everything with you. I did. And I do. It's just that the subject is so awkward that words are hard to find.

However, let me now make a big effort to "deliver my soul," as the Victorian preachers used to say. Actually I think it'll be easier in a letter because I can always tear it up and start again if I get in a muddle. Or if I can't immediately think of the right word I can sit and wait for it to come. So here goes—I shall tell you the whole truth about all the aspects of my past which you've found so baffling. Darling, believe me, I long to be completely honest with you.

Let me start with the phenomenon which you call my "multiple personality." There is in fact only one personality, me, but I've gone through different phases. As you know, I've travelled a very long way in my life on an upward social curve, and like a motor car ascending a steep gradient I've periodically had to change gears. In other words, I've had to adjust my personality in order to keep pace with my changing circumstances, and I've mentally labelled each readjustment with a new name (Nevilles One, Two, Three, Four and Stephen). Some of these *personae* have been better integrated, as the psychologists say, than others, but rest assured that Neville Four is perfectly integrated and "the real me"! Neville One was an innocent—naive and shy. In contrast, Neville Two was a pushy, ambitious creation of whom I came to disapprove profoundly. Neville Three was my attempt to contain him, but the attempt was not altogether successful. Stephen, on the other hand, had been a good creation; he's without doubt my mature self, but he's always cost me a lot of effort to maintain. What's so wonderful about the emergence of Neville Four is that he's just as good as Stephen but he costs me no effort. That's why I feel I've uncovered my real self at last. I feel I've achieved a perfect inner harmony.

Whenever I "change gears"—that is, move into a new *persona*—I like to forget all that's gone before. This is because adjustment to a new life is easier once one's wiped the slate clean. Also, to forget is a form of psychological survival. I had hard times in my youth after my father died bankrupt. My first marriage ended in the tragedy of Grace's death. My marriage with Dido began awkwardly and was only set right when I was reborn as Stephen. My life has in many ways been very difficult—although I don't want to turn this letter into a prolonged moan! Charles Raven, the hero of my younger days in the Church, used to say that until a man has been down into hell he's not fully mature, and I believe that to be true. It's part of the mystery of suffering. I know I'm fully mature, but sometimes I can't help reflecting what a price I've had to pay for that maturity.

This must be where I talk about Dido.

(Later) I've just spent ten minutes writing nothing and now feel I must put down at least something, no matter how inadequate, in order to overcome my writer's block! Let me start by saying this: my first wife was so wonderful and so perfect that after she died I knew I had to marry her exact opposite. I couldn't have stood some lesser version of Grace, perpetually reminding me of what I'd lost. And I knew I had to remarry. I was well aware that I wasn't designed by God to be a Victorian hero chastely mourning his lost love for the rest of his life.

I must also state that I felt very guilty about Grace's death. As you know, she died of pneumonia during a family holiday. We always took our family holiday in Devon, but that year I insisted on a change of plan and we went to the Lake District. It was a long way from our rented cottage to the shops and one morning Grace got soaked to the skin and a chill set in. It could never have happened in Devon where our cottage stood next to the village shop. So after she died, I felt responsible. It even seemed I'd destroyed her, although I concede this was taking an extreme view of what happened. However, gradually I conceived the idea not only of marrying her exact opposite but of marrying someone whom I could rescue, look after and keep safe—I saw it as a way of atoning for what I'd done.

I thought of Dido straight away. I'd actually met her before Grace died, although of course we were mere social acquaintances then; there was no romance of any kind between us while Grace was still alive. When I eventually approached Dido she didn't want to marry me, but that only made me keener—I've always liked a challenge! I realised she had a lot of problems but that merely reinforced my conviction that I was being called to look after her, and later, when she did come to love me, my call seemed even clearer. Love is one of the ultimate prizes of life. One can't just tear it up and chuck it in the wastepaper basket. Once Dido had come to love me I knew I had to cherish her and preserve her from destruction. There was no choice. You don't argue with a call from God. You simply roll up your sleeves, get down to work and do the best you can.

And I did. My reward has been not only Elizabeth and Pip, to whom I'm devoted, but the three children who died either shortly before or shortly after birth. These lost sons of mine I named Arthur (after my father), George (after Bishop Bell) and Aidan (after an elderly clergyman I deeply respected). Dido was never interested in choosing names for them and couldn't understand why I bothered, but to me the naming was important; it was an acknowledgement of their reality, perhaps even a symbol of thanksgiving for their very short existences, certainly a statement that they had been welcomed, not rejected, by their parents.

At first Dido did accompany me to the cemetery to visit their grave, but once she had her living boy and girl she lost interest in the dead—whom she always saw, I'm afraid, as representing her failure to reproduce successfully—and now I go to the cemetery on my own. I've never lost interest in those children. They're very real to me, even though I may never speak of them. I see them all quite clearly. They're never tiresome or difficult as living children inevitably are sometimes; they're always happy, always bright, always perfect. When Arthur had his seventeenth birthday the other day I thought: how amazing that Arthur should be seventeen! And I could see him at once, looking like me but tall and slim like my father. But of course I can't talk about him to Dido. She'd think I was being morbid, but how can a shining dream be morbid? I love my shining dreams, my world of might-have-been.

In novels dead babies always seem to draw a couple together, but that didn't happen in our case. Quite the reverse. But I try not to blame Dido too much for her attitude because she always found childbirth an ordeal and perhaps the births were traumas which ultimately she could only surmount by blocking out her most painful memories. I never wanted her to go on having children like that, but she had to have her boy and her girl. I overheard Primrose saying once to one of her Gang that Dido had to have five children in order to keep up with Grace, but that wasn't true. Dido didn't want Aidan at all because by then she already had Elizabeth and Pip; Aidan was an accident. But she wouldn't have an abortion, which was what the doctor recommended and which I certainly didn't oppose, since her life was in danger. I think possibly she wanted to die. She was in a very bad mental state at the time and afterwards she did have a severe breakdown. But at least she survived, thank God, and I didn't have to live with the knowledge that I'd destroyed her with that pregnancy. No more babies after that, of course. While they were doing the Caesarean they sorted out that problem. During the breakdown afterwards Dido used to sob for hours and say she'd been deprived of her femininity, but they didn't take anything out, they just tied something up. I explained that over and over again but she only went on sobbing. It was a very bad breakdown. I felt so sorry for her. She was so pitiful, so pathetic. Her life has in many ways been a tragic one.

That's why I was so impatient with you when you seemed to be jealous of Dido earlier. If only you'd known! You have so much: your youth, your health, a good temperament free of neurosis, looks, brains, charm, a talent for getting on well with people instead of putting their backs up . . . And Dido has so little, just her children and—well, yes, she has me. Or rather, she has Stephen. But she doesn't have *me,* Neville Four. I belong entirely to you, and what goes on between Stephen and Dido just doesn't count, it's of no significance—why, it doesn't even happen! Everything important, everything that's *crucial* doesn't happen with Dido at all. Of that you can be quite certain.

Well, there it is, darling—the plain, unvarnished truth at last. As you see, I'm at heart a very simple, honest person, but I admit I do sometimes have difficulty finding the words to explain myself, particularly if the explanations involve deep emotions. (When we meet, please don't ask about Arthur, George and Aidan unless I raise the subject first.)

I suppose the earnest disciples of Freud and Jung would want to know all about my parents and my Uncle Willoughby, but I hardly feel that sort of ancient history's relevant to us now in 1963, and anyway an old codger's sentimental reminiscences about his extreme past could only be monumentally boring to anyone under thirty! Suffice it to say that my father, my mother and my uncle were all wonderful, all perfect, and they loved me as much as I loved them.

And talking of love I shall now close this letter by telling you that you're the most miraculous thing that's ever happened to me and I hardly know how to wait until I can take you in my arms again. Be sure to write me a line as soon as you return to the Archdeacon's lap on Monday morning! My darling, I remain always—till the day I die—your most devoted and adoring

N.

13

"*DARLING* Neville," I wrote.

Thanks so much for your marvellous letter—I can't tell you how much better I feel now that you've explained everything, all I can say is that I feel as if a vast load as big as six elephants has finally rolled off my mind. To be quite honest, I've been absolutely *torturing* myself about D. However, if nothing of crucial importance ever happens between you and her, then my torment is at an end and I can simply feel sorry for her. I'm sure you're right and she's pathetic. It must be awful to yearn to be a social success and yet wind up loathed by so many people. As you say, she's had a tragic life.

I do think you overreacted a bit to your first wife's death—after all, it was hardly your fault that the heavens opened and she got soaked! However I quite understand that in the aftermath of such a catastrophe you would have been obsessed by the thought of women being destroyed and longed to do your share of conscientious preservation. I must be quite honest and say I don't think your behaviour was exactly *rational*—in fact if this were a book I'd find your explanation somewhat implausible—but real life is full of oddities and of course great tragedy does make people behave irrationally and succumb to various *idées fixes*.

I promise not to speak a word about Arthur, George and Aidan unless you mention them, but I must write, even if I can't say, that in my opinion you're quite entitled to your "shining dreams" and I don't think you're being morbid at all. I think it's admirable (not quite the right word, but I can't think of a better one) that you feel so deeply connected to them; it makes you seem so loving and compassionate, and in some strange way *wise*—you clearly know how to value and cherish things which other, lesser men might pass off as unimportant, and by loving those lost children you bring them to life. I feel I can picture Arthur exactly, looking just like you but elongated!

Of course I understand completely now about your different *personae. Persona* is the word for mask, isn't it, the mask an actor used to wear in a Greek play. Your identities are not really identities at all but different masks and underneath is the real you—whom I know as Neville Four. Being a self-made man, constantly obliged to remake your mask in order to keep up with your changing circumstances, must be very exhausting. But perhaps we're all self-made to some extent, all engaged periodically in "shifting gears" and remaking our masks. I know I remade Venetia's mask when I went to stay with Marina at the Chantry, and I believe I've remade it yet again with you— although in your company the mask is the real me, just as Neville Four is the real you. What an odd thing personality is. Was it you who told me that the Greeks and Romans had no word for "personality" in its modern sense? Or was it my father? I can't remember. I get confused between the two of you sometimes.

Can't wait for Wednesday, darling—shall we chance the Crusader's car-park again?

Lots and lots of love,

v.

I 4

"MY darling," wrote Aysgarth in reply.

I fell upon your letter this morning like a starving man pouncing on a crust of bread, and devoured every crumb with a sensuous delight! I was also much touched by your kind, sensitive, understanding paragraph about Arthur, George and Aidan. It's such a psychological luxury to be able to share them with someone at last.

Yes, you're quite right about "personality" being a modern concept. That's why people get in such a tangle with the creeds when they read that God is three persons in one—they fall into the heresy of tritheism (where are you, Bishop Ashworth!) and think that God is three separate individuals, whereas in fact the word person in that context means *persona,* the mask. There's one person with three masks: the Idea (God), the manifestation of the Idea in a form comprehensible to man (Jesus) and the continuing influence of that Idea throughout the world (the Holy Spirit). But I must set aside theology and say how glad I am that you now understand about Stephen and the Nevilles—and about Dido too, of course. I do desperately want to be open and frank with you in every way.

How I wish you could have travelled back to Starbridge with me on Sunday morning! Your presence would have given me some much needed extra strength to cope with the Bone-Pelham crisis, now billowing wildly out of control. No sooner had I finished presiding at Matins when Eddie buttonholed me in the vestry with the truly appalling news that Lady B-P has produced a letter from Dean Carter acknowledging the receipt of the £3,000! But I *cannot* believe it of Carter. Neither can Fitzgerald, who says there must be an explanation and he'll interrogate Carter's widow in Budleigh Salterton. Meanwhile the undertakers are getting restless, Lady B-P is still hot against a burial in the cemetery, and her doctor (milked for information by Fitzgerald during a lavish lunch at the Quill Pen) says she's eccentric but not, in his opinion, certifiable. As I so often sigh to you: what a life! My darling, I long with an almost unbearable intensity to see you—yes, let's meet again at the Crusader.

All my love, always and forever,

N.

1 5

I BROWSED pleasurably among the sentences of this letter for some time. Then it dimly occurred to me that apart from the paragraph on the babies and the lines responding to my enquiry about the word "personality" he had made no attempt to answer my letter in depth at all. I had thought he might respond to my very bald remarks about Dido and the distinctly critical note I had struck when commenting on the source of his *idée fixe,* but it seemed these were matters he preferred to gloss over. And why not? Surely there was no need for him to expand on the explanations which he kept saying he found so difficult.

It was at this point that Mrs. Ashworth telephoned.

"Charles tells me you're coming in this afternoon at five," she said after we had exchanged pleasantries, "and I'm just phoning to say do stay on for a drink if you can. I've got a tea-party but with luck everyone will be gone by six."

I accepted the invitation with alacrity.

"How are you?" she added in her kindest voice. "It seems ages since we last met for a gossip."

"Oh, I'm fine," I said. "Absolutely fine."

But was I?

Unlocking my writing-case I retrieved the long letter Aysgarth had written earlier on Sunday morning before his departure from Flaxton Hall. Again I noted the reference to Dido's sterilisation, a fact which exploded my theory that he was abstaining from marital sex because he was afraid of destroying her with another pregnancy. Then I reached the part where he was mixing up his current *personae* in such a way that he implied nothing ever happened with Dido. I read that passage over and over again until it no longer seemed a model of honest clarity but a convoluted masterpiece which was capable of more than one interpretation.

The glass shuddered again in my hall of mirrors.

I began to wonder if I was going mad.

XV

"Having disposed of God as a separate Being or Person, Dr. Robinson is in difficulties over many Christian activities, including prayer. How does one pray to 'ultimate reality'?"

ANONYMOUS,
in The Honest to God Debate

I

"DIVERT me," said Mrs. Ashworth, as we began to sip our gin-and-tonics, "by telling me all about your glorious love-life. Mrs. Lindsay said you were away last weekend—were you sailing at Bosham with your young man?"

"No, just checking up on my parents at Flaxton Pauncefoot. As a matter of fact the Perry romance has cooled—he seems to be more interested in boats than in girls."

"Too bad! But I'm sure someone else will soon turn up now that you're looking so glamorous. By the way, how I envy you that thick, wavy hair! I'd have to spend half my life at the hairdresser's to get that effect."

We talked about hair for a time. Mrs. Ashworth revealed that she had her hair "coloured" by the smartest salon in Starbridge. "Clergymen's wives, of course, never have their hair 'dyed,' " she said with her deadpan humour. I expressed deep interest in the "colouring" and said I was sure the Bishop had never guessed. Mrs. Ashworth commented indulgently that men were so innocent sometimes. Sipping our gins we became steadily cosier.

". . . and talking of men," said Mrs. Ashworth, "what happened to the man who lured your poor friend Dinkie into that most unfortunate romance?"

"Oh, he's still dead keen on her," I said, "but I think she's recently come to realise it's a dead-end street."

"Good. That must represent progress."

"Does it? She still can't imagine ever giving him up."

"Tell her to take a holiday—go back to America for a while, perhaps—so that she can see the situation from a fresh perspective."

"That would be quite difficult. He depends on hearing from her every day, and—"

"How appalling! This sounds like a really dangerous situation—an emotional dependency which is fast swinging out of control. Has he opened his heart to Dinkie yet about his marriage?"

"Yes, but . . . to be quite frank, Mrs. Ashworth, I don't think he's levelling with her. Dinkie believes every word he says, of course, but the more he writes to her that he wants to be absolutely honest—"

"If he's running two women at once I'd think he was lying to the back teeth. Living in two different worlds necessarily involves considerable verbal juggling."

"I don't think he's living in two different worlds," I said slowly. "The three of them are all in the same world. But he's living as two separate people."

"That's the most terrifying thing you've said yet," said Mrs. Ashworth at once. "Tell Dinkie that a split personality leading a split-level life is big, big trouble."

"You think he's mad?"

"Well, obviously Dinkie would realise if he was raving, so the short answer to that question must be no, but I do think he sounds spiritually, if not mentally, unbalanced. One has to be whole, not divided, in order to be spiritually healthy . . . Did Jon Darrow say that to me once? I can't remember. Maybe it was Charles."

Automatically I said: "I met Father Darrow the other evening at the Starbridge Playhouse."

"Oh yes, *Present Laughter*. Amusing, wasn't it?"

"Tremendously . . . Mrs. Ashworth, Father Darrow's rather weird, isn't he?"

"I don't think I'd use the word 'weird.' Unusual, perhaps. But he's very wise and good. Charles thinks the world of him."

My voice said woodenly: "He does?"

"Jon's been his spiritual director for over twenty-five years."

After a pause I managed to say: "So he's not a crank—not a charlatan?"

"Good heavens, no! He's a most distinguished man. Who's been telling you he's a charlatan?"

Far away in the hall the front door opened and the Bishop, true to his long-established custom, shouted: "Darling!" as he returned to the house. After our session of dictation he had departed to visit his chaplain, who lived in a cottage nearby.

"Have another drink," Mrs. Ashworth said to me as he entered the room to join us, but I excused myself, feeling far too disturbed to prolong the conversation.

Then I stumbled back to my flat.

2

I POURED out the gin and sat sipping it in the twilight as the clock of St. Martin's-in-Cripplegate tolled the hour. The little flat was shadowed and still.

After a while I began to wonder if the Ground of My Being was staging a conservation battle against the Great Pollutant.

No, I didn't. I wondered if God and the Devil were fighting for the possession of my soul.

Strange how much more chilling—how much more *real*—the battle seemed when described by the old terminology. One couldn't get very worked up about something called the Ground of One's Being, that was the trouble. And how on earth did one pray to it?

I thought: someone should tell John Robinson that.

Eventually, after a lot of gin, I started to cry.

3

"DEAR Eddie," I wrote.

What's cooking? I see you're the canon in residence for August, so I shall look forward to hearing you preach at Matins next Sunday. Make sure you keep me awake!

Yours,
VENETIA.

4

"I THOUGHT we might have a change from Chancton Wood," said Aysgarth as I slid into the passenger seat of his car the next day, "so in a fit of inspiration I bought an Ordnance Survey map which marks every place of interest in the diocese and found an ancient monument called Castle Brigga not far from Starwater Abbey. I think it must be one of the old hill-forts built by the Starobrigantes—shall we go and have a look?"

We drove away out of the city.

"We're all in such a state over this Bone-Pelham crisis," he was saying as the spire of the Cathedral receded into the distance behind us. "Fitzgerald drives to Budleigh Salterton tomorrow to talk to Dean Carter's widow. I must say, Fitzgerald can be extraordinarily dynamic so long as the situation isn't connected with sex."

"I thought everything was connected with sex."

We laughed.

"My darling!" said Neville Four, who of course never slept with his wife, and reached out to put his left hand on my thigh.

But what had Stephen been getting up to with Dido?

5

THE hill-fort, a vast mound ringed by two broad ditches, afforded plenty of seclusion. We settled ourselves in the shade of a clump of bushes conveniently placed in a hollow far from the path, and soon the glass in the hall of mirrors no longer reflected terrifying distortions but a clear radiant reality, the only reality that had any meaning. Eventually rain drove us back to the car, but by that time I felt nothing could mar my happiness. We lit cigarettes; then he entertained me by reminiscing about his days as a canon of Westminster Abbey when he had regularly prowled the corridors of Church House.

". . . and the Archbishop stormed in saying: 'If I were still a headmaster I'd cane him, I swear I would!' and of course all the time the lawyer who'd drafted the offending clause was hiding in the broom-cupboard! The secretaries, two nice old girls with grey hair and double-chins, nearly had kittens on the spot. Well, someone lured Fisher away and we opened the cupboard and the lawyer keeled out like a corpse in a horror film—"

I laughed and laughed. Outside the car the world was grey with rain but I no longer noticed.

"—and someone shrieked: 'Is there a doctor in the house?' and my friend Derek gasped: 'My God, he's dead!' but the very next moment the corpse groaned: 'Brandy!' and the old girls screamed: 'He's alive!' So I skipped out across Dean's Yard, dived into my house in Little Cloister, shoved the brandy in a shopping bag, raced back to Church House—and bumped straight into the Archbishop who was about to leave for Lambeth . . ."

As I started laughing again I asked myself why I had written to Eddie but I no longer knew. I tried to recall my doubts and suspicions but found they no longer existed. All I knew was that I was in ecstasy and that I wanted the afternoon to last for ever.

". . . and the net result was that we all polished off the brandy. The old girls were quite tiddly in the end . . . Heavens, look at the time! We must go."

Without warning my laughter dissolved into tears of despair.

"Venetia—darling—" He was at once immensely distressed.

I got a grip on myself. "Sorry," said my voice. "Temporary aberration. Bit of a strain, seeing you so seldom and for such a short time." And suddenly, as the confusion began to pour back into my mind, I heard myself say rapidly: "Neville, I'm beginning to think it might be a good idea if I went away for a while to London—not permanently, of course, but I'm getting so muddled here and I feel I need the chance to—"

"For God's sake!" he said ashen, and as he spoke I knew—I just knew, I was wholly convinced—that he no longer had sex with his wife. "Don't leave Starbridge! Please, Venetia, please—I absolutely rely on these meetings—the meetings and the letters—they keep me going, I don't know what I'd do without them—oh my darling, I love you so much, I adore you, I can't imagine how I ever existed without you, how could you ever think of leaving me even temporarily, I thought you loved me, I thought you understood—"

I collapsed in floods of tears again and swore I would never leave.

6

"*DEAR* Venetia," wrote Eddie by return of post.

I shall look forward to spotting you in the congregation next Sunday. My text will be: "Be not deceived; God is not mocked: for whatsoever a man soweth, that shall he also reap." I used to reflect often on that text when I was a POW in May '45. However, in my sermon I shall substitute the decadence sown by secular society for the devastation sown by Hitler.

Yours,
EDDIE.

P.S. Any chance of you dropping in for a drink some time this week? I've got a rather interesting bottle of Château Lafite which I've been saving for a rainy day.

DEAR Eddie,

Passionate about the Château Lafite but this week's a bit difficult. Can
we "take a raincheck," as Dinkie would say?

Yours,

VENETIA.

P.S. Marina tells me Dinkie's having a mad affair with Katie's brother
Simon. I wouldn't have thought brainless hulks were in her line, but
Americans are notorious for their lack of discrimination.

P.P.S. Thanks for warning me about the extremely sinister text on
which you intend to preach. I shall bring a hip-flask of brandy in case
I feel faint with terror.

8

"MY darling," wrote Aysgarth.

I didn't sleep a wink all last night because I was so worried about you,
and so far I've written three letters but torn them all up. Your distress
appalled me. What can I do to put things right? It would kill me to
give you up but I'd rather be dead than make you unhappy. One day,
as I've said before, I *will* have to give you up; you'll meet someone
of your own generation who'll make you the best possible husband—
you may even meet this Great Paragon tomorrow, for all I know, but
darling, make sure he *is* the Great Paragon because it would break my
heart if you wasted yourself on someone who was unworthy of you.

Forgive all this turgid agonising, but I fear you might be thinking
me selfish, begging you to stay in Starbridge, and I'm anxious to
demonstrate that I *am* capable of putting your welfare above my selfish
longings. What I want more than anything else is for you to be happy.
That's how I can face the knowledge that one day I shall have to cede
you to the Great Paragon. However, meanwhile you're free, and until
that terrible day when my great prize is irrevocably lost I feel I can't
bear to part from you even temporarily. In fact I—

(Later) Fitzgerald's just rung up. The Widow Carter says she knows
nothing of her late husband's financial affairs—she never even had a
cheque-book until he died—but she does remember that their retire-

ment bungalow in Budleigh Salterton cost £3,000 more than they could afford and that her husband was thrilled when he managed to get the money from somewhere.

This is, of course, horrific and the potential for scandal is enough to give any Dean and Chapter a collective nervous breakdown. Imagine Carter, one of the premier deans in England, taking a bribe like that! Fitzgerald and Dalton still doggedly refuse to believe it. Eddie, always the optimist, says it can only be a matter of hours now before the tabloid press hear Lady Bone-Pelham shrieking that the Dean and Chapter have welshed on the deal to give her heroic husband the distinguished last resting-place he deserves. Meanwhile Sir George is still lying in state at the undertakers', and the undertakers themselves are getting very shirty indeed. I confess I'm sorely tempted to dig up a little patch of the cloisters' lawn in order to bury Carter's iniquity along with Sir George's corpse, but if I start bending the rules all the nobs will want to be buried there and I'll have the Health Department trying to prosecute me for operating an insanitary establishment. (Or does this only apply to restaurants?) The whole thing's a nightmare.

Must close, darling—I'll try not to be so selfish in future, I promise—I really do accept that I can't keep you for ever, but meanwhile let's not think of the future, let's blot it out, let's just live in the present, let's have our shining dream, because I love you more than words can ever express and the thought of living without you is absolutely, utterly and entirely *unbearable*. All my love, my darling, my angel, my adored one, for ever and ever,

N.

9

DEAR Venetia,

I'm extremely surprised to hear that Dinkie was having an affair with Simon. According to Perry Palmer, who invited me to Albany for a drink when I was visiting my London dentist last week, she's ended up as a scalp in Michael Ashworth's collection. Incidentally, Perry asked when you were coming to see his coal-cellar.

Yours,
EDDIE.

P.S. I'll try not to terrify you from the pulpit! Any chance of seeing you for a cup of coffee after Matins? I think I can get out of the Sung

Communion by putting pressure on Tommy Fitzgerald—I substituted for him in May when he had to waltz off to wait upon his widowed mother.

P.P.S. I shan't be missing Communion altogether on Sunday, of course—I'll be the celebrant at the Early Service. (I don't want you to think I'm lax!)

10

DEAR Eddie,

Having drained my hip-flask during your sermon, I shall without doubt require black coffee afterwards to revive me. Thanks. By the way, Perry's got it quite wrong and it was Emma-Louise who wound up as a scalp. She's now flirting hard with Robert Welbeck who, so Marina tells me, is dying of unrequited love for her (Marina). Marina herself, of course, is still welded to the frame of her asexual triangle with Christian and Katie and avoiding the furious pounces of Michael Ashworth who can't bear to think that such a gorgeous scalp might elude his collection. Just as an afterthought: do you think Perry's queer? I'm trying to decide whether the coal-cellar's worth a visit.

Yours,
VENETIA.

11

DARLING, darling Neville,

I cried when I read your letter, wept for hours, because you were trying so hard to be noble when all I really deserved was a kick on the bottom for being so *cruel* as to talk as I did. Of course I'll never leave you, never—except later this month when I have to go up to town for my mother's seventieth birthday. No way out of that, I'm afraid, but don't worry—I'll come straight back to Starbridge. And again, don't worry—I don't want to marry anyone except you, and if you're never free, then I'll never marry. So please, *please* treat my silly remark about leaving as if it had never been uttered, and *do* stop talking about that repulsive Great Paragon, because I adore you, I couldn't live without you and there couldn't possibly be anyone else, not now, *not ever* . . .

"*THIS* is amazingly good coffee, Eddie. Congratulations."

"It takes a foreigner to make decent coffee in England! Well, tell me the worst—what did you think of the sermon?"

"Great fun. Can't wait to reap what I've sown."

Eddie laughed. We were sitting in the drawing-room of his little house in the North Walk and beyond the bow window the Cathedral basked in the hot August sun. The room was carefully furnished with reproduction antiques, and the walls were lined with English sporting prints; all books were confined to the study across the hall. Eddie himself was still wearing his cassock and looked like a huge black pear.

". . . and I simply must take this opportunity to tell you how grateful I am that you never treat me as a clergyman," he was saying earnestly. "After being continually addressed by the elderly inhabitants of the Close as 'dear Canon' and viewed as if I were a stainless-steel robot, it's so refreshing to receive letters from someone who has no hesitation in writing about affairs and asexual triangles and pounces and queers—"

"That reminds me, do you think Perry's queer as a coot?"

"I find it quite impossible to tell. In fact I don't believe it's possible to know much about anyone's sex-life unless one happens to be a priest who hears confessions."

I said vaguely: "You don't hear confessions, do you, Eddie?" and was surprised when he said he did. "I share the job with Tommy Fitzgerald," he added. "I'm not High Church by inclination as Tommy is, but I had plenty of experience of the confessional when I was running my Anglo-Catholic parish at Langley Bottom."

"Yes, I remember your triumph among the bells and smells. But Eddie, since confession isn't compulsory in the Church of England and since it's regarded by the majority as a High Church fad, I'm amazed to hear the Dean allows such goings-on in his Cathedral!"

"Oh, *he'd* never hear anyone, of course! The very word 'confession' makes him regress instantly to his Non-Conformist upbringing!"

"Then who performed the impossible feat of persuading him to allow confessions?"

"The Bishop. Charles is the kind of priest who's difficult to classify: his churchmanship's middle-of-the-road, but he can preach like an Evangelical once he gets going on sin and he's as fervent about confessions as any Anglo-Catholic."

"But how on earth did the Bishop force Aysgarth to—"

"Oh, the clash was resolved without too much trouble because Charles had Cathedral tradition on his side and Tommy was already there, willing to hear confessions. Stephen soon decided it would be prudent not to meddle too violently with the status quo—he'd only just been appointed Dean—and later he did come to see that the Cathedral, as the mother-church of the diocese, really does have to provide a confessor for the occasional penitent who turns up. But we've got another big churchmanship clash brewing, and this one won't be resolved so easily. Charles is in favour of experimenting with the idea of making the Eucharist the main service on Sunday morning, but Stephen just says: 'Over my dead body.' "

"What do you three canons say?"

"Nothing. We're far too busy praying for a resolution to our eternal problem."

"What eternal problem?"

"How to prevent our Bishop and our Dean killing each other."

"But good heavens, Eddie, are you saying these clashes go on all the time?"

"Oh, we live dangerously in this Cathedral Close! It's blood and thunder all the way! I hesitate to say this to you, Venetia—and perhaps I can say it only because I know you're as devoted to Stephen as I am—but he really does behave very foolishly sometimes."

"What do you mean by 'foolishly'?"

"Well, he's got this odd, reckless streak. He takes such risks."

"Scandalous risks?"

"Potentially, yes." Eddie hesitated but when I interposed: "Go on, you can trust me," he said: "Let me give you an example of the most fearful crisis which has recently blown up as the result of a risk he took. He commissioned a sculpture for the Cathedral churchyard, and he did it without consulting the Chapter. Of course he quickly asked us for our approval, showed us some vague sketches and produced an impressive title for the work—'Modern Man in Search of God'—but that didn't alter the fact that he was imposing his decision on us. Apparently he'd met this attractive young sculptress Harriet March—maybe you know her?—at one of Dido's Art Evenings, and she'd charmed him so much that he'd offered her the commission on the spot. But he knew nothing about her work, nothing at all! What a risk to take, what a potential scandal! However, fortunately for him the Tate were prepared to vouch for her so it seemed he'd brought off the gamble, although Tommy and Paul remained livid about the lack of consultation and Tommy made a very cutting remark about Stephen's penchant for young women—which, as you and I both know, is a perfectly harmless idiosyncrasy that he's been indulging in innocently for years. Anyway, just when we'd decided we'd all learn to love the sculpture, Mrs. March sent some photographs of the work in progress and it was quite obvious that the masterpiece will be pornographic."

"Help! Naked ladies?"

"Naked men—and only one portion of their anatomy is portrayed."

"Glory!"

"Well, of course we can't possibly have it in the churchyard—the gutter-press would feast off the story for days and we'd be the laughing-stock of the Church of England. I realise that, Paul realises that, Tommy realises that, but thanks to Tommy playing his cards wrong and roping in the Archdeacon, Stephen's got locked in a power-struggle with the Bishop and that's absolutely *fatal.* I tell you, Venetia, those two should never be living in the same Cathedral Close. They're not only theologically incompatible; they're temperamentally mismatched. Stephen can really only get on with cuddly, pliable old bishops like the late Dr. Ottershaw back in the forties, but Charles is neither cuddly nor pliable nor even particularly old. God knows where it'll all end . . . I say, Venetia, would you like a drink? It somehow seems to have turned into twelve o'clock. I've got rather an intriguing bottle of Hock in the fridge—"

"Lovely. Thanks. But Eddie"—automatically I followed him into the kitchen—"this is horrific. I didn't quite realise—I mean, I had no idea—"

"No, of course not—how could you have known? I shouldn't really be telling you, but to be honest I'm just so worried that it's the most unutterable relief to confide in someone I can trust. I can't really discuss the situation with Paul and Tommy because I'm afraid of seeming disloyal to Stephen."

"Well, you can trust me to the hilt and I swear I'll never think you're being disloyal. Supposing this ghastly mess does get splashed all over the worst front pages in Fleet Street? What would happen then?"

"Disaster. The Bishop would be down on us like a ton of bricks. He'd make a visitation."

"What's that?"

"Well, it certainly wouldn't just be dropping in at the Cathedral for elevenses. What does the chairman of the board do when his biggest branch office goes off the rails? He turns up with the auditors and lawyers, tracks down the source of the catastrophe and sacks the man responsible."

"My God." I had to lean against the doorpost, but fortunately Eddie was unaware of the full dimensions of my horror; he was too busy extracting the cork from the bottle. "But surely Ashworth can't fire Aysgarth!"

"No, he can't, not directly, because the deanery's a Crown appointment, but if a really serious mess is uncovered"—Eddie began to pour out the Hock—"Charles will go to the Archbishop of Canterbury. There'd be no trial in the Church Courts, of course—much too scandalous—but Archbishop Ramsey, with the Crown, as it were, in the pocket of his purple cassock, would gently suggest a retirement with full pension rights on the grounds of ill health."

I was speechless. It was only when we had returned with the wine to the drawing-room that I managed to say: "Eddie, if you're deliberately piling on the gloom and doom in order to frighten me—"

"Let me cheer you up by saying that although the sculpture could turn into a fiasco big enough to warrant a visitation, the Cathedral itself is still bowling along in an acceptable fashion—or in other words, I don't believe a visitation would turn up a mess serious enough to justify an appeal to the Archbishop."

"Thank God!"

"But what really worries me," said Eddie, barely listening, "is that this is only the latest of a long series of clashes between the Bishop and the Dean, and now Charles could well have reached the point where he'd seize any opportunity to pull out the long knife. If he can't drive home a charge of mismanagement, he'll be itching to prove a charge of personal misconduct, and although Stephen may wriggle out of this present tight corner, where on earth will his gambler's streak lead him next? Thank goodness he's at least cut back on the drink recently. I can't even begin to describe the scandalous risks he's taken during his long love-affair with the bottle . . . Hm, this Hock's really very passable! Have a sip, Venetia."

I sipped the Hock. It tasted of nothing. When I replaced the glass on the table I was aware that my hand was trembling. "Now you really are exaggerating, Eddie!" said my voice brightly. "I know our Mr. Dean drinks quite a bit, but—"

"*Quite a bit?* Sorry—excuse the heavy irony. But perhaps I'd better not say any more, it'd be a mistake, I'd regret it later—"

"Oh no," I said. "No, you tell me everything. Good for you to get it off your chest. And don't worry, I swear I'll never tell a soul."

"Well, you won't believe half of what I say," said Eddie, knocking back his Hock. "You simply won't believe it, but . . ."

He embarked on his revelations.

And then the horrors really began to unfold.

"*HE'S* been a heavy drinker for years," said Eddie, "and like many heavy drinkers he's skilled at covering it up, but every so often he goes over the top. Then we have to protect him—and we've all done it, even Tommy."

"Over the top? You mean—"

"Drunk for services. Evensong's the worst. He probably starts drinking at lunch and then goes on. Whoever's canon in residence keeps an eye on him and if Stephen can't walk straight the canon volunteers to take the service on his own. As you know, we usually field at least two of the senior clergy at each Evensong, one for the readings and one for the prayers and versicles, but it's a flexible arrangement and sometimes during the week the canon either copes on his own or gets one of the minor canons to assist him. However, if it's one of the months when the Dean himself is in residence, we three canons make very sure someone's always there to partner him and if necessary take over."

"But surely he must know when he's drunk! How does he have the nerve to turn up?"

"Oh, he thinks he can get away with anything! It's actually very difficult to coax him not to take part in a service; the trick is to tell him he looks exhausted and say one's only too pleased to do him a favour when he's obviously been working so hard. You'd think he'd go in for absenteeism in a big way, but no, he's very conscientious about attendance. I think he believes that so long as he shows up he's got everything in control. Funnily enough for the past three months or so he really has seemed to have everything in control, although why he should suddenly be drinking less I've no idea. He hasn't been drunk at a service since before Easter. But the real horror-story happened last Christmas. He turned up so drunk for the Midnight Eucharist that he passed out in the Dean's stall."

I said: "I don't believe it," and drained my glass of Hock.

"I told you that you wouldn't believe half of what I said." He gave me a refill. "The Bishop, thank God, was preaching. Stephen would never have made it to the pulpit."

"The Bishop!" I was so appalled that I could barely speak. "Are you trying to tell me that Aysgarth passed out at a service where the *Bishop* was present?"

"Yes, but we canons performed the most fantastic rescue-act and I don't think Charles noticed anything. Before the service he was the last to enter the vestry, and as soon as he came in Paul button-holed him and steered him away from Stephen while Tommy and I acted as a screen. Luckily there were masses of people milling around, not just the Choir and the Vergers but the retired clergy who help administer the sacrament at Christmas, so it wasn't so difficult to keep the Dean and the Bishop separated."

"Surely you tried to persuade Aysgarth not to take part!"

"Of course, but as it was one of the biggest services of the year he absolutely refused to step down. He's a great one for keeping up appearances—only this time he was so drunk he could barely keep upright. In the end we entered the Cathedral with Tommy on one side of him and me on the other to ensure we'd steady him if he stumbled, although normally he'd have been on his own, walking ahead of the Bishop, while Tommy and I—or Paul—would have been walking together in front of him."

"But surely the Bishop must have realised—"

"I don't think so. He probably thought our formation was odd but I suspect he'd have been too busy glancing around the congregation and mentally recapping his sermon to pay the oddity much attention."

"So Aysgarth made it to the stall—"

"Yes, and once he was there he was out of sight of almost everyone except the people in the extreme west wing of the choir. The Bishop was the celebrant and Tommy was reading the lessons, so Stephen didn't actually have to do anything until the administration of the sacrament."

"What happened then?"

"Our worst dreams came true. Remember, this was the Midnight Eucharist, which is always like the feeding of the five thousand: a packed Cathedral, hordes of communicants and so much going on that a dean could go missing for a while without his absence being noticed. We had two tables in operation, one at the head of the nave, where the Bishop and Paul and half the clerical assistants were working, and one at the high altar where Tommy and I were labouring away with the other half of the helpers. Stephen was supposed to be at our table and of course we both noticed he wasn't. Tommy said: 'Let him be—much better that he stays where he is,' and I certainly wasn't going to argue with him, but after a while I said: 'It's odd he hasn't at least attempted to join us.' 'Just what I was thinking,' said Tommy, and using the excuse that he was going to get some more consecrated wine from the Bishop's table, he nipped away to investigate. However he never reached the Bishop's table. He was back in a flash, and the moment I saw his face I knew the worst had happened.

"Well, I palmed off my wafers on the nearest clerical assistant and

followed Tommy to the Dean's stall. Stephen was out, absolutely unconscious, we couldn't rouse him. Tommy said: 'We've got to get him away,
before Charles passes by,' but of course that was easier said than done,
even though, as you'll remember, there's an exit from the choir into the
side-aisle by the vestry. So the route was obvious. What wasn't so obvious
was how on earth we were going to get him out. Tommy and I are both
around six feet tall and not exactly weaklings, but Stephen's heavy—or
at least he was before he lost weight recently—and we feared he'd be
difficult to manoeuvre. In the end Tommy just said: 'It's speed that's
important. We can't cover up the fact that he's being whisked out. All
we can do is whisk him out in double-quick time.' So I took his left side
and Tommy took his right and then Tommy said: 'All right, Eddie—say
your prayers'—and I assure you that didn't seem in the least blasphemous
because we were both sweating blood by that time, I can remember my
heart banging away, I don't think I've been so consumed with horror
since I was captured in Normandy in '44.

"Well, we did it, we draped his arms around our shoulders and we
whipped him out with his feet two inches from the ground, and I don't
think too many people noticed; all the attention was focused on the
Bishop at the central table, and no one was anticipating any action in the
choir. However Dido and the family saw us, of course; they'd noticed,
even if no one else had, that he hadn't emerged from the stall earlier and
they were wondering what was wrong. Dido came straight to the vestry
with all four sons of the first marriage, and so fortunately there were
plenty of strong helpers to smuggle him home. But none of the boys ever
spoke of the incident afterwards, and Dido just treated it as an unfortunate
case of food poisoning."

"But what on earth did Aysgarth say the next day to you and
Fitzgerald?"

"He claimed he'd had no sleep the night before and that the heavy
Christmas Eve dinner had overpowered him."

"But surely Fitzgerald made some sort of protest—"

"Of course—to me. Tommy's actually a little frightened of Stephen,
and so's Paul. Stephen's a very strong personality. But both Tommy and
Paul said after the catastrophe that I'd have to talk bluntly to Stephen—
they knew he'd always listen to me even if he wouldn't listen to them—
but as it turned out, nothing needed to be said. The disaster had given
him the most colossal fright. He drank only sodawater after that for three
weeks."

There was a pause. Eddie refilled our glasses again before adding:
"Fortunately, as I mentioned earlier, he seems to be drinking less at
present—in fact he's in amazingly high spirits, although considering the

current batch of Cathedral crises I can't imagine why he should be so cheerful. He's almost treating the sculpture fiasco as a joke."

"Well, I suppose it does have its funny side—"

"It doesn't, you know. There's nothing funny about increasing the Bishop's desire to pull out the long knife."

"But Eddie—"

"A scandalous risk that doesn't come off—that's all Charles needs now to close in for the kill, and we're not home and dry on this sculpture yet, not by a long chalk. In fact I've even wondered—and now I'm really scraping the bottom of the barrel of horror—I've even wondered if Stephen's harmless penchant for young women has swung right out of control and he's indulging in some sort of crazy flirtation with Harriet March."

"Oh, that's impossible."

"Yes, I suppose it is. It would explain why he's in such high spirits, but . . . no, he couldn't, surely, be that much of a fool."

"What on earth gave you the idea?"

"He was rather wild in one of our Chapter meetings not so long ago—I forget the exact context, but he described the Cathedral's spire as a phallic symbol. Afterwards I heard Tommy say to Paul: 'I do hope this sculpture fiasco doesn't turn out to be a case of *cherchez la femme,*' and as soon as he'd spoken I felt my blood run cold—"

"I think Fitzgerald's round the bend. I say, Eddie, while we're on the subject of sex . . . well, there's something I can't resist asking just out of sheer vulgar curiosity: what the hell do you think goes on between Aysgarth and Dido?"

"Anything from nightly copulation to absolutely nothing," said Eddie gloomily, polishing off the Hock, "and with his history of heavy drinking I think the most likely answer is nothing. But who can tell? Only God can possibly know what goes on in that marriage. The whole thing's a complete mystery."

But it no longer seemed such a mystery to me. Aysgarth's drinking could well have had a malign effect on his relationship with Dido, and even now that his alcohol intake had been reduced and his body had unmistakably recovered, he no longer needed to sleep with her because he had me; a psychological block prevented him from fully consummating our affair, but at least I was able to provide him with sexual satisfaction. The mystery had at last been unravelled and now I could relax— except that relaxation had simultaneously become impossible.

I started to torment myself with images of the Bishop, itching to pull out the long knife and close in for the kill.

"*MY* darling," wrote Aysgarth.

I'm scribbling this in the weekly staff meeting which we always hold
at eleven o'clock every Monday—the senior members of staff sit
around a table in the sacristy (that's the large room where the ceremonial robes are kept). I'm at the top and my minions sit in no
particular order on either side. Today I've got the Clerk of the
Works on my left and the senior Verger on my right. The three
residentiary Canons are here, of course (or, to give them their proper
titles as canons of a cathedral of the Old Foundation: the Precentor,
the Chancellor—to be distinguished from the Chancellor of the diocese who grants faculties—and the Treasurer). Then we have the
Choirmaster, the Organist, the Master-Mason, the senior Cathedral
Guide, the Manager of the Cathedral shop, the Architect, the Librarian and the Vicar of the Close (who does the day-to-day pastoral
work for me among the people who live within the precincts). Neither the Accountant nor the Estate Agent nor the Investment Manager is present today because the agenda doesn't require their special
skills. This is just going to be a cosy little chat, very Barchester,
about various domestic matters such as how far we pamper the tourists. (This is known as the Great Cafeteria Question.) However at the
moment the senior Verger and the Organist are waffling about *The
Archers.* I'll have to rein them in.

(Later) We embarked on our discussion of the proposed cafeteria,
but we've somehow got back to *The Archers* and Gilbert the Librarian
is saying it's not as good as *Mrs. Dale's Diary.* Why we're so fixated
on wireless serials this morning I can't imagine. I'll have to rein them
in again.

(Later) Horrors! The Vicar of the Close, who's finally been allowed
to get a word in, has suggested that before we spend money building
a cafeteria we'd better start glueing together the west front—apparently he was on the sward yesterday when an American tourist was
grazed by a piece of falling masonry the size of a brick which dropped
off one of the statues high up on the west wall. Runcival the Master-
Mason says that's nothing new, the west front's been on the verge of
disintegration for years, and didn't he say only six months ago . . . etc.,
etc. The Clerk of the Works says we'd better shove up some scaffold-
ing before an entire statue falls out of a niche with lethal results. That's

all I need, of course: a dead tourist adorning the west front steps. Fitzgerald says to Runcival: "How much money are we talking about here?" and Runcival answers in his most sepulchral voice: "A thousand for a temporary safety measure and thousands for the full repairs." That means an appeal, which is always hell. The last one indirectly finished off Dean Carter. But before we can even launch an appeal I've got to raise a quick thousand to ensure a temporary safety. This is somewhat tricky because—

(Later) Had to stop because everyone was having hysterics at the thought of an appeal. However the Architect is now burbling on about quarrying the right kind of stone for the repairs. As I was saying, raising a quick thousand is going to be slightly tricky. The Cathedral finances are handled primarily by the Accountant and me. (Forget Eddie's formal title of Treasurer—he does liaise with the Accountant, but the title's a hang-over from the old days and means he has to keep an eye on the Cathedral treasures.) The Accountant deals with most of the money, but I have a private account, which I call the Dean's Fund, at the Cathedral's bank. I use it for what I call "glorifying the Cathedral"—buying miscellaneous articles of great artistic merit. Harriet's sculpture falls into this category, of course, but so also do small items such as the magnificent pair of cut-glass vases which we use for flowers.

The money's raised mainly by staging concerts in the nave, but I made a packet when I got the Starbridge Playhouse to put on *Murder in the Cathedral* here a couple of years ago and I have various other fund-raising tricks up my sleeve. But these take time to pull off and time is just what I don't have at the moment as the thousand for the west front needs to be raised at once. It shouldn't actually come from the Dean's Fund at all, but the official funds are in low water at the moment, in fact they're in the red, and to tell the truth the Dean's Fund owes the main Cathedral account money which I've got to repay before the auditors move in for their next session. So what do I do? Heaven only knows, but the temptation to follow in Carter's footsteps and sell off burial plots in the cloisters is fast becoming irresistible!

Must close, Fitzgerald's obviously wondering what I'm scribbling, desperate love,

N.

"*DEAR* Venetia," wrote Eddie.

I'm scrawling this at the weekly staff meeting where the possibility of killing off all the tiresome tourists is being discussed. Apparently we only have to let the west front disintegrate a little more and then all the statues will fall out of their niches with very effective results. Look, it was marvellous seeing you yesterday. Any chance of dinner at the Quill Pen this week? They have quite a dashing little Piesporter Goldtröpchen on the wine-list.

> Yours gratefully (for listening so sympathetically yesterday),
> EDDIE.

P.S. Stephen appears to be writing a three-volume novel. He shouldn't do it, people notice. Quick notes only!

"*ARE* you all right, Venetia?" said the Bishop suddenly after he had dictated his last sentence of the afternoon. "You seem a little *distraite*."

"Well, as a matter of fact I'm rather worried about a friend of mine who seems to be drifting deeper and deeper into a catastrophic mess. Sorry if I wasn't quite with-it today."

"Come and have some tea. My wife should be around somewhere—"

"How nice of you, Bishop, but I really have to dash back. So if you'll excuse me . . ."

I fled.

I WAS just pouring myself a stiff brandy and wondering what the legal definition of embezzlement was, when my brother Oliver telephoned about my mother's seventieth birthday.

". . . and Sylvia's found a silver rose-bowl at Garrard's. The only difficulty is that everyone turns out to be absolutely broke and we were wondering, old girl, since you happen to be the only member of the family who has no worries or anxieties of any kind—"

"Look, pal," I said, "if everyone can't come up with their share you can count me out."

"I say, Venetia, is anything the matter? You sound a bit—"

"Oh, run off and play at being an M.P.!" I hung up, then left the receiver off the hook.

The dim room darkened as night began to fall.

1 8

"MY darling, I thought we might go back to that nice little hollow at Castle Brigga—"

"I'm dreadfully sorry, Neville, but I've got to cancel—I'm feeling like death."

He was painfully concerned. We had met in the car-park of the Crusader Hotel and I had just collapsed on the Humber's front seat.

"But how awful to think you had to drag yourself over here when you were unwell! Why didn't you phone the Deanery?"

"I did. Dido answered."

"Damn. Darling, I'm so sorry . . . Are you registered with a doctor?"

"Don't need one. It's just a touch of food poisoning." It was a hang-over. I had drunk myself into a stupor the night before because I was so worried about him.

"If only I could look after you, make you tea—"

"No, don't worry, I just want to snooze."

He drove me to the door of my flat and parted from me in an agony of anxiety. His last feverish words were: "I'll write!"

Closing the front door I groped my way upstairs to bed and prayed he would somehow be saved from ruin.

XVI

". . . there is a great deal of loose thinking in Honest to God."

JOHN LAWRENCE,
in The Honest to God Debate

"A false spirituality of this kind has always haunted the thinking of clever men . . ."

GLYN SIMON,
in The Honest to God Debate

I

"ANY news of Dinkie?" inquired Mrs. Ashworth over coffee at the South Canonry the next morning.

"Yes, but it's suddenly become so ghastly that I'm not sure I can talk about it."

"She's not suicidal, is she?"

"No, but it turns out her married man's on the brink of catastrophe, and she's so paralysed with horror that she can't work out what she should do next."

"She should leave him."

"Then he'll keel over into the abyss, she says."

"On the contrary, the shock would probably prompt him to pull himself together."

"That could be true, certainly. But in my view the most potent argument in favour of her leaving him is that Dinkie herself is a great danger to this man, possibly the greatest danger of all. If their affair's exposed he could wind up as ruined as Profumo."

"The person who's in the greatest danger of all," said Mrs. Ashworth, "is Dinkie. Tell her he's got a good chance of survival if she leaves him, but neither of them will survive if she stays."

"Yes, I think I could coax Dinkie to believe that, but the trouble—the nightmare—the really spine-chilling truth is that he's now so heavily involved that I don't think he could bear to let her go. He'd never accept that the affair was over unless—" I stopped. Then I said: "I'm sorry, Mrs.

Ashworth, I know I sound quite abnormally worried, but I really am very fond of Dinkie and one does get so fraught when one's friends are in a fix."

"Of course," said Mrs. Ashworth. "That's what friendship's all about, isn't it? I understand."

Changing the subject abruptly I asked her for news of Charley.

2

MY darling,

It was *agony* only being able to see you for such a short time this afternoon, I feel utterly stunned—and also, of course, demented to think of you suffering all alone in your flat with no one to look after you. I only wish I could send flowers and grapes by the ton, but I can only send you this letter—which comes as always with my very best love. I do hope you're now feeling better. I'd ring you but I do prefer to avoid the telephone, such a dangerous instrument, particularly since D's new hobby seems to be listening in on the extension.

Can we meet on Friday afternoon instead? I've got an appointment but I can cancel it. It's only with the surveyors. Let the whole west front fall down! I just want to be with you in our dear little hollow. If you can make it but aren't well enough to reply to this letter by return, ring me at 7.00 a.m. on Friday. (D will never rouse herself at that hour, not even to listen in.) If I don't hear from you I'll know it's no good, but my darling, *please* drop everything, even the Bishop, because if I don't see you I'll go mad and drink a bottle of brandy and pass out before I can get to Evensong. I feel absolutely *desperate*.

Deepest love,
N.

3

"*I CAN'T* tell you how glad I am to see you," said Eddie as we drank Piesporter Goldtröpchen and toyed with grilled trout at the Quill Pen on Thursday night. "You're fast becoming a life-line! We've got a big crisis blowing up over the west front. Three years ago it could have been repaired with minimal expense, but Stephen shrugged off the warning reports by saying that surveyors were always over-pessimistic about old buildings. Now, of course, the repairs will cost a fortune and what's worse is that Stephen's being vague about money."

"Vague about money?"

"The accounts are in a mess. Poor old Bob Carey, our accountant, is practically gibbering with terror, but Stephen just says don't worry, he'll sort everything out."

"But how on earth—"

"The whole trouble began three years ago when Stephen began to raise money for the Chagall window and opened a special account at the bank. It was all quite aboveboard, but later he kept on the account while he continued his fund-raising for more works of art, and the net result was that this gave him a fatal leeway to take financial risks—he was able to write cheques without obtaining a counter-signature."

"Don't tell me he—"

"He seems to have got careless and spent money before he'd actually raised it—Tommy's convinced Stephen lied to us about the cost of that sculpture. Anyway, what happened was that a few months ago Stephen borrowed some money for the Dean's Fund from the main Cathedral account. You may ask why Bob Carey didn't put his foot down, but he's such a nice old boy that I don't suppose he suspected anything was wrong—or perhaps he just didn't have the nerve to stand up to the Dean and say no. However, shortly after that the Cathedral dipped into the red when we had a problem with drainage under St. Anselm's Chapel. Bob asked for the repayment of the loan but Stephen put him off so the Cathedral's still in the red—although there's nothing particularly unusual about that, I hasten to add, because the Cathedral's often dipping into the red and out again as we struggle to keep up with the expenses. What's unusual about this particular sojourn in debt is that Stephen's directly to blame for it because he can't repay that loan."

"But what on earth's he going to do?"

"Oh, he'll raise the money eventually by giving concerts, no doubt about that, but meanwhile we're in the soup because we need money immediately to shore up the west front. I suppose we'll have to mortgage one of our city properties, although that's not going to look good, and if the Bishop hears—"

"Oh, my God—"

"No, it's all right, he wouldn't make a visitation just because we'd been driven to mortgage property, but of course we all want to keep the accounts mess from him. My really big nightmare is that Harriet March will sue us for breach of contract if—when—we reject that sculpture. Heaven only knows what the legal position is—"

"But surely with her reputation she'll be able to sell the piece elsewhere!"

"I think she ought to bury it. And talking of burials we're knee-deep in another absolutely scandalous situation . . ." He told me about the Bone-Pelham fiasco. I gave up attempting to eat my trout and concentrated on trying not to drink my Piesporter Goldtröpchen as if it were lemonade.

". . . and we simply can't start burying people again in the cloisters! The lawn's full up, chock-a-block with corpses going all the way back to the pre-Reformation canons—"

"But listen, Eddie, what do you think the real story is about this three thousand pounds that you say Sir George is reported to have paid to Dean Carter?"

"Tommy and Paul, who knew Carter very well, are quite sure he'd never have taken a bribe and I find it hard to believe too, but no matter what happened, the fact remains that Stephen's mishandled this business. He should never have got drawn into investigating the three thousand; it's essentially a red herring. He should have taken a very firm line with Lady Bone-Pelham right from the start and said sorry, I don't know what Dr. Carter arranged but it's impossible for us under public health regulations to bury anyone in the cloisters in 1963. Heaven only knows what the public health regulations are, of course, but that's a minor detail . . . I say, Venetia, is anything wrong with that trout?"

"No, it was divine but I'm just not particularly hungry. Marvellous wine, Eddie!"

"Very soothing, isn't it, and God knows I need soothing. The really important thing, as I see it, is to prevent word of this mess reaching the Bishop. If Lady Bone-Pelham blows her top—"

"She won't. Aysgarth will charm her somehow."

"I think he's running out of charm. I think he's running out of luck. I think he's running out of everything—"

"Always the little ray of sunshine, aren't you, Eddie? I say, do you think I could possibly have a drop of Rémy Martin instead of pudding?"

4

AT seven o'clock on Friday morning I telephoned the Deanery. Aysgarth grabbed the receiver halfway through the first ring.

"It's me," I said. "I can come."

"My darling, it's no good. I'm apoplectic with rage. Charles has summoned me to the South Canonry at three."

"Oh, my God—"

"No, it's all right! It'll only be about the Bone-Pelham fiasco—Lady Bone-Pelham finally couldn't resist screeching to him that I was a blackguard who ought to be defrocked, but I've now got the mess under control. Yesterday I talked to Carter's son, who's a very respectable chartered accountant in London, and he says the three thousand was almost certainly a gift from Sir George to the Starbridge Sunlight Home for Handicapped Children—apparently Carter did a lot of work in his spare time for the Home and was treasurer of a fund-raising appeal a few years ago. The Widow Carter had obviously forgotten this and confused the donation with a sum of three thousand pounds which her husband raised (so his son tells me) from a building society to finance the purchase of the bungalow in Budleigh Salterton. So the situation's now crystal clear: Dean Carter is exonerated, the Widow Bone-Pelham is certifiable, off goes Sir George's corpse to the cemetery and off the hook drop the Dean and Chapter. Happy ending!"

"Thank God! So the Bishop has nothing to complain about?"

"Certainly not! Game, set and match to the Dean!"

"*Thank God.* Oh Neville—"

"My darling, I've got to see you—Lady Mary after Evensong?"

"Can't wait . . ."

5

"MY dear Venetia," wrote Eddie in a note which was delivered by hand.

I really enjoyed our dinner yesterday at the Quill Pen. Sorry I got a bit gloomy at the end. You were wonderful, so calm, so serene, so endlessly sympathetic and understanding. You couldn't possibly drop in for a drink some time over the weekend, could you? I promise to open the Château Lafite this time! I don't know why I got diverted by the Hock the other day.

Love,
EDDIE.

6

"VENETIA, it's Arabella. Look, sweetie, I've got the most ghastly crisis on at the moment, I'm simply knee-deep in divorce lawyers and everyone's threatening to sue everyone else and the bills keep mounting up and I'm so desperate I've even cancelled my weekly order from the florist. So could you be an absolute darling and pay my share of the rose-bowl for the time being? There's no *long-term* problem because Sebastian (my new dreamboat) is so rich he never even carries money, but I don't want to bother him when his divorce is at a slightly delicate stage, so—"

"I've opted out of the rose-bowl unless everyone pays their own way. Tell Dreamboat to get acquainted with a bunch of five-pound notes."

"Venetia!" She was shattered.

I hung up.

7

DEAR Eddie,

Drooling at the thought of the Château Lafite. Do you have two bottles?

Love,
VENETIA.

Having slipped this note through Eddie's letter-box I crossed the Cathedral sward to the north porch. The bell was tolling for Evensong, and as the sidesman showed me to my usual place in the choir, the organ began to play. Five minutes later the procession emerged from the vestry, the congregation stood up—

But Aysgarth was nowhere to be seen.

After the service I did sit on Lady Mary for half an hour in the hope that he might still reach the cloisters, but no one came. I tried to work out what had happened. The appointment with the Bishop had been set for three o'clock. If Aysgarth was still at the South Canonry three and a half hours later, what on earth could be going on?

Returning home I poured myself a double brandy and prepared for a tense vigil by the phone.

8

HE rang just before eight. "Darling, I'm so sorry, I—" He stopped. Then he said to someone nearby: "Just talking to Primrose—I won't be a moment." Dido's voice droned in the background like a dentist's drill. Then he said to me: "Listen, Primrose, I must go—I'd forgotten we were dining out. I'll talk to you tomorrow." And the next moment I heard the click of the receiver being replaced and the buzz of the empty line.

9

"MY darling," wrote Aysgarth.

I had rather a rough ride at the South Canonry this afternoon, and when I got home Dido demanded a blow-by-blow description—which I didn't give her as she would have had hysterics, but nevertheless she suspected I wasn't being honest with her, and by the time I'd calmed her down and packed her off to her bedroom to nurse her headache it was nearly half-past five. I was just about to rush off to the Cathedral for Evensong when disaster struck: the Architect turned up on my doorstep to discuss the west front, and by the time I'd got rid of him I knew I must have missed you, but I did dash to Lady Mary anyway, just to make sure. Gnashing my teeth at the thought that we'd probably only missed each other by seconds I raced back to phone you—only to find that some more visitors had arrived to see me, and although I did my best to liquidate them they lingered infuriatingly on. Then just as I finally got you on the line Dido surfaced to remind me that we were expected at the Chantry for dinner in five minutes! At that point, I can tell you, I was ready to climb every wall in sight and needed a very hefty Scotch to help me keep both feet firmly on the ground. Darling, I'm sorry, sorry, sorry—what a disaster! I felt demented.

Charles really wheeled on the big guns at the South Canonry. His power-mania is now running riot to such an extent that I feel his true home is in a City boardroom—he's the kind of potentate who would enjoy raising an eyebrow and seeing the Stock Market plunge in consequence. Thank God he's missed out on Canterbury! The Church of England's had a lucky escape.

Of course I hardly expected the interview to be easy; he'd signalled the episcopal displeasure by summoning me not by phone ("Hullo, Stephen old boy—any chance of seeing you for a tot of Tio Pepe?") but by a letter, *typed,* if you please, by the hag Peabody and signed with the official episcopal signature—a cross (for bishop), then "Charles" and finally "Staro" (for Starbridge). The full text of this icy missive ran: "My dear Dean, I should be greatly obliged if you could come to the South Canonry at 3.00 p.m. to discuss a matter which requires an urgent resolution. Yours sincerely, † CHARLES STARO."

Very nasty. Well, I togged myself up in my best clerical suit and then I *drove* the three hundred yards to the South Canonry. (No turning up on foot like a suppliant.) The lay-chaplain admitted me in vilely aloof style and ushered me into the episcopal study with a sniff. (Why was I admitted by the *lay*-chaplain? Why not by the chaplain himself? That was a subtle piece of downgrading!) Charles, sitting behind his desk and exuding his very worst public-school/Cambridge snootiness, *didn't stand up*. Damn rude. He just looked at me as if I were some idle undergraduate who hadn't been studying for his exams and said: "Good afternoon, Stephen. Please sit down. I'm afraid we've reached the point where we must settle the fate of the Harriet March sculpture."

I nearly passed out. I was all set to drag the rug from under his feet on the Bone-Pelham crisis. However, I pulled myself together, sat down and kept my mouth shut. Sometimes silence can be a disconcerting weapon, but Charles didn't turn a hair. He just said bluntly: "The diocesan committee's now been selected for the purpose of advising the Chancellor on this matter, but I see no point in them ever meeting. My mind's made up; I can no longer afford to procrastinate in the hope that you'll see reason. We just can't afford to air this case in the Consistory Court, and I must insist that you withdraw your application for a faculty."

I said: "I dispute your decision, I dispute the wisdom of your attitude and I dispute your despotic attempt to deprive me of my rights under ecclesiastical law. I demand a hearing before the Chancellor." I thought that would stop him dead in his tracks, but he blasted back: "I deplore your hostility, I deplore your pigheadedness and above all I deplore your refusal to face reality. Do you seriously believe you'd ever be granted a faculty for that junk-heap?"

I said: "Whether I'm granted a faculty or not is irrelevant. The fact remains that I'm entitled to a hearing in the Consistory Court, and no bishop is entitled to dispense with the law."

"Don't flaunt that flabby liberal idealism at me!" exploded Charles. "You're just using it to cover up the fact that you're too proud to back down! You know as well as I do that all you'll achieve by a court hearing is nation-wide publicity in the gutter-press, and if you really think I'm going to stand by and let the unchurched masses split their sides laughing over the pornographic taste of the Dean of Starbridge, you'd better think again!"

I shot back: "If you're so power-mad that you believe you're above the law, I'm complaining to the Archbishop of Canterbury!"

"I'm the one who'll be complaining to the Archbishop of Canterbury!" shouts Charles. "Either you wash your hands of that sculpture or I'm making a visitation!"

Silence. I'm winded. I feel as if I've wound up in a pool of blood on the floor, and for a moment I'm so shocked I can't speak. A visitation would be very nasty. In fact it would be very, very nasty indeed in my present circumstances. The last thing I want is the Bishop arriving on the doorstep like the wrath of God, particularly when I've got the west front falling down with the result that I'm obliged to do some juggling with the accounts. (If only I wasn't already juggling! It's true that commissioning the sculpture *was* a trifle more expensive than I'd anticipated, but I knew I could make up the deficit eventually. How was I to know I'd suddenly need a quick thousand to shore up the west front?)

I see now what must have happened: Charles had the confidence to bludgeon me into a bloodstained heap because he knew I was vulnerable over the accounts. That *traitor* Fitzgerald! He'd tipped off the Archdeacon again.

Well, I mopped up the blood (metaphorically) and I staggered to my feet (literally) and I said with dignity: "I'm sorry that you should find it necessary to threaten me in such an extremely unedifying manner, and even sorrier that your order puts me in a most awkward moral predicament. Perhaps, as my Bishop, you can advise me how I can face Mrs. March with a clear conscience when I repudiate the contract for the sculpture."

I thought that might make him give an embarrassed twitch, but no, he strokes his pectoral cross—I can't stand it when he does that, I'm sure he only does it to underline the fact that he's reached the episcopal bench in the House of Lords and I haven't—and he retorts: "If you can commission a sculpture on impulse, without consulting your Chapter, from an attractive young woman who batted her eyelashes at you over the dry-martini cocktails, I wouldn't have thought your conscience was too clear in the first place. Pay Mrs. March in full so that she has no legal redress and then sever your connection with her. That, I think, will ensure your conscience is a little clearer in future than it is at present."

I could have hit him.

But I didn't. Successful clergymen don't go around hitting people and no clergyman in his right mind takes a swing at his bishop. I'm in my right mind. I didn't take a swing. But by heaven, I don't know how I restrained myself.

When I trusted myself to speak I said: "I've already denied to you that my association with Mrs. March is in any way improper. I must tell you that I strongly resent you raking up this slander a second time."

"And I must tell you," said Charles, "that I've recently heard yet another rumour which implies your association with Mrs. March is an improper one. I'm prepared to believe your denials, but I put it to you that the dean of a great cathedral is required to be as far above suspicion as Caesar's wife, and I must frankly declare that I don't wish to hear such scandalous gossip ever again."

Well, of course, I knew I had to stand up to him, put up a tough front, so I said: "I'm much obliged to you for continuing to believe me innocent of adultery. In the circumstances I suppose I should regard that as an unprecedented favour."

He just looked at me. I hoped he was going to give me details of this new rumour—naturally I wanted to demolish it—but to my disappointment he changed the subject and said: "Someone was asking about you the other day, someone who always takes an interest in you and wishes you well. Do you ever think of calling on Jon Darrow?"

I was very surprised. However it was a relief to drop the subject of adultery, so I said amiably enough that I'd planned to look in at Starrington Manor next Christmas, and wasn't it marvellous that the old boy was still ticking over.

Charles said: "Don't leave it till Christmas. Go soon—he'd really like to see you." And then having allowed himself this little piece of chit-chat in order to ease the truly appalling atmosphere between us, he said tersely: "But to return to the sculpture: I trust I can now rely on you to terminate the arrangement with Mrs. March immediately and in a manner which generates no publicity of any kind."

"As you wish," I said equally tersely, "but I'm sorry. The sculpture's a fine work of modern art—in the opinion of those who have the taste to appreciate it." Then I waited, but when he didn't offer me either his hand or a reply I walked out.

Well, all I can say is that I've staved off a disastrous visitation. But what a scene! I feel as if he beat me up with that pectoral cross of his. I'd like to—but no, I must get a grip on myself. Violent feelings are utterly wrong for a clergyman. Perhaps I can work mine off by punching a pillow for ten minutes! No, on second thoughts I think it's time for a triple-whisky. (The dinner-party tonight was an awful bore but at least the port flowed freely.)

I haven't yet worked out what to say to Harriet, but I'm sure she'll be decent about the fiasco if I put all the blame squarely on Charles. The stupid part about the rumours is that I'm quite certain she's not interested in carrying on with any man at the moment because she's still wedded to the memory of her hero-husband who was killed on Everest. That fact makes this new rumour all the more startling—and worrying too. Where did the story come from and how on earth did it get started? I don't think I can blame Fitzgerald for this one. Scandalous facts—yes. Romantic fiction—no. Not his line of country at all.

But I must now leave the mystery unsolved and conclude this letter. I'll slip out early tomorrow morning, take the car to Butchers' Alley and pop the envelope through your door—I'll be tempted to ring the bell, I know, but you'd be in your nightdress and I might feel tempted to rip it off. I already feel like ripping everything in sight and giving primeval howls of rage. That **** of a Bishop! I can't *bear* being worsted in a power-struggle like that, I long to WIN! My darling, write *soon*—I feel so starved of your company that I can hardly endure it, vastest, devotedest love,

N.

10

"*ACCORDING* to Stephen," said Eddie as we sipped Château Lafite in his drawing-room and watched the Cathedral turn golden in the evening light, "he and Charles had a stylish fencing match which Stephen eventually won by graciously withdrawing the sculpture in order to do the pathetically harassed Bishop a favour. I don't believe a word of it."

"You don't?"

"No. I think Charles, as Dinkie would say, 'took him to the cleaners.' How *is* Dinkie, by the way?"

"Oh, she's in a ghastly state. She's having an affair with a married man who—" I stopped. I had only drunk half a glass of wine. I said: "I think I'm going mad."

"I thought Dinkie was carrying on with—"

"—with Simon, yes. Sorry. Mental aberration."

"I say, Venetia, you wouldn't by any possible chance be free for the rest of the evening, would you? I've discovered this nice little restaurant where they have a most provocative Pouilly-Fuissé—"

I agreed to go out to dinner.

11

"*WELL,* thanks, Eddie—it's been fun—"

"Any chance of seeing you next week?"

"Why not? I might as well live it up a little before I have to face the ghastly family reunion at Lord North Street."

"I'm glad your brother was finally able to buy the rose-bowl on credit."

"God knows what he bought it on—I think he had to take someone to lunch at the Ritz in order to get the loan. The entire episode with all its shoddy scrounging and revolting extravagance makes me wonder why the British haven't long since guillotined their aristocracy."

This amused Eddie. "We seem to have reversed our roles!" he remarked. "Now that the sculpture crisis is over I'm calm and cheerful, whereas now that you're facing the family reunion you're gloom personified!"

"Well, don't get too cheerful—there's still the problem of how you're going to raise the quick thousand to shore up the west front."

Eddie said startled at once: "How did you know about that?"

My stomach seemed to turn a full circle in a single second. My voice said: "You told me."

"I know I told you about the west front but I never mentioned any exact sum of money."

"Then I must have got it from Primrose—you know how the Dean tells her everything."

"I'm surprised he told her about the Chapter meeting yesterday morning. It developed into a real slanging-match when Stephen had to reveal he'd led us astray about the cost of the sculpture."

I said quickly: "Primrose was talking about the staff meeting last Monday. Wasn't it Runcival who said the temporary repairs would cost a thousand?"

"Yes, it was, but that slang phrase you used, 'a quick thousand,' wasn't used by Runcival. As English isn't my native tongue I'm very sensitive to slang, and I know that particular colloquialism only surfaced at yesterday's Chapter meeting."

"Well, now it's surfacing again," I said. "I don't see why the Dean and Chapter should have a monopoly on the well-worn phrase 'a quick thousand.' Heavens, look at the time, I mustn't keep you hanging around on the doorstep a second longer—"

"But we haven't yet made a date for—"

"Phone me," I said, and escaped.

I 2

MY dearest Venetia,

Last night was *tremendous!* I really enjoyed your dashing witticisms about Simone de Beauvoir and Jean-Paul Sartre. Listen, I've just seen in *The Starbridge Weekly News* that the latest Ingmar Bergman film is playing at the Rialto. Interested?

Much love,
EDDIE.

13

DEAR Eddie,

Glad you weren't appalled by my philosophical didacticism at dinner—I'm afraid I was tight as Old Harry after all the divine Château Lafite and the even diviner Pouilly-Fuissé. I really shouldn't have had that Rémy Martin afterwards, but never mind, we only live once (on earth, I mean) so one might as well forge ahead with élan. However I don't think I could quite forge ahead to Ingmar Bergman at present—I'm not in the mood for Scandinavian gloom and doom. Why don't I buy some fish and chips and a bottle of hooch so that we can indulge in the sin of gluttony at my flat? After demolishing Sartre's existentialism, I think it's time I behaved like a zombie. We might watch Martin Darrow on TV.

Much love,
VENETIA.

14

... *AND* my darling, I couldn't help noticing at Castle Brigga this afternoon that you weren't quite yourself—although of course looking as beautiful as ever and being just as wonderfully sympathetic as always—and suddenly I had the dreadful thought that maybe you'd met the Great Paragon. Even though you were so generous to me in our dear little hollow I had the impression that you were somehow separated from me by something, and after we'd parted I felt in a cold panic for hours—although perhaps my imagination's running riot merely because I'm so dreading losing you. But my darling, if ever there *was* someone else, you would tell me, wouldn't you? I do like to think that we tell each other everything. Of course it would slaughter me to know that the Great Paragon had finally arrived, but I'd rather know than not know—even though I can't imagine how I'd ever survive without you, I love you so much and no words could ever express how grateful I am to you for so utterly restoring my self-esteem after my recent hellish confrontations with the Bishop and the Chapter. You've been so sweet, so understanding, so loving, so kind, so—

1 5

"*THIS* is very nice *vin ordinaire,* Venetia. A most interesting bouquet. It goes well with the fish and chips."

"Shut up, Eddie, and let's enjoy Martin Darrow."

"Will you kick me out if I hold your hand?"

"You sound as if you'd prefer to be kicked."

"Oh Venetia, I—"

"*Shut up!* I want to have thirty minutes of absolute quiet while I goggle at the box."

Eddie shut up.

We watched one of the summer repeats of *Down at the Surgery.* Martin Darrow, dark, debonair and richly amusing, lit up the screen with his presence. After a while Eddie reached out and encircled my fingers with his huge hot clammy paw.

I somehow managed to keep my fish and chips in my stomach.

1 6

...*AND* darling, *darling* Neville, I just don't know how you could have received such an utterly false impression—if I seemed *distraite* at Castle Brigga it was only because I was so worried about you. Of course there's no one else! I love you and no one but you, I'll love you for ever and ever—in fact, I love you so much that *I'd even lay down my life to save you,* so don't talk to me any more about loving someone else, never even think of it because *you're* the Great Paragon, *you,* my adored one, my dearest love, my *darling* Mr. Dean—

1 7

DARLING Venetia,

I'm scribbling this in the Monday staff meeting because I've just had a tremendous idea and I can't wait to let you know about it: why don't

I come up to town on the day after your mother's seventieth birthday and take you out to dinner at the Savoy? Say yes and I shall be in ecstasy.

Passionate love,
EDDIE.

18

MY darling,

I'm scrawling this in the Monday staff meeting where Runcival the Master-Mason is going on and on and on about the blank-blank west front. My undying thanks for your magnificent and moving letter which made me want to sing the Hallelujah Chorus at the top of my voice on the Cathedral sward—only the thought of the sopranos' top notes deterred me! But thank God, darling, you're never likely to be in a position where you have to sacrifice your life to keep me safe.

I think I'm recovering from *that bishop.* I've had a top secret conference with the bank manager about raising the quick thousand and I'm now sure I can pull off a loan without mortgaging any property—I've promised him I'll stage a really gargantuan performance of *The Messiah* this Christmas to recoup my losses. Fitzgerald's bound to growl: "I thought we were running a cathedral, not a concert hall," but he can't raise any serious objection to *The Messiah,* and I know I'll win through in the end.

(Later) The Clerk of the Works has just been reading us a doomsday script about the state of the fabric, and declares that in twenty years' time the spire will fall down. This gives a completely new twist, I must say, to the famous pronouncement: *Après nous le déluge!* Eddie's now scribbling furiously, probably eager to produce some earnest memorandum. Poor old Eddie, he's been a bit excitable lately—I think the sculpture crisis has told on him. When we met this morning he said he wanted to go up to London after Sunday Evensong for a reunion with some old chums from the Anglo-German Churchmen's Fellowship, and could I stand in for him at the early services on Monday. Well, of course officially he's supposed to be tethered to the Cathedral this month as he's the canon in residence, but I think he deserves a short break and I'm very willing to help him out. What a tower of strength he's been to me recently! After Fitzgerald's betrayals I've got to the stage where I really appreciate loyalty, and as I told you once not so very long ago, at least I can always rely on Eddie never to stab me in the back. All my love, my darling, my angel, my—

19

DEAR Eddie,

Okay. Dinner at the Savoy on Sunday night. But I warn you, I'll be a basket-case after my mother's party and may well be unable to speak. You'd better come to Lord North Street at around six-thirty to have a drink and say "hiya" to the parents.

Meanwhile there's something I want to ask you: when is a confession not a confession? An old school-friend of mine, Margaret Wharton, saw an Anglo-Catholic priest the other day and told him a lot of things about her married lover. Afterwards she found out to her horror that the priest counsels her lover's boss. Margaret wasn't actually in the confessional with this priest, she was just chatting. Is there a remote possibility that the priest could pass on to the boss the fact that the married lover is up to his neck in adultery? Margaret can't sleep a wink at night for worrying about this. Please advise instantly.

Lots of love,
v.

20

MY darling Venetia,

If the priest betrays a single syllable he should be reported to his bishop. Confidential conversations aren't confined to the confessional.

Many thanks for the invitation to Lord North Street. I'll bring your mother a belated birthday present. She's very keen on plants, isn't she? In tremendous spirits, *much* love,

EDDIE.

MY darling Neville,

I'm glad to report with enormous relief that the great family orgy is over and we now have ten years to recover before my mother reaches eighty. Everyone behaved well, although that idiot Harold made a revoltingly sentimental speech—my father and I looked at each other and knew instantly that we both wanted to throttle him—and Oliver arrived slightly tight from the Reform Club—and Henrietta would keep boring us with stories about her dogs—and Sylvia talked on and on about her pregnancy (if I were pregnant I hope I'd have the good taste to keep my mouth shut and not go so nauseously mumsy-wumsy)—and Absolutely-the-Bottom Arabella kept tossing her newly-blonded hair all over the place as she prattled about Sebastian, her current "dreamboat," who must be just about the most brainless hunk on earth to fall for all that rubbish.

Mama was thrilled with the rose-bowl which Sylvia had tricked out with those ghastly scentless roses which always look like plastic. In fact Mama adored the whole circus and even shed a tear after Harold's frightful speech and said how lucky she was to have such a wonderful glorious family, and we all slobbered over her shamelessly and told her how lucky we were to have such a wonderful glorious mother. God knows how much champagne we all drank. Papa even started declaiming in classical Greek. The whole evening was a huge success.

This morning I'm slightly hung-over but I did just want to dash off a letter so that you wouldn't feel "starved." Darling, I'm thinking of you constantly and counting the hours that separate us—in fact I hardly know how to wait until we're at Castle Brigga once more . . .

22

"HOW very clever it was of you," I said to Eddie as we dined at the Savoy, "to give my mother that book. Victorian water-colours of plants! She'll be your friend for life now."

"I hope so," said Eddie blandly, sipping his champagne.

Silence fell. I toyed with my grilled sole and wished I felt hungry. Frantically I searched for a new topic of conversation. "Well, don't keep me in suspense!" I said brightly, making an artistic mound of my spinach. "I've been deprived of the Starbridge news for two whole days! What's the latest shattering development?"

"Dido came to see me."

My knife clattered on my plate. I tried to grasp the handle again but something seemed to have happened to my fingers. Casually my voice said: "Oh yes? What a bore! What did she want to talk about?"

"Stephen."

"Well, that's hardly a new departure, I suppose." I took a large gulp of champagne and managed to get my knife under control. "But what did the old girl say?"

"She's terrified of the Bishop."

"Oh God, don't tell me she had hysterics all over your drawing-room!"

"No, she was well in control of herself, although I wouldn't have been surprised to see a touch of hysteria. I think she's right to be terrified."

"But why? The Bone-Pelham crisis was defused, the sculpture mess has now been swept under the rug and I'm sure the Dean will somehow raise the money to shore up the west front—why should Dido suddenly start twittering in terror?"

"Because my worst nightmare's come true and there's a rumour going around that Stephen's having an affair with Harriet March."

I managed to say after only a fractional pause: "You mean because he commissioned the sculpture on an impulse while she was simpering at him during a party?"

"No, there's a new rumour, and Dido says it's already reached the South Canonry. Apparently (and Stephen didn't tell me this) Charles indicated during their big showdown that the story was known to him. Of course Stephen must have denied everything, but I think this could finally be the point where the Bishop pulls out the long knife. We all know what he's like on the subject of sexual morality. He may overlook heavy drinking, commissioning pornographic sculpture and juggling with the accounts, but he's not going to turn a blind eye to a sexual indiscretion."

I drained my glass. As a passing waiter immediately refilled it I said: "What I'd like to know is how this bloody silly new rumour ever got off the ground." Automatically I started drinking again.

"According to Dido, Stephen's been seen driving around with a glamorous, long-haired young woman on his day off—and of course that description does fit Harriet March."

"Obviously someone's mistakenly identified the man as the Dean."

"No, there's no question of mistaken identity. Apparently Stephen almost caused a traffic accident in Chasuble Lane a few weeks ago, and the policeman who happened to be passing by not only recognised him but spoke to him. Before joining the force this man had worked in the stonemasons' yard at the Cathedral, so—"

"But how did the story reach Dido if the policeman no longer has any connection with the Close?"

"Oh, a good story will always grow wings and fly! The policeman told his former work-mates in the pub that a young woman like a film star with long, wavy dark hair had jumped out of the Dean's car and vanished as if she was anxious to avoid publicity. The enthralled work-mates told Runcival who told the Clerk of the Works who told Tommy Fitzgerald who told Paul Dalton who told his sister who told Dido—"

"—who told you. I see. But then who told the Bishop?"

"It was almost certainly the Archdeacon. Tommy tipped him off about the sculpture, and the odds are he tipped him off again about the rumour. And of course once the Archdeacon knew—"

"But surely there could be a perfectly innocent explanation? For instance, two of the Archdeacon's daughters have long wavy hair, and Sally, if not Julie, could certainly be described as glamorous. Why shouldn't the Dean have been giving her a lift? And why, when he got stuck with the policeman in Chasuble Lane, shouldn't she have nipped out and popped home to the vicarage down Butchers' Alley?"

"Funnily enough I offered Dido the same explanation, but she just said that no matter how many innocent explanations were offered, the Bishop would continue to think the worst."

"That sounds as if she's secretly suspecting the worst herself!"

"No, Dido seems absolutely convinced that Stephen would never have a fully consummated love affair with anyone. But of course a clergyman can get in a scandalous mess without committing an act which is legally defined as adultery, and what Dido's afraid of is that Stephen's dabbled in a flirtation that's somehow got out of control."

"I just can't believe he'd be quite such a fool." I drained my glass of champagne again. "Dare I ask how this interview with Dido ended, or will that spoil the punchline of your story?"

"She asked me to intervene. She said none of the sons had ever been able to talk to him and I was the only man who could possibly help. That's true, of course. Funny how Dido always gets the personal relationships dead right—"

"But what on earth does she expect you to say?"

"She wants me to spell out the cold hard facts of life and bring him down to earth. She's convinced that having lost touch with reality by indulging in this heavy flirtation, he's now in the most frightful danger— and I'm bound to say," said Eddie as he too finished his glass of champagne, "I think she's absolutely right."

"I think she's round the bend."

"No, Venetia. You've got Dido dead wrong. I know she's tormented by a neurotic temperament, but she's honest, she's loyal and she's brave— brave enough to face this appalling crisis without flinching. She wants to save Stephen. And so do I. And so, I think, do you."

"Well, of course I do! I'm just boggling at her melodramatic suggestion that you should stage some monstrous scene in which you spell out the cold hard facts of life like a teacher trying to educate a sub-normal pupil! You're not really going to do as she suggests, are you?"

"I've already done it," said Eddie.

I nearly passed out. "You mean you've seen him?"

"No. Not him. I came to the conclusion," said Eddie, laying down his knife and fork, "that it wasn't actually Stephen I had to see."

And as I stared, too shocked to move or speak, he raised his head and looked me straight in the eyes.

XVII

"It is in his chapter on the 'New Morality' that Catholics would feel themselves unable to go far with Dr. Robinson."

ANONYMOUS,
in The Honest to God Debate

I

I LOOKED away.

I stared at my mangled fish. I stared at my sculpted spinach. I stared at the shining cutlery and the snow-white table-cloth and the champagne bottle in the ice-bucket and the carnation in the vase.

There was a long, long silence.

Then Eddie spoke again. He spoke quietly, and as I listened I noticed that a small potato remained on his plate. It's strange what the mind registers in moments of overpowering horror and fear.

Eddie said: "Marry me."

The outline of the dinner-plate began to blur.

He said: "It's all right. I understand. It's all right."

My hands were twisting my napkin into a lump in my lap. I was unable to reply.

"We'll have fun," he said. "I know we would. We'd be good friends. It would work. And we'd live in London, not just because you wouldn't want to live permanently in the provinces, but because . . . well, I could no longer work in Starbridge, and London's the place where I'd be most likely to land a good job. I've worked there before and my *curriculum vitae*'s excellent."

I managed to nod but still I could not speak.

"You could share in my career or you could be quite independent. I'm used to coping with the work on my own so I wouldn't insist that you converted yourself into a clerical wife."

My voice said with difficulty: "Sounds reasonable."

"Think it over," said Eddie as the waiter removed our plates. "Of course I hardly need add that you have the complete freedom to say no—this isn't a bizarre attempt to blackmail you into marriage—but I honestly do think that you and I—"

"Quite." I reached for my glass but it was empty. "The trouble is," I said, "I can't imagine ever leaving Starbridge."

"It'll be horrifically difficult for both of us. But even if you don't marry me, something's got to be done, Venetia. Things can't go on as they are."

"Oh, I quite see that." I fidgeted with my glass before adding: "I don't love you."

"I think you could. I'll take the risk."

"All these scandalous risks—"

"There's nothing scandalous about marrying a girl one's loved for a long time, and I think it's a gamble that'll come off. We like each other, we get on—"

"Yes," I said. "Happy ending. Soaring violins. Golden sunset." I started to cry.

"Darling Venetia—my dear, I'm so sorry, don't cry—please—everything's going to be all right—"

"Not for him. That Bishop—"

"The Bishop as yet has no proof. No witness has identified you as the girl in the Dean's car, and as you pointed out a moment ago, that girl could have been one of Malcolm Lindsay's daughters. The Bishop may suspect you—although in fact I can't think why he should—but if you now leave Starbridge he'll never know for certain."

I tried to wipe away my tears with my napkin. At last I said: "Does Dido suspect, do you think?"

"I'm sure of it. She never mentioned your name but I'm convinced she must know."

"But how could she?" I was appalled. "He was always so careful!"

"Yes, but Dido's so shrewd about personal relationships, and there was a lot of evidence lying around."

"What evidence?"

"The sort of evidence which I can now clearly see with the wisdom of hindsight but which Dido would have picked up much earlier. I'd guess she suspected as soon as you stayed on in Starbridge but severed yourself from Primrose. It was all so odd, so mysterious . . . and you looked so stunning, so radiant, yet there was apparently no man in your life. I myself had no trouble swallowing the theory that you'd undergone a religious conversion—it's a well-known phenomenon and it does result in both radical change and enhanced vitality—but I doubt if Dido would have swallowed it so easily. Then there was the fact that Stephen was so buoyant at a time when he should have been bowed down by the Cathedral crises. This would have been glaringly obvious to Dido—it was glaringly obvious to me, but because I was wrapped up in the wrong theory I never actually connected you with Stephen until—"

"The quick thousand for the west front." I dragged my napkin across my aching eyes.

"It just seemed such a coincidence that you should have used that same raffish phrase. And then as soon as the truth occurred to me everything seemed blindingly obvious."

I realised I had ruined my make-up as usual. Black streaks marred the white napkin.

Mumbling an excuse I groped my way to my feet and stumbled to the cloakroom.

2

AFTER I had finished vomiting I cleaned my face, but my hands were trembling so much that I was unable to reapply my eye make-up.

"I'll take you home," said Eddie as soon as he saw my haggard appearance.

"I'm terribly sorry—"

"No need to apologise."

Halfway down Whitehall I said: "I don't know what you think he and I got up to, but—"

"It doesn't matter."

"—we didn't—"

"I don't want to know."

I started to cry again. "It'll kill him if I break it off."

"No, it'll save him. It'll wake him from the dream."

"He'll die of grief—"

"No, that only happens in books. He'll live. He'll only be destroyed if you stay and wreck his career."

"But how terrible that it should be you—and I—who have to—"

"Sometimes you have to shed blood in order to save lives. Think of surgeons."

But I could not think of surgeons. I could only think of my doomed Mr. Dean. I began to weep uncontrollably.

"Lord North Street!" pronounced the taxi-driver glumly after we had remained stationary for some time.

"Drive around Smith Square, please," said Eddie, "and drive slowly."

As the car crawled on I succeeded in drying my eyes, but the realisation that I was almost home made me panic. "My God, what can I look like? If my parents see me—"

"Shall I come in and create a diversion while you rush upstairs to bed?"

But I knew I could bear his company no longer. I told him I would manage.

"Travel back with me tomorrow," he said. "I'm getting the ten-fifteen."

"No, I've got to be alone, I've got to think."

"All right, but phone me if you change your mind. I'm staying at the Stafford."

Having circled Smith Square at a funeral pace we wound up back in Lord North Street.

"Darling . . ." He gave me such a brief kiss that I barely noticed it. "Remember: I love you. We'll have fun. It'll work."

We parted. The taxi disappeared. Turning the key in the lock with shaking fingers I crept into the hall. Raucous laughter from the drawing-room upstairs indicated that a social gathering was in progress, but as I tiptoed past, praying that my presence in the house would not be immediately discovered, the door opened and my mother appeared. She exclaimed: "Ah, Venetia!" But then her expression changed and she said no more.

I muttered: "Rather tired. Long day. 'Night." And fled to my room.

Later my mother tapped on my locked door and said: "Anything I can do, darling?" but I pretended to be asleep and she went away.

3

DARLING Eddie,

I've thought it over and concluded that you're right. We'd have fun. It'd work. But don't rush me. I've got to figure out how to tell him. That may take a little time and meanwhile please tell *no one* how things stand between us. Thanks for being so nice when I wrecked dinner.

Lots of love,
VENETIA.

4

MY darling Neville,

I can't wait to see you—staying on an extra day in London was a big mistake. A party of us went to dine at the Savoy but I hated every moment and when I got home I lay awake all night longing for you. In fact I've missed you so much that I've felt quite ill, but at least these two days in London have proved to me beyond any doubt that I love you more than anyone else in the world, and I'm now utterly convinced that so long as you're drawing breath on this earth I could never be happy with anyone else. My darling Mr. Dean, I hardly know how to wait for Wednesday but meanwhile this comes to you with undying—yes, *undying*—love from your adoring and devoted

V.

I SENT both letters from the post office in Tufton Street, and as soon as Eddie's envelope slipped from my fingers I wanted to claw it back.

Yet even if I had been able to retrieve the letter I would have had no choice but to post it again. Unless I converted myself into a lost prize, Aysgarth would never let go of me and then without doubt he would be destroyed.

On my way home I reached the church in the centre of Smith Square. Round and round the church I walked, the church of St. John the Evangelist. " 'In the beginning was the Word,' " Father Darrow had said, quoting St. John's Gospel, but it was a word I could no longer hear.

My head was throbbing. I could barely see. I hardly knew what I was doing.

"Darling Eddie . . . We'd have fun. It'd work . . ."

"My darling Neville, I can't wait to see you . . ."

Two people, I was being divided between two people, but no, I was dividing *into* two people, it was as if someone was hacking away with a meat cleaver and splitting my personality from top to bottom. I saw clearly then not only that I was mad but that we were all three of us mad, Aysgarth, Eddie and I—all mad and all in hell—and all the time the Great Pollutant was spewing its filth across our lives.

AS I prepared to leave, my mother said again: "Is there anything I can do, darling?" but I answered kindly: "No, you run along and attend to your plants." No point in bothering the old girl, particularly when she had just enjoyed such a splendid birthday with all her wonderful, glorious children.

My father said: "Goodbye, Venetia. I enjoyed meeting Hoffenberg again. A thoroughly nice chap," and patted me encouragingly on the shoulder, but of course he was always hopeless with women.

I caught the eleven-fifteen train and arrived in Starbridge ninety minutes later. At the flat I found a shoal of letters from Aysgarth. He was writing morning, noon and night, and suddenly the colossal weight of his love seemed suffocating; I felt as if not only all the breath but all the blood was being squeezed from my body. I couldn't even open the letters. I could only sit on the edge of the sofa and clutch the envelopes.

Eventually I managed to phone Eddie. "Look," I said, "this morning I posted you a revoltingly graceless note saying I'd go ahead. I just want to say I'm sorry it was so revoltingly graceless. You deserve better."

"Venetia!"

"I want very much to marry you and I'm quite sure it's the right thing to do."

"But this is sensational! I—"

"I'm seeing him on Wednesday. I'll end it all then."

"Darling, I'm so happy, so—"

I got rid of him but just as I was reaching for the gin bottle the phone rang. Wretched Eddie no doubt wanted to rush to the flat and slobber over me. Wanting only to be alone I grabbed the receiver in a rage. "Yes?"

"My darling."

My rage was wiped out. All memory of Eddie was wiped out. Everything was wiped out except the sound of that voice. Blindly I sank down on the sofa.

"I had to phone," he said. "Couldn't stop myself. Had to hear your voice."

"Darling—oh Neville—"

"I can't wait till Wednesday, I've got to see you. Lady Mary after Evensong?"

I agreed to meet him in the cloisters that evening.

WELL, of course, I couldn't do it, could I? I couldn't end the affair. I couldn't end it in the cloisters that evening, I couldn't end it on Wednesday at Castle Brigga, I couldn't end it when I wrote to him every day. I couldn't end it, and all the time Eddie was hovering in an agony of anxiety as I repeatedly promised him: "I'll do it. I really will."

At Castle Brigga I said idly to Aysgarth when he mentioned the subject of Primrose's limp friendship with Tait: "Do you think Maurice has ever proposed?" and when to my surprise I received an affirmative answer, I asked: "But do you think she's right to turn him down?"

"Of course!" He was shocked. "No girl should ever marry a man she doesn't love."

"But Maurice would nonetheless be a husband, wouldn't he? He'd give her status and self-respect and a real life at last."

"Without love all that would be meaningless."

"But she'd probably come to love him later."

"That doesn't necessarily follow at all. I told Primrose: 'Never marry a man you don't care for with passion,' and she promised me she never would."

"But darling, Prim doesn't exactly have the suitors queuing up, does she, and time's ticking on—"

"I'd rather she stayed a spinster than married without love."

"Isn't that much too idealistic? Have you, a very masculine man, any real grasp of what spinsterhood actually means?"

But he only said stubbornly: "One must have one's ideals; that's what separates us from the animals. To marry without love is a crime."

That was the moment when I should have said: "It's a crime I'm about to commit," but I could only exclaim warmly: "Darling Neville, what a romantic you are!"—and yet again poor Eddie slipped far to the back of my mind.

8

"YOU'VE got to tell him, Venetia," said Eddie. "I'm sorry, I know you don't want to be pushed but the time's come when I don't just have to push—I have to give you the biggest possible shove. He's in greater danger with every day that passes. Tommy Fitzgerald said to me today: 'I think the Dean writes letters to a lady-love during the staff meetings.

When I put on my distance-glasses I could see the words "My darling" at the top of the page.' "

"Oh my God—"

"And if Tommy chooses to pass on *that* piece of information to the Archdeacon—"

"I'll end it tomorrow at Castle Brigga," I said.

But I didn't see how I ever could.

I drank myself senseless with gin and passed out some time before dawn.

9

"NEVILLE! Thank God I've managed to get you on the phone. Look, I can't make it this afternoon, I feel appalling—no, don't panic, it's nothing for you to worry about, just menstruation-de-luxe—really, I can't think why God couldn't have made female organs more cleverly, they're nothing but trouble, even worse than teeth."

"My poor darling, I'm so sorry—but I've got to see you soon or I'll go mad. What about tomorrow? I'll cancel everything—"

"No, tomorrow's no good, I've got to work for the Bishop. How about Friday?"

We agreed to meet in the car-park of the Rialto cinema on Friday afternoon. That gave me two days to decide how I was going to do the impossible, and for the first time in my life I began to understand why people committed suicide. But of course I wasn't the suicidal type.

Or was I?

Taking two aspirins to kill my hangover I reached again for the gin bottle.

It was five minutes past seven in the morning.

I 0

"AND now," said the Bishop, smooth, powerful and dangerous in a pitch-black suit, "having completed all the chapters except the one on ethics, I think it's finally time to demolish the New Morality."

The sweat prickled on my forehead.

"We'll start," said Dr. Ashworth after a pause to survey the battlefield, "with some random observations as usual. Are you ready?"

"Yes, Bishop." My mouth was bone-dry.

"Number one: Dr. Robinson is attempting to apply the principle of

Situationethik—" He spelled the word before interpolating: "Better to use the German designation, I think, as that calls attention to the original writing on the subject—a theory of morals according to which there is no human action which would be morally wrong in every circumstance. This theory parts company with the traditional teaching of the Catholic Church which, while acknowledging that vast numbers of moral decisions are determined by the 'situation'—that is, the circumstances of each particular case—nonetheless holds that some actions are intrinsically wrong and can never under any circumstances be justified.

"Dr. Robinson contends that when attempting to resolve a moral dilemma nothing is prescribed—except love. The Catholic Church would agree with this, *but*—underline the 'but,' please—it would say that this prescription must take into account certain absolute limits to conduct; the maintaining of such absolute limits is a safeguard against the sinfulness and fallibility of man. Dr. Robinson, however, rejecting objective standards in advocating a subjective approach, declares that a solution to each moral dilemma can be discovered merely by surveying all the facts with loving compassion.

"This is, of course, impossible.

"Human beings are not omniscient, and only God can ever know all the facts in any given case. For example, a well-meaning counsellor may approach a case with enormous loving compassion yet because of either ignorance or wishful thinking or misunderstanding or just plain stupidity come to a conclusion which is entirely wrong. Love is not enough. We must have objective standards which provide the poor, faltering, limited human race with at least some indication of how we should conduct ourselves in order to avoid misery and destruction. The Bishop, I fear, has far too high an opinion of modern man's ability to soar above his sinful, fallible nature and play God in ethical matters with impunity.

"Number two: the Bishop writes as if Christianity were no more than a weak love ethic. Christianity is indeed about love but it is also about salvation and redemption. It is directed not towards a so-called modern man who lives some idyllic existence in which every problem can be solved with a kiss and a cuddle. It deals with people as they are—and very often they're suffering, floundering amidst tragedy, perhaps even screaming in agony as the result of their wrong actions and the wrong actions of others. What has Dr. Robinson to say to these people? Absolutely nothing. You must say rather more than: 'All you need is love!' to someone who is tortured by guilt, racked with grief or overpowered by despair. When a man is being crucified during his personal Good Friday, he needs someone who symbolises Easter Sunday and the redemptive love of Christ, not some sunny-natured fool who bounces around at the foot of the cross and showers him with sentimental good will.

"Number three: the Bishop theorises a great deal about human relationships but seems to have only the sketchiest idea about how his theories would work in practice. If a young man and a young woman are in love, he suggests, the young man will ask himself not: do I sleep with her? But: do I love her? According to Dr. Robinson, if the answer is yes, then the young man, glorified by his passion, will abstain from sexual intercourse in order not to take advantage of his girlfriend. However, I put it to Dr. Robinson that this is sheer romantic idealism which has no relation to reality. The young man, in reality, will ask himself: do I sleep with her? And immediately he'll answer: you bet—if I can! He may be full of good intentions; he may sincerely believe he loves the girl; he may even wish to marry her eventually, but if a sexual attraction exists he'll want to take the young lady to bed. And perhaps he will marry her. And perhaps they will indeed live happily ever after. One must always allow for cases where both parties are blessed by extraordinary good luck. But perhaps, alternatively, he'll tire of her; perhaps he'll abuse her love; perhaps she'll abuse his; perhaps there'll be an abortion, a breakdown, even suicide. There are any number of possibilities inherent in this situation, but two things at least are certain: first, sex is the most powerful drive known to man and any ethical theory that fails to take this into account must be seriously deficient. And second, such a powerful force can lay waste, maim and kill as efficiently as a powerful force such as a hurricane or an earthquake. Bearing this fact of life in mind, it would seem prudent to devise rules and safeguards which will help to minimise the potential damage. Dr. Robinson has very much more confidence than I have in both the wisdom of inexperienced young people and their ability to protect themselves from serious harm.

"Number four: the Bishop tells us we find God in loving relationships. Certainly we do. But supposing someone, through no fault of his own, has no loving relationships in his life; are we to say that in his loneliness he has no access to God? Or supposing a loving relationship comes to an end; are we to say that the parties concerned must part from God as well as each other? God cannot, I suggest, be confined merely to loving relationships, and I would also suggest that it is not only God who can be found there. The Devil can infiltrate any situation, and it's quite possible to have an extremely loving relationship which is absolutely wrong and utterly destructive, not only for the parties themselves but for the innocent people who depend on them. The classic example of this, of course," said Dr. Ashworth, pausing in his peregrinations to hover at my side, "is adultery. Have you got that, Venetia?"

"Yes, Bishop."

"You don't seem to be writing."

"I . . ."

"Never mind, these are only rough notes. I'll go more slowly. The classic example (as I was saying) is adultery. Number five: by adopting this subjective approach to ethics the Bishop seems to be aligning himself with those people who declare that the real obscenity in our society today is not sex but violence. Sex, I agree, is not an obscenity. But the abuse of sex, I would argue, is deeply obscene. I think it not surprising that at this stage of the century there should be a backlash against strict standards in sexual conduct, but I prophesy that the people who are now busy tearing up the old rules will reap rather more than they bargained for. I also venture to suggest that more harm, more grief and more soul-destroying misery are caused to more people by the abuse of the sexual rules than by the use of violence. For example, anyone who has ever witnessed the carnage wrought by a devastating adulterous liaison could never forget the horror of seeing people slowly driven mad by their—Venetia! My dear girl, what's the matter?"

I finally broke down.

I I

"RIGHT," said the Bishop swiftly, "don't move. Take this"—a handkerchief was stuffed into my shaking hand—"and hold on. Help's coming." And sweeping to the door he flung it open and shouted: "Darling!" just as he did when he returned home from an outing.

I sat glued to my chair and clutched his handkerchief and shuddered with dry, hoarse, racking sobs. Clear-eyed I stared at my open notebook and the shorthand which I knew I could never read back.

Voices sounded in the hall. I heard the Bishop say urgently: "It's Venetia," and I also heard Mrs. Ashworth's lightning response: "Leave this to me."

Hurrying into the room she stooped over me and put an arm around my shoulders. "You're exhausted, aren't you?" she said briskly. "You must have a complete rest. I'll tell everyone you've got flu."

Tears finally streamed down my cheeks. I clutched her. But I was unable to speak.

"Come along," said Mrs. Ashworth, mercifully unemotional. "I'll put you to bed and give you a couple of sleeping pills so that you can switch off and pass out. Much the best thing to do."

She helped me to my feet and steered me upstairs. No one was in the hall. The telephone started to ring but someone answered it. The stairs seemed to go on for ever. "You can have the best spare-room," said Mrs. Ashworth. "It's got a beautiful view of the meadows, very soothing and restful. I'll just get you a pair of Charley's pyjamas. I'm afraid my nightdress wouldn't fit you."

I sat down on the spare-room bed. The view was indeed very beautiful, and I thought how tactful it was of her not to give me a room which faced the Cathedral. But then I remembered she had no idea why I should now find any view of the Cathedral unbearable. The lapse frightened me. I had to remember I was among the enemy; I had to take fanatical care to make no mistakes.

Still shivering from head to toe I began to plot a plausible excuse for my collapse.

1 2

"SO sorry to be such a bore," I said to Mrs. Ashworth unsteadily when she brought me the sleeping tablets, "but the truth is I didn't level with you earlier about Perry Palmer. I'm madly in love with him but he gave me a terrible time when I went up to London for my mother's birthday and I've done nothing but drink gin ever since. All rather a nightmare. But I'm sure I'll sort myself out eventually."

"Poor Venetia," said Mrs. Ashworth, sounding sincerely sympathetic but remaining expressionless. "I'm so very sorry. Now do please take these tablets and pass out."

Downing the pills I keeled over out of torment into oblivion.

1 3

"CAN I make any phone calls for you?" offered Mrs. Ashworth as she brought me tea that evening. "Is there anyone who might ring your flat and be concerned when there was no reply?"

I had to struggle to think. My brain was still sluggish from the pills but I thought of Aysgarth, receiving no letter from me at seven o'clock on the following morning and unable to contact me by phone. Then with horror I remembered that I was due to meet him in the afternoon for our postponed outing. If I failed to appear he would be demented.

"What's the matter?" said Mrs. Ashworth sharply.

"Nothing." My panic was so great I could hardly breathe.

"Now Venetia, that's quite obviously not true. You're white as a ghost and you look terrified—"

"Mrs. Ashworth, I've got to talk to Eddie Hoffenberg."

"I'll ring him for you."

"No, no—I've got to speak to him myself, I must, I shan't sleep a wink unless I speak to him!"

"Very well." Mrs. Ashworth said no more but led me into a light airy bedroom where a white telephone sat on a table by a large double-bed.

Having collapsed on the counterpane I waited till she had left the room and then feverishly started to dial.

"Eddie," I said as he answered, "listen carefully. This is an emergency. I collapsed at the South Canonry this afternoon—exhaustion, nothing more—and I'm staying here for a couple of days while Mrs. Ashworth announces to everyone that I have flu. I told her"—I hesitated, acutely aware that my words could be falling among eavesdroppers—"I told her about my awful love affair with Perry," I said. "I had to explain why I was in such a state."

"I understand," said Eddie without hesitation. "Would you like me to tell him you're temporarily out of circulation?"

"Could you? I'm meeting him tomorrow afternoon, and if I don't turn up—"

"Leave it to me. But Venetia, you'll really have to end this affair with Perry, you know."

"Yes, but—"

"You must write to him. I was a fool to think you could break it off in any other way."

"I'll write later, I promise—"

"No," said Eddie, "you'll write now. I'm not standing any more of this procrastination."

"But Eddie, I'm ill, I—"

"Once the letter's written you'll feel better."

"No, I can't do it now, I can't—"

"I tell you, *you must!* You'll ruin him, you'll ruin yourself, you'll ruin everyone if you go on like this one day longer!"

I started to sob.

"I'll be at the South Canonry at eleven o'clock tomorrow morning," said Eddie, "and if that letter's not written, I'll break the news to him myself."

"No!" I screamed but he had hung up.

I sobbed and sobbed.

Eventually Mrs. Ashworth appeared and without a word led me back to bed. I got rid of her by pretending to be asleep. Then I lay awake in agony until dawn.

"*MY* darling Neville, There's no kind, gentle way to say this, but . . ."
"Dear Neville, How I hate to write this, but . . ."
"Darling Neville, I can hardly bring myself to tell you this, but . . ."
"Dearest Neville, You'll never forgive me, but . . ."
I paused to burn all these attempts at confession in the ash-tray and tried yet again to find the words to express the unspeakable. It was now the morning after my collapse and I was still lying in bed. I had brushed my hair but made no attempt to apply make-up. Intermittently I wept. Charley's pyjamas, pale green cotton adorned with dark green piping, provided a touch of chic which was bizarrely at odds with my shadowed, drawn face. I looked like the worst kind of heroin addict, someone who could barely survive from one fix to the next. No wonder Mrs. Ashworth had instantly diagnosed me as exhausted, and no wonder she had instinctively decided that such a seamy disintegration had to be passed off as a socially acceptable bout of flu.

With terror I realised it was almost eleven o'clock and the letter was still unwritten. Picking up my pen I wrote in a mindless daze of panic and pain:

Neville, Forgive me but I can't go on, I'm marrying Eddie, I don't want to hurt you but I can't go on, sorry, sorry, sorry but I can't go on, there are no more words,

V.

There was a knock on the door, and as I started violently my hostess looked in. "Are you sure you feel up to seeing anyone?" she asked. "If I rang Eddie now I could probably catch him before—" She broke off as the doorbell rang downstairs. "That must be him," she said. "He's early. But Venetia, if you want to change your mind—"

"No." I was stuffing the letter into an envelope, sealing the flap. "I must see him." My fingers were very stiff and I hardly knew what I was doing but I laid the unaddressed envelope on the bedside table beside the ash-tray overflowing with cigarette butts. In the distance I was aware of voices followed by footsteps but I paid them no attention. I could only concentrate on straightening the bedclothes as if I thought that by smoothing the sheet I could smooth away my turmoil.

The next moment I had a shock: the door swung wide and the Bishop walked in. I had not seen him since my collapse, but no doubt that was because his wife had advised him to keep away. He was dressed formally in gaiters for some approaching official engagement, but by speaking in his kindest voice he avoided being intimidating.

"Well, Venetia," he said lightly, "it seems the clerical celebrities of Starbridge are all rushing to offer you sympathy!"

And as I looked past him I saw to my indescribable terror that not merely Eddie but Aysgarth had followed him up to my room.

1 5

IT was the most scandalous risk but he was faultlessly debonair, sauntering along with his hands in his pockets while his expression conveyed just the right amount of affectionate paternal concern, and beside him Eddie too was acting as if his life depended on it; he was exuding a sociable manner which flawlessly concealed what must have been an unadulterated horror and fear. Everyone was immaculately casual. The Bishop, who showed no inclination to leave, drifted to the window as if to check that the view was still there; Mrs. Ashworth, also unable to tear herself away, began to readjust a flower in the vase which she had brought to the room earlier; Eddie wandered to the bedside until he stood within inches of the unaddressed envelope; and Aysgarth, keeping a relentlessly chaste distance from me, lounged against the tall chest of drawers. The conversation, insofar as I could register it, seemed to be light and inconsequential, like the opening phase of a drawing-room comedy. I almost felt we were waiting for the audience to settle in their seats so that Martin Darrow could make his big entrance.

I struggled to concentrate on the dialogue.

". . . and when I happened to mention to Stephen that I was visiting you—" That was Eddie.

"—I decided it was time to pay a pastoral call!" That, of course, was Aysgarth.

"Quite right!" said the Bishop, very charming. "Why should the Vicar of the Close have all the fun?"

"My sentiments exactly!" said Aysgarth.

They beamed at each other, a model of Christian amiability. No other dean and no other bishop could possibly have been on better terms.

"It's sweet of you to come," I said, finally finding my place in the script. "I'm terribly honoured."

"How are you feeling?" enquired Eddie, looking straight at the envelope on the bedside table.

"Oh, just a trifle fragile."

"She has a temperature of a hundred and one," said Mrs. Ashworth, lying with effortless skill as she continued to remodel the flower arrangement.

"There's a lot of this flu about," said Aysgarth. "I hear the Archdeacon's daughters are going down like ninepins."

"What a curious vision that conjures up!" said Eddie.

There was much casual laughter in which I managed to join. Everyone was having a splendid time.

"This is all rather Victorian, isn't it?" I heard the Bishop remark after an interval during which I lost the thread of the conversation. I was trying to work out how I could slip the envelope to Eddie without Aysgarth noticing. "Wasn't there a novel by Trollope in which the heroine received a couple of clergymen when she was lying on her sick-bed?"

"The mother, I assume, was in attendance," said Mrs. Ashworth, finally abandoning the flowers and deciding for some reason to pick up the wastepaper basket.

"Was that *Orley Farm,* Charles?" asked Eddie with interest. "I seem to recall the hero and heroine being drawn together over a sick-bed, but the hero wasn't a clergyman, and—"

"Surely it must have been one of the Barchester novels!" said Aysgarth.

"It could have been *The Vicar of Bullhampton,*" said the Bishop, "but to be quite honest, I don't remember. Lyle, why are you wandering around with that wastepaper basket?"

"Just being a good housewife." She emptied my overflowing ash-tray.

"Very smart pyjamas, Venetia!"

"Thank you, Mr. Dean! They're Charley's."

"I seem to have seen them before somewhere—"

"Marks and Spencer's," said Mrs. Ashworth, looking around to see what she could tidy up next.

"Ah yes! Good old Marks—"

"How did we all live," mused the Bishop rhetorically, "before the advent of Marks and Spencer?"

"One of my daughters-in-law gave me a Marks and Spencer's string vest last Christmas," said Aysgarth. "I always feel very dashing when I'm wearing it."

"I'm rather keen on their shirts," said Eddie.

"They say the royal family shop there incognito," I said, finding my place in the script again. I suddenly noticed my hands. They were gripping the edge of the sheet so hard that my knuckles ached. I tried to relax my fingers one by one but by the time I had finished I realised I had once more lost the thread of the conversation.

"—Jermyn Street," said the Bishop, concluding a sentence. Recalling the conversation about clothes I made the brilliant deduction that he had been referring to the tailors who made his shirts.

"My father's been to the same tailor in Savile Row for fifty years," I said. "So unadventurous."

There was a pause. To my horror I realised that my deduction had been wrong and that the conversation had moved on from clothes. What else happened in Jermyn Street apart from the tailoring of expensive shirts? I racked my brains in panic but could only recall the back entrance of Fortnum's.

"Talking of your father, Venetia," said Eddie, rushing to the rescue, "how did that family dinner-party of yours go? I completely forgot to ask."

"Oh, it was fabulous!" I said, now feeling ill with the strain of keeping up with the conversation. "We were all awash with champagne and sentimentality!"

"Eddie paid a quick visit to London that weekend," said Aysgarth, "but he won't say much about it. I can't think why he should be so secretive."

I commented brightly: "We all have our secrets!" before it struck me that this was quite the wrong thing to say. Or did I merely think it was wrong because my secrets were so all-consuming? "I mean—what I'm trying to say is—"

"We ought to pay a quick visit to London ourselves, Lyle," said the Bishop as I floundered to a halt. "I want to see Thornton Wilder's play *The Ides of March.* Have you seen it, Venetia?"

"I think Venetia's flaking out," said Mrs. Ashworth, suddenly taking control of the scene, "and after receiving a bishop, a dean and a canon simultaneously, I'm not one bit surprised. Charles, would you like to lead the retreat?"

"I'll post this for you, Venetia," said Eddie, picking up the envelope on the bedside table.

"It's not addressed," said Aysgarth, who had also been watching the letter like a hawk.

"It's okay," I said much too loudly. "I—" But I had to stop. I was so terrified of saying the wrong thing. My mind went blank. Panic began to interfere with my breathing.

"It's a note for Lady Flaxton," said Eddie, pocketing the envelope. "Venetia told me about it on the phone last night. Don't worry, Venetia, I'll write the address and provide the stamp."

"Well!" said the Bishop, moving to the door. "Come along, gentlemen—the audience is at an end!"

I thought: I'm nearly there. I've only got to hold myself together for a few more seconds. We're all nearly there. No one's made any ghastly mistakes. We're going to survive.

". . . so get well soon, Venetia—" That was Aysgarth.

"Yes, get well soon—" That was Eddie.

Nearly there. Nearly home.

"Would you like Primrose to look in with some magazines?"

I found my voice. "Well, if she has five minutes to spare . . ." I was going to make it. Only seconds to go.

"I'll ring her at the office when I get home—"

"Lovely—thanks so much—"

The countdown to safety had now begun. Ten—nine—eight—

"I'll be in touch, Venetia," said Eddie. "Let me know if there's anything you need."

"Oh, I'll be all right now—"

Seven—six—five—four—

"Well, take care of yourself—"

"Yes, take care of yourself—"

Three—two—

" 'Bye, Venetia—"

" 'Bye, Venetia—"

One—*zero!* I'd done it. I'd survived. Thank God.

" 'Bye, Eddie," I said, almost fainting with relief. " 'Bye, Neville."

The world at once stopped turning as everyone froze in their tracks.

PART FOUR

THE LIGHT OF
THE WORLD

"Here was more than just a man: here was a window into God at work. For 'God was in Christ reconciling the world to himself.'"

JOHN A. T. ROBINSON
HONEST TO GOD

XVIII

*"It is this union-in-estrangement with the Ground of our being . . .
that we mean by hell."*

JOHN A. T. ROBINSON
HONEST TO GOD

I

SOMEONE was screaming.

I couldn't think who it was.

It wasn't the Bishop, motionless in the doorway. It wasn't Eddie, paralysed at the foot of the bed. It wasn't Aysgarth, carved in stone in the middle of the carpet. It wasn't Mrs. Ashworth, transfixed by the dressing-table.

But someone was screaming. Someone was shouting: "No, *no*, NO!" over and over again in a rising crescendo of hysteria.

Then I realised the voice was connected with me. It belonged to a fragment of my personality. I had begun to disintegrate and now I was splitting into a thousand pieces . . .

I screamed and screamed, but Mrs. Ashworth was coming to the rescue; I saw her move, saw her swing round on the three men and shout: *"Out!"* in a voice which made them jump. The curious part was that they all obeyed her instantly. Afterwards I never forgot that at the most crucial moment of my spiritual sickness the Church of England, that ancient bastion of male privilege, turned tail and fled *en masse*.

Mrs. Ashworth flung her arms around me. She cried in agony: "It's all right—don't reproach yourself—" but I could only weep: "I've ruined him—I've given it all away." Then huge sobs tore at my throat, but she only held me closer and as I clung to her in a frenzy of terror I heard her whisper: "Oh my darling child, do you think we hadn't guessed? I always knew you were Dinkie. I've suffered with you every inch of the way . . ."

AFTER a long while when I was calmer and we had used up the box of Kleenex wiping away our tears, we sat in silence, holding hands. I felt safer now that I knew I was no longer alone. I was still unable to think clearly but I could breathe in a normal manner and know that only one person was doing the breathing. Mrs. Ashworth had apparently glued together my fragmented self by enfolding me in a loving silence. Without words we were able to share the pain and thus, mysteriously, reduce it.

At last, after what seemed a great interval, I whispered five words. They were: "What will the Bishop do?"

"Enlist Jon Darrow's help."

"I know the Bishop dropped a hint earlier about Father Darrow, but Neville didn't seem to realise—"

"It's no good dropping delicate little hints to someone like Stephen. You have to slam him against a wall and shake him till his teeth rattle before he takes any notice. I told Charles that, but poor Charles! He does so hate taking a tough line!"

"Does he? But during that final row they had over the sculpture—"

"My dear, I was livid—*livid!* Charles was up all night afterwards, pacing the floor in a frenzy, and that sort of stress is extremely bad for him. He's got a very sensitive nature," said Mrs. Ashworth, exuding the fiery concern of a protective tigress, "and he can't bear fights."

"But he seems to be so good at them! I thought he was capable of pulling out a long knife at any moment and—"

"No, luckily for Stephen long knives aren't included in the regulation kit issued to bishops at their consecration."

"But surely *now*—"

"Oh, it'll be ultimatum time of course—'Rehabilitate yourself with the aid of a skilled director or else I'll go straight to the Archbishop'—but don't worry. Those old public-school boys who run the Church of England always prefer to bury a mess six feet deep and then play cricket on top of it. Charles will press for rehabilitation, and Stephen—who's quite the most relentless survivor I've ever met—will fall into line."

"So—"

"So assuming the affair's over, you shouldn't waste any more energy worrying about him." She reached for the cigarettes on my bedside table but the packet was empty. "Shall we smoke?" she said. "There's a packet in my bedroom—just a minute."

By the time she returned I had phrased my next question. "Mrs. Ashworth," I said, "when did you first realise what was going on?"

"Last May." She paused to light our cigarettes. "Charles told me he'd looked out of the window of the Cathedral library and seen the two of you holding hands in the cloisters. His comment was: 'I do wish Stephen would stop this idiotic flirting with young women. I've no doubt it's all quite harmless but it's definitely not appropriate behaviour for a senior cleric.' Then suddenly I had a twinge of feminine intuition. Of course I had no idea—how could I have had?—that Stephen might ever be capable of such serious clerical misconduct as adultery, but nevertheless I thought: supposing it's *not* harmless? And I suggested to Charles that we kept an eye on you. He hit on the idea of employing you as a secretary, and gradually as time passed—"

"It all became obvious."

"To me, yes. But Charles kept saying: 'We've no proof,' and trying not to believe the worst. Poor Charles—such a very Christian nature! However in my experience," said Mrs. Ashworth, blowing smoke casually at the ceiling, "the worst is usually true."

"Neville and I . . . we never actually . . . we didn't quite . . ."

"No? I wonder why he held back. I suppose it was just his way of fooling himself that he wasn't committing adultery."

"It seemed to be more complicated than that. He saw me as a great prize and he seemed to be frightened that if he won me he wouldn't want me any more."

"How bizarre! But no doubt his capture of Dido taught him how unpleasant winning a great prize could be."

"Oh, he never saw Dido as a prize! He married her out of compassion."

Mrs. Ashworth gave an incredulous laugh. "My dear, his *amour fou* for a society girl was the talk of the Church! He was mad about her."

There was a silence. Then slowly I said: "Perhaps he still is. After all, I know he didn't abstain from going all the way with me just because he was afraid of winning a great prize and finding it unsatisfactory; he also abstained because he believed it would save Dido from destruction."

"Well, of course I've long suspected that there's far more to that marriage than meets the eye. People are usually so busy noticing how obsessed she is with him that they overlook how utterly he's bound up with her."

"But in that case why did he—"

"—fall for you? Oh, for all the usual reasons, I'm sure, but also, I suspect, because you represented an escape from the Dido obsession and he'd reached the stage where he needed a holiday. After all, what's the most satisfactory way of escaping from an obsession? You escape into another obsession and run the two of them in tandem."

"So you think he didn't really love me at all?"

"On the contrary I'm sure he was mad about you, and that's why one should stress the peculiarity of his psychology. If he didn't consummate the affair there must have been very powerful mental forces holding him back."

"It seems so stupid," I said, "to have gone through all this without ever—"

"It could be important for your recovery. Human beings are really very fragile, emotionally and spiritually, and need to keep a certain private space around their deepest selves where they feel they can be in control against any invading force. If you can feel later that there was at least one part of your deepest self which was untouched by this destruction, you'll find the healing will take place more easily."

I said simply: "I don't think I'll ever be healed."

"My dearest Venetia—"

"I can't stop thinking about him. What on earth could have been said after they'd left the room?"

"Probably very little. They'd pretend your fatal slip never happened because they'd all need time to work out what they were going to do next."

"Neville must be in the most frightful panic—"

"I doubt it. He'll have knocked back the whisky by this time."

"My God, you mean you know about the drink?"

"Oh, we all know about that. The great thing is to hush it up, but fortunately those canons practise loyalty on a heroic scale . . . And talking of canons, Eddie's still very keen, isn't he?"

"I've actually agreed to marry him. I've just made the break with Neville. That letter Eddie took away—"

"Good heavens, now I see it all!"

I started to cry. "He'll get the letter tomorrow—I can't bear to think of it—he'll be so hurt, so shattered, so crushed—"

"For a little while, perhaps."

"But Mrs. Ashworth—"

"My dear, that one's tough as old boots. They simply don't make them any tougher up in Yorkshire."

"But if he loses me and loses his job—"

"He won't lose it. I've told you: he'll fall into line and trot off to Jon Darrow's spiritual workshop for a compulsory overhaul and comprehensive repairs. Of course if Stephen were a gentleman he'd do the decent thing and resign, but he'll never voluntarily give up that Deanery. It's much too big a prize to kiss goodbye."

"But he doesn't approve of spiritual directors and he calls Father Darrow an ecclesiastical pirate!"

"It's really amazing what one can learn to like," said Mrs. Ashworth, "when one's professional life is on the line. No, my dear, the big question here is not what's going to happen to Neville-Stephen; his future's clearly mapped out. The really big question is what's going to happen to you."

I wiped my tears from my swollen eyes and whispered: "What do you think I should do?" as if I now had a choice. But of course no new choice existed. I still had to end the affair to ensure Aysgarth's survival, and I knew there was only one way of making him let go.

"You really want to know what I think?" said Mrs. Ashworth. "I think you should marry the good, decent man who loves you."

I started weeping again. "But I don't love him."

"So long as you like him and respect him, I don't think the absence of romantic love is important. And as for the real love, that can come later."

"Can it?"

"Why not? When one's emerged from a disastrous affair, goodness and decency begin to seem immensely attractive."

I was reassured by her confidence, and suddenly the future seemed less chilling. "Mrs. Ashworth," I said, speaking reluctantly but driven on by a craving for further reassurance, "am I right in thinking you speak from personal experience? You seem so very certain . . . I'm sorry, I don't want to pry, but—"

Mrs. Ashworth said obliquely: "I never cease to thank God that Charles wanted to marry me even though I was then too battered to love him as he deserved."

"So before you met him—"

There was a knock at the door.

"Who is it?" called Mrs. Ashworth sharply, and the Bishop answered: "Me."

"Just a moment." She stubbed out her cigarette and left the room. I heard their voices murmur in the distance for some time but at last Mrs. Ashworth returned to say briskly: "Charles would very much like to see you on your own. It might be a good thing. He could convince you that the Christian response to Stephen's behaviour isn't to disembowel him with a long knife."

After a pause I said: "Okay."

"I'll wait in the corridor. If you want to turf him out, all you have to do is yell."

She slipped out and the Bishop slipped in. He was very quiet, very calm, very gentle. "This won't take long," he said, pulling up a chair and sitting down by the bed. "Sometimes in a crisis it's best if no words are spoken but I think if I were silent now I would only add to your very great anxiety, so I want to say this: I know the Church must often seem to a layman to be just another worldly corporation staffed by ambitious executives, but in our own inadequate, imperfect way the churchmen in authority do try, by remembering God every day and praying to Him for the grace to serve Him as He desires, to live according to Christian precepts. My job is to be a shepherd. That's why I carry the crozier, the shepherd's crook, in the Cathedral. I have to care for the sheep, all of them, not just the sheep who stay bunched together and never put a foot wrong, but the sheep who stray out of sight and can't find their way home. My duty in caring for the flock is not to run around with a whip and a knife, flogging the strays into line and cutting the throats of the ones who cause trouble. My duty is to go after the strays and find them and carry them back one by one to safety. So you see, although bishops may seem very grand people, particularly when they're dressed up in their uniform, and although their job may seem rooted in a complex web of power, yet at the heart of their lives lies this great simplicity, the simplicity of the shepherd who serves God by caring for others and helping them when they're in distress."

He paused as if to consider whether he should say more but then rose to his feet and silently replaced the chair. It was only when he reached the door that he spoke again. He said: "I expect it's too difficult for you to talk to me, but if you should wish later when you're better to talk to a clergyman, I can easily arrange a meeting. Meanwhile I'm sure my wife is far more able to help you than I am." And he slipped out again into the corridor.

Feeling that no man could possibly be of any use to me at that moment I reflected vaguely that it was a pity there were no women priests. But of course those old public-school boys who ran the Church of England would never permit a woman to play cricket on their hallowed turf.

"Still conscious?" said Mrs. Ashworth, returning to the room.

"Yes. He was rather sweet," I said vaguely in a hopeless attempt to express my gratitude for the Bishop's kindness, and then overcome by my exhaustion I again started to cry.

3

WHEN the tears finally stopped I felt as a patient must feel when he has been prepared for an operation and knows that he is powerless to do anything except wait for the ordeal to be over. I lay lifelessly in bed. Mrs. Ashworth offered me a selection of novels but I was unable to read them. I could only listen to her transistor radio and thumb through some magazines.

In the afternoon a letter arrived, delivered by hand. The address on the envelope had been typed in order to preserve the author's anonymity among the prying eyes at the South Canonry. I could hardly bear to break the seal but I had to know what he had written.

"My darling," I read.

> Just a brief note which you can burn immediately in the ash-tray. *Don't worry* about the slip. I said afterwards: "Venetia's obviously very ill and confused—why should she call me Neville when I specifically told her on holiday in the Hebrides that she could call me Stephen?" Eddie at once said: "Obviously she was almost delirious," and Charles said: "She's certainly most unwell." So that's all right. I thought it was rather clever of me to rake up the Hebrides—everyone always sinks into Christian names on holiday, and just because Eddie never actually heard you call me Stephen up there he can't prove I didn't invite you to dispense with formality. So my darling, *don't worry* and *get well soon.* Nobody suspects anything.
>
> Much, much, much love,
N.

Mrs. Ashworth burnt the letter in the ash-tray and produced a new box of Kleenex. Time dragged on and at intervals she would sit with me and knit. I wanted to ask her more about the man who had wrecked her life before the young Dr. Ashworth had arrived on the scene like a white knight, but I was unable to frame any question beyond a preliminary enquiry. I did say: "That story you told me about the young woman who was almost destroyed by a romance that went wrong—you were the young woman, weren't you, just as I was Dinkie," but when she answered: "It's best to draw a veil over that now," I realised that the subject was one which she had no wish to discuss. Yet because I knew she had been through an experience similar to mine I was able to say to her: "One of the most baffling aspects of the whole affair is that I feel I never really knew him. I just knew a *persona,* a mask. He claimed it was the real him, but I suspect there were acres and acres of the real him that I never traversed at all; I suspect I just saw one corner of a vast field."

"Oh, that's a very common feature of love affairs. Romance and fantasy fence off the cosy corner and leave reality out in the cold beyond the pale."

"But what *was* reality here? How do I come to terms with it? How do I sort it all out in my mind when so much is either unknown or a mystery? You talked of twin obsessions running in tandem, but—"

"—but I was speculating. Yes, I do understand what you mean, but all you can do is concentrate on the facts which are beyond dispute: he was married; the two of you became emotionally involved with each other; he brought you to breakdown. Then you can expand a little on those basic facts with some degree of certainty: he was probably under stress for various reasons—and perhaps you too were under stress in some way, with the result that you each found an escape from your problems in the other; then during this great escape he displayed a passion which could well have been genuine but could also have been part of an elaborate fantasy generated by the journey away from reality. That all sounds very stark, I know, but that's really all it's possible to say."

"I just feel that if only I knew the whole truth—"

"My dear, we never know the whole truth about anyone. Only God can ever know the whole truth. All we can do is struggle to grasp that part of the truth which God has made accessible to us and accept that not all mysteries are solvable."

"But surely you know the whole truth about the Bishop?"

Mrs. Ashworth smiled. Then she said: "When I first met Charles long ago in 1937 he seemed very straightforward, a successful young clergyman from a comfortable middle-class home. But the reality behind the glittering image was far more complex, I assure you, than I could ever have imagined, and even now I daresay there are still mysteries in his past which I shall never unravel." She hesitated but added: "He was a widower when I met him. He's talked to me about that first marriage, but not in a way that has ever encouraged me to dig deep into what actually happened. I'd like to know more, of course, but I've accepted that there's nothing more he has to say; I've accepted that there's a limit on our knowledge of even those who are closest to us. The older one gets the more one realises how saturated life is in mystery, and the biggest mystery of all, it often seems to me, is the mystery of the human personality."

I meditated on this conversation for some time while the sunshine dwindled into twilight and darkness began to fall. Later the Bishop looked in to see how I was. Later still Mrs. Ashworth brought me a mug of cocoa and some more pills. Once again I sank thankfully into oblivion, but the next morning at seven o'clock I was awake, every muscle in my body aching with tension as I pictured the postman walking up to the front door of the Deanery with my letter in his hand.

4

AT eight o'clock Mrs. Ashworth came to my room with Aysgarth's reply. All she said was: "He's just delivered this. I heard the car in the drive and thought it might be him. He looked much as usual."

My fingers were trembling so much that I was unable to open the envelope. Without a word she took it from my hands, ripped open the flap and handed me the folded sheet of paper within.

He had written:

This breaks my heart. I'm now standing in the worst wasteland I've ever known. I can only pray that God will bless you and keep you safe and ultimately grant you the happiness you deserve.

There was no opening "my darling," no signature, no love sent, only the three bleak sentences which, carefully written in his clear handwriting, suggested a survivor in ruthless control of himself.

I wept with relief.

It was finally over.

Or was it?

5

MY darling,

I feel I'm going stark staring mad. Can you not write *just one word?* Please, please, if you've ever loved me at all—which now seems doubtful—send me JUST ONE WORD.

N.

6

DARLING Neville,

You know how much I love you, but I'm ending our affair because there's no alternative; if I don't end it you'll be ruined. Please try to understand. I'm doing this—*all of it*—so that you can be saved.

V.

7

MY darling,

I was so utterly appalled by your letter that I nearly passed out. Listen, you *mustn't marry him,* you absolutely mustn't—the very idea that you could be marrying Eddie in order to save me is so horrific that I can't maintain a noble silence on the subject a second longer, I just can't, I'd wind up in a lunatic asylum.

Darling, Eddie's dead wrong for you. God knows, no one's fonder of Eddie than I am—oh, the nightmare of it, the sheer unadulterated *hell* that I should be betrayed by the two people who are closest to me, I feel as if I've been disembowelled and abandoned to bleed to death, but never mind that now, I don't count, what's it matter if I bleed to death, what have I got to live for, but *you* count, *you* matter, you have *everything* to live for, and I can't bear that you should throw yourself away like this, CAN'T BEAR IT.

The truth is poor Eddie's a very damaged sort of fellow—it's the result of his war experiences and losing all his family—and he's so neurotic, so enslaved by hypochondria and introspection, that he could only wear you down in no time if you married him. HE'S NOT GOOD ENOUGH FOR YOU. I've always tried to resign myself to the fact that you would marry one day but I wanted you to marry someone who was worthy of you, and he's not worthy, he'll never be worthy, and besides—I hate to say this because the images it conjures up are so revolting, but nevertheless it has to be said—how can you conceivably marry a man whom you find physically repulsive? It's all the most ghastly mistake and it'll wreck your life. Even if you go into the marriage with the idea of divorcing him eventually, you'll still have to live through an experience which could scar you for ever.

Darling, I'll give you up, I'll never see you again, I'll never even write one letter, but please, *please,* PLEASE swear to me by return of post that you'll break off this absolutely *disastrous* engagement. Always your most devoted and loving

N.

8

"DEAR Mr. Dean," dictated Mrs. Ashworth as the tears streamed down my face and the pen shook in my hand,

I'm afraid you must take it as settled that Eddie and I will be marrying shortly. I know this is very difficult for you and I'm sorry. But the sooner you accept the situation the sooner all three of us will begin to recover from this horrific ordeal.

Yours sincerely,
VENETIA.

MY darling,

I can't believe you could have written that letter, and I refuse to take *anything* as settled. I'm going to fight to save you from tragedy. Eternal love from your devoted

N.

MY dear Stephen,

Venetia has asked me to reply to your last letter. I assure you that it is indeed settled that she is to marry Eddie, and Charles and I both think that your correspondence with her should now cease.

Yours sincerely,
LYLE.

"...*SO* unable to stand the suspense any longer I turned up at the Deanery," wrote Eddie.

Dido showed me straight into his study. It was a shock for him but he recovered quickly and was perfectly civil. He looked tired but sober. Certainly there was no whisky in sight. I told him of my intention to work in London and said I planned to marry you next month at St. Margaret's Westminster. He nodded and said would I like him to write to the Bishop of London, but I said no, that was all right, Charles had already offered to pull strings on my behalf. That reply produced a deafening silence but I raced on and asked if he wanted me to resign the canonry straight away or whether he was content for me to stay on until the wedding.

Then he became very proud, very grand, and said that was nothing to do with him, that was something I should discuss with the Bishop, he had no strong feelings on the subject, as far as he was concerned I could do exactly as I liked. So I said I didn't want to leave the

Cathedral in the lurch by a sudden resignation and it might also be a good thing, from the point of view of avoiding gossip, if I stayed on until my marriage. Then I added that after the wedding we'd be renting a flat in London until I got the house which will go with my new job. I thought perhaps I should make it clear that we shan't be returning to the Starbridge diocese, even temporarily.

He said politely: "Quite. I wish you every happiness," and suddenly I couldn't bear it, I just had to say: "Stephen, I'm so very sorry, but believe me, whatever happens either now or in the future, you'll always be the hero who saved me from despair in that POW camp and looked after me later as if I were your own son."

He just sighed. Then he said in an exasperated voice: "You'll never be an Englishman, will you, Eddie? Englishmen just don't make that kind of remark," and I laughed—I think he did mean me to laugh, don't you?—and thanked him for seeing me and that was the end of the conversation. But he seemed well in control of himself and I think he's going to be all right . . .

I 2

MY dear Venetia,

Eddie has just been here and, as you would say, "slobbered all over me." Why can't foreigners behave properly? However, I accept that he meant well. I also accept that I've lost my Great Prize and that our correspondence must inevitably end.

I won't ask you to thank Lyle for her letter. What an old battle-axe that woman's turned into! She has a real talent for wielding what Eddie, with his Nazi memories, would call "the long knife." I could tell you a thing or two about her. But I won't. I may be just a Yorkshire draper's son but I trust I know when and how to behave like a gentleman.

I went to see that old pirate Jon Darrow today. Thought I really ought to look in on the old boy as he was asking after me so persistently. I must say, old age has improved him; he's quieter now, more sedate. We had a little chat about this and that, talked about the past, just as one inevitably does with the elderly. By the way, I think he secretly took a fancy to you at the Starbridge Playhouse! "A most interesting girl!" he said, eyes gleaming. Funny old pirate. I promised I'd drop in on him again soon—and in fact I think I might drop in on him regularly for a while. He seemed so pathetically glad to receive a visitor, and one really does have a Christian duty to be kind to old people.

I hope you're now completely recovered from the flu. Primrose has just succumbed—there's certainly a lot of it about—and has returned from her flat to her old room at the Deanery in order to be properly cosseted. Perhaps you might look in on her before you leave for London to make the wedding arrangements. It would be prudent, I think, if you made some small gesture towards renewing that friendship, because Primrose continues to wonder why you dropped her so abruptly and she needs the chance to write off your withdrawal as a mere temporary aberration resulting from Eddie's courtship.

In sending you my best regards I hope I may sign myself your well-wisher,

STEPHEN AYSGARTH.

13

ARRIVING at the Deanery clutching a box of chocolates and the latest edition of *Punch,* I was admitted by Dido's companion-housekeeper Miss Carp and ushered upstairs to Primrose's room. Lying wanly in bed Primrose opened her eyes as I put my head around the door.

"Receiving callers, Prim?"

"Venetia! Good heavens, I *am* honoured." She hauled herself up on the pillows and gave me a chilly smile. Her lank brown hair, frizzy at the ends, fell in strands towards her shoulders and her pink nightdress, possibly one of Dorothy Perkins' more unfortunate products, clung limply to her flat chest.

Leaving my offerings on the bed I enquired: "Feeling ghastly?"

"Yes, but better than yesterday. Oh, *Punch*! How nice—thanks . . . Well, I suppose I ought to congratulate you, oughtn't I? We've all seen the announcement in today's *Times.*"

"Please don't feel obliged to congratulate me if you don't want to, Primrose."

"Well, to be quite frank, Father and I think it's a very big mistake. We think you could do better for yourself."

I was just wondering whether I should give up and walk out when the door behind me was swept wide open and Dido streamed into the room. It at once occurred to me that she had crept along the corridor to eavesdrop as soon as Miss Carp had informed her of my arrival.

"What utter nonsense, Primrose!" she exclaimed. "You should be ashamed of yourself, sulking away so ungraciously in bed just because Venetia's getting married and you're still lying on the shelf!" And before this brutal remark could draw forth a stinging retort she added crisply: "Venetia, how very kind of you to call on poor Primrose—I always did say you were a nice girl *au fond,* even though the *fond* was so seldom on display—and my dear! Too, too lovely about your engagement, I'm thrilled for you both! Take no notice of Primrose's sour grapes, because I assure you, my dear, that far from disapproving of your engagement Stephen told me last night—and of course he always tells me every-thing—that in his opinion marriage would be the making of both you *and* dear Eddie!"

"He doesn't tell you a damn thing!" said Primrose incensed. *"I'm* the one he confides in, and he told me this morning—"

"Well, obviously when he saw you were so *devoured* by jealousy he pretended to disapprove of the engagement so that you wouldn't feel quite such a failure!"

My voice said politely: "I think I ought to be going now," but when I turned towards the door I found that Aysgarth himself was standing on the threshold.

"Oh, there you are, darling!" cried Dido radiantly as I flinched and stopped dead in my tracks. "Come on in and join the party! Primrose, silly girl, is refusing to believe you're in favour of Venetia's marriage—do tell her you're all for it!"

"I certainly wish Venetia every happiness." He gave me a smile which was no more than a subtle upturning of his thin mouth. His blue eyes were expressionless.

"Father," said Primrose, now pale with rage, "you distinctly said to me—"

"Oh, dear, *dear* child," said Dido in a voice which vibrated with exasperation, "when are you ever going to abandon this pathetic illusion that you're in your father's confidence?"

"Darling," said Aysgarth quietly to her. "Please."

"Father never lies to me, and he said—"

"Never lies to you? My God, that's a laugh! If you only knew the half of what's been going on in his life lately—"

Aysgarth and I spoke at the same moment. He said strongly: "Dido, that's enough!" while I exclaimed with a dreadful false brightness: "Well, I simply *must* be going!"

"Your trouble, Dido," cried Primrose, outshouting us both, "is that you're the one who's 'devoured' by jealousy because I'm in his confidence and you're not! Why, he said to me only the other day: 'Primrose,' he said, 'of course I know you'll marry eventually, but how am I going to bear it when you go away and I have no one to talk to?' And that's why you're quite wrong in thinking I'm jealous of Venetia—I don't want to get married, I'm never going to get married, I've made up my mind that I'm going to stay with Father and be a comfort to him in his marital hell!"

"Primrose, be quiet!" said Aysgarth violently, but the scene was now quite out of control and as I stood paralysed with horror Dido, throwing all self-restraint to the winds, tossed the lighted match into the keg of dynamite which we had all been circling for so long.

"My poor pet!" she said to Primrose in her most withering voice. "You've been grossly deceived! He's just been playing a role for you, the role of the doting father, but in fact he's long past caring what you do with yourself. He's too busy doting elsewhere—as Venetia will be the first to testify!"

Primrose said blankly: "Venetia?" at the exact same moment as Aysgarth whispered: "That's enough—that's enough, I tell you—"

"You see?" said Dido to Primrose. "You know nothing—nothing, nothing, nothing! But Venetia could tell you things you could never in your wildest dreams imagine, Venetia could tell you—"

I said in a loud voice: "I'm going!" but quick as a flash Dido barred my path to the door.

"Oh no, you're not!" she said. "I've *had* it with this girl, mooning over her father as if he were her lover and making my life hell for year after year, and this is it, this is where I refuse to tolerate her behaviour a second longer, this is where I draw the line." She spun to face Primrose. "Venetia's your father's little piece of nonsense. Not his mistress—she's still *virgo intacta*—but his trivial little plaything which he uses for relaxation during his leisure hours. It's been going on for some months. He takes her out on his afternoon off and they drive to some deserted spot—Castle Brigga, isn't it, Venetia dear?—and there they indulge in their amusing little sex-games—"

"I don't believe it," said Primrose. She was now ashen. "That's the foulest lie I've ever heard." She looked at her father. "Why don't you deny it?" she said in a shaking voice. "Why are you just standing there? Why don't you say it's a lie?"

"Because it's the truth," said Dido. She jerked my arm. "It's all true, isn't it, Venetia? My God, look at you! I suppose you thought I didn't know anything about it! I suppose you thought I'd never heard of Castle Brigga! Who told her, you're thinking, who told her—and how does she know I'm still a virgin? Well, my dear, this is where you get your big surprise, the surprise you'll remember all your life, because STEPHEN TELLS ME *EVERYTHING*. He always has and he always will—and do you know where he tells me everything, Venetia? In bed!

And after sex! I suppose you thought, silly, ignorant girl, that you had him all to yourself; I suppose you thought you knew him through and through—but you were wrong. You never knew *Stephen* at all. You just knew a masked actor who indulged in some shallow play-acting, but I know *Stephen* and *Stephen* makes love only to *me*. He's always promised that there was one act he'd never do with anyone else, and that promise was given because he's dedicated his whole life to making me feel cherished and fulfilled. So what do I care about his little weaknesses? What do I care about all the drink and the masked actor who amuses himself with young girls? All that matters is that *he's mine* and *he loves me* and I love him a thousand times better than *any other woman ever could!*" And turning her back on me abruptly she marched out with her head held high.

The door banged.

There was a silence.

I remember Primrose, blue eyes huge in her white shocked face. I remember Aysgarth, grey and drawn, the suffering etched deep in the heavy lines about his mouth. I remember the copy of *Punch* on the bed and the unopened box of chocolates and the curtains fluttering lightly in the breeze from the open window.

At last Aysgarth said unevenly to Primrose—not to me, but to Primrose, it was Primrose he turned to first: "It's not true, I give you my word."

"Of course it couldn't possibly be true," said Primrose stiff-lipped. "Not possibly." She was unable to look at either of us.

Then Aysgarth turned to me and said: "I apologise, Venetia, for all her lies. She's had a fixation about Castle Brigga ever since she discovered that I'd circled it on the Ordnance Survey map. I'd planned to take Pip there one day for an outing."

"I see," I said. "Yes."

The silence closed in on us again, and suddenly I saw the full dimensions of the destruction that had been wrought. Neither Primrose nor I could know for certain whether or not he spoke the truth. We would want to believe him, but the more we tried the more clearly we would remember Dido, fearlessly outspoken, shrewd about personal relationships, passionately devoted to her husband, voicing the horrors which we could never be sure were false. She had told the truth to Primrose about my affair with Aysgarth. How could I ever convince myself beyond doubt that she had lied to me about her marriage? I knew that logically it was possible that she had told the truth to Primrose and lied to me, but it was equally possible that she had told the truth to both of us. Faith had been wrecked, trust destroyed, love annihilated. Now indeed we all stood in a wasteland which stretched as far as the eye could see.

"My darling——"

I gave a start, but he was talking to Primrose—not to me but to Primrose—and as I glimpsed some seamy psychological shadow fall backwards across the past I felt my blood run cold with repulsion.

"——my darling, you must believe me, you must——"

"But of course I believe you!" said Primrose, somehow managing to look at him at last, but as soon as I saw the expression on her face I knew he had lost her for ever.

He knew it too. He had been moving towards her but now he swung back to face me. "Venetia, tell her," he said stricken, stammering in his agony. "Tell her it's not true!"

"It's not true," I said to Primrose in my politest voice, and walked away without looking back.

I 4

MY dear Venetia,

I'm sorry to trouble you when you must be so busy with your wedding preparations, but I really felt I couldn't let that appalling scene at the Deanery pass without comment. Dido seems to have jumped to conclusions on the minimum of evidence. Of course I never told her anything about us. But she did find out I'd circled Castle Brigga on the map, she did find out that I was disappearing with the car on my afternoon off, and when she heard the rumour that I'd been seen in Chasuble Lane (at the end of my ill-fated attempt to play Juan Fangio) with a young woman, she realised it was you and not, as was popularly supposed, Harriet March.

Her disclosure that I had promised never to consummate an extra-marital affair is true (and explains why she was confident you were still *virgo intacta*) but her allegation that I have a habit of gossiping garrulously in bed after sexual intercourse is, I assure you, a fable. In such circumstances I prefer to smoke a cigarette and pass out. No doubt there's more you'd like me to say on that particular subject, but I believe I've now implied all that requires to be said: namely that Dido's not above mixing truth with lies when she's ruthlessly pursuing her own ends.

Yours sincerely,
STEPHEN.

I NEVER replied to that letter because I was too busy in London assembling my trousseau. Later he wrote to my sister Sylvia and asked for news of me. Sylvia was rather touched by this avuncular interest and struck up a correspondence with him; it helped pass the time as she waited for the baby to arrive. She showed me a couple of his letters. They were very amusing and charming, but I doubted that Sylvia could match this sparkling style in her replies.

He did write me one more letter. It read:

My dearest Venetia,

The time has come when I must wish you well in your new life and assure you that I shall be praying hard for your happiness. I suspect you no longer believe this, but you really were the very greatest prize I ever encountered, the love of my life, and now that I look back from a grey cold present into that brilliant past we shared together, I realise how very privileged I was to experience, no matter how fleetingly, such absolute perfection. I shall always cherish the memory of those walks through the woods and those kisses in the hollow—and even those prosaic journeys in the car when we merely laughed and gossiped together. What glorious times we had! I shall never forget them, never, I swear it—till my dying day I'll always dream of those shining hours when I loved the best girl in all the world and travelled with her through paradise. May God bless you, my darling, and in sending you all my love as always, I remain, now and forever, your most devoted

MR. DEAN.

The letter arrived on my wedding-day.
It wrecked my eye make-up and nearly ruined my white gown.
God knows how I ever made it to the church.

XIX

*"But equally it is the union-in-love with the Ground of our being such as we see
in Jesus Christ, that is the meaning of heaven. And it is the offer of that life, in all
its divine depth, to overcome the estrangement and alienation of existence as we
know it that the New Testament speaks of as the 'new creation.'"*

JOHN A. T. ROBINSON
HONEST TO GOD

I

EDDIE landed a very acceptable job as the rector of a smart Kensington
parish, and the rectory was acceptable too, a cream-coloured, early Victorian, double-fronted town house with plenty of space for entertaining.
I bought my heart's desire in the country later. It was in Norfolk, a little
out of the way perhaps, but the fine, austere, classical mansion had a lake
at the bottom of the back lawn, and the members of the Coterie adored
streaming down there from London at weekends. I never bothered with
parish life, but I was always careful to keep up appearances by behaving
properly in London—or if I did misbehave I made damned sure I was
discreet.

The marriage, of course, was a disaster.

The 1960s were a disaster too, as those who were lucky enough to
survive knew all too well. "All you need is love!" sang the Beatles, as
the Great Pollutant, seeping into the gap created by the absence of a
strong religion, began systematically to poison our lives. Pascal wrote:
"It is natural for the mind to believe and for the will to love; so that for
want of true objects, they must attach themselves to false." The true
objects all went under in that part of the 1960s where I wasted what
remained of my youth, and only the false gods survived to ensure our
ruin.

The ranks of the Coterie were decimated. Dinkie overdosed on heroin,
Emma-Louise crashed through three marriages, that nice Holly Carr
committed suicide, Norman Aysgarth took to drink, man-eating Cynthia

had a nervous breakdown, Robert Welbeck was crippled in a motorway smash-up, Simon drowned in a swimming-pool after freaking out on LSD, Don Latham dropped out of the BBC in order to meditate in India, Katie Aysgarth took to spiritualism and went peculiar, Christian—

Now, that was a great mystery. They say Nick Darrow unravelled that one in the end, Nick Darrow treading his mystical paths with his crystal ball in one hand and his crucifix in the other. He survived, of course. So, more surprisingly, did Michael Ashworth and Marina, who married each other and lived (so far as I could tell) happily ever after. Michael still pounced around occasionally but Marina always became a devoted friend of any mistress who lasted longer than six months. Some people really are extraordinary.

Primrose's wedding took place a month after mine, and with an ambitious wife egging him on, Maurice Tait wound up running the Choir School. They had four children and Primrose was always reported to be radiant—as was Dido once she had finally got rid of her step-daughter. It was nice to know that the appalling scene at the Deanery eventually made Dido, Primrose and, presumably, Maurice ecstatically happy.

Eddie died young, just as he had so often threatened he would, but before the end came I tried to make amends to him for my shortcomings by having a baby. God knows who the father was but all that mattered was that Eddie thought the child was his. It turned out to be a girl, rather a bright little bit of fluff, but I never had much gift for being a mother.

The Bishop published his book *A Modern Heresy for Modern Man* to critical acclaim but minimal sales. However, later his distinguished good looks were discovered by television and he used to appear, gorgeous in purple, pectoral cross flashing, on various discussion programmes. Unlike other eminent prelates who flirted with the medium, he always took a very firm line with hedonistic pop stars.

I found I could never bear to watch him for more than a few seconds, but I was glad that in the Church of England, then enduring one of its most demoralised phases, there was at least someone who had the guts to speak up for the unfashionable views which he believed to be right.

I eventually severed all my Starbridge connections. Once I met Mrs. Ashworth for lunch in London but that was a mistake and afterwards she said: "I'm sorry, I remind you of it all, don't I? Don't worry, I understand."

I liked that woman. I could never hold it against her that she had given me the wrong advice. How could she have known that what had been right for her and the Bishop would be wrong for Eddie and me? At least she had cared deeply about my welfare and I knew she saw me as the daughter she had never had. At that lunch in London she told me that in 1945 when her husband had returned from the war she had tried to have another baby but without success. That had obviously been a sadness to her, but at least both her sons did well.

Charley, surprisingly, turned out to be almost as sexy as his brother in the end—those golden eyes were really very compelling—and he married one of those ghastly wonder-women spawned by the Women's Movement, someone who was capable of tossing off a master's thesis, bringing up a shoal of successful children and producing a gourmet dinner for eight—all with one hand tied behind her back while she continued to look like a film star. I loathe women like that, but perhaps I'm jealous because they made the most of their opportunities while I threw all mine away. And perhaps I'm jealous too of Charley's wonder-woman because I sometimes think I might have found Charley an entertaining husband. If only I could have hung on and waited while he completed his transformation from ugly duckling to sexy swan! But I couldn't have waited, could I? I had to save my Mr. Dean.

I never recovered from him, of course. No man I met ever measured up to him. I often wondered if I would have been less enslaved by his memory if our love affair had been fully consummated; naturally no real-life consummation could ever match the glittering dream which existed for all time in my imagination, but perhaps even if the affair had been completed in a conventional manner I would still have been unable to forget the memory of those "shining hours" which Aysgarth had described in his final letter.

He ruined me, that was the truth of it. He ruined me, he ruined my marriage, he ruined every attempt I made to find happiness elsewhere. Religion? Oh, he ruined that for me too; I turned away from theology and I turned away from the Church. He and his New Reformation! I wanted no part of it, not after all I'd been through in Starbridge. The last thing I did before I left my home in Lord North Street for my wedding at St. Margaret's was to tear up *Honest to God* and chuck the pieces in the wastepaper basket.

So the '60s came to an end and the '70s began for those who had survived. I certainly thought of myself as surviving; I hadn't O.D.'d on heroin or freaked out on LSD or died of cirrhosis of the liver. But as I see so clearly now, my survival was an illusion. The Great Pollutant had claimed another victim, and from my spiritual grave I could only look back in rage at the man whom I held responsible for my death.

Then one day in 1975 when I was in Norfolk, one day when the summer sun was shining on the lake, one day when I was a widow of thirty-eight, a letter arrived out of the blue.

MY dear Venetia,

I have now reached the advanced age of seventy-three and look at least a hundred, even though in my head I feel no more than forty-five! What a curious phenomenon growing old is. I'm not able to go out and about much nowadays, but I've made a good recovery from my stroke—still *compos mentis* (or am I deluding myself?!)—and I can walk with the aid of two sticks. It was wonderful to wave the wheelchair goodbye. I was goaded into staging this spectacular recovery by the formidable alliance of Dido (still going strong, needless to say) and my new ladyfriend, Mrs. Jenny Hayman, a charming young widow who lives near us in Surrey and who drops in almost every day to chat with me and occasionally (if I'm very good) to hold my hand. Dido is devoted to Jenny, whose visits give her (D) the chance to escape from the useless old hulk (me) and roar round the village infuriating everyone in sight, so I have now followed the example of my mentor Alex Jardine (Bishop of Starbridge 1932–1937) and wound up in an irreproachably seemly *ménage à trois*.

Anyway, when I was in the wheelchair and feeling a trifle glum, Dido and Jenny hatched a scheme to lure me off my bottom: Jenny offered to take me on an excursion to Norwich to see the Cotman exhibition. As you know, I've always been interested in art (I'm sure you've never forgotten that fatally ambivalent box of cigars!) and I particularly liked the thought of a little holiday in Norwich, such a beautiful city with such a magnificent cathedral. So to cut a long story short I shall merely add that the carrot dangled before the donkey proved too luscious to resist, and the donkey will soon be doddering through Norfolk.

My darling, if you can't face me I shall understand, but I have only one desire at the moment and that's to see you again—just once more—before I die. Of course I may live for years (poor old Dido!) but if I'm called to meet my Maker before I've had the chance to fulfill this last alluring whim, I shall without doubt stage a tantrum in heaven. (Hell is out of the question, of course, since no good Liberal Protestant Modernist believes in it—although on reflection I recall there *are* no good Liberal Protestant Modernists nowadays, only a bunch of boring radical theologians who don't believe in anything—and I'm certainly not one of those!)

Let me know what you think. Whatever your decision nothing can change the fact that I shall love you till the day I die. I remain—still—after all these many years—your most loyal and devoted

MR. DEAN.

3

HE was very stout and very old. His face had a high colour, possibly as the result of heart disease, and his white hair was thinner and wispier. He moved very slowly with his two sticks. His eyes were now only a faded blue, but his mouth still turned downwards in a sultry curve when his face was in repose.

As soon as I saw how impaired he was I knew beyond doubt that this visit was no mere exercise in nostalgia, no bizarre extension of the fantasy and illusion of 1963. He had struggled to see me at the very end of his life because his love was genuine, and once this truth had dawned all my anger vanished as if it had never existed. I ran out to meet him, and although he merely held out his hand I flung wide my arms and we hugged each other.

"Well!" he said afterwards. For a moment no other words were possible. "Well!" He beamed at me.

I said only: "My darling Mr. Dean."

The new ladyfriend was a pleasant woman, very middle-class, but then not everyone can be born with a silver spoon in their mouth, and anyway every time I looked in the glass I despised the aristocracy. I think she was nervous of me. God knows what he had told her. I had invited another old friend to stay (homosexual, so restful) in case the going proved sticky, but there were no problems and we all chattered away happily throughout dinner. We had arranged that they should stay the night before travelling on to Norwich.

The only difficult moment came when Nanny brought in Vanessa, then aged four. Aysgarth said: "So this is the child," and when his faded eyes filled with tears I knew he was looking at the world of might-have-been, the world we would have inhabited if Dido had conveniently died and left him a widower. I had often thought of this world and had concluded in my anger that he would have made me very miserable once victory had finally dulled his appetite for his great prize, but now I knew I was looking, just as he was, at the lasting happiness we had been denied.

The next morning after breakfast he said to me: "I'd so much like to walk to that seat overlooking the lake," so we set off at a snail's pace across the lawn. Little Mrs. Hayman stayed tactfully in the house, but no doubt he had given her orders beforehand about making herself scarce at the right moment.

When we were finally settled on the seat by the lake we held hands and waited in silence until he had recovered his breath. It was a clear, warm morning. The water was as still as glass. Birds skimmed over the surface and vanished in the reeds. Everywhere was very quiet.

At last he said with a smile: "You've been very kind to me, haven't you?"

"For heaven's sake! What else did you expect?"

"Perhaps formal politeness masking a bitter resentment."

I said at once with an incredulous laugh: "You silly man, what on earth are you talking about?"

"My darling Venetia," he said, "do you think I never realised, as I listened to the gossip on the grapevine, that I ruined you? And do you really think that I—with my deep horror of destroying women—could ever die in peace unless I had made some attempt, no matter how feeble, to put right the great wrong that I've done?"

Tears sprang to my eyes. Then pressing his gnarled old hand against my cheek I passionately denied my own destruction.

4

THERE was so much I had planned to discuss with him. I wanted to examine all the dark corners of our affair so that the mysteries were finally clarified. I wanted him to tell me truthfully, without prevarication, in words of one syllable, exactly what his relationship with Dido had been not only in 1963 but from the day he married her. I wanted to discover why he had been so "bound up," as Mrs. Ashworth had put it, with such an impossible woman who was so absolutely wrong for him. That was the real mystery, of course. In 1963 I had been so young and inexperienced that I had gone off at a tangent chasing a solution to the wrong problem. The mystery had not been whether he had slept with Dido while chasing me. Obviously he had. (Or had he?) At the age of twenty-six I would have found it a massive betrayal if he had been sleeping with another woman, but now I could see that any sex he might have had with her could have been of no more emotional significance than one of his "triple-whiskies," a mere tranquilliser which helped keep him calm in stressful times. No, the real mystery was not whether he had slept with Dido but how he had come to be so incurably entangled with her, and it was this question which I was determined he should now answer.

But once again he eluded me. He always did, I realise that now. And

Mrs. Ashworth was right. We're not meant to know everything about other people, even those who are closest to us, and we have to accept at the end of the day that not all mysteries are solvable.

Meanwhile he was busy saying he had destroyed me.

"Darling . . ." I suddenly realised the tears were streaming down my face. He was displaying all his old talent for wrecking my make-up. "It wasn't your fault," I said. "You mustn't reproach yourself. And I'm not ruined, I did survive, I'm fine." Finding a handkerchief I started mopping my cheeks. Fortunately I now used a waterproof mascara.

"Promiscuity is so often a mark of dislocation," he said, "of boredom, alienation and despair. One very seldom realises that when one's young, of course, because the transient pleasure's so overwhelming. But later the pleasure no longer heals, and then, as in all cases of alienation, one yearns for the putting-right, the making-whole, the unification of the frag-mented self."

Trying to speak lightly I said: "This sounds like the theology of atonement!"

"That's right. At-one-ment. Do you ever go to church?"

I shook my head. No point in saying anything. Nothing worthwhile to say.

"God's not there any more?"

I made a big effort. All hostesses have a duty to be sociable, even with retired clergymen who are so *louche* as to talk about God at the wrong moment. "Oh, God's there!" I said brightly, as if we were discussing some eccentric mutual friend, "but He's not interested in me and I'm not interested in Him. We're irrelevant to each other nowadays."

"If you love someone they never become irrelevant."

"Well, obviously He and I don't love each other." I did hope the old pet wasn't going to become tiresome and spoil our very successful reun-ion. I tried to work out how I could tell him tactfully that I hated discussing religion because it always reminded me of Starbridge, but then I realised that any such admission would only confirm his belief that he was responsible for my spiritual destruction. I was still floundering for the words which would direct the conversation away from God when he said with strength: "You're saying you're estranged from God. You're saying you're alienated in the wasteland. But that's the tragedy of man-kind which lies at the heart not only of the doctrine of atonement but the doctrine of the Incarnation. We may be estranged from God, but God's never estranged from us. He came into the world to be at one with us and share our suffering so that mankind may be raised up, reconciled and redeemed. 'God was in Christ,' as the famous quotation goes, 'recon-ciling the world to Himself.' "

"Yes, I know all that, darling, and of course it's lovely, so idealistic, but what relation does it have to real life as we live it today in 1975?"

"I'll tell you exactly." He was getting stronger and stronger. The years were falling away, the clock was being put back, and for a moment I could almost believe we were sitting together again on Lady Mary. "I'll give you an example," he said, "an example of the principle of atonement in action, of the spirit of the Incarnation still ceaselessly on the move, of how pain and alienation and estrangement, no matter how deep, can be transmuted and healed by the power of love—which is the power of God. I wanted to put things right between us. I came here out of love, and when you saw me you knew that. Then you didn't just open the door and say hullo. You opened the door and you smiled and you ran down the steps and you took me in your arms and you hugged me—and the demons of alienation and estrangement were vanquished at last because my love and your response had cast them out. That old pirate Jon Darrow would have said: 'No demon can withstand the power of Christ!' but as a Modernist I prefer to say: 'This is the Christian principle in action!' In the end Love—Love with a capital L—is the only thing that matters. I was very wrong about many things back in 1963, but at least I was right about that."

"You're saying Charles Ashworth won the battle but John Robinson won the war?" I said, again struggling to keep my emotions at bay by adopting a light, amused tone, but he only said urgently: "The real truth lies far beyond Ashworth and Robinson—the real truth lies with God Himself. The power of His love is such that although you may consider yourself estranged from Him, He could never consider Himself estranged from you. He's always longing for the reconciliation—the moment when you turn back to Him, as you turned back to me, and fling wide your arms and vanquish the demon of alienation."

"Quite. Well, this theological talk is just like the old days, but—"

He refused to give up. Stubborn, pigheaded old Yorkshireman. I might have known he'd battle on. Abruptly he said: "You remember Holman Hunt's painting, 'The Light of the World'?"

"Oh darling, such an awful old piece of Victorian tat!"

"The style may be dated, but the *kerygma,* the message, is eternal. Christ stands outside the closed door, the door with no handle, and waits with his lamp for admittance to the human heart beyond—"

"All right, it's *not* just an awful old piece of Victorian tat—I was being revoltingly over-sophisticated. But again, what does all this mean in practical terms today in 1975? I know I've made a complete and utter mess of my life, but it's far too late now to start all over again!"

"It's never too late. That's the point. It's always possible to rise from the grave of pain, alienation and despair."

"Even when one's buried beneath a concrete slab?"

"Yes! Certainly! Even then!"

"But how do I achieve this resurrection? Go back to the Church?"

At once he became sombre. "I know the Church failed you. The Church is as fallible and imperfect as the men who run it, and I could never blame you, after all your experiences, if you hold the Church in contempt. But if you could look past the Church now to the eternal truths which lie beyond—"

"Yes, they're still there, I realise that, but how do I connect with them, how do I tune in, how do I dial their number?"

"They're not at the end of a telephone line. They're waiting on your doorstep, and all you have to do is open the great closed door, the door that Holman Hunt painted, the door that has to be opened from within."

There was a pause. Then I astonished myself by saying: "I can picture Christ standing at the great closed door. But I can't see myself on the inside. I think I'm on the outside, watching him, and beyond the door is my new resurrected life, but I can't figure out how to get there. So it's no good Christ just standing by the door with his lamp. That's too passive. He's got to act—he's got to stretch out his hand and grab me so that he can heave me over the threshold."

"Then that's what will happen. One day—and I shall pray it's one day soon—you'll see him standing at the great closed door and then as you watch he'll turn and stretch out his hand."

"Darling!" I had to give him a kiss. He was trying so hard and I loved him so much. "All right," I said, wanting to make him feel he had succeeded, "I'll pray for that too—we'll both pray for my much-needed resurrection, but darling, I can't have you blaming yourself any more for my futile existence. And for God's sake, don't think I'm secretly seething with anger towards you. I've been angry in the past, I admit, but I promise you I blame you for nothing now."

It was true. I had forgiven him. But I had to blame someone for my wasted life so all the anger which I had directed outward I now turned in upon myself. With a new ferocity I continued the all-consuming task of blotting out the pain of alienation, and although occasionally I remembered that image of the outstretched hand by the great closed door, no light pierced the darkness of the wasteland where the Great Pollutant still oozed its filth across my soul.

5

THEN in 1988, thirteen years after my last meeting with Aysgarth and twenty-five years after the publication of *Honest to God,* I took that wrong turning on the motorway and saw once again as if in a dream the spire of Starbridge Cathedral soaring towards the sky to lure me back to my lost paradise of long ago. And it was there in the cloisters, where Lady Mary's seat was no longer to be found, that I saw among the milling crowds the man whom I still called my Talisman, the man who then led me into the deserted garden of the Choir School, and it was there, as we sat overlooking the river, that I wept yet again for the life that had been destroyed.

6

"WELL, the trouble was," I said in a voice devoid of emotion as I confessed the emotion I could never forget, "I became so very, very fond of my darling Mr. Dean." Then I broke down, quietly, with the minimum of fuss, and shed two or three discreet tears into a tastefully embroidered handkerchief. In my opinion middle-aged women, who will always look revolting in distress, have absolutely no excuse for bawling away like young girls who will inevitably wind up looking dewy-eyed and lovely.

Nick was very still. He was forty-five now; I was fifty-one. The gap in our ages which had seemed such an abyss a quarter of a century ago had been wiped out. We were merely middle-aged contemporaries who had shared fragments of the past. Without the owlish spectacles which had given him such a serious air in his youth, his face had an angular individuality which was striking, and as always, he was intensely watchable. He was wearing off-white slacks, a casually styled black jacket and one of those modern clerical shirts, pale grey with a thin strip of plastic woven around the neck to symbolise the stiff collar. The informality of his appearance conveyed the impression of a clergyman on the fringes of the Church, someone unconventional, daring, possibly a trifle unorthodox. I wondered vaguely how his life had turned out but I knew little about him beyond the fact that he worked at one of the Guild churches in the City of London. Somebody had told me he counselled AIDS cases, but that rumour was hardly surprising. Everyone counselled AIDS cases nowadays. It was the fashion.

"Sorry," I said, giving my eyes one last dab with the tasteful handkerchief. "Silly of me. Take no notice."

He said again as he had said a few moments before: "Forgive."

"I did forgive him. Long ago."

"But have you forgiven the most important person of all?"

"Who's that?"

"Yourself."

I was transfixed. Then I scrabbled for my powder compact and tried to hide my confusion by giving my nose a quick pat with the puff. Despite the fact that my tears had been shed so discreetly, I had still wound up looking revolting. Poor Nick, landed with a middle-aged fright! I resolved to adopt a bright new sociable manner to extricate us both from embarrassment.

"What are you doing down here?" I enquired agreeably, dropping the powder compact back in my bag.

"I'm a consultant to the diocese of Starbridge. The Bishop calls me in sometimes."

"Oh yes? What's your special expertise?"

"The paranormal."

I boggled but made a quick recovery. "Still treading your mystical paths?"

He smiled but said nothing.

"Laid any good ghosts lately?" I said gaily as if I were chatting to a difficult guest at a cocktail party.

"I'm beginning to think you yourself are a ghost," he said, "a spirit crying out to be laid to rest."

"Well, darling, you can lay me any time you please! My pleasure." I stood up, intent on giving the impression that I was well in command of myself again, and added briskly: "Were you on your way to the South Canonry to see the Bishop when you rescued me?"

"No, I'd already been to the South Canonry and I'd decided to kill time in the cloisters while I waited for Evensong ... Will you stroll back with me to the north porch?"

We began to walk up the path away from the river to the door in the wall which separated us from the stonemasons' yard. After a long silence in which I was wholly absorbed in remembering the Evensongs of 1963, he said: "Why did you yourself come to Starbridge today?"

"God knows. But my dear, never mind about me—I'm just languishing on my own private scrap-heap! Tell me all about the Church of England in 1988—does anyone still remember *Honest to God*?"

"Some books have just been published to mark the twenty-fifth anniversary. A few middle-aged churchmen are getting nostalgic, but I suspect the younger generation are largely indifferent to the dated theology of the sixties."

"So all that starry-eyed radicalism which was going to create the New Reformation—"

"—expired. The New Reformation ran aground on the rocks of apathy, the Radicals are now thrashing about in a dead end and the Liberals are being knocked so hard that they can only reel punch-drunk from one crisis to the next. This is the day of the conservatives, and the Evangelicals are finally on the march."

"My God, that's exactly what Charley Ashworth prophesied in 1963!"

"Ah well," said Nick dryly, opening the door in the wall, "it would be hard to find someone more conservative than Charley."

"And where do you stand amidst all these warring factions?"

"Beyond them."

We moved into the stonemasons' yard and as Nick closed the door behind us I said: "I remember your father talking of the religion that was beyond fashion. But if you represent timeless mysticism and Charley represents the Evangelicals, who among our former acquaintances now stands for the Liberal-Radical wing?"

"Ah, that would be Primrose Tait," said Nick. "She's a great power nowadays in the Movement for the Ordination of Women."

"Oh God!" I rolled my eyes heavenwards in mock-horror, just as I always did whenever a successful woman appeared on the horizon to make me despise myself for my lost opportunities. "Thank heavens I'm right outside it all! What a circus!"

Nick said swiftly: "So you're happy on your scrap-heap, are you?" but pride made me retort: "In total bliss, darling! It's the only place where a worthless old hag of a failure like me could ever feel thoroughly at home!"

"So that's how you see yourself, is it? Worthless? A failure? Unforgivable?"

"Well, be frank, Nick! How do you see me?"

"I follow a man," said my Talisman, "who believed that each one of us has worth, and that no one is unforgivable."

To my horror I found I was unable to deliver a glib reply—or indeed any reply at all.

We re-entered the Close by the main entrance of the stonemasons' yard, and as we began to move around the vast west front of the Cathedral towards the north porch, I became painfully aware that although I was near enough to touch the walls I was utterly severed from the great mystery beyond them. Then at last the alienation and estrangement, that famous *angst* of twentieth-century man, seemed unbearable.

My soul ached. I longed to shed the pollution which poisoned it, but I was so weak. I could only say mildly, absurdly, to Nick: "Did you ever see *Ben-Hur*?" No cry for help could ever have been more obscure.

"The Charlton Heston version?"

"Yes, there was one part I always remember and it wasn't that bloody chariot race. It was when Christ was preaching to the crowd—although one never saw the face of Christ, only his back, and one never heard him, they merely played a special kind of music—"

"I remember."

"—and Ben-Hur appeared on the edge of the crowd. He was right in the background and one saw him move around the outer fringes—just as we're doing now, moving around the edge of the Cathedral—and as Ben-Hur moved, Christ moved too and one realised that Christ was watching him—"

"Yes, that was a very dramatic moment."

"—but I can't quite remember what happened next."

"Ben-Hur was drawn in from the fringes."

"He was? But not in that scene, surely."

"Then it was later."

We turned the corner and saw the north porch. Above us, somewhere in the tower below the spire, the bell was tolling for Evensong.

"Well!" I said brightly, pausing by the porch and wondering what on earth had driven me to ramble on so disjointedly about an ancient Hollywood epic. "It's been heavenly to see you again—keep treading those mystical paths! I suppose you'll eventually waft back into my orbit some day, just as you always do."

In reply he took out his wallet, produced a card and handed it to me. The card read: "The Reverend Nicholas Darrow, St. Benet's-by-the-Wall, Egg Street, London E.C.2." "Give me a call," he said, "when you get back to town."

"My dear, what fun! But I mustn't distract you from all your paranormal phenomena!" I was acutely aware that he had asked for neither my phone number nor my address. The card was a mere gesture of politeness, nothing more, a move which could be labelled "concerned" and "caring," a minor spiritual charade which would salve his Christian conscience.

"So long, Venetia," he was saying with a smile as he turned away into the north porch. He even added that most meaningless of all American-isms: "Take care."

"Goodbye, Nick." I remained outside, staring after him, his card already screwed up in my hand for deposit in the nearest litter-bin.

Then he stopped. He had reached the huge oak door which led into the Cathedral, and for one long moment he stood there—he stood there as if waiting by the great closed door, and suddenly I thought: Holman Hunt. "The Light of the World."

I knew then what was going to happen next, but I didn't dare believe it. My voice cried in my head: he won't, he can't, he couldn't—

But he did. And as I stared through my tears in wonder, unable to move or speak, he turned back to me and he stretched out his hand.

Author's Note

SCANDALOUS RISKS is the fourth in a series of six novels about the Church of England in the twentieth century; each book is designed to be read independently of the the others, but the more books are read the wider will be the view of the multi-sided reality which is being presented.

The first novel, *Glittering Images,* narrated by Charles Ashworth, was set in 1937. *Glamorous Powers,* narrated by Jon Darrow, opened in 1940, and *Ultimate Prizes* was narrated by Neville Aysgarth after the war. The fifth novel, *Mystical Paths,* will examine the Church in 1968 from the point of view of Nicholas Darrow.

AYSGARTH'S thought (though not his private life) derives from the writings of John Arthur Thomas Robinson (1919–1983) in the 1960s. Robinson was born in the shadow of Canterbury Cathedral where his father was a canon, and educated at Marlborough and at Jesus College, Cambridge; he gained a degree in Classics, a first in Theology and a doctorate in Philosophy. After he was ordained in 1945 he was a curate at Bristol and a chaplain at Wells Theological College before he became Dean of Clare College, Cambridge, and Lecturer in New Testament in the University Faculty of Divinity in 1951. He was still under forty when he was asked by Dr. Mervyn Stockwood, then Bishop of Southwark, to be his suffragan (assistant) bishop at Woolwich. The Archbishop of Canterbury, Dr. Geoffrey Fisher, was opposed to this appointment, mainly on the ground that Robinson was too young for episcopal rank, but Stockwood persisted and Robinson became Bishop of Woolwich in 1959. By this time he had been married for some years and had four children.

In 1960 he gained nationwide notoriety during the Crown's prosecution of Penguin Books for publishing an alleged obscene novel, the unexpurgated edition of *Lady Chatterley's Lover* by D. H. Lawrence. Robinson agreed to be a witness for the defence, but some of his opinions, taken out of context, provided sensational headlines for the press; his remark that sex was an act of holy communion (widely misinterpreted as Holy Communion) dates from this time. Archbishop Fisher commented: "In my judgement the Bishop was mistaken to think that he could take part in the trial without becoming a stumbling-block to many ordinary Christians."

Less than three years later, in March 1963, Robinson was hitting the national headlines again when the SCM Press published his most famous work, *Honest to God.* In the seven months following publication, 350,000 copies were sold and seven translations were about to be published. It was, so its publisher David L. Edwards claimed, the fastest-selling book of serious theology in the history of the world, and clearly by trying to restate Christianity in an up-to-date form and by introducing the general public to the writings of modern theologians Robinson connected with a vast religious interest buried deep in what was too often assumed to be a largely godless and secular society. Dr. Michael Ramsey, who had succeeded Dr. Fisher as Archbishop of Canterbury, was at first hostile to the book but later revised this initial reaction and admitted: "I was soon to grasp how many were the contemporary gropings and quests which lay behind *Honest to God.*" Robinson received over four thousand letters, some of which were published in *The Honest to God Debate,* edited by David L. Edwards, in October 1963. This book also contained, in addition to favourable reviews, strong criticism of the book from professional theologians.

After ten years as Bishop of Woolwich Robinson returned to Cambridge as Dean of Chapel at Trinity. This appointment was not altogether a success and Robinson did not become the prophetic voice of the 1970s as many in the Church had hoped that he would. It was noticeable that his New Testament scholarship became increasingly conservative. In 1983 he was diagnosed as suffering from cancer and he died in the December of that year. His last book, *The Priority of John,* was published posthumously, and in reviewing it Canon Leslie Houlden wrote: "The public reputation of John Robinson . . . was at its height in the sixties. On the theological scene he seemed to epitomise the spirit of that period as well as anyone . . . yet to see him as a thrillingly shocking radical was a misconception . . . He hunted with no pack for long but went his own way . . . Those who have seen him as a late Victorian radical born out of due time are perhaps the most discerning."

Honest to God is still in print, and in 1988 the SCM Press published *God's Truth,* a collection of essays to celebrate the twenty-fifth anniversary of this landmark in the history of the twentieth-century Church of England.

PERMISSIONS ACKNOWLEDGEMENTS

*Grateful acknowledgement is made to the following for
permission to reprint previously published material:*

Dandy Dittys and Warner/Chappell Music, Inc.: *Excerpt
from "Got a Lot O' Livin' to Do" by Aaron Schroeder and
Benjamin Weissman. Copyright © 1957 (Renewed 1985)
Rachel's Own Music & Gladys Music (ASCAP). All rights
on behalf of Gladys Music administered by Chappell & Co. All
rights on behalf of Rachel's Own Music administered by
Dandy Dittys. All rights reserved. Used by permission.*

SCM Press: *Excerpts from articles by various writers (John
Lawrence, Glyn Simon, David Jenkins, R. P. C. Hanson,
T. E. Hutley, and an anonymous writer) from* The Honest to
God Debate, *edited by John A. T. Robinson and David L.
Edwards, 1963. Reprinted by permission.*

Westminster/John Knox Press and SCM Press: *Excerpts
from* Honest to God *by John A. T. Robinson. Copyright ©
1963 by SCM Press Ltd. Rights in the U.S. administered by
The Westminster Press. Reprinted by permission of
Westminster/John Knox Press, Louisville, Ky., and SCM
Press, London.*

*Excerpts from article by John A. T. Robinson from the
Sunday Mirror (April 7, 1963) are included in this work.*

A NOTE ON THE TYPE

THE text of this book was set in Bembo, a facsimile of a typeface cut by one of the most celebrated goldsmiths of his time, Francesco Griffo, for Aldus Manutius, the Venetian printer, in 1495. The face was named for Pietro Bembo, the author of the small treatise entitled De Aetna in which it first appeared. Through the research of Stanley Morison, it is now acknowledged that all old-face type designs up to the time of William Caslon can be traced to the Bembo cut.

THE present-day version of Bembo was introduced by the Monotype Corporation, London, in 1929. Sturdy, well balanced, and finely proportioned, Bembo is a face of rare beauty and great legibility in all of its sizes.

COMPOSED by ComCom, a division of
The Haddon Craftsmen, Inc.,
Allentown, Pennsylvania
Printed and bound by R. R. Donnelley & Sons,
Harrisonburg, Virginia
Book and ornament designed by Margaret Wagner